THE GOD
CONSPIRACY

DEREK P. GILBERT

The God Conspiracy
By Derek P. Gilbert

AVENUE FICTION
514 ROSE AVENUE, CRANE, MO 65633

Published by Rose Avenue Fiction
www.roseavenuefiction.com

ISBN 978-0-9980967-7-3

Cover artwork by Jeffrey Mardis
Printed in the United States of America

First Print Edition April 2009
First Electronic Edition April 2009

For Sharon:
You've inspired me to dream and be
more than I ever thought possible.

PROLOGUE

Kevin Snedeker pulled a tissue from a small travel pack and blew his nose for the fourth time in five minutes. His sinuses were in open rebellion and taking no prisoners.

"I'm sorry," Snedeker said. His boss, a man he knew only as Green, stared at him through a fog of cigarette smoke from the other side of the dimly lit conference room.

Snedeker stuffed the used Kleenex into his jeans pocket, next to an ancient thumb drive he carried for luck. It was a souvenir, a slow USB 1.0 drive he'd used as a teen to keep pictures he downloaded from a website he would never have admitted to visiting.

The siren song of computer hacking had directed the course of Snedeker's life for the last twenty years, finally landing him here, his dream job—great money and equipment beyond state of the art. A few more months and he'd finally have his student loans paid off. Maybe he'd even trade his twelve-year-old Subaru for something made in this decade.

The money made up for the fact that the office was underneath a mountain. And for his boss's lack of people skills.

"I'm sorry, you were saying?" Snedeker sniffed as his nose threatened to drip again.

"The package has been sent?" Green, his sharp features highlighted by the orange glow from his cigarette, spoke with a deep, raspy voice that sounded as though it had been worked over with a wire brush.

"Yes," Snedeker said, pushing his glasses back up his nose. "One email, sent through anonymous proxies to the address list you gave me." His eyes itched, and he wanted nothing more than to get back to his desk, where he kept his stash of eye drops, decongestants, and saline nasal spray.

Green nodded, the orange beacon of his cigarette bobbing up and down through the haze as he inhaled.

"I compiled that list of people, too," Snedeker continued. "Just like you asked—names and addresses of everybody who's getting the note. But, Mister Green? I have to ask—is that—well, can we *do* that?"

"That is not your concern."

"I mean, some of those people, you know, are on 'do not call' lists…"

"I said," Green repeated, eyes flashing, "That is not your concern." He exhaled another squall line of smoke.

"Okay," Snedeker managed around a cough.

"Relax, Mister Snedeker," his boss said. "You've been very useful. I believe we're done here."

"So I can go now?"

A hint of a smile crossed Green's face, just a twitch at the corner of his lips. "We're done."

As Snedeker tried to stand, a powerful hand on his shoulder forced him back down into the chair. Surprised, he spun around— and noticed for the first time the very large man who'd been standing behind him.

A moment later, he saw the small-caliber pistol in the man's gloved right hand.

Outside the conference room, Green flicked his expensive silver lighter and lit a fresh Bentley. He exhaled slowly, turning the lighter over in his hand, admiring the curved, twisting pattern perfectly engraved in its gleaming titanium case. He ran his thumb gently, almost lovingly over the cryptic, archaic design.

Green waited near the open door just long enough to hear the telltale *pop* that announced the insertion of a twenty-two-caliber bullet into Kevin Snedeker's brain.

ONE

The day had already lasted ten minutes longer than forever. Eric John Moore stared through the classroom window at Mayfield Elementary School and dreamed of dragons in the October sky over Iowa. His fourth-grade teacher droned on, demonstrating the effect of heat on the air pressure inside a balloon.

"Eric? Would you care to rejoin us on planet Earth?" Mrs. Holcomb, a stern-faced woman with hair too dark and lips too red for her age, stood with hands on her grandmotherly hips. Eric's face turned hot, and he stared at his desk while his freckled cheeks approached the color of his bright red hair.

One of the girls in the next row giggled, and Eric risked a glance to see who it was. His heart sank—it was Courtney Hill, the prettiest girl in school, at least in Eric's eyes.

"Can you tell me why the balloon got bigger when I heated it?"

Eric was smart enough to understand that Mrs. Holcomb was trying to embarrass him further for daydreaming, but he was also smart enough to know the answer. "The gas molecules move faster when the temperature is higher, so there's more space in between. That makes the balloon bigger."

Mrs. Holcomb glared for a moment before responding. "Correct," she said. "Now, class, the opposite is true when we lower the temperature…"

Her voice faded in Eric's ears as though someone slowly turned a hidden volume knob on Mrs. Holcomb all the way to "off." He carefully edged a spiral notebook out from beneath his science book and tried to resume work on his design for an interstellar spaceship. After doodling for a minute, he put down his mechanical pencil. No inspiration.

Eric looked up at the ponderous hands of the big, round clock on the wall behind Mrs. Holcomb. Twenty minutes to freedom. He sighed. The day would never end.

"Come on, hit those ropes! You can do it! Let's go, let's go, let's go!"

Tony Harris yelled encouragement to the eighth grade boys in his last gym class of the day. "Good job, Juan! Way to go! Come on, Donny, you can do it! Let's go, go, go!"

Four lines of thirteen- and fourteen-year-old boys waited for their turn at the ancient ropes that dangled from the gym ceiling. It wasn't the kind of thing one saw in newer schools, but William Jennings Bryan Elementary had been built when the medicine ball was still part of a child's fitness program. A couple of them still took up space in the equipment room.

"Pick it up, Larry. Come on, now, you can do it," Harris called. An overweight young man struggled to get a few feet of clearance between his feet and the floor.

"What's the matter, Lardey?"

"Too much junk in the trunk, dude." The shouted taunts came from the back of the nearest line of boys, triggering stifled giggles from the rest.

"Who said that?" A group of five near the end worked hard to look innocent. Any teacher with more than two weeks' experience knew the look; the boys might as well have been covered with Day-Glo orange body paint. Harris didn't know what was more aggravating—that the boys mocked a classmate or that they thought he was too stupid to figure out who did it.

"I'll ask you one more time. Who said that?" The prime suspects sniggered and shuffled their feet.

"Okay," Harris said. "You, you, you, you, and you. Twenty-five pushups. Now."

The boys groaned and complained, but only for a moment. One look at their gym teacher convinced them he wasn't in the mood for appeals. One by one, they dropped to the floor and began grunting and groaning through the reps.

"Come on, are you men or boys? Keep your backs straight! Like this!" Harris dropped to the floor and raced through the pushups, his powerful shoulders and upper arms working like pistons, lifting his five-eleven, two hundred and twenty-five pound frame quickly and effortlessly off the floor in rapid succession. He finished his twenty-five while the fastest of the boys struggled with number eighteen.

Jumping to his feet, Harris waited until the last of the boys collapsed at sixteen. As the boy stood, Harris stared at the culprits until all of them hung their heads, eyes focused on the floor between them. "What's the matter, ladies? I'm an old man of thirty-five. You can't beat an old man?" The group stood silent and sullen.

"You see, there's always somebody out there who can whip your butt," Harris said. "From now on, do your best and keep your mouth shut. Leave these other guys alone. Besides," he said quietly, "it doesn't take guts when it's five on one."

The harsh clang of the bell ended the lecture, and the class hurried for the gym doors and freedom. "See you clowns Monday. Hey, Larry," Harris called, as the dejected target of the boys' abuse walked past, "Good work. You're getting stronger. I can see it. Keep it up." The boy gave Harris half a smile and followed the class out the door.

Cleaning up the gym after the last class of the week was always a good feeling. Bryan Elementary's other gym teacher, Janice Hodgson, who'd been working with the eighth grade girls on the other side of the gym, walked over and asked, "What was that all about?"

"The usual," Harris said. "Pick on the fat kid. What do they call it now—body shaming? Typical guy stuff."

Janice, a tall woman who stood nearly eye-to-eye with Harris, shook her head. "Kids," she said. "The girls do it, too. It's a rough time of life."

Harris chuckled. "You couldn't pay me enough to go back."

"Not even if it meant new knees?"

Smiling ruefully, Harris said, "Not even for that."

A few years earlier, he would have made the trade in an instant. Nine years ago, a bad knee ended Tony Harris' career as a third-string running back for the Chicago Bears after only four seasons. It took three years of surgeries, rehab, and tryout camps to admit he was through. Even the Canadian Football League hadn't been interested.

That was a tough time. Football defined Tony Harris. After years of being the strongest, fastest, and best, accepting that he was no longer physically qualified to play had been nearly impossible. Alcohol, broken relationships, and an eight-year-old son he'd refused to acknowledge as his responsibility were the markers he'd left to show his passage through life after football.

He was glad his father hadn't lived long enough to see it.

Finally, disgusted with himself, Harris put his degree in Phys Ed to use and found a job as a gym teacher at an elementary school on Chicago's northwest side. He'd quit drinking, got back into shape, and made it clear to his former girlfriend that he was ready to step up and play a role in their son's life. Shareece wasn't making it easy, but he'd expected that. Deserved it.

"Do you have your son this weekend?" Janice asked.

"No," Harris said. "Next weekend's mine. One weekend a month. Hardly enough for a boy to get to know his father."

"No big plans?"

"No," he continued, "Just me and the TV for game one of the Series, that's it. It's going to be a quiet weekend."

Bob Moore sighed as he stared at the numbers on the computer screen. The new small business software saved a lot of work in tallying the balance sheet of his small grocery store, but that was the only good thing about it. The numbers didn't lie—he had to do something different or they'd be out of business in less than a year.

Bob pushed the rolling office chair away from the computer desk in the back room of the Mayfield Family Grocery, a business that had been in the Moore family for three generations. His grandfather had opened it when he got back from Europe after World War II. The little farm town of Mayfield, Iowa had seen good times and bad over the last seventy-five years, and the white-frame grocery at the corner of Third and Main had been there to provide basic necessities through it all.

After the Mayfield tornado of 1974, Bob's grandfather, Jim, kept the store open all night, serving coffee and sandwiches to rescue workers from all over east-central Iowa. The massive twister leveled two dozen houses on the west side of Route 3. Jim Moore never asked for a dime, even after the governor declared the county a disaster area. But the landmark grocery store now faced forces more powerful and relentless than an Iowa tornado.

Since the discount superstore opened at the edge of town ten years earlier, there'd been a steady decline in the grocery's monthly gross. Then a new dollar store chain planted a location right in town, just a few blocks away. It specialized in staples—bread, milk, basic household and personal care items—at prices even the superstore couldn't match. It was a perfect storm of competition. His stomach clenched into knots when he let himself think too long about why he hadn't seen it coming.

Even worse were the guilty looks from his neighbors. Bob couldn't blame them for saving a buck a gallon on milk—but he couldn't help feeling a little betrayed.

It didn't help that some of his neighbors had been hit hard by a nasty strain of avian flu. Every chicken in Kiowa County had been slaughtered in the spring by order of the government, and there was talk that hogs might have to be culled, too. At least the flu hadn't spread to humans. Not yet.

About the only good thing Bob could see was the pretty, full-color graph his new software created to illustrate his store's slow, agonizing death.

The screen door at the front of the store slammed shut. Bob glanced up at the ancient wall clock, an advertisement for a soda company long gone: Two-forty. E.J. was home.

"Hey, buddy," Bob called, as he shut down the program. "How was your day?"

"Okay," Eric said.

"What'd you learn today?"

"The usual."

"Usual?"

"Yeah, you know. Stuff."

Bob leaned back in the office chair, scratching the light brown beard he'd grown last year, partly to cover a chin that had softened as he neared forty and partly to compensate for the thinning hair on top of his head. "Ohhh," he said, knowingly. "Stuff."

"Dad," Eric said, with the tone of voice familiar to all parents that said, *Don't be goofy*.

"Any homework?" Bob asked.

"A little," Eric said. "A math worksheet."

"Okay. You can have the desk. I've got some work to do in the store. Get that done and we can play a little catch before your mom gets home."

Eric watched his dad disappear through the doorway and around the corner into the small store. Living behind and above a grocery had its advantages. You never ran out of ice cream, for one thing.

The office at the back of the store was a square room about fourteen feet on each side, with shelves of office supplies and boxes of some of the non-perishables, like gum and cigarettes, around three of the walls. A door directly opposite the entry to the store led back to the Moore's kitchen. Next to the door, positioned so that Bob or his wife Cindy could see it from the store, was the desk that housed the family's iMac.

Eric had hoped for a four-point-seven gig eight-core gaming machine with a top of the line GPU, but his parents overruled him. Still, the iMac was pretty fast, even if there weren't as many games for it. And at least his parents had broadband.

Glancing over his shoulder, Eric decided his dad was too busy to notice if he checked his email before starting on the math assignment. Besides, the worksheet was easy. Probably wouldn't take more than ten minutes.

Eric opened the web browser and logged into his webmail account. It was slower than using the computer's mail app, but it kept his parents from reading all his email. Not that he had anything to hide. They had his username and password anyway, but it was nice to enjoy the illusion of privacy.

Two messages waited for him. One promised an inexpensive all-natural supplement for "male enhancement". Eric made a face and clicked "delete."

The subject line of the other caught his attention. It looked like spam, but it didn't have a bunch of misspelled words to fool the junk mail filter. He clicked on the message to read it. As he did, his eyes grew big.

> *The time is near.*
> *The great and terrible day of the Lord has come.*
> *You are one of the Chosen.*
> *Tell no one.*
> ***GOD***

TWO

The engine of the 2010 Camaro SS growled like a hungry beast as Tony Harris waited for the light to change at the corner of Narragansett and Irving Park. The early October afternoon was bright and clear, and the cool air felt good through his open window. There were still a few weeks before the clocks were set back. Harris wasn't looking forward to returning to Standard Time; by the time he'd get home to his modest bungalow near Hanson Park there would be barely any daylight left.

The muscle car was a souvenir of his younger days, when he still drew an NFL salary. Harris knew it would be smart to replace it with something more sensible, but he hadn't been able to let go of one of the few remnants of his fading youth.

He switched on the radio, preset to one of the "smooth jazz" stations in Chicago. The dichotomy between the raw power of his ride and the soft clarinet easing through its quad speakers made Harris smile. The car's high-end stereo ought to be thumping loud enough to shake street lights, just for appearance, but the older he got, the less he tolerated the noise.

The music faded, replaced by an announcer with an impossibly deep voice.

"WWJZ, Chicago's smooth jazz. It's four o'clock in Chi-town, and I'm Darius Miles. Stay right here for another hour of the Windy City's best jazz right after the news with Shannon Reed."

"Thank you, Darius. Israel's Prime Minister Moshe Perleman is warning the United Nations that recent attacks by Hamas and Islamic insurgents will bring severe consequences. Twenty-seven Israelis were killed last week in a rocket attack in southern

Israel, near the border with Gaza, and a suicide bomber in Tel Aviv claimed twenty-three lives yesterday. Hamas has claimed responsibility for both attacks. UN peacekeeping forces, trying to keep order in the region after a massive earthquake destroyed Damascus earlier this year, have been unable to stop a string of terror attacks launched from inside Syria in recent weeks."

Harris switched off the radio again. *Lord, what a mess we made of this world.*

Eric Moore stared at his computer screen for a long time trying to decide what to make of the strange message. *One of the Chosen? What could that mean?*

Was it a joke? He screwed up his face and thought about asking his dad what he thought, but that would mean admitting he hadn't started his homework yet.

Eric finally decided the email didn't mean anything. It was probably a stupid trick by one of his friends, or one of the kids at school who made fun of him because he went to church with his parents every Sunday and youth group every Wednesday. So he decided to forward the email to a few other friends, just to see if anybody mentioned it at school the next day. Then he closed the browser, opened up his backpack, and pulled out his math homework.

"They're moving in the Golan Heights!" Jared Gruner hunched and squinted to see the fine details on the monitor a little better. His heavy frame and wildly disorganized dark hair were evidence of too many hours staring into a computer screen. "I could tell what it is, Stauffer, if you'd spend a few bucks on a quality monitor!"

"Come on, man, it's a twenty-seven inch 4K screen. What more do you want?" Scott Stauffer, a thin young man with thick glasses and a Moe Howard haircut, leaned over Jared's shoulder. "What are you looking at, anyway?"

Gruner's pudgy face was screwed into a contortion of concentration. "I could tell you for sure if you'd drop a few bucks for higher resolution. They make 8K now, you know."

"Yeah, but my van needs the money more. What is that?" Stauffer pointed at a mysterious blob on the screen.

Gruner stared at it for a moment. Then he leaned forward, reached up inside his black T-shirt and wiped it away. "Pizza. Sorry, man."

"Stauffer, thou hast encountered a slavering grue. What say thee, varlet: fight or run?" Terry Norlock sat at the table in the area of Stauffer's three-room apartment designated the dining room, mainly because it was next to the kitchen and had a light fixture. Norlock held a card he'd drawn from a deck on the table after deciphering the twelve-sided dice Stauffer had just rolled.

"Uh, wait a minute," Stauffer said, his squint mimicking Gruner's.

Norlock sighed loudly. "Well, do you want to play or not? What are you guys doing?"

A voice with a heavy Indian accent called from the kitchen. "What is happening?" Vijay Sampurnananda, a coworker of Stauffer's and a recent addition to their weekly gaming sessions, had taken a break from the game to search the refrigerator for a snack.

"Stauffer encountered a slavering grue," Norlock said.

"Am I there?"

"No, you're still above ground, in the mysterious wood."

"Where is the grue?"

"In the subterranean—hey, why am I the only one who's paying attention?" Norlock, whose pale complexion was emphasized by his long blond hair, was about halfway to a full-blown snit.

Gruner sighed. Norlock was a member of the Association for Renaissance Martial Arts, a bunch of medieval re-enactors who liked to dress funny and practice fighting with five-hundred-year-old weapons. His fascination with the Middle Ages was probably why Norlock took their weekly games so seriously.

A friend of Gruner's who knew a guy with a cousin at the Defense Intelligence Agency had slipped him the informations needed to access images from a Defense Department satellite in orbit over the Middle East. The situation there was melting down in a hurry. Syria had fallen back into anarchy after the big quake in the spring. Jihadist groups controlled most of the country, but they were desperate since outside financial support had dried up as that strain of avian flu spread through the region.

Across the border, Israel was sick of getting hit by rockets and mortars. The Israelis had threatened to put an end to it once and for all. That set off Arab governments in the Middle East, not to mention Islamic terror groups. Sunnis and Shias might even quit fighting each other for the first time in centuries.

Stauffer leaned annoyingly close over Gruner's right shoulder. "What's the deal with the Golan Heights? Why does Israel have it, anyway? Isn't it part of Syria?"

"Why should it be?" Gruner replied, edging sideways to create a little more personal space. "The Israelis took it after they were attacked in sixty-seven. Since when does a country that wins a war started by the other guys have to give back what it took in self-defense? Never happened before, but the whole world, except America practically, wants Israel to give it back. That would be stupid."

"Why?"

"Look." Gruner hit alt-tab on the keyboard to bring up Google Earth. "The Golan is high ground. See the way it slopes down to the Sea of Galilee? If Israel gives it up, the whole north of the country would practically be in mortar range."

"Mm." Stauffer stared at the map, the monitor's reflection in his glasses making them look like windows in a low Earth orbit satellite.

Jared Gruner wasn't religious, but he was fascinated with apocalyptic prophecy. The feuds in that part of the world were so old and ran so deep that some groups there would gladly drag the whole world into a nuclear war as long as they got to kill a few of the enemy. Gruner was convinced that fighting there could easily lead to something like Armageddon.

But now, just as he accessed the newest secret satellite images of the area, Norlock was throwing a hissy over a game. A kid's game, if he was honest. He looked back at his friend. "Just give us a minute, okay, Terry? This is important."

"Look, if you guys don't want to play, just say so and I'll…"

Vijay interrupted from the kitchen. "Scott, may I have a cola?"

"Sure, go ahead, Veej."

"If you guys don't want to play…" Norlock started again, but Gruner cut him off.

"Look at this!" He jabbed at the screen. "Right there! You know what that is?"

"Dude," Stauffer said. "You're getting fingerprints on it."

Norlock flipped the card into the air and heaved a world-weary sigh.

"And a peanut butter sandwich?" Vijay called from the kitchen.

"Yeah, sure," Stauffer answered.

"Please, where is the peanut butter?"

"Hold on," Stauffer said to Gruner. "Coming, Veej."

Norlock got up from the table, his six feet and five inches seeming even taller in the cramped apartment. He wandered over to the computer desk, where an intense Jared Gruner was trying to manipulate the computer image with a graphics program to sharpen its details. "What is that?" Norlock asked.

"Not sure," Gruner said, "But I think it's mechanized armor."

"What?"

"Tanks. IDF. Moving toward Syria."

"Wow," Norlock said. "For real?"

Gruner just raised a bushy eyebrow in annoyance.

"Where did you get this?"

"Buddy of mine with connections," Gruner said. "It's off a DIA satellite."

"They can't trace the IP of the downloading computer, can they?"

Gruner's ample stomach churned. In his rush to hack into the DOD computers, he'd forgotten to route the connection through a proxy. He pursed his lips and slowly turned his attention back to the screen.

"Oh, crap."

From the air, it looked like a minor government installation, perhaps a weather station or a power substation nestled among the rolling greenery of the mountains on the border between Pennsylvania and Maryland.

It was much more than that.

Designated Site R, it served as the communications nexus for Army, Navy, and Air Force operations on the East Coast. All messages between Washington, D.C. and the North American Aerospace Defense Command in Colorado were routed through Site R.

Situated six hundred and fifty feet below a greenstone behemoth called Raven Rock Mountain, near Waynesboro, Pennsylvania, Site R also served as the Emergency Operations Center for the United States military. If the plane that slammed into the Pentagon on September 11, 2001 had inflicted enough damage, command and control functions would have shifted to Site R with little more than a hiccup. Within hours of the first strike, Vice President Dick Cheney arrived at Site R in a convoy of four helicopters to coordinate America's response to the attack.

Despite its innocuous name, Site R was the nerve center of the government of the United States of America.

It was also a Continuity of Government redoubt, one of several semi-secret, underground bunkers where those empowered to rebuild American life after a catastrophe would be protected while the rest of the country took its chances on the surface. Not coincidentally, it was only seven miles from the president's retreat at Camp David.

A competent researcher could confirm Site R information with a few minutes of searching on the Internet. However, hidden beneath Site R lay secret facilities that no search engine would find—areas that even the majority of Site R's military staff knew nothing about. There, deep beneath the surface, Green used the communication capabilities of the complex above to stay informed. *Scientia est potentia*—knowledge is power.

Green called his subordinates, each responsible for a specific area of intelligence analysis, to a conference room decorated in the same bland industrial style as the rest of the complex. Holding the center of the room were two standard-issue Formica-topped tables placed end-to-end, surrounded by thirteen black office chairs. The windowless, soundproof room was illuminated by the harsh glow of a rectangular fluorescent fixture suspended above the table. Army Captain Thomas Wetzel, the last to enter the room, took the chair just to Green's right.

"Anything new, gentlemen?" Green, seated at the head of the long table, scanned the faces of his twelve assistants. They were all career military, selected from the various branches of service for intelligence and dedication. None of them had strong family attachments that might lead to conflicting loyalties in a time of crisis. If a critical situation developed topside that required immediate evacuation of the government to the Federal Relocation Arc, a ring of underground shelters surrounding the capital, Green would not be shorthanded just because somebody wanted to check on family.

The twelve looked around the table at one another, shaking their heads.

"All right. You know what to watch for. I have reason to believe that an incident is imminent. There is too much at stake for us to miss anything. I want to be notified at once. Wetzel," Green fixed him with his dark eyes, "Let me know immediately if PRISM hits on anything."

Green's stare was intense, unblinking. Wetzel struggled to maintain eye contact with his boss. "We're monitoring as much web traffic as we can, sir," he said. "But sir, with the volume on the web, we're having trouble keeping up."

"We have the tools, do we not?"

"Yes, sir, to intercept. But—"

"But what?"

"Sir. I thought this new IT contractor was going to update our data mining capabilities to streamline the process. Right now, we're trying to drink from a fire hose."

Green's eyes bored into Wetzel like twin lasers. "Mister Snedeker's services are no longer available to us."

"Yes, sir." Wetzel resigned himself to another long day. And Green's stare made it clear that it was better not to ask what he'd meant.

The twelve junior men stood and quietly filed out of the room to return to their desks in the communications center. As Wetzel left the room, he glanced back at his boss. Green stared toward the ceiling at nothing in particular, lost in thought. Then, with a trace of a smile, Green pulled a cigarette from the silver case in his jacket pocket, leaned back in his chair, and lit up.

Wetzel fought down an involuntary shudder as he turned to leave.

It was October 13th, the end of a long and mostly unproductive week for Special Agent Joseph Unes. As one of the newer agents assigned to the Saint Louis field office, he'd drawn the mundane chore of examining the telephone logs of yet another investment banker suspected of playing fast and loose with accounts. It wasn't exactly what he'd envisioned when he signed up with the bureau twelve years earlier. His eyes and his mind were tired, and he wanted to go home.

Unes took off his glasses and rubbed his eyes. Staring at the tiny print on the phone company's records was a strain. Maybe it was time for bifocals, he thought, or laser eye surgery.

He put the thought out of his mind. Forty-six wasn't *that* old. Besides, the thought of cutting into his eyes, even with lasers, made him queasy.

Unes made a mental note to stop at International Foods on South Grand before heading home to Manchester, one of Saint Louis' western suburbs. It was out of the way, but it was the best place in the area for a good leg of lamb. He had promised Cathy and the girls that he'd make *kibbeh b'sounieh* tonight, a baked dish of minced lamb, burghul wheat, spices and oil—a sort of Lebanese meat loaf.

He preferred *kibbeh nayeh*—raw *kibbeh*—but his wife and daughters had never acquired the taste. That's what he got for marrying an Irish girl.

Unes checked his watch. Four-fifty. Late enough, especially since he'd come in at seven to try to finish this part of the investigation.

His hope of a clean getaway faded when he heard his name over the office intercom—sort of.

"Joe Unes, line two. Joe Unes, line two, please." The new receptionist, Michelle, still pronounced 'Unes' with one syllable, as though it rhymed with 'tunes.' Joe's partner, Mark Hopkins, snickered from his desk across the room.

Unes sighed. He'd stop on the way out and remind Michelle— *again*—that Unes had two syllables, emphasis on the first: *YOO-niss*.

Joe picked up the handset and punched the flashing button on his desk phone. "Agent Unes. Oh, hey, Tommy. What? Where?" He grabbed a legal pad and furiously began taking notes. "Are you sure? Who's on the scene now? Mm, hmm. County on the way? Okay. We'll be there in thirty minutes."

"What's up?" Hopkins asked.

"Some lunatic has hostages at a Grandy's out in Valley Park."

"Why are they calling us?"

"Possible terrorist connection," Joe said, checking his pistol to make sure it was loaded.

"Terrorist? At a supermarket? In freakin' Valley Park?" Hopkins, an athletic man of thirty-three, slipped into his sportcoat. Unlike Joe, who walked on the treadmill three nights a week to keep his weight barely under control, Hopkins managed to look like a GQ model even when he was in a rush.

"Yeah," Joe said, struggling into his jacket. "Guy's armed, wearing a bomb belt, and he's shouting about the end of the world."

"Sir?" Wetzel entered Green's office and found his boss seated behind an expansive wooden desk, unadorned except for an unusual geometric symbol carved on the panel facing the door. The off-white walls in the dimly lit room held a few nondescript pieces of mass-produced art and a framed photograph of the White House. A cigarette smoldered in a large bronze ashtray near Green's right hand.

Green looked up from what appeared to be an intelligence briefing. Closing the folder, he said, "Yes?"

"We have one," Wetzel said.

"Details."

"Saint Louis," Captain Wetzel continued. "Hostage situation. Male Caucasian with a handgun and a bomb belt has taken hostages in a grocery store."

Green nodded and made a note on a legal pad. "Call Washington. Get me the Secretary of DHS and the Director of FEMA. Put them through as soon as you have them."

THREE

Cindy Moore hadn't meant to be so late getting home. Lois Clossen kept her chatting for nearly two hours when all Cindy wanted to do was drop off her latest order of Brenda Faye cosmetics.

The sky had darkened by the time Cindy pulled into the gravel drive behind the Mayfield Family Grocery. The lights over the sign out front were on, and the floodlight on the detached garage, triggered by Cindy's car, spread a wide, welcoming glow between the drive and the back of the store.

As she stepped out of the car, she saw a flare of light near the backdoor of the house. The smell of ground beef over charcoal announced a dinner of Bob's famous hamburgers. Cindy smiled to herself. Just like Bob to take the initiative instead of waiting for her to get home and then complaining about a late meal.

These long days were fewer and farther between, lately. Cindy's side business of selling cosmetics and notions to friends from church, customers of the store, and people she'd grown up with was fairly successful. Products in the Brenda Faye catalog were things women couldn't find anywhere this side of Des Moines, which was an hour and a half drive each way. At least, not until the MegaMart opened.

Not that the stuff at MegaMart was better, or even as good. But the prices at MegaMart were so much cheaper that some of her most loyal customers had opted to make do. And then there was Amazon. Better prices and delivered by the mailman.

Cindy carried her case full of samples and catalogs through the unlocked backdoor and into the kitchen. E.J. sat at the table reading a science fiction novel and Bob stood over a boiling pot of—something. Vegetable, by the smell.

"Hi, honey," Bob said. "Lois Clossen keep you talking?"

Cindy, an inch taller than her husband, leaned to kiss his cheek—and to look over his shoulder. It was green beans. Good. Beans were hard to ruin.

"Yes, she did," Cindy said. "Poor woman. She's been really lonely since Knute passed on."

Bob nodded and continued stirring the beans while Cindy crossed the kitchen to the office to set down her case. "Did you have a good day at school, E.J.?" she asked.

"Uh huh."

"Learn anything?"

"Uh huh."

"Anything fun?"

"Uh uh."

"Speak English?"

Eric finally looked up from his book with the same "don't be goofy" look he'd given his father earlier. Cindy winked and smiled.

"It's considered good manners to answer in complete sentences," she said.

"Sorry, Mom."

"What's this?" Cindy retrieved a piece of pink paper from the table.

"Oh," Eric said. "Something from the school nurse about flu shots."

Hmm," Cindy said, setting it on the countertop to read later. "Go wash your hands for dinner. Those burgers smell about done."

Mark Hopkins slammed his hand against the steering wheel of his silver Chevy Impala and swore in frustration. Joe Unes raised an eyebrow. Highway Forty—Unes still hadn't figured out why nobody in Saint Louis called it "I-Sixty-Four"—always slowed down at this time of day.

The highway was a compromise, eight lanes of concrete shoehorned into space for four. Here at Lindbergh Boulevard, maybe a third of the distance they needed to cover, things always got dicey at rush hour. The interchange was ancient, designed for the cars and traffic volume of a day long gone.

Unes wished he was driving. The two agents had agreed to take Hopkins' car to the hostage scene. Unes lived about two miles from the Grandy's supermarket. It was more convenient for Hopkins to drop him off before heading home than for Joe to run all the way back downtown for Hopkins' car.

"Easy, Mark," Unes said. "It's always like this at five o'clock." Hopkins lived in South County. He didn't travel this way to get home.

"I know, I know," Hopkins said. "What's going on there, that's what I want to know."

Impatient, Unes thought. Not a good trait in their line of work. Unes was less than eager to face a lunatic with high explosives.

A man with a wife and kids had a lot to lose. Any man who said otherwise was either a liar or a jerk. Joe Unes preferred solving the puzzles left behind at crime scenes. Let hotshots like Hopkins handle shootouts.

Unes decided to take advantage of the traffic delay to call Cathy and tell her to plan on something else for dinner.

Traffic finally eased enough for Hopkins pick up some speed. The younger agent turned on the radio and switched to an all-news station.

The topic was the Middle East. *"The latest report from Tel Aviv confirms an earlier unofficial report from Amman, Jordan, that cities in northern Israel have been hit by artillery shells filled with poison gas, possibly chlorine, apparently fired by Islamic militants in southern Lebanon. There is no word on casualties at this hour, although an Israeli government spokesman described the situation as 'grave.'"*

"Arabs!" Hopkins spat. "We oughta nuke 'em. Just turn the whole Middle East to a frickin' sheet of glass!"

"Mark," Unes said, *"I'm* an Arab."

"You—what?"

"I am an Arab-American," Joe said, louder. "My parents are from Lebanon. That's one of the places Arabs live. I still have cousins there."

Hopkins stared straight ahead, apparently focused on the traffic. "Huh. You look Italian. I figured you were from The Hill."

"Come on. How many Italians do you know with a name like Unes? Hey, watch the pickup!"

Hopkins swerved to miss a green and gray Mazda. "Hey, sorry. So, you got camels in the old country?"

"It's Lebanon, not Arabia," Unes said. "There's no sand in Lebanon except on the beaches."

The highway was a slow-moving river of steel. Nearly twenty minutes passed before Unes and Hopkins finally arrived at the parking lot of a supermarket under siege.

Like most modern supermarkets, Grandy's Foods was a low, wide building of brick and glass. It dominated a corner of one of the busiest intersections in southwestern Saint Louis County, anchoring the strip mall it shared with two sit-down restaurants, two sandwich shops, a takeout pizza place, a dry cleaners, a tax accountant, a hair styling academy, a nail salon, and a dentist's office. On a typical Friday afternoon, the store would be filled with shoppers loading up for the weekend. Now the lot was clear except for a dozen police cars, three fire trucks, and a couple dozen vehicles belonging to people who got caught shopping in the wrong place at the wrong time.

Unes was almost out of the car before the engine shut down completely. He and Hopkins quickly identified the officer in charge, a captain with the Saint Louis County Police Department. It was the county's jurisdiction, since the tiny village of Twin Oaks, which encompassed the strip mall and not much more, didn't have a police force of its own.

The captain—Warner, according to his badge—stood behind a barricade of patrol cars arranged in a semicircle that faced the front of the store. He was about Joe's height, six-two, but probably thirty pounds lighter. With his dark brown hair cropped close and a bristling mustache, Captain Warner resembled Tom Selleck in his *Magnum, P.I.* days.

"Captain? Special Agent Joe Unes. This is Special Agent Mark Hopkins. Saint Louis field office." Unes extended his hand to Warner, who gripped it firmly. "What's the situation?"

"Male Caucasian, about thirty-five, barricaded inside with about thirty hostages," the captain said, without taking his eyes off the store. "He's got a sawed-off shotgun, we presume loaded, and a belt he claims is dynamite. We assume he's telling the truth."

"Any demands?" Hopkins asked.

"No. Just keeps yelling about the end of the world. Threatens to blow the belt if we get too close."

"Only thirty hostages?" Unes said. "I would have thought the store would be busier at this time on a Friday."

"It was," Warner said. "Some of the smarter or luckier ones got out when he first pulled out the gun. Workers in the back of the store—salad bar, stock room, butchers—they left through the back. Got some of the customers out with 'em. Plus he let some of the kids go."

"Any pattern to the people he kept?"

"We don't know who he kept," Warner said, finally turning to face Unes. "What's the Bureau's interest?"

"It's your show," Unes said. "We were called to investigate a possible terror connection."

"Figures," Warner said. "Used to be lunatics were loners. Now we have to worry about whole networks of lunatics." The captain turned back to the store. "I don't know about al Qaeda, but he's got those people in there terrified."

Captain Warner was interrupted by gunfire inside the store. Two blasts from a shotgun. Unes jumped, the noise hitting like cannon fire.

As one, the law enforcement officers frantically searched for a target. A panel of glass in the front of the store spidered and collapsed outward to the sidewalk.

"Oh Lord God, to whom vengeance belongeth! O God, to whom vengeance belongeth, show thyself!" A voice, high-pitched and strained, filtered through the hole in the glass, but Joe couldn't see its owner. Whoever he was, he didn't offer a target to the sharpshooters deployed around the outside of the store.

"Lift up thyself, thou judge of the earth! Render a reward to the proud! Lord, how long shall the wicked, how long shall the wicked triumph?"

Unes, crouched behind a county patrol car between Warner and Mark Hopkins, peered around the rear bumper to get a look at the store. No sign of the man inside. The captain muttered, "Lunatic. Freaking nuts."

Unes scratched the afternoon stubble on his chin, thinking. He'd heard the shooter's words before. It dawned on the agent that it was a psalm he once heard at mass.

Again, the voice cried from inside the store, "How long, O Lord, holy and true, dost thou not judge and avenge our blood on them that dwell on the earth?"

Hopkins snorted. "Crazy son of a—Joe? This guy maybe think he's another David Koresh?"

Unes just raised his eyebrows. Who could tell what this guy was thinking?

"And I will show wonders in the heavens and in the earth, blood, and fire, and pillars of smoke," the voice cried, cracking again with fatigue, emotion, or perhaps the strain of keeping a fingerhold on reality. "The sun shall be turned into darkness, and the moon into blood, before the great and the terrible day of the Lord!"

Captain Warner began to turn toward Unes, a question on his lips, when they were suddenly slammed to the asphalt.

In an instant, the world around Joe Unes erupted in blood, and fire, and pillars of smoke.

"What was *that?*" At Scott Stauffer's apartment, four miles northwest of Grandy's, Jared Gruner and Terry Norlock stared at each other, eyes wide.

"Thunder?" Norlock offered.

"No clouds," Gruner said.

"No kidding. What *was* that?" Stauffer asked again as he and Vijay Sampurnananda emerged from Scott's tiny kitchen, snacks forgotten.

"Thunder?" Norlock repeated.

"I do not think so," Vijay said. "It is a cloudless day."

Gruner snorted. "That's what I said."

"Explosion?" Stauffer ventured.

"Sounded big," Norlock said.

"Sounded close," said Gruner.

"Much too close," said Vijay.

"Can you see anything outside?" Norlock asked.

Stauffer immediately went to the sliding glass door that opened onto a minuscule balcony overlooking the apartment community's parking lot. Mature oaks and maples surrounded the apartments, screening the single-family homes nearby from the complex, which in turn buffered the homes from the noise of busy Manchester Road. The autumn leaves and the fading light of late afternoon made seeing a smoke plume difficult at best.

Even so...

"Uh, guys? The sky is glowing." Stauffer's three friends thundered across the living room like thoroughbreds at Fairmount Park. The wooden platform groaned as they jostled for position. Slavering grues and underground kingdoms were forgotten as the four men gaped at the orange and yellow glow in the southwestern sky.

Vijay asked, "What would cause such a thing?" His question sparked a feverish round of speculation.

"Natural gas?"

"Too big."

"Car bomb?"

"Truck bomb?"

"Ammonium nitrate?"

"It'd take a lot."

"C-4, maybe."

"C-4? Plastic explosive?"

"Possible."

"Where?"

"Why?"

Four sets of eyes turned to the southwest again as the four friends considered an explanation for the ominous glow in the sky.

"There's only one way to find out, gentlemen," Gruner said. "Stofe, you got gas in your van?"

FOUR

There's nothing quite as good as coming home and opening your front door after work on a Friday afternoon. This was one of the things Tony Harris had learned to appreciate during his reintegration into normal society.

Harris threw his car keys into an empty candy dish on an end table next to his leather recliner and stretched. He looked forward to enjoying an evening of absolutely nothing important.

The lady he'd been dating the last few months, Wanda Tompkins, was out with friends, but she'd promised to call later. Harris decided to take advantage of his free evening to watch TV and catch up on some laundry.

He smiled to himself. Ten years ago, if someone had told him there'd be a day when he'd look forward to a quiet Friday night at home alone, he'd have locked himself in the trainer's room at Soldier Field and drowned himself in the whirlpool.

That was a different life. If he'd saved his money, if he'd been smarter. If he hadn't tried to cut back on that kick return in Green Bay—when his body changed direction and his left knee didn't. In one pivotal moment, he'd gone from good money and loose women to slogging toward a pension from the Chicago Board of Education.

That moment probably saved his life.

Harris scooped up the mail from the floor of the foyer and closed the door of the two-bedroom brick bungalow.

He switched on the living room light and flipped through the day's mail: Bill, junk, junk, sports magazine, and a letter from his C.O. in the National Guard.

He dropped the rest of the mail onto the kitchen table and tore open the letter from Captain Poverello. Captain P always sent a short note to his team to remind them of their monthly weekend of duty, and to ask about family, career, and so on. A good man.

Harris had served under Poverello during their six-month stint at Camp Liberty in Baghdad during the Iraq War. Poverello had a knack for getting his men to work harder than they thought they could.

Especially impressive was that Captain Poverello pulled it off with Harris, even though he was three years older, two inches taller, and about forty pounds heavier than his captain.

Harris joined the Guard as a reaction to the self-loathing that grew out of a two-year pity party following his forced retirement. The man he saw in the mirror was not who he wanted to be. An ad for the Guard caught him at a moment when he was looking for something to prove he could still rise to a challenge. He was at a recruiting office the next day.

Harris had to do some talking to get in—most recruits were a lot younger than twenty-nine—but he didn't regret a decision that had surprised a lot of people. He regained his self-respect, came to feel comfortable in his own skin again, and reconciled himself at last to life after football.

As bumpy as it was, the road Harris traveled after his last game was a lot easier than for a lot of other guys he knew.

He dropped the captain's note on top of the rest of the day's mail and reminded himself to call his sergeants tomorrow. The fridge offered up what was left of some General Tso's chicken he'd brought home three nights ago. That and a bottle of water would do nicely for dinner during the news. Then, game one of the World Series, only the Cubs' second trip to the Series since World War II. Harris found the remote on the couch and flicked on the TV while he prepared to settle into his recliner.

The devastation that greeted Harris on the fifty-five-inch screen stopped him cold. The scene looked like pictures he'd seen of a car bombing in Karbala. Except these shots were live. They moved. And the text on the upper left of the screen read, "SAINT LOUIS."

A grocery store. Rubble, a flaming ruin. Thirty people, hostages, all dead. A couple of cops outside, too.

Harris collapsed into the chair, not wanting to believe his eyes. It was one thing to see pictures like this from Baghdad or Damascus, but it was altogether different coming from the heartland of America. *Lord, what is going on? What are we doing to ourselves down here?*

He stared, horrified, and yet fascinated. All of the cable news networks were hooked into feeds from local Saint Louis stations. The supermarket looked like it had been shelled. Whatever the bomber used had been powerful.

For forty-five minutes, Harris switched between the cable networks, checking for updates. He knew a couple of guys who'd played for Saint Louis before the Rams moved back to L.A.

Then Channel 5 broke in with a bright red graphic, one of those that warn viewers to pay attention because something big is coming. The perfectly coiffed brunette announced, with a catch in her voice, that someone had opened fire with an automatic weapon at a mall just outside Philadelphia. Eighteen people were reported dead, but that wasn't confirmed.

He switched to a different station to see if they had more details. Instead, he saw fire and smoke billowing from a gaping hole in what looked like…

"Hell, no!" Harris jumped from his chair. The camera pulled back to reveal the ruined but unmistakable brick and ivy outfield wall at Wrigley Field, where, minutes before, tens of thousands of exuberant Cubs fans had anxiously awaited the first pitch of the World Series.

He woke up coughing. Joe Unes lay face down on the asphalt outside what used to be a Grandy's supermarket, trying to remember where he was. Dust from the explosion clogged his nose, and by breathing through his mouth he'd pulled in a lungful of dust.

The shrill ringing in his ears drowned out everything but the sirens, which sounded miles away. His head felt like it had been used for T-ball practice. His cheek was wet, and Unes didn't know whether it was saliva, blood, or something else. His chest spasmed with the effort of trying to clear his lungs.

Unes' head slowly cleared. He needed to get up, assess the situation. Their suspect probably wasn't going anywhere after that blast, but there were almost certainly people around him who needed help. And the air had to be better somewhere else.

Slowly, he lifted his head, testing each muscle and bone as he moved. Everything seemed to work except his ears. He coughed again, and spat a wad of chalky mucus. His eyes burned, and his back felt uncomfortably warm.

Glasses. Where are my glasses? Unes fumbled through the rubble until his fingers brushed a plastic earpiece. He picked them up and squinted at them in the orange glow that came from behind him. Scratched, but not broken.

Blowing dust off the lenses, Unes put on his glasses and pushed himself up, struggling to keep his balance. He turned toward the glow.

Where the Grandy's had been minutes before, an inferno raged.

The fire engines closest to the store were damaged beyond use. No sign of the crews. Flashing lights on Big Bend Road announced the arrival of more emergency vehicles.

Unes tried to walk and stumbled. He looked down and saw that he was about to step on Captain Warner. He knelt and placed two fingers on the captain's neck, but Unes was so shaken he couldn't tell whether Warner had a pulse.

Warner's cough answered that question.

Unes straightened to his feet, hoping to flag an EMT from one of the arriving ambulances.

As he stood, Unes wiped his damp cheek, surprised when the back of his hand came away red. He touched his cheek again. It stung, probably scraped open by the asphalt when he hit.

Then the parking lot spun, and Unes shifted his feet for balance. His upper lip was wet, and he realized his nose was bleeding, too.

An ambulance pulled into the far side of the lot. Tilting his head back to keep the blood from dripping down his face, Unes managed three faltering steps before tripping over another object.

He caught himself with both hands as he tumbled forward, badly scraping his palms on an asphalt full of splintered glass and rubble from the blast. Unes pushed himself up, blood flowing freely from his nose now, and he gritted his teeth at the fresh wounds on his hands.

The agent turned to find the obstacle that sent him crashing to the ground. It took his brain a few seconds to process the mangled mass at his feet.

He recognized the suit.

It was Mark Hopkins. And his face was gone.

"Stauffer, don't you ever put gas in this thing?"

Jared Gruner was steamed, and it showed on every one of his two hundred and ninety-five pounds. He could not fathom how his friend since high school could go out in public in a Ford Econoline older than the dinosaur bones in its gas tank.

Unfortunately, the faded blue van—that is, blue where it wasn't rusted through, with darker shadows on the doors where adhesive letters had once spelled out *Rent-a-Husband*—was the only vehicle any of them owned that was big enough for Gruner plus company.

"Yes, it's got gas!" Stauffer yelled back. "It's just missing some other things!"

"Please," Vijay interjected from the bench seat in the back. "How can we help?"

"It needs a push," Stauffer said.

"You gotta be kidding," Gruner fumed.

"No. I'll pop the clutch when it's rolling and we're good."

"I'm not pushing."

"I'm not pushing if he's in the van," Norlock said, nodding toward Gruner.

The side door slid open. "I will push," said Vijay, climbing out. Norlock rolled his eyes and followed.

Stauffer stared at Gruner until he withered, grunting as he pushed himself out of the passenger seat.

"Okay," Stauffer called, out his window. "We need to back it out of the parking space so we can get it rolling forward, down the hill toward the street."

"We're not stupid," Gruner grumbled.

"Chill, dude," said Norlock.

The three passengers heaved to and slowly forced the van to give ground. It took less than a minute, but all three were sweating despite the cool October evening.

"Okay," Stauffer called. "Now give it a push from behind until it starts rolling downhill on its own."

Gruner continued to gripe, mocking Stauffer's voice as the three switched sides. "Give it a push, give it a push."

"Look, man," Norlock said. "This was your idea. We could go back inside and finish Underground Kingdom."

Gruner gave Norlock a blistering look. "On three. One, two…"

Stauffer's battered Econoline put up a fight, but Vijay, Norlock, and Gruner prevailed, rousing the van from its slumber and propelling it down the gentle slope of the Gaslight Square Apartments parking lot. Halfway to the street, with barely fifty feet to spare, the engine finally gasped itself awake, like a cave troll with sleep apnea. An acrid cloud of blue-gray smoke fouled the air as the van roared a warning to anything that might get in its way, now that its sleep had been disturbed.

"Is that normal?" asked Vijay.

"Is anything about Stauffer normal?" asked Gruner.

Crickets sang a chorus as an orange sun melted below the horizon. The chirping had a soothing effect on Bob Moore's soul.

They'd had a good dinner—anything grilled over charcoal was okay with Bob—followed by an entertaining round of Boggle. Now, while E.J. got ready for bed, Bob enjoyed the cool evening air out on the patio.

The light, westerly breeze carried a hint of burning leaves, a pleasant smell that summoned memories of autumns past. Closing his eyes, Bob let the smoky perfume transport him to a Friday night nearly twenty years before; to a high school football game played less than five miles from where he stood: Mayfield High and its arch-rival, Harrisonville. It was the night he'd finally worked up the nerve to ask a tall, radiant girl from his third period math class for a date.

He'd never been so scared in his life.

To his eternal surprise and gratitude, Cynthia Ferguson accepted. They hadn't been apart for more than three days at a time since.

"Whatcha thinking 'bout, babe?" Cindy Moore slipped her arm around Bob's waist and joined him on the patio, listening to the cricket symphony.

"Oh, nothing," Bob said, wrapping his arm around her shoulder. After a pause, he said, "Well, yeah. I ran the numbers for the store this afternoon."

"Not too good, huh?"

"No, not too good."

"How bad?" she asked.

"At the rate things are going, ten months, maybe."

Cindy leaned her head against Bob's shoulder. Husband and wife stood quietly, gazing into the darkness. An owl hooted nearby, and a distant police siren floated on the breeze, like a mournful spirit searching for a place to rest.

After a long while, Cindy said, "I've been praying about it. You know what verse came up in my devotional today?"

"What?"

"From Matthew six: 'So I tell you to stop worrying about what you will eat, drink, or wear. Isn't life more than food and the body more than clothes? Look at the birds. They don't plant, harvest, or gather the harvest into barns. Yet, your heavenly Father feeds them. Aren't you worth more than they?'"

"Hmm."

"Hmm?"

"Timely."

Cindy turned and put her other arm around her husband. "He will take care of us. No matter what."

Bob pulled Cindy close and nodded. "I know. It's just easier hearing that verse when you're not staring bankruptcy in the face."

He was quiet for a moment. "And it hurts losing what my dad and grandpa worked so hard to build."

Cindy squeezed tighter. "I love you, Bob."

"Me too, you."

Patience is a virtue, according to the old saying. If true, then Green was a very virtuous man.

Summaries of news reports beaming into the homes of shocked television viewers around the country were piled neatly on the desk in front of him. A second stack of reports referenced violent, deadly events that had yet to reach news outlets. Even social media, fed by an ever-present army of attention hounds with video phones, was not yet aware of the unfolding horror.

A legal pad with a list of tasks, some checked as complete, sat beside the pages from the laser printer next to his desk. Green removed a cigarette from an engraved silver case in the top right-hand drawer of his desk and lit it, savoring the calming sensation of smoke in his lungs.

Another man, when presented with news of unspeakable carnage taking place in his country, would be disturbed, angry. Green was not. All was as it should be—as it *must* be.

A muted buzz signaled a call from his staff in the outer office. "Yes?"

It was Wetzel. "We have those addresses, sir."

"Good," Green said, exhaling a plume of blue-gray smoke into the dimly lit room. "Get me Fort Campbell."

FIVE

The drive from Scott Stauffer's apartment to Grandy's normally took about ten minutes. Today, the Friday afternoon traffic, swelled by curiosity seekers and emergency vehicles, stretched the trip to nearly twenty.

Gruner groaned impatiently. Life in suburban Saint Louis was usually predictable to the point of driving him crazy. Now, finally, they had a chance to be on the scene of something of national importance. He was glad he remembered to grab Stauffer's palm-sized action camera before they left the apartment. It shot 4K video at sixty frames per second with top-of-its-class image stabilization. Gruner couldn't wait to try it—if they ever got close enough to whatever happened to actually shoot some video.

As the ancient van trundled down a cross street to bypass some of the rush, Gruner muttered, "Can't you make this beast move any faster?" Stauffer ignored him. Gruner decided he'd tell Stauffer about the camera later.

The dirty orange glow in the sky ate away at the darkening blue as Stauffer urged the Econoline east along Big Bend. The traffic light at Hanna Road had switched to a four-way red flasher. Stauffer paused cautiously, then rumbled ahead, braking hard as he nearly slammed into a twisting chain of red taillights.

A quarter of a mile east, nearly every police car in West County had arrived and were diverting traffic onto the ramps for Route 141—which meant away from Grandy's.

"Roadblock," Stauffer announced. "The cops closed off the street."

"Get on the shoulder and pull into the subdivision up there." Gruner pointed ahead and to the right.

"Why? What? I can't drive on the shoulder, man. It's illegal!"

"Who's gonna tag you, huh? The cops are busy. Do it."

"And then what?

"We walk."

"Walk? Are you nuts?" Norlock leaned forward from the back seat. "To get over there, we'll have to cross One-Forty-One. On foot."

Gruner looked over his shoulder. "So?"

Norlock glared. "We'll be killed!"

Gruner rolled his eyes and turned to Stauffer. "Here, turn here."

Stauffer yanked the van into the subdivision, an upscale neighborhood of rustic, cedar-sided two-story homes.

"Not too conspicuous, are we?" Norlock asked.

"Don't worry about it," Gruner said. "I know a perfect place to park."

"Where?" Stauffer asked.

"End of the street," Gruner said mysteriously. "It's a dead end with trees all around. No one will notice."

Two minutes later, the rest of them saw why. The street came to a dead end in the middle of the Shady Rest Pet Cemetery.

Stauffer's eyes were wide as he maneuvered the van into a small parking area at the front of the burial ground. "Who puts a pet cemetery in the middle of a subdivision?"

"Ah, quiet, Stofe," Gruner said. "It's out of sight. The *end* of the subdivision. Nobody ever comes back here at night."

Stauffer gave him a peculiar look. "Exactly how do you know that?"

No good answer presented itself. "Never mind," said Gruner. "Let's go."

The four extracted themselves from the cracked and peeling vinyl upholstery, climbed out of the van, and started back up the street toward the cemetery's entrance.

"Do you mean to say," Vijay asked, "That in this country, people give their pet a ceremonial burial as if it were a member of the family?"

"Not usually," Norlock said.

It took five minutes to cross the cemetery and find a good place to cut between houses toward Route 141, a pair of homes with no lights on inside and no backyard fences.

The darkness was a blessing and a curse. It prevented prying eyes from noticing four strange men in their late twenties, haphazardly dressed, sneaking across private property after sundown. But it also made it impossible for Terry Norlock to notice an errant loop of garden hose trailing across the ground between the two homes.

"Whoa!"

Norlock's size fourteen Nikes tangled with the hose and each other, catapulting his six-foot-five-inch frame into Vijay. Only five-seven, Vijay went down like a quarterback blindsided by a blitzing linebacker.

"Aaggrrah!" *Thud!* "Get off me! Get off—please—now!"

Vijay was nervous most of the time and he strongly disliked surprises. He kept yelling even after Norlock pulled him to his feet.

Panicked, Sampurnananda bolted into the night toward the glow from the fire.

Norlock rushed after his friend, realizing Vijay might run into something even more dangerous than a water hose. "Wait!"

The noise disturbed the guardian of a split-level home to their right, a dog with a deep bark who clearly took homeyard security seriously. A furious howling mixed with grunts and growls erupted inside a screen porch just ten feet away, shredding the night air with a cry that could be heard for blocks.

It was enough to motivate Stauffer and Gruner, who rarely moved quickly for anything. They followed Vijay and Norlock at a dead run.

Fortunately, the yard held no additional surprises. They were soon far enough from the noise to slow down and carefully pick their way through a buffer of white pines that separated the subdivision from a huge, high-spired Presbyterian church. Neighborhood spectators filled the parking lot in front of the building—staring helplessly at the burning supermarket.

Norlock put out a hand and stopped the others. "We should probably go around the back way."

"It would have to be Presbyterian," Gruner muttered, catching his breath.

"What do you mean?" Vijay gasped, his own heart still thumping.

"The Presbyterians and Catholics have all the biggest churches in Saint Louis," Gruner said as he gestured toward the expanse of parking lot before them. "If this was, like, independent Baptist, we wouldn't have to walk so far."

Watching news for hours on end was not how Tony Harris usually spent an evening at home. Football, yes; baseball, sometimes; even a decent movie could keep him in a chair for a couple of hours at a time. But not news. Too much of the same thing night after night, especially since twenty-four hour news networks had spread like crabgrass across the middle numbers of his cable box. Years ago, when cable news channels actually reported news, it was convenient for catching up on what was going on. Now it was all talking heads shouting at each other, especially on slow news days when they were desperate for eyeballs.

Today was anything but a slow news day.

The death toll at Wrigley Field was estimated at over two thousand, and that was probably going to get worse as more of the critically injured lost the fight for life. Thousands of wounded had been rushed to hospitals all over Cook County. Emergency rooms overflowed with the dead, dying, and dumbstruck.

Someone had smuggled a bomb into the bleachers. Maybe more than one. Borrowing a trick from the Middle East, it had been made even more lethal with thousands of nails and sharp metal fragments packed around the device. One of the medical personnel speculated, based on the condition of the victims at the scene, that the shrapnel was coated with rat poison or a similar toxic substance.

It was like watching the aftermath of a wreck on the Kennedy or Dan Ryan. Harris couldn't tear his eyes away from the television screen. Between the death and agony at Wrigley Field, the King of Prussia Mall, and the supermarket near Saint Louis, news producers had a career's worth of raw and bloody images packed into a few short hours of hell.

To intensify the fear, foreign journalists reported military movements in the Middle East. Expert observers of the age-old chess match said this signaled an invasion of Syria by Israel.

The world had gone mad.

The ring of Harris's telephone made him jump. "Hold on," he muttered, struggling to get the phone out of his pants pocket.

"Hello?"

"Lieutenant Harris?" A male voice, probably in his early twenties. Harris didn't recognize it.

"Yes?"

"This is Lieutenant Walters with HQ. You are to report within forty-eight hours to your company rendezvous for…"

"Whoa, Lieutenant! I'm not scheduled to go back out for another two weeks!"

"I'm sorry, Lieutenant, but these are my orders. This is not training—the Three-Sixty-Ninth MPs are being called up immediately."

"*Called up?* Are you sure?"

"Yes."

"For how long?"

"I don't know. Sorry."

"All right, Lieutenant. Thanks for the call—I know it's not an easy one to make." Harris stared at his phone for a long moment. *How can a lump of plastic and silicon totally rearrange a man's life?* Then he thought of the men, women, and children—*children, for Godsake!*—who would never again watch a ballgame or make a phone call. "Sweet Jesus, help us all," he whispered.

Somebody had to answer for the live horror show that was playing in America's living rooms tonight.

Suddenly, Harris felt an odd sense of calm, of pride—of responsibility and determination. Someone would pay. And he, and the entire 369th, were getting in on the payback.

Even though he wore only a T-shirt and baggy shorts, the cool night air didn't keep Jared Gruner from sweating. The distance from the pet cemetery to the four-lane divided highway they faced was as far as he'd walked in one stretch all year. And that was at a *Babylon Five* fan convention, to get Mira Furlan's autograph. He'd waited two hours to spend ten seconds in her presence. It had been totally worth it.

The obstacle in front of him now wasn't nearly as appealing.

Route 141 was the main north-south corridor in western Saint Louis County. It looped from Arnold, south of Saint Louis, to the well-to-do West County suburb of Chesterfield. It connected some of the fastest-growing areas in the state of Missouri.

To Gruner, it looked like everyone who lived there was trying to get home at once.

"Are you sure you wanna do this?" Norlock asked.

"Do you want to see what happened up there?" The glow from the fire on the other side of the road was bright enough to read by. Gruner was determined to see it for himself. Something very bad had gone down in his backyard and he wanted to know what.

"Well," Stauffer said, looking both ways, "At least they're slowing down to look."

"Okay," Gruner said. "It's in the timing. We just need a gap."

The four fixed on the southbound traffic, waiting for their opportunity. It wasn't long in coming. About two minutes after reaching the side of the road, a window opened in the flow of cars and trucks that allowed the four men to practically walk across the two southbound lanes.

"See? That was easy," Gruner said.

Stauffer looked at the northbound traffic and grimaced. It was at least twice as heavy. "What is the airspeed velocity of an unladen swallow?"

The others stared at him as if he'd suddenly burst into song.

"I do not understand," Vijay said.

"Monty Python," Norlock said. "You wouldn't."

"Oh, *The Holy Grail*. I have only seen it once," Vijay said. "In India. Maybe the translation lost something."

Gruner suddenly yelled, "NOW!"

The other three turned to see Gruner charge onto the concrete ribbon with the grace of an enraged rhinoceros. The others, in spite of the two-second jump, easily beat him to the other side.

Gruner finally arrived at the shoulder, gasping for air, just before a semi-trailer barreled through the space he'd occupied a couple of seconds earlier.

"Hey! You coulda been toast, man," Norlock said.

"Had plenty...to spare," Gruner wheezed, leaning forward with his hands on his knees to catch his breath. "No...problem."

"Look, guys," Stauffer said, "Let's get off the road. We're exposed."

Stauffer started up the slope toward the Grandy's, followed by Vijay and Norlock. To Gruner, their silhouettes against the scorched, pulsating sky, tinted orange by the flames from the ruined store, made it appear as though his friends were walking straight into the very mouth of hell.

Jared Gruner began to wonder whether this was a good idea after all.

Joe Unes opened his eyes with a start. He'd passed out. *Funny how you only notice after it happens*, he thought.

The sight of Mark Hopkins had buckled his knees. Hopkins had been facing the store when it blew. A chunk of something must have caught him straight on. Unes hoped it had been quick and painless.

He lay on his side, facing away from the store. The fire burned angrily, and it was much too warm. Unes rolled to his back and tried to sit up, but the effort made him dizzy. He slowly lowered himself to the asphalt again. The sky reflected the blaze, the low clouds a canvas that captured the fire's demonic rage. The world around Joe Unes throbbed and pulsed a sickly, reddish orange like a diseased blister.

Coughing again from the dust, Unes rolled to his left side and almost crushed his glasses. He picked them up and put them on again. The police cars encircling the front of Grandy's had been knocked out of position, as if some enormous child had tired of his toys and swept them away with a careless hand. Hopkins' Impala sat about twenty feet away, its windshield spider-webbed with cracks. One of the headlights was broken, and fluid dripped from the engine.

Unes stared at the drip for what seemed like a long time, trying to decide whether it was antifreeze, oil, or gasoline.

It was time to move, regardless. He was roasting. And even though he still heard sirens, far away, muffled by the ringing in his ears, no one was coming his way to help.

Movement at the corner of his eye drew his attention back to the burning store.

Unes blinked, his eyes watering and distorting the images. It couldn't be, but he thought he saw men walking out of the flames. Had to be his imagination. Had he hit his head hard enough to hallucinate? *Fire's too hot. Nothing could have lived through that.*

But there they were. Three—no, four figures walking out of the fire. *Like a trailer for a bad action film.*

An odd thought. Unes closed his eyes hard and tried to sit up, but the parking lot seemed to bend and warp beneath him. He grabbed at it, scratching for a finger hold to keep from falling off.

Unes closed his eyes and breathed deeply, struggling against nausea. Sweat rolled down his face as heat washed over him like waves ahead of a hurricane. He opened his eyes, and the shapes were closer. One tall, one short, one wide, one…none of the above. Black shadows silhouetted against the inferno. Coming for him.

Is this how God sends for you when you die? Unes shut his eyes again, wishing desperately to get away from the fire. *God, I'm hot.*

"Hey, over here!" The voice was urgent and close.

Unes felt hands under his arms, pulling him up. He found himself being half-carried by two men, the tall one and the wide one. A cool breeze brushed his face, and he realized that his time wasn't up, not yet. He hurt. *You don't hurt when you're dead, do you?*

Maybe he'd still be able to find out who did this, or at least why.

He was lowered again to the ground, but this time there was a pillow under his head instead of debris-choked asphalt. Unes opened his eyes and saw a man in white kneeling over him. The EMT pulled back, and his face was replaced by four others that looked like they'd come straight from the local GameStop: a tall, blond man wearing an Apple Store T-shirt; a square, stocky face framed by hair that hadn't seen a comb in years; an earnest young Indian or Pakistani; and a short guy with glasses who looked like a cross between Moe Howard and Elvis Costello.

Joe Unes closed his eyes and began to laugh. He hurt all over, but he was most definitely alive—and he'd just been pulled from the flames of hell by the Four Nerdsmen of the Apocalypse.

SIX

The telephone rang in the Moores' kitchen. E.J. had gone to bed just ten minutes before, so Bob, who'd come downstairs for ice cream, picked it up on the second ring.

"Hello?"

"Bob? Ted Thornton." Ted was the sheriff for Kiowa County. Bob had known him since grammar school. He and his family attended Mayfield Bible Church, where Bob served as an elder.

"Hi, Ted. What can I do for you?"

"Bob, this is going to sound strange, but you're going to have to trust me." Sheriff Thornton's voice was low and intense, as though he had company he didn't want listening in.

"What is it, Ted?"

"You need to get your family and get out of your house, now."

"What?"

"You heard me," the sheriff repeated. "Take what you can. Food, clothing, blankets, water. Get out of the house. Now."

"Wha— Why?" This made no sense. Ted Thornton was a sensible, honest man. He had a good sense of humor, but practical jokes were not in character.

"Bob," Sheriff Thornton said, "You're going to have to trust me. Something funny is going on. I don't know what it is. I'm here at the office. Some men just called me away from dinner. Government men, and they want you. Now, Bob, I don't know these men, and I don't trust them. And Bob, they do *not* look like they're playing around. My advice to you, *unofficially*, is that you and your family hightail it right now for the most remote place you can think of until I can sort this out."

Bob couldn't believe his ears. He still wondered if Ted might be pulling his leg. "What would they want with me?"

"I don't know!" Thornton's voice dropped to an urgent whisper. "Bob, for God's sake, these men are not state troopers or FBI. I don't know what branch of the government they are or if they're government at all. But they've got paperwork from Homeland Security and they're armed. I'm talking automatic weapons here. And they don't look like they're going to bother with little details like reading you your rights. I bought you a little time, sent them off in the wrong direction. But they're gonna figure out I lied pretty quick and that's gonna make 'em mad. Now listen to me, and get—" The line suddenly went dead.

"Hello? Hello?" Bob listened for a few seconds. Nothing. Not even static.

His mind reeled. Ted Thornton was not the kind to use his office to pull a gag.

What to do? Standing in the middle of his kitchen, wearing a T-shirt, plaid lounge pants and a pair of house slippers, Bob closed his eyes and prayed.

Lord, I need a little guidance here. We're supposed to obey the government. Romans, chapter thirteen. What do I do?

An image of Joseph and Mary leaving Bethlehem and fleeing to Egypt ahead of Herod's soldiers came to his mind. And Ted Thornton was a government employee, too.

Bob made up his mind. He ran up the stairs two at a time.

"Who were you speaking to, sir?"

This was the cherry on the cake of Ted Thornton's day. Instead of enjoying a Friday night at the Mayfield High football game, he'd been called in by a deputy to deal with armed men who'd come to his office asking for directions.

Now Sheriff Thornton faced two men, late twenties or early thirties he guessed, dressed in black, wearing body armor and carrying M4 carbines. They nearly filled Thornton's small wood-paneled office, which was tucked into the back of the county administration building like an afterthought. His misdirection hadn't fooled them for more than a couple of minutes. He hoped it was enough.

"Tell me who you are, exactly," Thornton said.

"We're with the government." The taller one had a square chin, intense gray eyes, and looked to be in top physical condition. Thornton tried to keep fit by jogging and had seen his share of fights, but he judged the man on the other side of his desk could take him apart with his bare hands.

"You said that before," Thornton said. "Who with?"

"Homeland Security."

"Uh huh. And just why are you in Kiowa County?"

"Classified. I'm asking again, sir, who were you speaking to?"

Thornton didn't like this guy one bit. All he knew was that this Captain Thiel led a dozen well-armed men looking for Bob Moore and he wasn't being very polite about it.

"County business," Thornton said. "Now will you tell me what's going on?"

"No, sir, I am not authorized—"

Thornton cut him off. "I am the senior law enforcement official in this county," he said, leaning forward and putting his hands on his desk. "Unless you can show me some reason why your mission here supersedes my authority—"

"It does," Thiel interrupted. "Sir, we are under a state of emergency declared by the president of the United States. The administrator of FEMA Region Seven in Kansas City is now the ranking law enforcement official in this area. We are here on his authority."

Thornton couldn't believe his ears. "Emergency? What emergency?"

"Terrorism, sir. At least five separate incidents around the country. Maybe more that we don't know about yet. We're trying to prevent more. Now, sir—"

"What kind of a crock is this?" His temper was getting the better of him, but Thornton didn't care. Pushing away from the desk, he fumed, "You can't just come into my county and arrest a man I've known for more than twenty years without some kind of legal—"

"Sir, I am losing patience."

Sheriff Ted Thornton suddenly stared into the five-point-five-eight millimeter abyss that was the barrel of an M4. Captain Thiel never raised his voice, but Thornton got the sense of a coiled spring that was about to let go.

Or a coiled serpent.

"What do you want?" Thornton's voice was suddenly dry, rasping.

"I extended you the courtesy of coming to see you prior to apprehending Mister Moore," Thiel said. "This is, or *was*, your jurisdiction. It took us five minutes to determine that you were either misinformed or lying. GPS doesn't lie, and it is our business to find people in pitch dark. You mistook my courtesy for stupidity. And now I have to ask, why?"

Thornton felt his sweat soaking through his undershirt. What in the world could Bob Moore have done to put men like this on his tail? Not FBI. Thiel was a captain. Not an FBI rank. What, then? Delta Force? *Inside the United States?*

Thornton licked his lips. "You from Fort Benning?"

"Sheriff," Captain Thiel said, "Who were you speaking to?"

"Because I knew some guys at Benning back when I was in the service," Thornton said. "Crazy, all of 'em. But I guess you gotta be to do what you do, right?"

"Sheriff, I won't ask again," Thiel said, keeping his weapon on Thornton. "I will take you into custody, too."

"You'll what?"

"Sir, you may have aided the escape of a terrorist, someone we believe is part of a plot to bring down the government of the United States. As such, you would be considered an enemy of the state and subject to the same rules of engagement."

"Captain," Thornton said, "I volunteered and served a tour in the infantry. Afghanistan. Came back home, and I've been in law enforcement for fifteen years. The last thing I want to see is anybody get away with an attack on this country. But if you think Bob Moore—"

"Sir, slowly place your revolver on your desk and put your hands on top of your head."

"You're kidding."

"No, sir, I am not."

Thornton stared into the captain's gray eyes for several seconds before speaking. "No, I guess you're not."

Very slowly, and with one finger, Thornton removed his gun from its holster and set it on top of his desk. Thiel's assistant, who'd been hovering in the background, stepped in and took it.

Just as Thornton's fingers interlocked on top of his head, his mobile phone rang. Thiel picked it up from the desk and answered.

"Yes?" He listened for a moment, his face never changing expression. "Sheriff. It's for you."

Ted Thornton cautiously reached for the phone. "Sheriff!" The voice was frantic, almost hysterical. "I did it. Oh, God, I did it!"

"Did what? Who is this?"

"I didn't want to, but I did, and now they're dead! Oh, God, it's the end of the world! The end!"

"Who is this?" Thornton grabbed a pen from a coffee mug he used as a desk organizer and looked at the caller ID on his phone: *BELCHER ED M.*

"Ed? Ed Belcher?" Big guy, six-four, farmer with a couple thousand acres out on Highway W. Wife, three small children. Inherited the farm from his dad about eight years ago. Forced to slaughter his entire stock of hogs a couple months back because of the bird flu scare.

"Sheriff, I didn't want to, I didn't, but I did, and they're dead!" Belcher's voice trailed upward in a wail of pain or grief—or madness.

"Ed, you gotta calm down. Now, tell me what's going on. Are you all right? Is your family all right?" Thornton blocked out the black-clad men with their weapons trained on him. "Come on, Ed, talk to me! Tell me what happened."

"End of the world, end, end, end," Belcher moaned, an eerie, hollow sound that seemed to come from his very soul—a soul convinced that it was beyond hope of redemption. A rattling sound suggested that Belcher had dropped his phone.

"Ed! This is Sheriff Thornton. It's going to be okay, but you have to talk to me. Ed? I need you to tell me—"

An explosion of noise halted Thornton in mid-sentence. The sheriff jumped, his ear ringing, horrified by what he feared had just happened at the Belcher farm.

"Ed! Ed!" Thornton shouted into the phone, but he knew with a cold, sick certainty there would be no answer.

The sheriff looked up at the Special Forces captain. "All hell is breaking loose," Thornton said. "Ed Belcher. Good man. His family's farmed that piece of ground since before the Civil War. You heard the gunshot?"

Thiel nodded.

"All right," Thornton said. "You want the truth? I was on the phone with Bob Moore. Where is he going? I don't know, but I hope to hell you don't find him. Now, you boys want to handle this call, too, or can I have my gun, get a couple of deputies, and see if anyone's still alive out there?"

"Sheriff, what did he say to you?"

"Who, Belcher?"

Thiel nodded.

"He was yelling about the end of the world. He didn't want to do it but he did, and now they're all dead." Sheriff Thornton's mind worked overtime to keep his imagination from picturing the horror that waited at the Belcher place. His face was drawn. "He's got three kids, ten years old and younger. They're five miles out. And you are wasting their time."

Thiel's mouth tightened at the corners. "Sheriff," he said, "We're coming with you."

Thornton frowned. "Why?"

Thiel turned and directed his response to his assistant. "There are more of them here than we were told."

One good thing about packing for the Guards, Harris thought, was that you never had to worry about which clothes to bring. He had his duffel ready to go within an hour of the phone call from Lieutenant Walters.

The television blared in the background, delivering a stream of news that had steadily grown worse. The attacks already made 9/11 look like child's play. Besides Philadelphia, Chicago, and

Saint Louis, thousands more were probably dead in Los Angeles, Denver, Houston, and Tampa. The Houston blast had taken out an entire refinery complex near Baytown. That was especially bad. It would be days before the fires were under control, and by then there wouldn't be enough left of the bodies to identify many of the victims.

It was like the United States had plunged off a cliff into a bottomless pit of complete anarchy. Experts called in on short notice by the cable news networks were full of speculation but not much useful analysis. None of the incidents seemed connected except by the timing. And, Harris realized, the guys who really knew anything useful were too busy to talk to reporters.

As he zipped his duffel bag closed, another "breaking news" bumper caught his attention. When the announcer returned, he was clearly disturbed by the report he delivered.

"We've just had word that what appear to be the opening shots in a Middle East war have been fired. Shortly before dawn local time, tanks from the Israel Defense Force mobilized from positions in the Golan Heights and entered Syrian territory near the border crossing at Quneitra. Witnesses report a number of large explosions on the Syrian side of the border, but it is unclear whether they were caused by Israeli aircraft or artillery. A video statement posted to an Islamic State channel on YouTube calls it a 'blatant act of aggression by the Zionist occupiers of Palestine' and promises a fight to the last man. There has been no comment so far from the Israeli government."

Harris switched off the television. Information overload. No more death, no more talking heads guessing at what it meant. Hell in a hand basket, was his opinion.

He was packed, but he had until Sunday night to report. No rush. He'd have to take care of some housekeeping details in the morning; stop his mail with the post office, set the furnace at fifty-five degrees, store the Camaro properly in the garage, making sure it was locked up tight.

Now came the tough part. *Might as well get it done and over with.*

He sat down in his chair, pulled out his phone and called the mother of his son, Demetrius. Beautiful Shareece, a trophy to impress his teammates. Except that she'd had their child just as he began to realize that his professional football career was over. He'd been so wrapped up in self-pity that he had nothing left of for Shareece and Demetrius. She'd made him pay ever since.

She answered on the third ring. "Hello?"

"Shareece? It's Tony." A deep chill radiated through the phone.

"What do you want?" she asked icily.

"I've just been called up for active duty. I'm not going to be able to take Demetrius next weekend."

"What? How can you do this? I have plans!"

"Hey," Harris said. "I'm not *doing* anything. My unit's been called up. I have to go."

A pause. "How long?"

"I don't know."

He held the phone away from his ear as she let loose a shrill burst of foul language.

"Shareece, I really don't want this—"

"You're always doing this to me!"

"That's not true," he said. "Okay, once it was, but that part of my life is over. I'm doing the best I can, Shareece. I don't drink. Been at the same job four years now. I'm here whenever he needs me."

"Except for when you run off to play soldier," Shareece said. "You were gone nine months last time."

"Not my call, Shareece. A lot of guys were in Iraq longer than that."

"Fine. Where you going to be, so I can see if you're coming back?"

Nice, Harris thought. "I don't know," he said. "I'll let you know as soon as they tell us where we're going. Might be the Middle East again. You been watching the news tonight?"

"No. Why?"

"Never mind. Can I see Demetrius tomorrow or Sunday?"

"Judge said you get the third weekend of the month."

"Yeah, I know, Shareece, but I have to report Sunday night."

"Third weekend, Tony," Shareece said, sounding smug. "Ain't my fault if you're not here."

"Come on, Shareece," Harris said, trying to keep his anger contained. "Demetrius needs to know he's got a daddy who loves him."

"Loved him so much he couldn't be bothered when he was being born. Left his mama alone in the hospital. Didn't see his little boy until he was two weeks old. And not again for two years."

Harris took a deep breath. This was an old, painful wound. "Shareece, I am sorry for those days, really sorry. I would do it different if I could. For Demetrius and for you. What I did was wrong, and I deserve whatever you throw at me. I earned it. Why do you think I let you bust on me every time we talk? I don't take this from anybody but you. But let me ask you this, Shareece: Who gets hurt if Demetrius grows up thinking his daddy don't love him? Not you, Shareece. Not you. Him."

There was a long silence on the phone, and Harris began to believe he might have persuaded Shareece, just this once, to give him a break.

"Good-bye, Tony." The connection died—and with it, another small piece of Tony Harris' heart.

The pounding in Joe Unes' head had begun to subside and the ringing in his ears had faded to where he could hear people talking to him without straining. An EMT had checked him over and found that Unes' only injuries, miraculously, were skinned palms, a scratch on his cheek, a bump on his head from the asphalt, and a bloody nose.

Thirty-seven others, including his partner, had not been so blessed.

Why not me? Unes wondered. *Not that I'm complaining, God.*

Standing nearby were the four young men who'd pulled him away from the heat of the blaze, which was nearly under control. Fire crews from as far away as Eureka, way out I-44 near the big amusement park. The big guy held a small digital video camera.

Unes stood, slowly, a bottle of water in one hand and a cold compress for the lump on his forehead in the other.

"I want to thank you guys for pulling me away from that mess over there," he said. "It was getting warm."

"Glad to help," the big one said. "I'm Jared Gruner."

The little one stuck out his hand. "Scott Stauffer."

"Terry Norlock," said the tall one.

"I am Vijay," said the Indian.

Unes reached into the pocket of his torn and soiled jacket. His ID was still there. He showed it and introduced himself. "Special Agent Joe Unes, FBI. I hate to ask, since you fellas were kind enough to keep me from roasting, but why are you here?"

The big guy's eyebrows lifted a little and the kid with the Moe Howard haircut flinched.

"We heard the explosion and wanted to see what happened," Norlock said.

"Just happened to be driving by," Stauffer added. "We pulled off back there and walked up."

"Through the police line," Unes observed.

"You see, Agent Unes," Gruner said, "We were thinking this might be something big. Something that, uh, we might be able to help in some way."

Unes nodded. The big guy was twitchy. "Where did you park?"

"The pet cemetery," said Vijay. "A most unusual place."

His three friends glared at him as though he'd just confessed to detonating the bomb.

"The pet cemetery? On the far side of the church?" Unes asked.

"You know it?" Vijay smiled. "I do not understand the custom. It is not something we do in India."

"Sure, I know it," Unes said. Vijay's friends tried to find a discreet way to shut him up, but Vijay wasn't picking up on the non-verbal signals. "So you guys crossed the highway, then?"

"Yes," Vijay said. "It was very exciting." He obviously enjoyed being helpful. The other three looked everywhere but at Unes.

"I'll tell you what," Unes said. "Stay here a minute. We need to talk, but I have to find a working phone. I need to call my wife and mine's dead."

Stauffer said, "Do you want me to look at it? I'm pretty good with things like that."

"Be my guest." Unes pulled the phone from the left inside pocket of his sport coat and handed it over.

Turning it over in his hands, Scott Stauffer squinted as he examined the phone for signs of damage. He held it back up to Unes, turning it to catch the light from the burning building. "Here's your problem, right here."

How did I miss that? The back of his cell phone had a hole as big around as the tip of his little finger. Stauffer shook the phone, and Unes just barely heard a metallic rattle above the ringing in his ears.

"Where was your phone when the place blew?" Stauffer asked.

"Here," Unes said, the short hairs on the back of his neck standing at attention. "Right here." He looked down and pointed to a small hole in his jacket, directly above his heart.

SEVEN

Eric Moore had never in his ten years seen his father scared. It was really...*weird* was the only word he could think of, but that really didn't cover it.

Most children believe their fathers are invulnerable. Inevitably, though, the day comes when that illusion is shattered. It's a profound awakening. The sudden shock of realizing that one's father is human, subject to uncertainties, flaws, and self-doubt turns a kid's world upside-down. Tonight, it was Eric Moore's turn to grapple with that epiphany, and his ten-year-old vocabulary wasn't up to putting his emotions into words.

All he knew was that he didn't like it.

When his bedroom door burst open, Eric thought his dad was coming in to scold him for reading in bed again. But he knew right away that wasn't it. Eric's system for hiding the glow of his flashlight under the covers was foolproof. Instead, his dad switched on the light, and his bearded face had a look Eric had never seen before.

"Get dressed, son. Fast as you can. Right now!" And then he turned and ran—*ran!*—up the hall to his own bedroom. He always yelled when Eric ran in the house.

"Dad?" Eric sat up in bed, confused. The look on his father's face was—well, weird, but Eric was pretty sure his dad was serious. He slid to the floor and started up the hall to find out. He heard voices, low and urgent, behind his parents' door.

"Dad? What's the matter?" The door to his parents' room opened, and his dad stepped into the hall wearing a T-shirt and a pair of jeans. He was barefoot.

"E.J.? I said get dressed, and I mean it! Right now! Don't ask, just go!" And then he ducked back into their room without even closing the door for privacy.

"Dad?" A dozen scenarios ran through his mind, but they gave no hint as to what was happening. Eric turned and walked slowly back to his room. He'd just started removing his pajama top when his dad came running down the hall.

"E.J.? Why aren't you—" His dad stopped, took a deep breath and started again. "Look, buddy, I'm sorry I yelled. We haven't got much time. Sheriff Thornton called. He thinks we're in trouble, and we need to leave the house right away. We only have a few minutes. So get dressed as quick as you can and meet us downstairs. Can you do that?"

Eric nodded, stunned.

"Good. Grab a few books, nothing too heavy. We might be gone awhile. Okay?"

Eric nodded again and continued undressing, much faster. He threw on his favorite T-shirt, the one with the picture of the cartoon alien invader from TV, jeans, and his favorite sneakers. He grabbed his Iowa Hawkeyes cap, the book stashed under his blanket, two more he planned to read, and tumbled downstairs in less than three minutes.

His dad carried a load of stuff from the store in a big cardboard box. Eric saw cans, boxes, a roll of aluminum foil, some batteries and a flashlight. He heard a footstep on the stairs and turned to see his mom trying to maneuver around the turn at the landing with a big box in her arms.

"Eric," his father said, huffing into the kitchen with another armload of cans, "Do you remember the sleeping bags in the storage room upstairs?"

Eric nodded.

"Run up and get those, will you? Cindy, anything you can think of? Non-perishable food, stuff we can eat without too much preparation? Soap? First aid kit?"

"Matches, can opener, utility knife," Cindy Moore said. "Prescriptions, other meds, all in this box. Bob, how much time have we got? These plans won't help if they get here before we go."

"One more trip," Bob said, disappearing through the office and back into the store. Eric ran up the stairs and down the hall to the storage closet, a door to the unfinished part of the attic. The space was about fifteen feet wide and about twenty-five feet long, about half the length of the second floor. Eric's grandfather had put plywood on top of the joists to give the family some extra storage space.

Generations of treasure, things collected by the family through the years, and some that had been handed down from Eric's grandfather and great-grandfather, were packed into neatly labeled boxes along either side of the space. Eric ignored them now, motivated by his parents' urgency.

The sleeping bags were on a wooden shelving unit toward the back of the attic. He pulled down two and wrestled them out of the attic and into the hall. Dropping them just outside the door, Eric went back and quickly grabbed the third. Out in the hall again, Eric kicked the sleeping bags, first one and then the others, until he reached the stairs. Then he yelled, "Watch out!"

The first bag rolled down the stairs nicely, three hops and a thump when it hit the kitchen floor. The second bag followed— *bounce, bounce, bounce, thump!* Eric carried the last one down himself.

Eric entered the kitchen as his dad struggled with four one-gallon jugs of water. A light blinked on in the darkness outside. Eric's stomach jumped until he realized it was only his mother opening the door to their SUV.

"Where do you want these, Dad?" Eric asked.

"Outside, outside," his dad said. "We need to get it into the car and go."

Picking up a second sleeping bag, Eric stepped out into the cool night air. In a way, this was like an adventure. Maybe this would be fun, something to tell the guys about Monday at school.

Then he remembered the scared look in his dad's eyes. Eric didn't think he was going to like this at all.

It was a little after ten p.m. when Ted Thornton arrived at Ed Belcher's farm. Chief Deputy Ann Jurasik, who'd been looking forward to only one more hour on her shift before heading over to the Quad Cities to visit family for the weekend, sat next to him in his prowler, a three-year-old white Chevy Tahoe, a frown compressing her thin lips into a straight line. Captain Thiel and his team were right behind them in two GMVs, the lightweight all-terrain vehicles preferred by special ops units.

The house was a white frame foursquare built just after World War I. Set back about two hundred feet from the two-lane asphalt of Highway W, it had been home to four generations of Belchers. Behind it lay two thousand acres of rich topsoil that had been cleared, plowed and loved by Belcher men for a hundred and fifty years. Ed Belcher was proud of who he was, one of a dying breed. The small family farm in America was going the way of the horse-drawn carriage.

The lights were on inside the house, but the shades were drawn. A dog barked out back. Jud, Thornton remembered, the Belchers' black lab. Probably on his tether. Good dog, but tended to roam after dark. Ed kept Jud tied up at night so the neighbors up the road could rule him out as a suspect if chickens went missing.

Thornton shoved the door open and jumped out of the Tahoe, listening for anything besides Jud, who kept up a steady bark. It was as though he knew something was terribly, horribly wrong, and his frantic bark was a cry for help.

Poor fella, Thornton thought. *He may be coming home with me tonight.*

"Well, let's go," Thornton said. "Look sharp. You go around back. I'll take the front door." Sheriff and deputy approached the house side by side, both with guns drawn. The gravel of the unpaved drive shifted under their feet, crunching with each step, unnaturally loud.

The contrast between the sheriff's beefy six-one frame and his deputy's trim five-foot-six was almost comical, but there was no one in the department he trusted more. Ann Jurasik had eleven years on the force, and she was far and away the best officer Thornton had. There had been no EEOC consideration when she was promoted to Chief Deputy. She'd earned it.

Behind them, soldiers piled out of their GMVs, moving quickly and silently as they surrounded the property. Captain Thiel caught up to Thornton. "Sheriff," he said, "My team will enter and secure the building."

"Not in this lifetime," Thornton growled, without slowing or turning his head. "This is my job. These are my people."

"With all due respect, sir, we're better trained for this."

"With all due respect, captain, stay the hell out of my way." Thornton cleared the three steps to the front porch in one bound. He called, "Ed! Ed Belcher!"

The only sound was Jud's nonstop barking, louder now with the arrival of so many strangers.

Thornton didn't wait. He tried the knob. Unlocked. He turned it and pushed the door open, slowly.

It was worse than he could have imagined.

Sheriff Ted Thornton stepped into the front room of a nightmare. The three children—Ed Junior, Traci, and Mikey—sat on the living room couch in their pajamas. They slumped to one side, little Ed leaning against the wall, Traci against his shoulder, and Mikey lying on his side with his head in Traci's lap. They might have been three children who'd stayed up too late and fallen asleep watching television, except that their hands and feet were bound with duct tape—and they all had gaping, bloody holes where their middles used to be.

"Oh, my God," Thornton said softly. In fifteen-plus years of law enforcement, he'd never confronted a scene as heartbreaking as this.

"Sheriff!" It was Jurasik, calling from the kitchen, her voice strained. "Sheriff, Belcher's in here."

Thornton quickly moved through the dining room and around to the kitchen on the right. He held out some small hope that Belcher was still alive, that maybe he could make some sense of the horror in the living room.

That hope died a split second after he reached the kitchen.

The normally white walls and cabinets were splattered with reddish-brown gore. Ed Belcher's brains.

Belcher was sprawled on the floor, head against the base cabinet beneath the sink, his shotgun on the floor next to him. It seemed clear that he'd set down the phone, put the business end of his shotgun in his mouth, and pulled the trigger with his thumb.

Deputy Jurasik stood with her hand over her mouth. She'd known Ed Belcher a long time, too. Graduated in the same high school class. A tragedy.

"Ann," Thornton said, his mouth dry, "You all right?"

"Yeah," Jurasik said, wiping a tear from her eye with the back of her hand. "Yeah, I'll be all right. Did you find Sarah?"

Belcher's wife. "No. God. Maybe she got out." He hoped so.

He heard footsteps upstairs, several sets. A chair scraped against the floor. *The bastards are searching the house!*

Thornton turned on Captain Thiel. "Your people upstairs?" he demanded.

"Yes, sir." Thiel's no-nonsense expression hadn't changed since he'd walked into the sheriff's office an hour earlier.

This was too much. The sheriff's stomach knotted. "This is not a military operation, you snot-nosed punk! This is a crime scene! We have to document what happened here and present it to a court of law. And you are contaminating this crime scene."

"It looks cut and dried to me."

"Maybe," Thornton said, "But if we start finding prints and fibers that lead to you or your team, well, then, we'll have a hell of a problem, won't we?"

"No, sir," Thiel said. "We will not."

"You don't know much about the law, do you?"

Captain Thiel fixed him with steel-gray eyes. "I know enough to advise you against getting in my way," he said. "It would be a waste of your time."

Thornton's face grew hot. He was close to not caring whether he did something stupid. "Is that so? Let me tell you this: If I find one *shred* of evidence, just *one piece* of furniture out of place, I will have you back here so fast—"

"Sir." Thiel stopped him with a word, raising his voice for the first time all evening. "Do you know what 'unconditional immunity' means?"

Thornton glared at the younger man.

"Because I have it." Thiel continued. "By presidential directive. Unconditional immunity. Unless *you* do, I suggest you concentrate on your crime scene and forget we were here. Even if you find a shred of evidence."

"Sir." George Burgos, Thiel's warrant officer, entered the kitchen from the dining room. "The woman is upstairs. Hands and feet duct-taped, just like the kids. Face down on the bed. One shot, back of the head."

"Good Lord," Thornton said. Jurasik caught her breath, trying to hold back her tears in front of these intruders in black.

"Anything else?" Thiel asked.

"Yes, sir. We got it," Burgos said enigmatically.

"That's all, then," Thiel said, turning to Thornton. "We're leaving. Sheriff, remember what I said. We're at war, and you need to choose which side you're on." Thiel followed Burgos out of the house, leaving the sheriff and his deputy in the kitchen with the body of Ed Belcher.

"What did he mean by that, Sheriff? 'We got it'?" Jurasik asked. "Got what? What are they doing here?"

Thornton shook his head. "I don't know. 'Homeland Security' is what he said. But I have no earthly idea why DHS would use Special Forces to arrest people in the middle of Iowa."

"Special Forces?" Jurasik asked, eyes wide.

"Have to be. Too military for FBI. The gear, the vehicles— that's not law enforcement. That's who we send to bad places to get bad people." Thornton stared through the kitchen window into the black night, lost in thought.

Finally, Jurasik asked, "Should I call the coroner?"

Thornton sighed. "Yeah, go ahead," he said. "Get Robbie and Farns out here, too, just in case we need to keep people away. It's going to be a long night for everybody. I better call my wife." The sheriff pulled a cell phone from a holster on his belt while Jurasik went to the car to raise county dispatch.

Susie answered on the second ring. "Hello?"

"Hey, babe."

"Is it bad?" she asked simply.

Ted Thornton had given up trying to hide his feelings from his wife within the first three years of their marriage. Seventeen more years of practice had only made her better at gauging his mood by the sound of his voice.

"Yeah," he said, wandering back through the living room. "Real bad. The worst."

"Oh, no," she said. "The whole family? Everyone?"

"Everyone," he said. "I never figured Ed Belcher for this." Thornton began climbing the stairs.

"How long will you be there?"

"At least until we get a forensics team out here and the coroner removes the bodies," he said. "Gonna be a long night."

"I'll be praying, honey."

"Thanks, babe," he said. "I need it tonight. I'll be home as soon as I can."

"I love you, Ted."

"I love you, too, sweetheart. Good night."

Thornton surveyed the three bedrooms upstairs. The kids' rooms looked untouched. The master bedroom, though, was a mess.

The room Ed and Sarah Belcher slept in was small, not more than twelve by twelve, with a cramped closet on the wall it shared with one of the children's rooms. The bed was to the right of the open door, against the far wall. A small desk sat in front of the window almost directly opposite the door. Some personal items from the dresser next to the door had been knocked to the floor; apparently Sarah Belcher put up a fight before Ed dropped her on their bed and put his shotgun to the back of her neck.

"Sheriff? The coroner says he'll be down here in forty-five minutes." Deputy Jurasik was back inside, downstairs in the kitchen.

"Ann," Thornton said, "Will you come up here?"

He waited in silence, listening to the muted thud of her footsteps through the dining and living rooms, the creaking of the stairs, and the echoes of her progress through the upstairs hall. "Here's Sarah Belcher," Thornton said. "Just like that punk said."

Jurasik nodded, her face wooden. She looked as numb as he felt.

"Anything look like it's been moved or out of place in here?" Thornton had already spotted it. He wanted to see if his deputy noticed the same thing. She had a talent.

"Over there on the desk," she said. "Clean spot in the middle of the dust."

"What would have been there?" Thornton said.

"Desk blotter?"

"Maybe. Kinda small."

She moved to the desk for a closer look. "No, wait. Here," she said, pointing. "They wouldn't have a printer on the desk without a computer."

"Does that desk chair have wheels?" he asked, remembering the noise he'd heard.

"No," Jurasik said, scraping it across the hardwood floor.

Thornton grunted. So that was it. Thiel had come with them tonight to steal Ed Belcher's computer.

Gruner was going to have a serious talk with Vijay after they got out of this, if he didn't strangle the helpful little pigeon right in front of the FBI agent. Sure, they'd avoided a police barricade to get an up-close look at the blast, but you didn't tell that to the cops!

Lucky for us, Gruner thought, *the FBI guy seems cool*. He didn't look FBI. More like a banker. A little on the heavy side, dark hair, glasses, rounded face. Not what Gruner expected from the Bureau. And then he realized—the TV image of FBI agents, perfectly coifed and wardrobed, was what they wanted people to expect. That way, *real* agents could blend in. Smart. Very smart.

"So, uh, Agent Unes, are we in trouble for being here or anything?" He felt Stauffer's eyes bore into him, but he ignored him. Best to get things out in the open.

"No, not necessarily," Unes said, still holding an ice-filled towel to his head. "We need to talk, but now is not the best time."

"Oh, right. Sure."

"One other thing. Jared—it is Jared, right?"

Gruner nodded.

Unes managed a thin smile. "I'm going to have to ask for your video of the building."

"Why?" Gruner asked.

"What?" Stauffer interrupted, unaware Gruner even had the camera. "He wants what?"

"Later," Gruner said to his friend.

"The video is evidence," Unes said. "You'll get it back, eventually. But the bureau will want to see if we can find anything that might give us a clue about who did this and why."

"What video?" Stauffer pressed Gruner.

"*Later*," Gruner hissed.

"It might be helpful," Unes continued. "When we analyze a crime scene, we look at everything we can. You might have something in there the forensics guys miss."

"Really? Wow," Gruner said. "I could, uh, I could take some more if you want."

"With what?" Stauffer asked, staring at Gruner.

"Lay-ter," Gruner said again, emphasizing the word with raised eyebrows.

"Not now," the agent said. "Now, I just want to get home."

"I think you're going home by way of Saint Christopher's, Joe." A tall man in a dark suit had walked up behind Unes and put his hand on the agent's shoulder. The man's hair was short, and his long, lean face had a pinched, bureaucratic look. Now, *he* looked FBI.

"You need to be checked out," the tall man continued.

Unes nodded. "The EMTs looked me over, but yeah—okay. Let me get some names and phone numbers first. And I'll need a ride. Hopkins' car—"

"I saw," the tall man said, his mouth hard. "Hopkins, too. Don't wait too long to get to the hospital. Ride with one of the ambulances."

Unes nodded and the tall man walked away.

"Who was that?" Gruner asked.

"Special Agent in Charge Stephen Clay," Unes said. "Head of the Saint Louis field office.

"So this *is* a terror attack," Stauffer said. Agent Unes raised an eyebrow.

With his free hand, Unes fished a small spiral-ring notepad and a pen from the pocket of his dust-covered jacket. "Let's get some information," he said, setting the towel down on the back bumper of the ambulance. "Jared, what do you do?"

"I, uh, well, I'm between jobs right now," he answered. "I mean, I write some, and I'm trying to sell a couple of manuscripts. I thought I had a deal, too, but it fell apart at the last minute."

"Manuscripts," Unes said. "Books?"

"Yeah, and movies," Gruner said. "Conspiracy stuff. Secret societies, deep state, stuff like that."

"Uh huh," Unes said, scribbling on his notepad.

Curiosity overcame Gruner's reluctance to talk to an agent of the government. "Um, Agent Unes? Why do you think this guy did it?"

Unes shook his head. "I have no idea. We were called out to investigate. That's all I know right now."

"Why would a terrorist explode a bomb at a supermarket?" Vijay asked.

"To show people they can strike anywhere, any time," Norlock said.

"Cause panic," Stauffer said.

"That's possible," Unes said.

"But wouldn't you expect a higher profile target than a supermarket?" Gruner asked. "Especially in Saint Louis."

"Why?" Unes asked.

"Well, why not the Arch?" Norlock said.

"Or the NGA offices on South Second," Gruner added.

Unes lifted an eyebrow again. "What?"

"National Geospatial-Intelligence Agency," Gruner explained. "Down by 55 and Broadway. Makes sense as a target, if you ask me. That's where the government coordinates satellite and aerial images for all the intelligence agencies. They took pictures of Saint Louis a few years ago to set up security for the Pope."

"Mm hmm," Unes said. "You do a lot of research in this area?"

"Oh, yeah." Gruner began to forget he was talking to a federal agent. "The NGA put up about a quarter of the money that the CIA's venture capital division, In-Q-Tel, put into a company called Keyhole. They wrote the software that became Google Earth. Of course, the app for your iPad or laptop doesn't give you the same resolution from those satellite images that the agency gets. Convenient, huh?"

"Okay," Unes said. "What's your theory?"

"Um, okay." Gruner thought for a moment. "Okay. It could just be the usual lone nut, a lunatic. Or, if it's part of a plan coordinated somewhere, it's a group that just wants to scare people, not bring down infrastructure or weaken the country's defenses. I mean, look," he said, warming to the task, "Why not Lambert Field? Or Scott Air Force Base? Home of the Defense Information Systems Agency. DISA, now *there's* a target. It's like the military's IT center for North America."

"Or Boeing," Stauffer reminded him.

"Right, right, the Boeing plant," Gruner said. "Any of those targets make more sense than a supermarket."

"Unless you're just trying to scare people," Norlock said. "If people think, like, military sites are the only targets, there's not as much fear. Unless you're *in* the military or know someone who's military."

"You guys actually sit around and think about stuff like this?" Unes asked.

"Well, yeah," Gruner said. "I mean, I do, anyway. Why not?"

"What were you guys really doing tonight before you came out here?"

"We were, uh, playing Underground Kingdom," Norlock said. "Never heard of it."

Stauffer started to explain. "It's an RPG based on—"

"Wait, wait," Unes interrupted. "Rocket-propelled grenade?"

"Role-playing game," Gruner corrected. "You play a character in an adventure, and you have to work through puzzles and stuff to get to the finish."

"Uh huh. And you went from playing a game to playing search and rescue at a bomb site."

Gruner looked at his three friends, trying to get a sense of where the FBI agent was going with his questions. Stauffer just shrugged.

"Yeah," Gruner said. "Is that weird?"

"You mean suspicious?" Unes asked.

"Um, yeah."

"Probably."

Gruner took a deep breath and let it out. "Ah, crap."

Unes smiled. "Succinctly put. Now, hand over your phone."

Joe Unes knew he wasn't following procedure by borrowing a cell phone from a young man without a good explanation for being at a crime scene, but his head hurt too much to care. SAC Clay was too far away and busy besides, so Unes took the chance that he'd eventually have to explain why his home number was on a log of phone calls from Jared Gruner's cell phone. All that mattered to Unes was letting Cathy know that he was okay and on his way to the ER at Saint Christopher's.

If he caught hell at the office later, fine. He'd already caught hell tonight. The office kind couldn't possibly come close.

The ride to the ER was as bad as the first few minutes awake with a major hangover. Every bump, noise, and change of direction was magnified tenfold, and they all hurt. His head ached, his ears rang, and he couldn't breathe for the dust and the blood in his nose. The twenty minutes in the ambulance felt like a couple of hours.

Still, it could have been much, much worse. The image of Mark Hopkins after the blast came to mind and Unes began to shake. This was evil, plain and simple.

He'd have to do more checking on his four rescuers. As harmless as they appeared, there was no real reason for them to be at the scene.

Later. First, he needed the pain to stop so he could think.

The car was packed quickly and carelessly with everything they could think of on short notice. Cindy Moore closed the back door of their home, the rear entry to the Mayfield Family Market. She had often wondered what life would be like somewhere else, maybe in Saint Louis or Minneapolis. Even Des Moines would be a big step up from their tiny farm community. But running out in the middle of the night with nowhere to go and no idea why you were going—this was not part of her daydream.

And suddenly, as she locked the door, she was struck by just how much she loved this old place.

She heard the gate of the Explorer slam shut. Bob called, "Are you ready, honey?"

"No," she whispered, tears welling in her eyes. She sniffed, blinked hard, and turned to her husband. "Yes. Just locking up."

"Come on, E.J., climb in," Bob said. Eric opened the rear passenger door and vaulted in.

Cindy walked around to the passenger door, where Bob stood waiting to close it for her. *Even at a time like this, he remembers the little things*, she thought.

Bob closed her door, hurried around to the driver's side and climbed in. "Well," he said, "Here we go."

"Where?" Eric asked from the back seat.

"I've been trying to think about that," Bob said. "The only ideas that come to mind are getting away from here and staying off the main roads."

"That sounds logical," Cindy said.

"Maybe to Missouri? The Ozark Mountains?" Eric said.

"Possible," Bob said. "Let's start, and we'll decide on the way. It's an adventure. Tomorrow morning, we'll try to find a pay phone somewhere to call Sheriff Thornton and find out what's going on."

"Couldn't we just use one of our phones?" Cindy asked.

"Mom," Eric said. "They can trace those."

"He's right," Bob said. "Good thinking, E.J. Hon, turn off your phone. They can track the GPS or maybe even the cell tower pings. We all need to keep thinking." He powered down his own phone before turning the key and reaching for the gearshift.

"Dad, wait!" Eric put his hand on his father's shoulder. "Aren't we going to pray first?"

"Buddy, we're really short on—"

"He's right, Bob," Cindy said, putting her hand on her husband's. "We don't have time to plan, so we'd better find time to trust."

Bob turned to her, looking directly into her eyes. He nodded. "You're both right. We never go anywhere without the Lord's protection."

Bowing his head, he said, "Father in heaven, we thank you for your Word which guides us and sustains us, even in times like this. We pray for Sheriff Thornton and ask you to protect him. And Father, we don't know what your will is, so we ask for wisdom to discern the right path. Keep us safe as we travel, Lord, and guide us with your Holy Spirit that we might honor you with our actions, no matter what. We ask this in Jesus' holy name, Amen."

Cindy and Eric echoed, "Amen." And she suddenly felt a sense of peace despite the turmoil surrounding them, as though she'd emerged into the tranquil eye of a monster storm.

The Explorer lurched as Bob shifted into reverse and backed the car out of their driveway.

She took one last look at their home, dimly lit by the blue mercury vapor lamp across the street, and then Cindy Moore and her family rolled forward into the darkness.

EIGHT

"Sir? It's spreading, just like you said." Captain Alan Thiel spoke quietly into a secure satellite phone.

"Like ripples in a pond, yes." The voice was deep and rough, with a hint of an accent Thiel couldn't place. It belonged to a man named Malthus, whose security clearance had to be at least as high as the president's.

Thiel continued, "The scene at the farmhouse was total. Perpetrator was the husband. Shot and killed his entire family and then himself."

"Did you retrieve the PC?"

"Yes, sir."

"Good," Malthus said. "Do not examine it. Bring it with you when you return it to base. It will be collected."

"Sir," Thiel said, "The family we were sent to apprehend was warned off by the local sheriff. They have a thirty- or forty-minute lead."

A pause. "What did you do with the sheriff?"

"Nothing, sir. He had the crime scene to attend to. His chief deputy was with him, and there were others who knew they were there. I warned him against interfering and left."

"Noted."

"Sir," Thiel said, "Do we pursue the family, and if so, what actions should we take to apprehend them?"

"Leave that to me," Malthus said. "We will find them. Go to their home. Get the computer."

"That will give them another thirty to sixty minutes, sir."

"Do you question me, Captain?"

"No, sir," Thiel said. "Consider it done, sir." He heard a click, and Malthus was gone.

"Where to, sir?" Burgos, driving the GMV, looked to his captain for directions.

"Mayfield," Thiel said. "We're supposed to search the house before giving chase."

"Same objective?"

"The same."

This ranked as one of the three worst days in Joe Unes' life, and the other two were so long ago they didn't count. He hadn't been especially close to Mark Hopkins, but they had worked together for two years and seeing someone you worked with forty or more hours a week blown to hell right in front of you was a shock no one should experience.

Unes lay on a bed in the emergency room at Saint Christopher's Hospital. He was tired, thirsty, his head throbbed, and his ears still rang painfully loud.

The ER physician had checked him over in much the same manner as the EMT. He'd cleaned the scrapes on Unes' cheek and hands, given him some pain meds, and expressed concern about a possible concussion. Aside from that, though, Joe had somehow escaped unharmed.

He still hadn't decided whether to show Cathy his cell phone.

Footsteps stopped just outside the curtains around his bed. The curtains parted to reveal his wife and their two teenage daughters. Cathy's normally dimpled, smiling face was clouded with worry.

"Joe? Are you all right?" She moved to the side of the bed and squeezed his right hand.

"Aah, ooh. Careful, hon," he said. "I'm fine. A few scrapes and bumps, that's all." He held up his hand to show the abrasions.

"Thank God." Cathy released a deep breath, her tension beginning to unwind. "We heard the explosion, and I was afraid you were there. It's all over the news."

"Yeah," he said, "but I'm still here. God must have something more on my 'to do' list."

Their daughters, Emily and Molly, stood by, not knowing how to act. It pained Unes to see how scared they were by the sight of their father in a hospital bed, but they held back, too old to run to his arms for comfort like they did when they were little.

He pushed himself to smile. "Sorry, ladies," he said. "No *kibbeh* tonight." That broke the ice, and the girls moved to the other side of the bed and put their hands in his.

Eric Moore had no idea of the time. It was too dark to read his watch, and he didn't want his mom and dad to know he was still awake.

Lying in the back seat of the Explorer, covered with a blanket his mother had draped over him, Eric was fully alert, listening to the hum of the SUV's tires against the asphalt of a two-lane county highway.

It was way past Eric's bedtime, but he wasn't sleepy. Confused, excited, and a little scared, he wondered what was going to happen next. Most nights he went to bed knowing exactly what to expect when he woke up the next day. It was a life that seemed excruciatingly dull compared to the sci-fi and fantasy books he liked. Especially *The Hobbit* and *The Lord of the Rings*. They were awesome. Every day was a new adventure, another epic battle between good and evil, everything bigger than life.

Now, Eric found himself living a *real* adventure, and he was learning that he'd rather be home in bed with a book.

His father and mother spoke with soft voices in the front seat so they wouldn't disturb him. That was another reason he was awake—like every kid given the chance, he wanted to know what grownups talked about when they thought the children weren't listening.

"Where can we go, Bob?" his mother asked.

"Well, let's think," his father said. "My sister is in North Carolina. Way too far. We'd never get there. Your sister in is Kansas City. *That's* probably too far. We shouldn't get your mother involved; she's too frail, and there's no place to park the car out of sight there anyway. We need someplace we can reach by morning."

"Why?"

"I'm just guessing, but if these guys are as well-equipped as Ted Thornton thinks, they may be able to spot our car during the day, especially out in the open. That might use drones, maybe, or even spy satellites."

"Spy satellites? Isn't that a stretch? We haven't *done* anything!"

"I know," his father said, "But you didn't hear Ted Thornton's voice. He didn't sound like he was kidding. Anyway, just to be safe, we should probably be parked somewhere under cover by morning."

There was a long stretch of silence. Eric watched the stars floating above them through the window and wondered if a spy satellite might be watching them right now.

"Okay," his mother said at last. "What about the church?"

"What? You mean *our* church?"

"Yes. Why not? If these men go to the house, they'll see we're not there and figure out that we left in a hurry. They'll see that we took things from the shelves and assume that we're planning to be gone for a long time. The last place they'll think to look for us is right back in Mayfield!"

"Let me think about that," his father said.

Eric didn't hear anything from the front seat for a while. Just as his eyes began to feel too heavy to resist the hypnotic duet of the rubber and the road, his father spoke.

"Ok. Agreed," he whispered. "Staying in Mayfield might be our best option."

"I think so, too," she said. "Pastor Schiebold will take us in, I'm sure. He can get in touch with Ted and find out who those men are and what they want. This has to be some kind of awful mistake, Bob. Pastor will help straighten things out. Besides, it won't hurt to have the church praying with us."

"You're right," his dad said. "Our strength is there, not in running."

Pastor Schiebold. *Of course*! Eric mentally kicked himself for not thinking of it first.

David Schiebold was the head pastor at the Mayfield Bible Church, where Eric's dad was an elder. He was about the same age as Eric's dad, a little taller, and he still had all his hair. He was pretty cool, too, not like some of the pastors his friends complained about. He preached from the Bible, but he stopped talking when he was done. And Eric had been surprised to find out at youth group that Pastor Schiebold's favorite kind of music was rock. Christian rock, but it was still rock.

Eric closed his eyes. His mom was pretty smart. This was the right thing to do. Within five minutes, he was fast asleep.

The family had left in a rush. That much was clear. Thiel and his team didn't waste time announcing their presence at the Moore home, and the locked doors barely slowed them down. Doors in Mayfield, Iowa, were rarely locked, and the kind that were used hadn't been designed to keep out Special Forces troops trained for nighttime snatch and grab missions.

Thiel stood in the kitchen of the Moore home, pursing his lips as he considered their next move.

Warrant Officer Burgos came in through the back door. He'd just completed a search of the property, including a storm cellar they'd almost overlooked. "No sign of them, Captain."

Sergeant Grevey followed Burgos. "Sir, there was a second vehicle out here. You can see the marks in the gravel drive."

"Probably a bigger car—SUV maybe," Thiel said. "Or a van. Burgos, check vehicle registrations for Robert Moore. Crosscheck his wife as well. All VINs and plate numbers. Something big enough to carry the food and water they took from the store. Must be figuring they'd be gone for a while and not able to stop for supplies. Smart."

"We'll find them, sir," Grevey said.

"Someone will," Thiel said. "Our orders are to confiscate the computer."

"Another one?" Burgos asked.

"Evidence," Thiel said.

"You wouldn't figure these people for terrorists, if this is the family," Grevey remarked.

"What's that, Sergeant?"

"I said, sir," Grevey said, pointing to an eight-by-ten framed portrait on the wall, "that the folks in this picture here don't look like fundie whack jobs."

Thiel crossed the kitchen to examine the picture. It showed a balding man with a light brown beard, late thirties or early forties, a pretty woman about the same age with short, frosted hair, and a young boy with glasses and bright red hair.

"That's the thing, Sergeant," Thiel said. "They look like anybody and everybody. That's why these people are going to be so tough to contain."

NINE

Bob Moore had been driving for nearly five hours. The air coming through the dashboard vents was cool enough to help keep him awake, but it made his eyes sting. His eyelids felt as though they were lined with 40-grit sandpaper and blinking only helped for a few seconds at a time.

Cindy was asleep, her jacket a makeshift pillow against the passenger window. Eric had dropped off right after they left home. Bob marveled at their ability to trust so completely in the protection of the Lord. And in him.

Moore felt a twinge of shame at his doubts. He remembered the verse from Matthew that Cindy quoted earlier, and he thought about the epistle of James: *Count it all joy when ye fall into divers temptations; Knowing this, that the trying of your faith worketh patience. But let patience have her perfect work, that ye may be perfect and entire, wanting nothing.*

James—now there was a fascinating character. Even though they grew up under the same roof, James and the Lord's other half-brothers, according to the gospel of John, did not believe in Jesus while he was alive.

But something happened. Something big. It must have been; Bob tried to imagine having enough faith to believe that his younger brother, Fred, was God in the flesh. There wasn't that much faith in the universe.

By the time had Paul returned to Jerusalem from Damascus around 38 or 39 AD, James was one of the leaders of the new Christian church. The Jewish historian Josephus recorded that

James had been stoned to death by order of the high priest Annas had around 62 AD.

What changed James' mind so profoundly that he willingly submitted to a hideous death?

Paul wrote to the church at Corinth that James was one of the men to whom Jesus appeared after the Crucifixion. Seeing your dead brother with your own eyes and touching him with your own hands might do it.

Whatever changed his worldview, he'd been willing to die for his faith afterward. Not knowing what was ahead for his family, Bob Moore prayed as he drove, asking the Lord for that kind of strength.

He stayed off the highways, sticking to county roads as he circled around Mayfield in a wide, clockwise arc from southwest to northeast. Bob had no idea what tools the men searching for them might use, but he hoped they'd concentrate on the main roads. Or maybe they'd just stake out the house and wait for them to come back. There was no way to know, and he didn't want to pass through any of the small towns close to Mayfield just yet. Local police might be looking for them, too.

Cindy was right. Dave Schiebold really was their best hope. He'd believe them where a state trooper might not—and that was only if they were lucky enough for police to catch them before the men who stopped at Ted Thornton's office tonight. And since Ted was in the congregation, contact between him and Pastor Schiebold wouldn't attract much attention.

Traffic had been unusually light the whole night. Bob hadn't expected much; he'd counted on it along these back roads. Still, Friday night should have brought at least a few people out—kids coming home from high school football games, or maybe a couple of yahoos with nothing better to do than drink beer and howl at the moon. But they'd passed only three cars all night, which was a blessing. His stomach was still knotted from the last one.

Over and over since Ted Thornton's call, Bob had tried to sort through what he might have done to attract the government's attention. He couldn't think of a thing.

With a start, Bob realized he'd drifted into the oncoming lane. He couldn't go much further. He was glad to see a landmark he recognized. It was only another couple of minutes to the church.

"Cindy? Cindy?" Bob kept his voice low to avoid waking E.J.

"Hmm?" She sat up. "Where are we?"

"Almost at the church."

"Any trouble?"

"Nope."

"Thank God." Cindy leaned against his shoulder.

Bob slowed the big SUV to a stop as the farm road ended at Route 3, the main road through Mayfield. He looked both ways carefully, although in the dead of night, he wouldn't see anything that didn't have high beams attached. For all he knew, a full company of the Iowa National Guard waited fifty feet down the road.

Turning right onto Route 3, Bob eased the Explorer forward. And then, realizing that the Mayfield city limit was less than a hundred yards ahead, he switched off the headlights and coasted at twenty miles an hour with only the parking lights.

"What are you doing, Bob?"

"We're coming into town," he said. "No need to advertise."

"Won't they see the parking lights anyway?"

"Maybe," Bob said. "I'm new at this stealth thing."

Mayfield Bible Church sat at the edge of town, a traditional white frame church with clapboard siding and Gothic windows, a sight common in small towns across America. The main building held the sanctuary, a small business office, and the pastor's study. The lower level was long ago converted into a fellowship hall that could be sectioned off into Sunday school classrooms with track-mounted folding dividers. An old two-bedroom brick bungalow on the Mayfield side of the church housed the youth ministry, while a vinyl-sided ranch behind the church served as the parsonage for Pastor Dave Schiebold and his wife, Michelle.

Pulling the SUV into the church's parking lot as slowly as he could, Bob's stomach did flips as the pea gravel crunched and swooshed beneath their tires. How far did the sound carry? Would anyone notice at three a.m.? Had their pursuers given up? Would Dave Schiebold really take them in?

Bob slowly maneuvered around the church and onto the driveway that led to the parsonage. Suddenly, a blinding spotlight in front of the car hit him right in the eyes.

He stepped on the brakes hard, and the car jerked to a sudden stop. Cindy gasped, and Eric rolled off the back seat and onto the floor. Bob's heart sank, sure that they'd been caught. He shaded his eyes, straining to see who waited for them at the one place in Iowa they thought they'd be safe.

There was no sound. No one came. Squinting, Bob looked closer.

It was the driveway light over the garage door. They'd triggered the motion sensor.

Cindy realized what had happened at the same moment as Bob, and they began to laugh.

"What's going on?" Eric's sleepy voice rose from the floor of the back seat as he struggled to untangle himself from the blanket Cindy had spread over him.

"Nothing, E.J.," Bob said. "We're at the church."

"Who's out there?" A man's voice, outside the car.

Cindy and Bob looked at each other. "Pastor," Bob said. "I'd better go talk to him."

"Who is that? Who's there?"

Bob opened his door and stepped down to the driveway. It felt good to stand up and stretch. "It's Bob Moore, Pastor. We need some help."

There was a long pause, and the preacher's voice came again from an open window on the far right of the plain brick ranch home. "Bob? Are you all right?"

"It's a long—no, it's a strange story," Bob said. "Cindy and Eric are out here, too."

"Oh." Silence for a moment. Then, "Hold on a sec. I'll open the door."

This had been one of the most brutal days in Sheriff Ted Thornton's career. No, scratch that—it was probably the worst day of his life.

The image of the three Belcher children slumped on the couch would haunt his sleep for weeks. Maybe forever.

Making the day even more unbearable was the confrontation with the Special Forces types who'd invaded his jurisdiction. He still couldn't think what they wanted with a man like Bob Moore. If the government thought Bob was a threat to Homeland Security, then the country was in a hell of a mess.

He prayed that Bob and his family were somewhere safe and far away. Ted only wished they'd had more time to talk; he was cut off before he could tell Bob not to call him at the office.

Thornton stood on the Belchers' front porch and sighed. There was nothing more he could do now. The Moores were in God's hands. *Funny how that's the last place we feel comfortable.*

About an hour after Captain Thiel and his team vanished into the night, the sheriff sent Chief Deputy Jurasik home. She'd put in a full day and then some, and she deserved the weekend visit to her family. She needed the sleep before she hit the road in the morning—not that she was likely to sleep much after what she'd seen.

Besides, she'd agreed to take Jud. The dog's constant barking, understandable under the circumstances, had given Thornton a headache.

While he waited for the coroner's man and the forensics team, Thornton broke crime scene protocol. He found some instant coffee and a mug in a cupboard and gingerly made a cup with hot water from the bathroom sink to take the edge off his headache, all the while struggling to ignore the spray of congealing gore around him that was Ed Belcher's final solution to whatever had possessed him during his last minutes on Earth.

Finally, near dawn, the forensics work was almost done. The assistant from the county morgue stood by with his own cup of instant coffee, bleary eyed, waiting to remove the five bodies from the house.

"Sheriff? Sheriff, you want to come look at this?" The forensics tech down from Iowa City, a good-looking kid who was probably barely out of college, called him from the living room into the kitchen. The kid pointed a gloved finger at a sliver of white sticking out of the pocket of Ed Belcher's blue work shirt.

"A note?" the tech asked.

"Wouldn't know," Thornton said. "I waited for you."

"Should I?" the tech asked.

"Please."

The tech reached gingerly into Belcher's pocket and pulled out a sheet of paper, neatly folded in quarters. There was small block lettering on one side. The kid stared at the paper for a long time.

"What's it say?" Thornton asked impatiently.

"Here." The kid handed him the scrap of paper.

Thornton read, *Woe unto you that desire the day of the* LORD! *To what end is it for you? The day of the* LORD *is darkness, and not light.*

Sheriff Thornton shook his head. He'd had enough. He had to get home and get some sleep. Maybe some of this would make sense in the light of day.

But he doubted it.

Dave Schiebold had spent many Friday nights when he was younger staying out until it was closer to dawn than sunset, but a changed heart and twelve years in ministry had cured him of that. Or maybe it was just that he was getting close to forty. It was a rare weekend these days that he saw the far side of midnight.

Whatever the reason, Schiebold needed a couple of minutes to wake up enough to appreciate that there were three people knocking on his door, asking for help.

The front door of the modest three-bedroom ranch that served as the parsonage for the Mayfield Bible Church creaked as Schiebold opened it; as though it, too, could use a few more hours of sleep. Schiebold ran his fingers through his thick brown hair, trying to erase the tousled look his Michelle called "bed head."

"Bob? Cindy? What are you doing out there?" As a pastor, Schiebold had seen a lot of things over the last dozen years. At this moment, though, he had no clue as to what could possibly drop an entire family on his doorstep at three o'clock in the morning.

"May we come in, Pastor?" Bob Moore looked pretty bleary, too.

"Well, sure, sure," Schiebold said. "Come right on in. Well, hi, Eric. A little past your bedtime, huh?" The redheaded boy returned a sleepy and embarrassed smile.

"Here, have a seat," Schiebold said, ushering them into the undersized front room. The Moores situated themselves on a long charcoal and beige striped couch that had seen better days. Eric leaned up against his dad, who wrapped a protective arm around his son's shoulders.

Pastor Schiebold sat in a swivel rocker that he and Michelle had rescued from the curb on large-item trash day last spring. A little frayed on the arms, but serviceable. "Well," he said, still wondering where to begin. "What brings you here?"

"Pastor," Bob said, "I want to apologize for waking you up so late—"

"Oh, don't worry about that. What's up?"

"Well," Bob said, "Ted Thornton called us a few hours ago." Schiebold nodded. "He said some men had come to his office, asking about us—about me. And that we should get out of the house right away."

"Now, wait. Why?"

"He said they told him they were with the government and they wanted to take me in, but he didn't like the looks of them so he advised us to leave."

Now Schiebold was really confused. "The sheriff called and told you to run from government men who want to arrest you?"

Bob nodded. "Men with automatic weapons. And Ted said he didn't know what branch of government they were with."

"Government men with automatic weapons?" Schiebold realized he was echoing Bob, as if hearing the words a second time would help them make sense.

Sighing, Bob said, "I know. Crazy. I have no idea what this is about. We pay our taxes, we—"

"What's going on out here?" Michelle Schiebold, the only person of Asian descent in Mayfield, and probably all of Kiowa County, emerged from the hall leading to the bedrooms, tying the sash on a terrycloth robe. Dave Schiebold marveled, as he did every time he saw her face, that after all these years, his heart still lifted whenever she entered the room.

"Oh, Michelle," Cindy said, "We're so sorry to disturb you. It was my idea. We had nowhere else to go."

"Ted Thornton called the Moores earlier tonight and told them to leave home," Schiebold explained.

"What?"

"Some men are after me, for some reason," Bob said. "I don't know why. But Ted sounded serious on the phone. He made it clear that he really thought we needed to hide for a few days until he could sort things out."

"So we threw some things in the car and left the house," Cindy said. "Bob kept to back roads, but we realized we'd never get anyplace where we knew people by morning, and who knows how many men are out there looking for us, or what they'd do if they found us?"

"Well, thank God for Ted Thornton. And thank God you got here without any trouble," Schiebold said, starting to get the lay of the land. "This has to be some kind of mistake. I'm sure we can get ahold of Ted in the morning and—"

"Dave," his wife interrupted. "Can't you see what they need right now is sleep? Talk about Ted in the morning. Let's get the cots set up downstairs, and Eric can sleep on the old couch down there. And maybe you should move your car out of the garage so we can park their car out of sight." Michelle Schiebold turned to Cindy with a knowing look. "Men. Always wanting to solve the problem in sixty seconds or less."

Dave Schiebold smiled, thankful that his wife was awake. Michelle was right. She usually was.

Standing outside his GMV in what passed for downtown Mayfield, Captain Alan Thiel wondered if Malthus ever slept. Thiel had never dialed his secure line without reaching him, regardless of the hour.

"Understood, Captain," Malthus said, after Thiel concluded a summary of the night's action. "Return to base. You've done your job."

"With all due respect, sir, we have not," Thiel said. "The family is still at large."

"ATF will handle it from here," Malthus said. "There is no need for the public to learn of your role. ATF will apprehend the suspects."

And provide plausible deniability for his team, Thiel knew. ATF agents dressed in black looked enough like his team that the use of a Special Forces unit on American soil wouldn't become public knowledge, not right away.

"Sir," Thiel said, "I believe we can complete our mission."

"It would be complete if you hadn't opted to visit the sheriff. The mission is over, captain," Malthus said, in a tone that brooked no argument. "There will be others in the days to come. Return to base. Is that clear?"

"Yes, sir."

"Good." Malthus terminated the connection.

The thought of returning home without the primary objective accomplished galled Captain Thiel. His men were the best trained and equipped soldiers in the world, and he was not prepared to allow the owner of a hick town grocery store slip through his fingers. Especially with ATF pukes ready to take credit for the grab.

Thiel grimaced. To him, ATF agents were pretenders, frauds who wanted to dress like his men and play with their toys without making the physical and emotional sacrifices to earn the right.

"What's the plan, Captain?" Burgos asked.

"Have Intel set up a listening post," Thiel said. "They're scared. They'll call a friend soon enough. We'll find them. Let's get them before we head back."

TEN

Scott Stauffer gawked at his computer screen, mouth literally hanging open in disbelief. He knew he'd gotten in late the night before, but he was stunned that so much had happened while he was out.

He scanned several of his favorite news sites, catching up on the horrors of Bloody Friday, as some pundits had dubbed it. Others had opted for the date: Ten-Thirteen. Besides the three-dozen at Grandy's, nearly four thousand others had died in random acts of violence from coast to coast.

Four thousand dead.

Stauffer couldn't wrap his head around it. This *couldn't* be random. How could so many attacks come off in so many places on the same night without a plan? It *must* have been coordinated.

Al Qaeda? Islamic State? Possible. They were still active, even after all the time and money spent hunting them. A couple of government officials had said as much this morning.

Gruner was normally the paranoid one, but even Stauffer didn't accept the al Qaeda/ISIS theory. For one thing, the terrorists who'd been identified so far seemed to be ordinary Americans— no connections to Islam or the Middle East at all. Unless a bunch of middle-class suburbanites had suddenly decided to recite the *shahada*, the Muslim profession of faith, this was Americans attacking Americans.

And that was scarier.

It was still early for Stauffer. He normally slept until noon on Saturdays, because he and his friends were usually locked in mortal combat with trolls, wizards, and dragons until the early morning hours. But something nagged at him this morning, picking at the back of his brain until he finally got up to shut it up or drown it out.

Now, two hours later, he knew what had bothered him: For the first time since he'd moved into Winchester Square Apartments two years earlier, Scott Stauffer didn't hear any traffic on Manchester Road, the most heavily traveled east-west route in Saint Louis' western suburbs. That was bizarre.

The time at the bottom right of his computer screen said eight-fifteen. Still early. It didn't matter. He had to call Gruner.

The phone rang fourteen times before Gruner picked up. "Hello?" He sounded like he'd fallen out of bed.

"Gruner? Scott."

"Scott." The word, at this moment, clearly held no meaning whatsoever for Jared Gruner.

"Scott. Scott Stauffer? Short guy, glasses, kicks your butt at Underground Kingdom?"

There was a long, heavy sigh as the data chugged through Gruner's barely connected synapses. Finally: "What time is it?"

"Quarter after eight."

"What is it?"

Stauffer chewed his lip for a moment, formatting his response. "Okay," he said. "Eighteen separate terror attacks last night, including the Grandy's, all over the country, apparently unconnected. About four thousand dead so far. Homeland Security has raised the terror alert to Threat Level Red."

There was a long pause while Gruner absorbed the news.

"Call Norlock," Gruner said at last. "Vijay, too. I'll be right over."

The world was coming apart at the seams. The news on TV was a wearying drone of death and destruction. It was official: 10/13 surpassed 9/11 as the worst day of terror in the history of the world. The toll had been revised upward to nearly four thousand, and there were dozens of reports of senseless acts of violence still trickling in from smaller communities.

The last news Tony Harris had seen from the Middle East before turning in last night was grim, too. When Israel launched its assault through the Golan Heights, Hezbollah rockets from Lebanon rained down on towns in northern Israel. The Israelis' Iron Dome missile defense caught most of the rockets, but not all. The pictures on TV were horrible.

Harris felt caged. He kept the TV and radio off all day and listened to CDs instead. Once he reported in, he'd get all the information he needed about the state of the world, and he wanted to hold it back for just a few hours. Meanwhile, he had to get out.

Today might be his last chance to drive the Camaro for a while, so Harris slipped on a light jacket, locked up the house, and headed out for no place in particular. The sky was blue this early Saturday morning, or as blue as it gets over Chicago, and the weather was in the upper fifties, just about perfect for October.

As he turned west onto Diversey, Harris switched on the radio for some good driving music to lift his mood. No dice. There was no escaping the news.

Even the music stations had broken format to talk about Wrigley Field and the other acts of terror the night before.

The World Series was on hold. If it was played at all, which wasn't a sure thing, the Cubs would give up home field advantage to the Red Sox and play the Chicago games at Guaranteed Rate Field, the White Sox' stadium. And Major League Baseball had better come up with tighter security.

Air traffic was locked down, just like after 9/11. Airports were full of stranded travelers. Shopping malls scrambled to install metal detectors secure the back doors used by store employees.

Not that anyone was shopping; Harris noticed that traffic was almost non-existent. Normally, midday Saturday would find Chicago's streets full of shoppers. Today, the only other vehicles Harris saw were a couple of CTA buses and lots of police cars.

One of which was behind him with its lights on.

Harris cursed under his breath. He should have stopped to think before he left the house. Driving around this morning was a bad idea. Maybe even illegal.

The officer was a burly man, a couple dozen donuts past healthy. Harris could probably outrun him, but the officer wasn't a guy he'd want to face in the ring, at least for the first few minutes.

Harris rolled down his window. "Morning, Officer. What can I do for you?" He'd learned early in life that the best response to a policeman was courtesy and cooperation. Especially when you're black.

"What's your business?" the officer asked. His hair was cropped so close his head might have been shaved. Harris couldn't see the cop's eyes through his darkly tinted aviator sunglasses. The name on his badge was Zeller.

"My business?"

"On the street," the officer said. "You know we're at a Red Terror Alert."

Harris chose to tell a tactical lie. "No, sir, I didn't. I haven't heard the news today."

"Threat Level Red," the patrolman repeated. "Issued by Homeland Security last night. No non-essential travel."

"So, I should stay home?"

"Under Threat Level Red, we assume anyone on the street without business is an enemy," Officer Zeller said. "If you have no business being out, I suggest you return to your home."

"Is that the law?" Harris knew better than to push a police officer, but he couldn't help himself. A bit of the old attitude had awakened and wouldn't back down.

"My orders are to arrest anyone who has no business being out," the officer said. "The Justice Department decides what to do with you then. If you have no business, go home. Am I clear?"

"Seriously? Can you do that?" Harris knew he should stop talking, but his mouth had two steps on his common sense and was heading for the end zone.

The officer raised his eyebrows. His right hand moved toward the holster on his belt. "Wanna find out?"

Harris took a deep breath and forced himself to calm down. He didn't want to explain to his CO that he failed to report because he got mouthy with a cop. "No, sir."

Officer Zeller nodded. "Go home, then."

It had been a rough night. Between the bruises and the ringing in his ears, sleep was long in coming to Joe Unes, even with the meds.

The hospital mattress and regular interruptions by nurses hadn't helped. Why did they wake up patients to give them sleeping pills?

The ER doctor had insisted on admitting him for observation. So Unes sat, propped up in the hospital bed, wishing desperately for a cup of strong coffee. He still hurt, but the ringing in his ears had faded to a tolerable level.

The whole event made little sense. The bomber had given police so little time, less than two hours. He'd issued no demands and made no threats. He'd just blown himself up—and taken thirty-five people with him.

And that shouting about the great and terrible day of the Lord—what was that all about?

The electronic chirp of the telephone next to the bed interrupted his thoughts. "Hello?"

"Joe? How are you feeling this morning?" It was Steve Clay, his boss.

"Okay," he said. "Sore. A couple of scratches and my ears are ringing. All in all, though, no complaints. It's a miracle I'm here."

"That's what it looked like. I'm sorry about Mark."

"Yeah. Me, too."

"Any impressions about the terrorist?"

"Impressions? Steve, are you saying the bureau decided this is ours to follow up?"

"Yeah, looks that way," his boss replied. "Washington has an ID on the guy. Conrad Reston, white male, forty-four, from Valley Park. No priors, but apparently a link to a loosely organized white supremacist group. Bureau wants us to check out the group."

"How did Washington come up with a name so quickly?"

"What do you mean?"

"No priors," Unes said. "And there couldn't have been enough left of the guy to identify. So how did they get a name?"

"County police made him from a security camera in the store."

"Okay," Unes said. "And they think there's a group behind it?"

"Yeah," Clay said. "Theory is that the stuff that happened last night was more coordinated than it looks."

"Stuff? What stuff?"

"Sorry, Joe, I thought you knew by now," Clay said. "There were eighteen terrorist attacks last night, about four thousand dead altogether. No obvious connections between them, not on the surface. Incidents from New York to Los Angeles. The supermarket was just one of them. Bastards nearly blew up Wrigley Field."

Unes whistled softly. "White supremacists?"

"Maybe. Right-wing cult, possibly. That's the theory for now. And I guess I don't have to tell you this is number one on our list of priorities."

The sound Unes heard inside his head was his desk sprouting a new stack of files. "You need me in the office today?"

"Absolutely not," Clay said. "Take the weekend, get some rest. Let the doctors clear you first. Monday will come soon enough—if you're up to it then."

"Thanks, Steve."

"No sweat, Joe. See you Monday."

Unes sipped at a glass of water left by a nurse with his last dose of pain meds. He stared out through the hospital room's window, thinking. Clouds outside threatened rain. Appropriate.

Eighteen separate terror attacks last night? The public would be in shock. Politicians would demand quick answers. This would be a long weekend. And Monday would be a very busy day.

Sheriff Ted Thornton sat up and wiped sleep from his eyes with the back of his hand. He needed a few more hours, but a glance at the alarm clock on his nightstand told him it was already afternoon. He didn't want to miss the entire day. A shower and strong coffee doesn't substitute for sleep, but it would have to do.

"Hi, honey." His wife stood in the hallway outside their bedroom. "Are you up? I tried not to wake you. I sent the kids downstairs to keep the noise down."

"No, that's fine, sweetheart," Thornton said. "I need to get up and see if forensics found any evidence at Belcher's that looks like anything besides what it looked like." He yawned, and then shook his head. "That didn't make much sense, did it? Sorry, it was a long night."

"I made you some coffee," Susie Thornton said, bringing the steaming mug into the room.

"You're a mind reader," Thornton said. "Thanks, babe. Lord Almighty, but that was the worst scene—those kids!—their faces!" His hand trembled slightly as he reached for the coffee, but he recovered. "I never want to see anything like that again."

Susie sat on the bed next to him and kissed his cheek. "I'm sorry you had to see it at all."

"Well, somebody had to," he said. "I asked for the job. That's the downside of being the people's choice."

Twenty minutes later, showered and dressed in a pair of jeans and an Iowa State T-shirt, Thornton made his way into the kitchen of their modest brick home. Situated in the center of Mayfield, a half-block off Main Street, it was a convenient two-minute drive from the county administration building.

As he poured himself a second cup of coffee, his phone rang. Susie answered; he'd left it with her in the living room while he showered.

"Oh, hi, Pastor," she said. "Sure, I'll get him. Ted? It's Pastor Schiebold."

Thornton set down his mug and collected the phone from Susie, who returned to the couch where she'd been reading a novel.

"Hi, Pastor, how are you today?"

"Fine, Ted, just fine," Pastor Schiebold said. "But I need some help and advice."

"Sure," Thornton said. "What can I do for you?"

"Well," Schiebold said, "I've heard from Bob and Cindy Moore."

Thornton set down his coffee mug and began searching the countertop for a pen and a piece of paper. "Go on," he said.

"They're okay, and they're in a safe place," Schiebold said. "They want to know—and so do I—what exactly is going on, and how long you think it might take to straighten things out."

"Those are good questions," Thornton said. "The short answers are 'I'm not sure' and 'I don't know.'" He found an old Bic that was missing its cap in a cracked coffee mug and a small notepad stuffed between the telephone book and the cookie tin.

"So you're not really sure who's after Bob?"

Sitting down at the table in the eat-in kitchen, Thornton said, "No, I'm really not. The way they handled themselves, their weapons, and the way they addressed their commanding officer, I'd say Special Forces. They didn't look like FBI or ATF agents. But that just doesn't make any sense." He thought again of the dead children—and the bloody holes where their middles should have been. Nothing made sense today.

There was a silence that stretched several seconds. "Well, maybe it does, Ted."

"What do you mean?"

"Have you seen the news today?"

"No," Thornton admitted. "I was up all night at a crime scene. I just woke up about twenty minutes ago. Should I have seen it?"

Schiebold paused a second then said. "Well, in a nutshell, America is under attack."

"What?"

"According to what I've seen on the news today, there were about eighteen or twenty different terror attacks last night. The reports indicate at least four thousand people have died. Homeland Security has declared a Red Terror Alert."

"Threat Level Red?" The lawman made a mental note to check with the county coordinator for emergency preparedness to find out what a 'red level' meant for his department. In fact, he'd have to make some calls to find out why no one had notified him.

"That's right. Red. And here's the weird part, Ted: they say the terrorists—the ones who've been identified so far, anyway—don't fit any kind of pattern," Schiebold said. "The media says they're mostly average American citizens." He paused for a moment, and then continued. "Actually, the media is spinning this as the work of right-wing fundamentalists."

"Now, that really makes no sense," Thornton said.

"Well, you know I agree with you, but there it is," Schiebold said. "There are a lot of people obsessed with the end times, and given the new war in the Middle East…"

"Whoa! Hold up!" Thornton interrupted. "*What* war?"

"I forgot, you've been asleep. It looks like Israel invaded Syria overnight."

Thornton grunted. "Good Lord."

"So," Schiebold continued, "The media is saying this might be a cult that wants to bring on Armageddon."

"Yeah," Thornton said, rubbing his eyes. "I'm sure I'll hear about it. The Red Terror Alert might explain why Special Forces are on the prowl, but I never thought I'd see the day. If Homeland Security is behind this, I'll have to find out how they get away with violating *posse comitatus*."

"Posse what?"

"Comitatus," Thornton said. "The Posse Comitatus Act was passed after the Civil War. 1878, if I remember right. It's illegal to use military for police work on American soil except under extraordinary circumstances."

"Hmm," Schiebold said. "And these guys didn't tell you anything about what they wanted?"

"No. Just wanted to know where the Moores lived, or where they might go," Thornton said. "I didn't like the looks of them. Felt wrong. That's why I called Bob."

"And you've no idea when they'll call off the dogs, huh?"

"Afraid not. I'll make some calls and try to get hold of people who can tell me what's going on, and maybe do something about it." Thornton thought for a moment, and decided to confide in the preacher. "Listen, Pastor, there was something else about these guys, and maybe Bob can shed some light on this if he gets in touch."

"Hypothetically speaking," Schiebold said slowly, "If I knew how to get in touch with Bob, is there something I should ask him? Hypothetically."

"Hypothetically," Thornton said, catching the pastor's subtext. *He knows where they are.* "Good. I don't like to lie, especially in an official capacity. Anyway, I was out on a call last night at Ed Belcher's place. You know Ed?"

"Sure," Schiebold said. "He has a farm out on Highway W."

"Right. This is not public knowledge. Last night, it looks like Ed took a twelve-gauge shotgun and killed his wife, his children, and then himself."

"Oh, dear Jesus!"

"Amen," Thornton said. "I don't know why, and the only clue so far is a little scrap of paper we found in his shirt pocket. Bible verses, I think. Come to think of it, I'd like to you look at it tomorrow and tell me what you think."

"I'll be happy to help," Pastor Schiebold said.

"Here's the thing," Thornton said. "I think what happened there is connected to the Moores."

"Ed Belcher, you mean?"

"Yeah," Thornton said. "Those men after Bob? They were in my office when I got a call from Ed. He was out of his mind. Shot himself during the call. It's gonna take a long time before I get Ed's voice out of my nightmares. Anyway, those guys followed me out there. Suddenly, they put looking for Bob on hold. I can't figure why."

"They don't think—no, Bob couldn't have anything to do with that," Schiebold said.

"No, I don't think so, either. But they were in the room when Ed's call came in, and suddenly that was their priority. So, hypothetically, if you were to find a way to contact Bob, you might ask him about Ed Belcher. Nothing specific—just if they had any contact recently." Thornton sighed. "Nothing since yesterday afternoon makes sense. I'll see you at church tomorrow. And please—don't tell anyone about the Moores just yet. Or the Belchers."

"You bet. See you later, Ted."

Sitting in a GMV on the other side of Mayfield, parked behind G & R Small Engine Repair to screen their vehicles from drivers on Route 3, Tech Sergeant Raymond Bako leaned forward from the back seat and said, "Got 'em, Captain."

Captain Thiel reached for the headset, removed his cap and slipped the earphones over his closely cropped dark brown hair. He listened for a moment until he heard what he needed to know.

"Good work," he said to Bako.

"You know where they are?"

"Not yet, but I know who does," Thiel said. "Their pastor. I should have guessed. Bible-thumpers are just as bad as Salafists. They're all dangerous."

"What's the plan, Cap?" Burgos asked.

"We'll drop in on church tomorrow," Thiel said. "Let's see how long the flock keeps a secret when their shepherd is taken away."

ELEVEN

Running from bad guys sounded a lot more exciting than it really was, Eric Moore decided. In his books, it was adventure after adventure, always one step ahead, a non-stop roller coaster of action and exhilaration. Since last night, though, he'd learned it was more like short bursts of gut-twisting fear followed by hours and hours of nothing to do.

He was glad he'd brought a few books from home, but he soon tired of being cooped up in the Schiebolds' downstairs family room. Sunlight streamed through the small basement windows high up on the wall and Eric itched to go outside.

His parents were handling it better than he was, Eric thought. His dad stretched out on an old couch taking a nap, and his mother sat in an armchair reading her Bible. Eric would never understand how adults could be happy spending so much time doing nothing.

Putting down his book, he got up from the chair and went in search of his backpack, hoping he still had some paper and a pen in there. He wasn't very good at drawing, but Eric could spend hours designing airplanes or, better yet, inventing maps of imaginary cities. He wasn't sure why, but maps were fascinating. He thought it was really cool the way streets and roads and highways and rivers and lakes could be translated into lines and squiggles on a map.

His parents had noticed his interest and had started letting him chart their route on family trips. His dad said it was good practice in case the GPS didn't work. Maybe Eric could find an atlas somewhere and plan an emergency getaway.

As he rummaged through his backpack, Pastor Schiebold came down the stairs. "Hello, down there," he called.

"Hi, Pastor," Eric's mother said.

Eric's dad sat up quickly on the couch, blinking and trying to look awake. "Hi," he yawned.

"Oh, Bob, I'm sorry," Pastor said, descending the last step into the room. "I didn't mean to disturb you."

"No, no, it's all right," Eric's dad said. "Just catching up."

"Is there anything I can get you?" Schiebold asked.

"No, I think we're fine," Eric's mother said.

"How about you, Eric?"

"May I have a soda?"

"Eric," his mother said, with that tone in her voice.

"Well, Eric," Pastor said, catching the hint, "That's up to your mother."

"I would prefer he have some milk, if you have some," Eric's mother said. And then, remembering, she turned to Eric's dad. "Milk. We should have brought powdered milk."

Pastor smiled. "You were a bit rushed. Hopefully we'll get all this cleared up and you won't need it. I'll bring down a glass in a minute. I, uh, talked with Ted Thornton a few minutes ago."

"You did?" Eric's father said. "What did he say?"

"He's still not sure why these men want you or how long it will take before they give up looking."

To Eric, it looked like somebody let the air out of his parents. They sagged.

"Don't worry, though," Pastor continued. "He said he's going to make some calls Monday morning first thing to find out who, what, and why, and to see if he can't get somebody to explain just what's going on."

Eric's dad nodded. He looked sad. "Thank you, Pastor."

"Hey, and don't you worry about how long it takes, brother. We'll get through it, with the Lord's help. 'All things work together for good to them that love God.'" Schiebold paused and half-smiled. "You know, that's a lot easier to say when tough times are happening to someone else."

"We appreciate that, Pastor," Eric's mother said.

"There is some bad news I need to share with you," Pastor said, his face turning grim. "Eric, normally I'd ask a young man your age to leave the room so I could speak privately with his parents. But in this case, since the sheriff thinks it's best to stay out of sight, and there isn't anyplace else to go down here, I'll share this with you, too. Do you think you can handle it?"

Eric nodded.

"Good," Pastor said. Turning to his parents, he asked, "Do you remember Ed Belcher?"

"Sure," his father said. "He's a regular customer at the store."

"Well," Pastor Schiebold said, "Sheriff Thornton said the men after you seemed to be very interested in him, too."

"Oh, no," Eric's mother said.

"Why?" Bob asked.

"I don't know," Pastor said. "The sheriff told me the men who were asking for you were in his office when he got a phone call, uh, from Ed Belcher. They suddenly changed their plans and went with the sheriff out to the Belcher farm."

Eric's dad and mom looked puzzled. "Why would they do that?" his mother asked.

His father shook his head. "That's very strange," he said. "What does Ted think?"

"He's stumped," Pastor said. "He wondered if you might have had contact with Ed, something that might help him figure things out."

Bob shook his head. "Nothing I can think of. He was in the store last week, but it was the usual talk—how's the harvest coming, that kind of thing."

Schiebold nodded. "Well, I told Ted I'd ask you about it. Sort of. Officially, he doesn't know that I know where you are." He smiled at Eric. "I'll run upstairs and get you that milk. Okay?"

"Okay," Eric said, but his mind was elsewhere. He felt like a giant had just jumped on his chest, and it was hard to breathe. Mike Belcher was his classmate at Mayfield Elementary School. They sat next to each other in Mrs. Holcomb's class. And now he was dead.

Mike Belcher was one of the kids to whom Eric sent that bogus email from God.

He was made for a time such as this. Jared Gruner believed the many nights he'd sacrificed sleep for journeys into the far reaches of cyberspace, digging out bits of information the government didn't want him to know, were finally going to be put to good use.

"I'm telling you, a domestic terror group doesn't make any sense," he said. Gruner had been sitting at the table in Scott Stauffer's so-called dining room for hours trying to get his three friends to see what was really happening. His theories had been discarded, often with heated dissent, and tempers were short. Making matters worse, not a single pizza place was willing to deliver. They were afraid their drivers would be stopped by police for being on the street during a Red Terror Alert.

Gruner had argued that the drivers were essential workers but the restaurant managers wouldn't bite. So the four friends were forced to make do with the supplies in Stauffer's kitchen, which was as well stocked as one could expect for a guy more likely to consider extra computer memory a staple than flour, sugar, butter, or milk.

"No," Gruner continued, reaching for another saltine, "I don't see it. What do we know besides what government spokesmen are spoon-feeding the media? There was no obvious connection between the perpetrators. No history of violence or government protest from any of them so far. Not a single one with a prior arrest. What kind of organization recruits people like that?"

"Perhaps a very smart one," Vijay ventured. "One that does not wish to be exposed until it is ready to strike."

"And that's just it," Gruner said. "These hits last night were all small potatoes."

"Dude!" Norlock said, shocked. "Four thousand dead is not small potatoes!"

Nodding, Gruner said, "Yeah, that's a lot of people. Okay. And the bomb at Wrigley was high profile. You're right. But think about it: if you're running a terror group, and your operatives are deep cover, embedded so deep in mainstream America that nobody, I mean nobody, has a clue about their real identities, are you going to expose your operation, one you've planned and financed for years and years, on a bunch of suicide strikes you could pull off with a few dozen guys smuggled across the Mexican border?"

The group didn't respond, so he pressed on.

"These people—the ones they've named, anyway—are all Americans," Gruner said. "Look at them: Kenyon, Smith, Wojciehowicz, Long, Schulte, O'Toole, and this guy up here at the Grandy's, Reston. As American as you can get. And, at the risk of being politically incorrect, as white-bread as you can get. Where's the motive? Where are the links to anti-American groups with any of these so-called terrorists? I don't buy it. Secret underground terror network, my eye."

Gruner lowered his voice and leaned forward. "On the other hand, I don't believe these people led normal, productive lives, and then suddenly last night, all over the country, all at once, they just snapped. No. No way. Can't be coincidence."

"What's your point?" Stauffer asked.

"My point," Gruner said, leaning forward, "Is that these attacks weren't coordinated. They were *triggered*."

"Triggered?" Norlock asked. "By what?"

"I don't know."

"By who?" Stauffer asked.

Gruner leaned back, satisfied that he'd finally brought them around. "That, my friends, is what we need to figure out."

If there had been even one reason to stay home, he would have. But Tony Harris hadn't been able to talk his ex-girlfriend into letting him spend a few hours with their son on a weekend that wasn't his. With his parents both gone and his brothers and sisters all out of state, he had nothing to do and no one to do it with. He'd already said good-bye to Wanda, so Harris set the thermostat to fifty-five, parked his beloved Camaro in the concrete block garage, locked the reinforced doors and set the security system, made arrangements with Mrs. Langley next door to take in his mail, hoisted his duffel, and walked to the end of the block to catch a Diversey Avenue bus—which he hoped was still running.

With transit on a reduced schedule, Harris waited nearly an hour at the stop before finally catching an eastbound bus. With a transfer to the "L" at Sheffield, only a mile south of Wrigley Field, and a couple more to southbound CTA buses, he was at the headquarters of his Guard unit on South Calumet in just under two hours. The bus deposited Harris in front of the old, three-story brick building that served as the Harrigan Armory, home of the 369th Military Police Company.

Master Sergeant Jason Podowsky greeted him at the front desk inside the main door. The office decor was typical government issue: bland off-white walls in need of scrubbing, patternless floor tile, and olive drab accents on every fixture and furnishing that was nailed down.

"Hey, Jace, how you doing?" Harris grinned at the big kid with the blond crew cut and square jaw.

"Lieutenant Harris," Sergeant Podowsky smiled, shuffling papers on an ancient wooden desk. "Wassaaaaahp?"

"Man, that is so twentieth century," Harris said. "What you been up to?"

"Same old, same old, Lieutenant," the sergeant replied. "Working for my dad's towing company on the North Side. Trying to get him to expand the operation, add a carrier to the fleet."

"How big is the fleet these days?"

"Two trucks." Both men laughed.

"So you're handling paperwork tonight?" Harris asked.

"Yes, sir," Podowsky said. "The captain will be in a little later. Most of the guys who checked in are reporting tomorrow."

"I would've too, if I had any reason to be somewhere else," Harris said.

Sergeant Podowsky raised his eyebrows slightly but let the comment pass. "Here are the standard forms, sir," he said. "You know the drill."

"Yep," Harris said. "So any word about where they're sending us?"

"Not official. The rumor is Saint Louis."

"Saint Louis? What for?"

"Scott Air Force Base," Podowsky said. "Don't know anything more than that."

"Security?"

Podowsky just shook his head. "Don't know. Guess we'll find out Monday."

It was a beautiful Sunday morning in Mayfield, the type that made you glad to be alive no matter what. The sun was up and the crisp morning air was a tonic. Dressed in his gray suit, one of two that he owned, Pastor Dave Schiebold arrived at church early, as he always did on Sunday mornings. The doors were unlocked, his sermon and Sunday school lesson prepared, and the church bulletins set out by the main entrance for the greeters.

Schiebold went over a mental checklist again and found nothing undone. He even remembered to turn on the heater under the baptismal, just in case someone made a decision to follow Jesus in that act of obedience this morning. He'd learned the hard way not to try to predict when the Holy Spirit would move. Lorene Thompson felt led to be baptized one January Sunday when he was still new as the pastor of Mayfield Bible Church, and getting into the water was like an electric shock. It was only after the service that one of the elders remembered to tell him that whoever installed the font years ago had forgotten to insulate beneath the tub.

Grace Tolleson was right on time as usual, which for her meant an hour before the nine o'clock Sunday school classes. Even though Grace had played the small church organ for thirty-seven years and probably knew every piece in the aged hymnal by heart, she made it a rule to practice each hymn for the service at least twice beforehand.

Herb Boettcher arrived a few minutes after Grace. He waved hello to Schiebold and went downstairs to prep the 40-cup coffeemaker for the fellowship time between Sunday school and worship. Like Grace, Herb had been a member of Mayfield Bible Church for nearly as long as Schiebold had been alive, and he made it his ministry to be there every Sunday to serve up coffee.

A small thing, some might think, but people like this formed the backbone of the church. True saints.

His Sunday school class dragged. The discussion was lively enough; after a few moments of indecision, he ditched his outline for the day, a discussion of the Olivet Discourse, to talk about the events of Friday night. Besides the events of Ten-Thirteen, news of the horror at the Belcher farm had spread through the small community and the congregation was struggling to make sense of it all. But Schiebold wanted to talk with Ted Thornton and it was difficult to focus. Thankfully, the class kept the discussion going in spite of his half-hearted participation.

He was even distracted and distant during fellowship time. As he held a cup of Herb Boettcher's coffee and stared vacantly at the back corner of the room, Michelle slipped up to him and tapped him on the shoulder. "Earth to Dave."

"Oh, hi," he said. "Is it that obvious?"

"To me," Michelle said, with a smile. "But I know you better than most of them."

"I hope so," Schiebold said, returning her smile.

"So what are you thinking about?"

"I don't know," he said. "No, that's not true. It's the weight of the day. It feels like it did the Sunday morning after Nine-Eleven. What answers do I give them? How do we reconcile the deaths of innocents with a loving and merciful God?"

Michelle searched his eyes. "You've dealt with those questions before," she said. "Many times. What's different about today?"

She was right. Again. And then he realized what had bothered him all morning. He glanced around to see if anyone was listening. "I'm waiting for the first person to ask me about the Moores. I still don't know what I'm going to say."

"Have you seen Ted Thornton yet?"

"No," Schiebold said. "And he more or less asked me not to tell him where they are. He doesn't want to have to lie, either."

Ted Thornton arrived with Susie and their two teens, Steve and Jennifer, too close to the start of the service to catch him alone. Schiebold made eye contact with the sheriff, who nodded. They'd get together after church.

Pastor Schiebold took his position at the front of the church, seated on a chair near the center of a raised platform that housed the lectern, the small choir loft, the baptismal, and the organ, where Grace Tolleson's skilled fingers wove the opening chords of the day's first hymn.

Just as the congregation began to sing the opening verse of "Sweet Hour of Prayer," the doors at the back of the church opened, and men dressed entirely in black—carrying weapons!—swiftly fanned out along the walls and surrounded the congregation. Grace, unsure of what to do, played a few more bars before gradually fading the music down until it was inaudible. Only gradually did the congregation realize that something out of the ordinary was happening.

Schiebold almost laughed at the absurdity of the scene. God love her, leave it to Grace Tolleson to find a musically pleasing way to segue into a hostage situation.

"Excuse me, ladies and gentleman, may I have your attention, please?" The first one through the door was a tall, fit young man, not much over thirty, with close-cropped dark hair beneath a baseball cap. Schiebold noted a small scar on the man's left cheek.

"Excuse me, please," the man repeated. "We are from the Department of Homeland Security. Please remain calm and in your seats. If you cooperate, there will be no trouble."

A chorus of gasps, shouts, and confused bits of conversation collided in a jumble of noise as people tried to grasp what was happening. As if it wasn't enough that the world had stopped making sense less than forty-eight hours ago, the fifty-odd souls in the small, white church now faced men wearing black and carrying automatic weapons.

Schiebold looked at Ted Thornton, who nodded in reply. *These are the men after Bob Moore.* The sheriff looked ready to spit nails.

Sensing the need for order, Pastor Schiebold stood and raised his hands. "People," he said, and stopped suddenly as half a dozen wicked-looking guns were trained on him. Breathing a silent prayer, Schiebold cleared his throat and continued. "People, I'm sure we can help these men with whatever they need. Now let's stay calm and find out how we can help. Sir?"

The leader turned to face him. There was ice in his gray eyes. "Are you David Schiebold?"

"Yes."

"Would you come with me, please?" There was another gasp and murmur of confusion from the congregation.

Schiebold frowned. "May I ask why?"

"We believe you have information as to the whereabouts of a suspect wanted in connection with the terror attacks Friday night."

"What?" *Terror? They can't mean Bob Moore!*

"I don't think I need to repeat myself."

"Captain," Schiebold said, trying to calm the situation, "I'll be happy to help you, but can this wait until after church? You know where I'll be for the next hour."

"I'm afraid not, Reverend."

"I can't just leave," Schiebold said, forcing a smile. "I'll never find someone to preach on such short notice."

"Now, Reverend! This is not a request." The leader was apparently not in the mood for humor.

Schiebold nodded. "All right." He turned to the congregation. "I'm sure we'll get all this straightened out in short order—and then I'll be back."

The leader came forward to escort Schiebold out of the church. Michelle Schiebold stood up in the second row as he stepped down to meet the captain. One of the younger men in black barked, "Sit down!"

Pastor Schiebold stopped and glared. "That is my wife."

"Unless she wants to come with you, she sits," the man said.

Michelle's eyes were big, questioning. "It'll be all right," Schiebold said. "'Fear not them which kill the body, but are not able to kill the soul.'" He turned and scanned the pews until he found Herb Boettcher. "Herb, would you lead the congregation in prayer? I don't know how long I'll be with these gentlemen, but I sure would appreciate your help while I'm gone."

"You bet," Herb said, starting to rise.

"Sit down," the young man said again.

"Where are you taking him?" Michelle asked the leader.

"You'll be notified," he said, taking Schiebold's arm and leading him down the aisle.

Ted Thornton had finally seen enough, and he exploded out of the pew. "You just can't do this!" he shouted, pointing a meaty finger at the leader. "You have no right!"

The leader nodded to two of his men standing along the wall near the sheriff. One quickly moved to the sheriff's side and stuck what looked like a pistol in his back. Schiebold heard the *zap* of an electric discharge, and Thornton instantly crumpled into the aisle, convulsing helplessly. Susie Thornton screamed and tried to go to Ted, but the other man in black quickly stepped between them. She struggled to get around, but the young man, not much taller than Susie, held her fast.

Steve Thornton, fifteen years old and nearly as tall as his father, stood with his fists clenched. The man with the taser quickly turned and brought it to within a foot of Steve's chest and squeezed the trigger. Steve jerked backward as the charge arced between the contact points, and the bright flash burned an angry violet afterimage in Pastor Schiebold's eyes.

"Do not interfere," the leader said with a loud voice. "David Schiebold is only wanted for questioning. He has information about the whereabouts of Robert Moore, who is wanted in connection with the terror attacks Friday night. Including," he emphasized, "The murder of Edward Belcher and his family."

Schiebold could almost hear heads spinning as the congregation struggled to connect those dots. The clamor rose again as people sought opinions from their neighbors. *Murder? I thought it was suicide… Bob Moore's not here this morning… You don't suppose… These men don't know Bob… Does Pastor know something about…*

"Friends," Schiebold said. "We'll get this straightened out. For now, just pray. We'll all be together again soon." He turned to Michelle. "It will be all right. I promise."

She had tears in her eyes. "I love you."

"I love you, too."

The group's leader tugged on his arm. "Let's go, Reverend." To his men, he said, "Help the sheriff up and bring him with us. He's in this, too."

"What's happening?"

Eric Moore wasn't tall enough to see out of the windows in the Schiebold's basement. His father had moved to the window when he heard the growl of the strange, tan-colored Jeep-like things pulling into the church parking area. He'd described to Eric and his mother how most of the men in black had entered the church. A few stayed outside, watching the two doors in the back.

"I'm not sure, E.J. I can't see much either," his father said. "The men are inside the church now."

"Do you think they're looking for us?"

"I don't know," his father said, but Eric could tell by his voice that he really did.

Eric hunched over on the old couch next to his mother, his knees pulled up to his chin. He wondered if now was a good time to spill his secret. Something told him he'd better, before it was too late.

"Dad? You know how Pastor told us that the men went to the Belchers'?"

"Yeah?" his dad answered without turning away from the window.

"You know when I was doing my math homework?"

"Yeah?"

"Well, I, um, checked my email first," Eric said. "And there was a weird note there."

His father turned slowly away from the window. "What kind of note?"

"Something about 'the time is coming' and 'you're one of the Chosen Ones,'" Eric said.

"What?"

"And it was signed, 'God'."

His father's eyebrows lifted. "Signed by—God. Okay."

"And, well, I sent it to some friends at school 'cause I thought it was a joke."

"Son, I don't see that has to with—"

"And one of them was Mike Belcher."

His father pursed his lips in thought, and his parents exchanged a look. Eric couldn't tell if that was good or bad.

Finally, his dad said, "Okay. It's okay. Thanks for telling us, E.J. It's probably a coincidence, but I'll tell Sheriff Thornton. I'm sure he'll want to know."

Footsteps on the gravel of the parking lot drew his father back to the window. Bob Moore's eyes widened. "Oh, no," he said.

"What is it, honey?" his wife asked.

"They're taking Pastor Schiebold!" his father gasped, his stomach tightening. "And—and Ted Thornton, too. Oh, no, no, no."

"What?"

"It looks like they're arresting them."

Eric's mother was stunned. "During church?"

His dad nodded and continued to stare out the window. Suddenly he turned and gave Eric a big hug, kissed his mother, and said to both of them, "I love you."

And then, before Eric or his mother could react, he ran up the stairs two at a time. A moment later, they heard the front door open.

Eric's heart did a double back flip into his stomach.

His dad was giving himself up to the men with the guns.

TWELVE

His legs still felt weak and his muscles were sore from the spasms induced by the taser, but Sheriff Ted Thornton was determined to walk on his own. He'd rather chew nails than let the young punk who zapped him have the satisfaction of seeing his weakness. Thornton was doubly glad there wasn't anything in his bladder when he got zapped. That would have been too much.

His guts twisted into knots at finding himself unarmed and in the custody of thugs who had the indecency to drag them out of church on Sunday morning. For that matter, this Captain Thiel hadn't shown him any identification—and that made Thornton even madder. As if he was just supposed to accept that they were with the government because of their attitude. For all he knew, these kids were the real terrorists.

Thornton sized up the one closest to him as they slowly walked to the three GMVs parked in the middle of the church lot. No, not terrorists. Their equipment was too good. Too well financed.

Sheriff Thornton wasn't sure which was more frightening— being dragged out of church at gunpoint by terrorists, or by his own government.

"You sure don't look like 'we the people" he grumbled, as they arrived at the Hummers.

"Shut up," said the soldier who'd tasered him.

"Excuse me, Captain," Pastor Schiebold said. "Where are we going?"

"Custody," Captain Thiel said. "Until you're ready to talk."

"What is Bob Moore charged with?"

"Charged?" Thiel raised his eyebrows slightly. "He isn't charged with anything at the moment. We just want to talk to him."

"So why you?" Thornton asked. "Why Special Forces?"

"Special Forces?" Thiel countered. "Who says we were Special Forces?"

"Gotta be," Thornton said. "I've worked with the Bureau and ATF a few times, and you're not them. You guys are a whole 'nother class. You boys dress like you know what you're doing, not because it makes you look tough."

Pastor Schiebold frowned. "I thought the military couldn't do things like this."

"But they can," Thornton said. "Can't you, Captain?"

Just as Thiel opened his mouth to answer, the front door of the parsonage burst open and Bob Moore stumbled out. "Wait! Wait! I'm Bob Moore! If you want me, here I am!"

Thornton's heart sank. He yelled, "Bob! No!" Thiel and his men shouted him down, ordering Bob to lie face down on the gravel drive, immediately.

As two men kept hold of Thornton and Pastor Schiebold, Thiel, with a wave of his hand, directed his team to encircle Bob Moore.

The sheriff shook his head sadly. *Doesn't he know they're not going to trade us for him?*

Some of the bolder and more curious members of the congregation pushed through the double doors of the church to see what was going on. Susie was there, and so was Michelle Schiebold. Poor Herb Boettcher, face turning red, didn't know whether to stand and watch or roll up his sleeves and teach these youngsters a lesson. He was Marinevet who'd served in Vietnam. Back in the day, Ted would have put the odds at even money, but Herb was on the high side of seventy. Desire does not always compensate for the ravages of age.

Thornton caught Herb's eye and shook his head. The sheriff suspected these particular youngsters would feel no remorse about breaking Herb in two if he got in their way, even though he was more than twice their age.

Bob Moore quickly complied with the order to lie down. Two men pounced on him and bound his hands behind him with zip tie restraints. The front door of the parsonage opened again, and Cindy and Eric Moore emerged to witness the drama unfolding outside.

Thornton ground his teeth. The men apprehending Bob were rougher than they needed to be. His glasses had been knocked off, and Bob was bleeding from his right cheek after his head had been shoved into the gravel of the parking lot. In front of his wife and kid. There was no need to humiliate the man.

"You guys are real tough, you know that?" Thornton spat.

"Shut up," said the soldier.

"Congratulations," Thornton said. "Special Forces came to Iowa and took down an unarmed, forty-year-old civilian. I hope you're proud. Right up there with taking out al-Baghdadi."

"Sheriff," Captain Thiel said, returning to the group next to the vehicles, "I am not in the mood. We're going to be together for a while, so do us both a favor—shut up and speak only when spoken to. Lieutenant, let's get these prisoners loaded in. One in each car."

"It'll be all right, Ted," Schiebold said, as they were led to the GMVs, "There's a purpose in this, even if we don't see it yet."

Thornton hoped his pastor was right. Still, as he was shoved into the back seat of one of the military vehicles, Ted Thornton found himself wondering why God chose him for this particular mission.

"Sir?" Captain Tom Wetzel stood in Green's smoky office with a legal pad full of notes in his hand. "We're getting some questions from Homeland Security about what's going on."

Green sat back in his leather desk chair, a fresh cigarette alight in his hand. "Questions? From who—*specifically*—at Homeland Security?"

"Sir," Wetzel said, "Let me rephrase that. The questions are coming from a couple of the regional directors of FEMA. They want to know what to tell the Secretary of DHS if he asks about what's going on."

Green took a pull on his cigarette before answering. "Tell the directors that threats to the homeland have been identified and steps are being taken to neutralize them. Perpetrators and conspirators are being apprehended and transported to detention centers for questioning. That's all they need to know."

"Yes, sir." Wetzel saluted and exited Green's office, closing the door behind him.

As he returned to his desk in the Comm Center, Wetzel wondered at Green's remarks. *If we're the intelligence clearinghouse for the government, why doesn't Homeland Security call us directly?*

Cindy Moore felt like she'd been kicked in the stomach. Bob was normally so steady, so reserved, that she was totally unprepared when he dashed outside. By the time she realized what was happening and followed, the men in black were already standing over him in the church parking lot.

Eric had followed her upstairs, and he threw his arms around her as they watched the armed men bind Bob's hands behind his back with a zip tie, yank him to his feet, and then bully him toward the three big GMVs. She wanted to run after her husband, but her son's embrace held her back. What if they arrested her, too? Who would take care of E.J.?

And somehow, she knew that Bob had thought about that before he ran out of the house.

Standing in front of the parsonage, oblivious to the stares from those of the congregation who'd dared to leave the church, Cindy Moore choked back tears as her husband, her pastor, and the sheriff were shoved into the GMVs and driven away. The men in black might as well have taken her heart with them.

"Cindy! Cindy!" Michelle Schiebold ran across the parking lot. Cindy opened her arms and wrapped the smaller woman in a desperate hug.

"What's happening? Why did they take Dave and Ted?" Cindy asked.

Stepping back, Michelle said, "I think—I think they must have listened in on our phone line. That's the only way they could have guessed that Dave knew where you were."

"They tapped your phone? Can they do that?"

"I don't know. Maybe. None of this makes sense," Michelle said. "Why do they want Bob?"

"I wish I knew!" Cindy said, tears beginning to flow down her cheeks. "Susie, what is going on?"

"Ladies, may I suggest something?" It was Herb Boettcher, his weathered, lined face filled with concern. "I think this morning's worship should be turned into a prayer meeting. If that's all right with you."

Michelle nodded. "Yes," she said. "Yes, you're right. Let's take this to the Lord."

Cindy, holding Eric's hand, followed Herb and Michelle back to the little white church. The walk seemed to last a lifetime. Her mind raced with speculation. But no matter how she turned the problem, it came down to one thing: why did the government—if that was really who sent the men in black—want her husband in custody? Was it a case of mistaken identity? She couldn't imagine that it was anything else. It *had* to be a mistake. There was no other answer.

Michelle Schiebold led Cindy and Eric into the church. The congregation, buzzing with confused chatter, appeared as stunned as she was. Susie Thornton was in tears; Fran Braunberger, a matronly woman with pure white hair, hovered at her side with a pocket-sized packet of tissues.

Letting go of Cindy's hand as they entered the sanctuary, Michelle made her way through the people standing in the center aisle to the platform up front. "Excuse me," she said. "May I have your attention?"

Gradually, the noise subsided, and the four-dozen people in the little church turned toward her.

"Thank you," she said. "Brother Herb suggested we forgo our normal Sunday service and spend the time in prayer, and I think that's a wonderful idea." There were murmurs of assent from the congregation.

"But before we do," Michelle continued, "I think we need to share a bit of what we know about what just happened here." She glanced at Cindy and Susie for support before pressing on. "Friday evening, Sheriff Thornton was contacted by the men who were just here. They demanded to know where Bob Moore could be found. Ted made a decision—and I think, based on what we just saw, he was right—to call the Moores and advise them to be somewhere else when these men got to their house. Late Friday night, the Moores came here, to us, asking for our help. We agreed, trusting that they were unjustly pursued, and the Moores have been in our basement since very early yesterday morning. We had hoped Ted could contact authorities to find out what was going on and get this resolved. However, it seems that these men somehow listened in on a phone call between Dave and Ted. They apparently guessed that Dave knew where to find the Moores and came here this morning to take Dave in for questioning. And you saw what happened."

As she spoke, Cindy could see the anger rising in Michelle. Her words became more precise, almost clipped, as if she were biting them off.

"Can they do that?" Paul Cook, a young farmer with land south of Mayfield, stood in one of the back pews. "I mean, they didn't have no warrant, and since when can they tap your phone without some kind of warrant or somethin'?"

"I don't know," Michelle said. "I guess they think they can, because they did."

"It grieves me to say this," said an older woman standing in one of the side aisles near the front of the church, "But they must have some reason to be after Brother Moore."

Cindy was stunned, not believing she'd actually heard those words. She looked more closely and saw that the speaker was Eileen Gilliam. It *would* be her. A woman with hair as gray as steel and a heart to match, a widow for nearly fifteen years.

Old-timers recalled a day when Eileen was a gentler soul, but that was before Walt Gilliam had been laid into an early grave. She wasn't a bad person, as such, but it seemed that some days she just couldn't help but drag others into her circle of misery.

"The government doesn't send men like that for just anybody," Eileen continued.

That was too much. "Excuse me? Now, wait just a minute!" Cindy pushed her way up the center aisle, blood pounding in her ears.

Michelle cut her off. "Thank you, Eileen. I'm sure this will be settled very soon."

"We can't have our pastor involved in something like this," Eileen persisted. "It's not right!"

Michelle Schiebold's jaw clenched. Cindy glanced around at the congregation. Most of them were aghast at Eileen Gilliam's outburst, but she noticed that a couple of other faces were tactfully neutral. Eileen's words had crossed their minds before she'd spoken.

Herb Boettcher jumped into the breach. "Now, Miss Eileen, do you really believe Brother Moore had anything to do with that horrible, horrible tragedy at the Belchers?"

Eileen frowned. "Well, I don't—"

"And do you really think Brother Thornton would for one minute help somebody he thought was responsible for the deaths of five innocent people?"

"No, I guess—"

"And Pastor was only trusting the sheriff's judgment," Herb said. "There has to be some mistake, and once they talk to everyone, I'm sure it will all be fine. Now, people," he said, stepping up to the platform next to Michelle, who literally shook with anger, "we don't know how this will end, but our Savior does. Let's bow our heads and lay this on the One who carries all our burdens."

Thank God for Herb Boettcher, Cindy thought, as she took Eric's hand and bowed her head. *Do they really think Bob killed the Belchers? Lord, if ever we needed You, it's right now.*

The Internet crackled with theories. Nothing had been settled yesterday at Stauffer's, but Jared Gruner was satisfied that the other three had started thinking in terms of a planned event. It just wasn't the type of event most people associated with terrorists.

He spent hours scouring the web, social media, and mail lists, piecing together a clearer picture of the world outside his small, two-bedroom home. Network news? Couldn't trust it. Most reporters were too lazy or stupid to do more than regurgitate government press releases. Besides, the corporate fat cats who owned the networks gained nothing by rocking the boat. That's why fluff like the latest celebrity meltdown dominated the news, while important stuff like presidential Executive Orders and United Nations initiatives were left to the alternative media.

The scariest thing about the night before last, as far as Gruner was concerned, was that the perps were mainly middle-class types. These were people you met at the mall or the grocery store or the post office every single day. How could you profile attackers like that?

There was only one response the government could make, and that was to crack down on everybody. The 24-hour news channels drove the point home. Most people welcomed the inconvenience, believing that you had nothing to worry about if you had nothing to hide.

Jared Gruner wasn't most people.

For example, most people didn't know that the president didn't even need to declare martial law to suspend *habeas corpus* or to deploy federal troops on American soil.

Most people didn't know that a series of Executive Orders issued since the Carter administration had given FEMA the power to take over the government and nearly all aspects of society during an emergency: transportation, communications, food distribution, and even security. Most people wouldn't have believed their government could, with the stroke of a pen, turn their lives over to ten regional dictators, who in turn reported to the unelected director of the Federal Emergency Management Agency.

Most people hadn't heard the rumors that a small branch of Special Forces had been officially detached from the military by a secret presidential directive—and therefore not even subject to the Posse Comitatus Act. There were also rumors that the directive granted the unit full legal immunity for anything it did inside the United States.

But Jared Gruner was not most people.

He didn't have anything solid, not yet, but something was definitely going on. A few people at a couple of news groups he visited claimed to have seen black helicopters in the air, and one or two claimed they were the big Chinook copters that ferry troops around, but Gruner couldn't pick out any pattern to the sightings.

Not enough data, and no way to tell what was real and what was planted.

Then there was the total departure from known terrorist tactics. Either the terror groups had done something completely new, or—or this was just something completely new altogether.

What was even more disturbing were the rumblings on social media that anti-fascist groups might hit the streets in major cities, building on the idea the media kept repeating that Ten-Thirteen was the work of some apocalyptic white supremacist group.

Gruner ran his fingers through his uncombed hair and sighed in frustration. His eyes were gummy and lack of sleep and exercise made his thoughts sluggish.

Time for a break.

He stood and stretched, and then he rotated his arms straight out from his shoulders in ever-growing circles; eight times to the front, eight times to the back. Good for getting the blood moving.

Lack of sleep was another problem. No time for a nap, so he decided on another Blast Cola ("Twice the caffeine of regular colas!"). On his way to the fridge, he punched the speed dial on his phone for Scott Stauffer. Maybe Stofe would have an idea that would get him going again.

He let it ring fifteen times before hanging up. Strange. Voice mail should have picked up the call. Maybe Stofe let the battery die on his mobile—but that would have triggered an error message.

Shrugging, Gruner set down his phone, turned his mind back to the puzzle and went back to work.

THIRTEEN

Monday morning traffic into downtown Saint Louis was always a headache. Over the last two years, since moving upriver from the field office in Sainte Genevieve, Joe Unes had grown to expect it and accept it. A steady drizzle made things just that much slower. Traffic volume was a little surprising today, though, considering that Homeland Security hadn't lowered the Red Terror Alert yet.

Details of the tragedies that struck America Friday night dominated the radio newscasts, with special emphasis on the thirty-six who died in the blast at Grandy's.

News from the Middle East wasn't any brighter. The Israeli push into Syria had moved to within fifteen miles of what was left of Damascus, determined to crush the Iran-backed rebels who'd taken advantage of the chaos after the massive earthquake in Syria earlier in the year. Muslim states in the region had demanded an immediate cease-fire and withdrawal. King Abdullah of Jordan had issued an unusually strong warning to Prime Minister Perleman. Iran's mullahs had already declared *jihad*, but they had their hands full with a new American offensive against Shiite militias in Iraq.

The questions on the minds of world leaders were whether the Iranian nuclear program had progressed far enough to develop weapons and whether the Israelis would take out the Iranian reactor before American troops reached it.

Turkey's newest would-be caliph, President Arslan, issued new threats about marching to Jerusalem. Remnants of the Islamic State issued threats from their new home base in Libya, which still wasn't a functioning state a decade after the fall of Gaddafi. In Egypt, al-Sisi was losing control over a reenergized Muslim

Brotherhood, and to hold on to power a little longer he might be forced to take harsh measures he'd otherwise have ruled out, and that was bad news for Coptic Christians. The rest of the Arab League, led by the Saudis and Kuwaitis, condemned Israel's "act of aggression," but it was unclear what they'd do to back up their words.

American GIs, meanwhile, found progress in Iraq more difficult than expected with Iraqis outraged at Israel's military offensive in Syria. All of Iraq had risen up again, Sunni and Shia, and even the previously stable Kurdish territories weren't safe for Americans anymore.

More ominous were the signals coming from further away. Muslim states such as Afghanistan, Malaysia, Indonesia, and Pakistan threatened to jump in on Syria's side, despite warnings from the U.S., Britain, and Australia. The fear that Pakistan might throw its nuclear weapons into the fight kept diplomats busy in virtually every time zone. If Pakistan jumped in, India would likely come to Israel's aid. India was a nuclear state, too.

With India in the fight, China and Russia might follow. The prospect of global nuclear war was suddenly all too real.

The Palestinian territories were in flames, of course, and Israel's security forces had their hands full with a fresh wave of homicide bombers. The IDF struck back with a series of shockingly savage reprisals using helicopter-launched rockets that destroyed dozens buildings in three days. The scores of dead included civilians who'd simply been in the wrong place when the rockets landed.

The news, coupled with the steady rain, turned his drive to the office into the most depressing commute Joe Unes had ever experienced.

Local police cruisers were more visible this morning. Officers in riot gear manned major intersections near government buildings. No doubt that was the reason for the slow traffic. Nobody wanted to get pulled over when the cops were so edgy.

The police had reason to be on edge. Although things had quieted after the orgy of death Friday night, isolated incidents still popped up with no pattern or warning. Cops had to wonder if every car or van they stopped was packed with explosives. And then there were the rumors about street protests. Saint Louis had been sensitive about that ever since the Ferguson riots.

Despite Cathy's orders to forget about work during his weekend at Saint Christopher's Hospital, Unes couldn't stay away from the news. He counted twenty-three incidents in the last sixty hours, but he still couldn't see any connections between the attacks.

After seventy-five minutes of slogging through traffic as thick as cold oatmeal, Unes finally pulled off Market Street into the parking lot of the FBI's Saint Louis field office. As he'd expected, a stack of new files waited on his desk.

First things first: Unes took off his jacket and draped it over the back of his chair, picked up his coffee mug, and headed for the break room. A cup of coffee before tackling the paperwork was an indispensable part of the morning routine. Unes liked routine.

"Good to see you up and around Joe. You got a minute?" Special Agent in Charge Steven Clay stood in the doorway of his office.

"Sure," Unes said, changing direction. Coffee would have to wait.

Clay was a tall man, three or four inches taller than Unes, with a head of thick, dark hair that made him look younger than his fifty-six years. His prominent nose and slightly weak chin gave him an owl-like appearance that was exaggerated when he put on his reading glasses.

"Close the door, Joe," Clay said, settling into the chair behind his desk. Unes did, taking the seat facing Clay's desk. "You feeling okay this morning?"

"My ears are still ringing and I've got a few bruises, but it could have been a lot worse," Unes said.

"Good, good." Clay nodded absently. "You saw the files on your desk, I take it." He opened a folder of his own and pulled the owlish reading glasses from his shirt pocket.

"Yeah. I figured today would be a busy day."

"You don't know the half of it," Clay said, peering over the top of his spectacles. "Washington wants all field offices to coordinate on what happened Friday. They want answers yesterday. You've had a weekend to process information. I'd like to know your take. What do you think?"

Unes took a deep breath and exhaled, trying to box his thoughts into a presentable package. Shaking his head, he said, "The attacks are scattered, random. I can't see where there's any apparent connection between them. Either a bunch of lone nuts snapped all at once, or we're dealing with a mastermind more brilliant than Lex Luthor."

Clay raised his eyebrows in question. He missed the reference.

"Superman's arch-enemy," Unes explained.

"Right." Clay gazed down at the report again. "We have a list of religious extremist groups we want you to start checking out. File's on your desk. Bureau thinks the connection might have something to do with the war in the Middle East."

"Religious," Unes repeated. "As in Muslim?"

"No," Clay said. "Right-wing fundamentalists. Apocalyptic types, trying to kick-start the end times. All this crap in the Middle East has them stirred up, thinking Armageddon is right around the corner. The Bureau did a threat analysis on the groups a few years back, before Y2K."

"Project Megiddo. I remember," Unes said.

"Made a copy of that for you," Clay said. "Based on the suspects we've been able to ID and stuff we're seeing on social media, that's the key. This could be a violent splinter group of dominionists—Christian *jihadis*, basically, who think Jesus won't come back until they take over the world. Washington wants quick answers." He returned to reading the file in his hands.

"Social media. Twitter?"

"Mainly," Clay said, focused on the top sheet from the stack of paperwork on his desk. "Some Facebook groups and pages, too. We've got teams on that in DC. If that's not enough, the anti-fascists might use this as an excuse to mobilize again. Same signs we saw on Twitter before the last couple rounds of protests against police brutality. Anarchists."

Sensing that the meeting was over, Unes nodded and stood to leave. "When will Homeland Security lower the threat level?"

Looking up, Clay said, "I guess that depends on how quickly we find out which of these groups is headed up by—what did you call him?—Lex Luthor."

Worst Monday ever.

Just one day before, Scott Stauffer had been minding his own business, taking a break from his computer and watching some late afternoon football on TV to relax.

It hadn't helped. Every time the cameras panned across row after row of empty seats, Stauffer was reminded that things were very different than they'd been a couple of days before.

Nobody wanted to end up like the people in the bleachers at Wrigley Field Friday night. It was surprising that the NFL was playing at all.

The game was in the third quarter. The Rams started slowly, playing the 49ers even for the first half, but Parker Haydon, the new rookie quarterback, got hot after halftime and led the team to a seven-point lead. And then someone knocked at his apartment door.

It wasn't one of the gang. They never bothered to knock.

Stauffer had gone to the door and opened it without unhooking the security chain. As soon as the door began to swing open, it exploded inward, ripping the chain from the doorframe.

The metal door caught Stauffer on the shoulder and knocked him to one side. Instantly, his apartment was flooded by a team of men dressed in black who yelled at him to stay down. They searched his rooms, none too gently, and then confiscated his computer and most of the rest of his electronic equipment.

A man with a shaved head and lousy manners handcuffed him. He and a buddy half-carried Stauffer out of his apartment, dragging him down three flights of stairs to the parking lot in full view of half a dozen curious neighbors. Without a word, they threw him into the back of a plain black SUV.

They hadn't even bothered to turn off his TV.

As they drove off, one of the men put a blindfold on Stauffer. All he knew was that he was in the car for about half an hour and then marched to a waiting helicopter.

The flight was the worst of his life. Stauffer hated flying. His mind refused to accept the illogical notion that a difference in air pressure between the top and bottom of an airfoil could lift a heavier-than-air object off the ground. On top of that, he was still blindfolded so the only sensations his mind could process were sound, smell, and touch. It was the most terrifying thirty minutes of his life.

It was dark when they'd arrived the night before, so he hadn't seen any details outside. Now, in the light—and hopefully *sanity*—of day, Stauffer tried to concentrate, to assess his situation.

He lay in an uncomfortable bed somewhere within an hour or so of Saint Louis in a barracks-like facility with steel mesh over the windows. He'd been left with what must have been a military MRE—Meal Ready to Eat—and a plastic spork. The barracks held about a hundred bunk beds in it, but as Stauffer looked around the room, he realized that he was the sole occupant.

What did these men want with him? It wasn't a robbery or a kidnapping. That meant they were probably government. But which branch? They hadn't identified themselves. Could be ATF or FBI, but if they arrested him, didn't the law require them to read him his rights?

But why should any agency arrest him—for what? Was it something to do with the grocery store bombing? *I'll bet that's it,* Stauffer thought grimly. *That FBI agent has our names and numbers. Gruner, Norlock, and Vijay will be here before lunch.*

Vijay Sampurnananda was first in the office Monday morning, as usual, ready to begin his day writing code at Symptomatic Software. He'd been hired for the job after responding to an online ad posted by Scott Stauffer, one of the founders and the Chief Technology Officer of the company. It turned out that Vijay's experience was right for the position, and, as it turned out, his unique view of the world fit well with Scott and his odd pair of friends, Jared and Terry.

As his co-workers filed in, some a few minutes before eight, some fashionably late, and a few with creative ideas about what "eight o'clock" actually meant, Vijay kept an eye open for Stauffer.

The drive home from Scott's apartment Saturday night had been adventuresome; a Saint Louis County Police officer mistook Vijay's dark skin and black hair as evidence of Arab ancestry, and it was several nerve-wracking minutes before he convinced the officer that he was actually Indian (and Hindu, not Muslim), and he was allowed to continue on his way home.

Vijay wanted to talk to Stauffer about the incident, to determine whether this was unusual in America. But Stauffer, who generally got to work precisely at eight, was now more than half an hour late. That was unlike him.

Vijay decided to call Stauffer to see if he was well or if he'd perhaps overslept. The call went directly to voice mail.

Well, maybe Scott had some trouble with his horrible van. Vijay decided to wait another hour before worrying.

The air transport from Midway Airport to Saint Louis had been delayed by weather. Finally, early Monday morning, Lieutenant Tony Harris and the 369th Military Police Company got into the air. The company still hadn't been told where they were headed. Captain Poverello said they'd know when they got there.

The flight itself wasn't the worst he'd ever had. The charter flight was fairly smooth once it was in the air, and the trip took just under ninety minutes.

After some delays in the air because of new security procedures, the DC-9 touched down with the Arch visible just across the Mississippi on the way down. *So, it's Scott after all*, Harris thought.

Weather nearly identical to what they'd left in Chicago greeted the company as they climbed down the stairs to the tarmac. Harris was met by a depressingly gray sky, a slow steady drizzle, and a forty-five degree temperature.

"I could do without this." Sergeant Kendall Williams, one of Harris' three squad leaders, stood beside him, adjusting his pack.

"You and me both, brother," Harris said, hopping down.

This was his first visit to Scott Air Force Base. The airfield featured a runway large enough for big transports, even though most of the planes based here were basically military Lear jets.

Captain Mike Poverello, first off the plane, was welcomed by another officer, a major, at the bottom of the stairway. The captain turned to his men as each climbed off the plane and waved them toward a line of waiting vans idling at the edge of the runway. Harris shifted his duffel to a more comfortable position and started in that direction at double time. No point in staying out in the rain.

In shifts, the big fifteen-passenger vans carted the 369th to what appeared to be a recently constructed camp just south of the main part of the base. About a dozen long, low barracks sat inside a compound marked off by an eight-foot chain-link fence topped with barbed wire. A couple more sat outside the enclosure, flanking a third building that must have been headquarters, because that's where the van's driver stopped to let them out.

The building was basic military, no frills outside or in; a long, rectangular box, one level on a concrete slab. Harris entered a door at the right corner of the building and immediately wrinkled his nose at the odor of cheap latex paint.

The place looked like a half-finished police station. An unmanned desk and chair faced the door, and a dozen more identical desks, equipped with phones and black all-in-one desktop PCs, were arranged in four rows of three in a large open area just inside. Technicians scurried between the desks, running wires and cables from the phones and computers to outlets in the walls, which were in the process of being painted a dull off-white.

At the far end of the room, several doors marked private offices. Captain Poverello would get one of those, Harris guessed.

"Move in! Give everybody a chance to get out of the rain." Poverello pushed past Harris and Sergeant Williams, dropped his duffel in front of a desk, took off his cap, and ran a hand through his short, dark hair. Harris looked around and found his other squad leaders, Sergeants Mark Keloski and Ernie Ortiz, coming in together. He waved them over.

"Nice of them to build this just for us, eh, Captain?" Williams said, threading his way through the desks and swinging his duffel to the floor along the back wall.

"Watch the walls, they're wet," one of the painters said.

The rest of the 369th hustled in from outside, laughing and joking. Their attitude was a tribute to the captain, Harris thought, considering that they'd only been given forty-eight hours to notify wives, families, and employers before reporting.

And they still hadn't been briefed on the assignment.

"Gentlemen," Poverello began softly, his voice barely cutting the chorus of voices. "Hey, listen up!"

Sergeant Podowsky shouted, "Ten-shun!" The company quickly snapped to.

"Okay, that's better," the captain continued. "Men, this is Colonel Hostler. He is our commanding officer. He'll tell us why we're here."

The man who moved through the company to Captain Poverello's side was stocky with thinning hair, a little taller than the captain and at least thirty pounds heavier. His uniform was on the rumpled side, and the rain had plastered his hair to his scalp. Dark rings rimmed his eyes and jowls sagged from a heavily lined face giving the colonel the appearance of an oversized bulldog; a man who'd look natural with a half-smoked cigar clenched between his teeth.

"At ease, men," Hostler began. "We appreciate your making it here on such short notice. This camp, as you most likely are aware, is just outside Saint Louis. It's a new facility, in some respects. In fact, it doesn't even have an official name yet. But the essentials have been here for some time, waiting for a need. Just such a need presented itself this past weekend. I don't need to tell you again about the tragedies this nation experienced Friday night and Saturday. This is a time unlike any in our nation's history, a time when an enemy has succeeded in striking on our soil to bring death to thousands of American men, women, and children. This, gentlemen, will not stand."

The colonel paused for a moment, scowling as if determined not to rest until he got five minutes alone with whoever was responsible. "Drastic measures are required to ensure the safety and security of our families and loved ones. As you know, the Department of Homeland Security elevated the Terror Threat Level to Red on Friday night, and we are remain at that level.

Under such conditions, the Justice Department will exercise its full authority under the law to apprehend those believed responsible for or connected to the events of this weekend. And that, gentlemen, is where we come in.

"The camp enclosure at the end of the airfield is a detention center, one of two dozen scattered across the country. The way this works is simple: FBI and local law enforcement will round them up and bring them here. FBI will question them. Our job is to make sure they don't get out. That's all for now. Direct your questions to Captain Poverello and he will bring them to me." He turned and saluted the captain.

"Ten-shun!" Podowsky shouted again as the colonel made his way back through the company and outside to a waiting car.

"At ease," Captain Poverello said. "Lieutenants Morgan, Harris, Long, and Shoemaker, please join me in my office. Have your platoon sergeants get your men situated in the barracks behind the compound. First and second platoons, take the far building, third and fourth, take the near building."

"So that's it? We been called in to guard a camp full of terrorists?" Williams asked Harris, as the company heaved their packs onto their backs for the trek across the field to the barracks.

"Looks that way, Sergeant," Harris replied. "Okay, Williams, Keloski, Ortiz, secure the men in their new home away from home. I'll meet with Cap and find out what the plans are. It didn't look like there was anybody over there, but they wouldn't drag us down here if they didn't expect guests. We better be ready."

Noon, and still no word from Scott Stauffer. This was very irregular. Vijay Sampurnananda expected some contact from his friend and employer. His broken-down van had failed him before, but Stauffer had a phone and always called the office to let them know what had happened. And usually to ask for a ride.

But today, nothing.

Vijay decided that he'd waited long enough. He turned from the project he was building on his workstation, picked up the phone on his desk, and dialed the number for Terry Norlock. Although Norlock was at work, Vijay knew that he was usually more dependable than Jared Gruner. Scott would probably have called him first.

"Terry Norlock."

"Hello, Terry, it is Vijay. Have you heard from Scott this morning?"

"What ho, Veej. No, I haven't. What's up?"

"He has not arrived at work and no one has heard from him at our office," Vijay said. "Can you think of where he might be?"

"No, not off the top of my head," Norlock said. "Have you tried Gruner? Maybe he knows."

"No, I have not," Vijay said. "I called you first."

"Let me know what you find out," Norlock said. "I've got a customer. I'll talk to you later."

Vijay tapped Gruner's number on his speed dial. As far as Vijay knew, Gruner was between projects. He was usually between projects.

"Yeah—hello. What is it?" Gruner's muffled voice sounded as though it came through his pillow.

"Hello, Jared, it is me, Vijay. Have you heard from Scott today?"

"Oh, yeah. Hey, Veej," Gruner said, suddenly more alert. "No. Why?"

"Well, he is not at work, and he has not called. That is not like him at all. I am concerned that he may be sick or was perhaps in an automobile accident."

"Oh yeah?" Gruner sounded puzzled. "I tried calling him last night, but he never picked up."

Vijay frowned. "I am trying not to be unnecessarily concerned, but I must admit, I am worried."

"Tell you what," Gruner said. "I'm not doing anything right now. I'll run over to Scott's and see if he's home."

"Thank you, Jared," Vijay said. "Please call me when you find out what is going on."

"Yeah, no trouble," Gruner said. "I'll call you from Scott's."

It was a five-minute drive from Jared Gruner's house to Scott Stauffer's apartment. Gruner noticed police on nearly every street between his house and Stauffer's. He kept his eighteeen-year-old Mazda Protegé just below the speed limit. No need to provoke the officers of the law during a Red Terror Alert.

As he pulled off Manchester Road into the parking lot of the Winchester Square Apartments, Gruner's instincts screamed that something was wrong. Stauffer's beat-up van was in its usual spot, right below his door on the third floor. Jared pried himself out of his car and huffed up the three flights.

Gruner listened outside the door to Stauffer's apartment for a few moments until he was absolutely sure. There was no mistaking it—coming from Stauffer's apartment was the sound of a TV soap opera. Unless Stauffer had a girlfriend he'd kept hidden from his three closest friends, that would never happen. And the probability of Stauffer meeting a girl without Gruner hearing all about it were smaller than the odds of *pi* being a whole number.

Stauffer kept a spare key hidden on top of the brick facade above the door. It took Gruner about three seconds to find it. He unlocked the apartment and went in. He was three steps in when his fears were confirmed.

The TV was on, the coffee pot had boiled dry and cracked, and most obvious to Gruner: *Stauffer's computer was missing.*

No doubt about it. This was serious.

FOURTEEN

Monday morning had always been one of her favorite times of the week. Cindy Moore normally felt excited and energized at the prospect of a new day, a new week, new opportunities and challenges. This morning, however, Cindy felt—heavy. Weighed down.

Getting out of bed was a chore. She hadn't slept well, and she didn't want to face the day.

But she had to get up. Although Mayfield schools had been closed for the day after the horror of Bloody Friday hit so close to home, Eric would be up sooner or later. Cindy wanted time to think through what she would say to him.

What could she say? She had no idea what had happened or why.

For once, Cindy was thankful that E.J. was a slow riser. Today, she would let him sleep. That would buy her a little time.

Slowly making her way downstairs, Cindy tried to think, to set a course of action. Events had moved so quickly yesterday that everything was still a blur. Cindy had spent the day at the parsonage with Susie Thornton and Michelle Schiebold. Thankfully, they didn't blame Bob for what happened to their husbands. Their children kept each other occupied while the three women sat in the Schiebolds' kitchen, talking, praying, and trying to overcome their shock.

The time for shock was over. Today, they needed to do something.

Cindy rinsed out the coffee pot and began scooping ground coffee into a filter. A slow thumping on the stairs announced E.J.'s arrival. *So much for time to think.*

Eric's red hair was mussed and his eyes were puffy. He hadn't slept much, either.

"Good morning, sunshine," Cindy said. Eric didn't answer. He just shuffled across the kitchen floor and wrapped his arms around her. "I know, I know," she whispered.

"What's gonna happen, Mom?" Eric asked, his voice muffled by her baggy sweatshirt.

"I don't know, E.J. We still need to find out where your dad's been taken, and why they thought they needed to arrest him in the first place. Then we can decide what to do."

Just then the telephone's ring interrupted the stillness of the gray Monday morning. Cindy gently detached her son so she was able to cross the kitchen to answer.

"Hello?"

"Cindy? This is Susie Thornton. How are you this morning? It's not too early, is it?"

"No, it's fine, Susie," Cindy said. "I couldn't sleep anyway. I'm just tired. It was a long night."

"Here, too," Susie said. "Hey, I've been going through Ted's address book, and I think I found someone who can help us."

"That would be wonderful. Who is it?"

"Our congressman," Susie said. "Harold Benson."

"Do you think he would?"

"I think so," Susie said. "At least he can get some answers from the FBI or whoever sent those goons. Ted's known him a long time. They've worked together on rallies and fundraisers and whatnot. In fact, Congressman Benson was the one who really encouraged Ted to run for sheriff the first time. Ted likes him."

"Oh, praise God! It would be wonderful if he could help," Cindy said. "Can you get in touch with him, do you think?"

"I think so," Susie said. "Ted has numbers in his address book for his Washington office and his home office up in Prairie View. I'll call as soon as the office in Washington opens, at eight our time."

"Thank you, Susie," Cindy said. "Do you want to call Michelle, or should I?"

"I will," Susie said. "If I don't keep working on something, I start thinking. And since I don't know anything, that drives me crazy. I'll call you back as soon as I get someone at the congressman's office."

"Thanks, Susie. Bye."

Cindy turned to finish loading the coffeemaker when she heard Eric's voice from the office between the kitchen and the store.

"Mom! The computer's gone!"

"What?" Cindy set down the coffee and went to look for herself. Sure enough, there was an empty spot on the desk where the computer had been the night before.

Or had it? She and E.J. hadn't gone in the office when they got home. For that matter, she hadn't been in the office since Friday when they abandoned the house.

Cindy switched on the lights in the store and made a quick circuit. Nothing else seemed to be missing except for the items they grabbed Friday night. She went back into the office and looked at the safe tucked unobtrusively under the desk. It hadn't been disturbed, but just to be sure, she spun the combination dial and opened the door. The change drawer from the cash register was still there, all the money intact.

The only thing missing from the house or store was the computer.

"Eric, what was that you said about the email you saw on Friday?"

Her son, standing next to the desk, repeated the odd story about the email from "God" that he forwarded to three of his friends. "Do you think it's important, Mom?" he asked.

Cindy shook her head. "I don't know. But I think I'd better call Mrs. Thornton back."

His captors hadn't extended any courtesy, that's for sure. Bob Moore endured an uncomfortable ride in a GMV with his hands bound behind his back. The open cut on his cheek had been left to bleed until it clotted.

Bob's questions were still unanswered. He didn't know why he'd been arrested, why the men felt compelled to take Pastor Schiebold and Sheriff Thornton, or where they were going.

They'd driven all through the day, though Bob didn't know where. His captors blindfolded him once they'd gotten into the vehicle and left him that way except for one brief stop at a small gas station. He'd been allowed a supervised trip to a filthy men's room that offered no clues about where they were. As soon as he was back in the GMV, the blindfold went right back on.

He spent the night in a tiny, bare room furnished only with a cot. The door was locked, and steel mesh covered the outside of the small window. Bob thought he might have had a chance of escape if he were mechanically inclined, but not knowing his location or even where Ted and Pastor Schiebold were, and not having much in the way of survival skills, Bob decided it was best to wait and pray.

At daybreak, his captors allowed Bob a quick shower before putting his clothes back on. The communal shower looked like something from an army barracks or a prison.

A meal of scrambled eggs, bacon, toast, and coffee was brought to his room on a tray after the shower. The eggs were reconstituted from powder and the bacon and coffee were cheap, but at least the toast wasn't burned. Bob forced himself to eat.

It was odd, Bob mused, that despite being chased from his home in the dead of night and yanked away from his family without cause, he felt a sense of peace. There wasn't much in his power to control at the moment, so Bob decided to leave it to God. He worried about Cindy and E.J., but he knew they were under the protection of the Lord. Whatever happened, it was in His hands, and God loved them even more than he did.

The lock in the door clacked and popped, and the door swung outward to reveal Captain Thiel.

"Ready to move?"

"I guess so," Bob said.

"Good. Let's go. Hands behind your back."

Once again, plastic restraints were cinched tight around his wrists. So far, that was the worst part of the last twenty-four hours.

Captain Thiel and one of his team walked on either side of Bob, directing him out of the building and onto a small airfield. Miles of flat, open ground surrounded them. Trees were visible in the distance in three directions. Behind him, the rectangular frame building he'd just left was flanked by four more, two on each side. *Definitely like a barracks*, Bob thought.

Behind him and off to his right, a cluster of plain, single-story, flat-roofed brick buildings housed what were probably administration offices. An American flag flew from a tall pole on the other side of the brick buildings, presumably outside the main entrance.

Radar or satellite dishes adorned a couple of roofs. Parked beyond the end of the line of brick buildings were two big, steel boxes sporting antennas mounted on trailers. They were connected to equipment that might have been generators.

A few moments later, four of Captain Thiel's men brought out Ted Thornton and Pastor Schiebold. "Good morning," Bob said.

"Mmph," Thornton grunted, looking around.

"This is the day that the Lord has made," Schiebold said, smiling. "How are you, Bob? How's that cut?"

"Okay, I think," Bob said. "I cleaned it this morning. It stings, but it's not deep."

"Quiet," Captain Thiel said. "The prisoners may not speak to one another."

Pastor Schiebold raised his eyebrows and looked away. Bob turned around and went back to looking at his surroundings. It might be Iowa, but they'd been in the GMVs long enough yesterday that they could be three hundred miles in any direction from Mayfield.

A low rumble from behind caught his attention. Bob turned to see a helicopter coming in over their heads, apparently set to land at the field.

"Huh," Thornton said. "I thought black helicopters were an urban legend."

"I won't tell you again," Captain Thiel said. "Keep quiet unless spoken to. Now, move. This is our transport."

Working this case was going to be a slow, ugly job, Joe Unes decided. Dealing with religious nuts was difficult, and with that new strain of bird flu spreading to humans and the situation in the Middle East escalating fast, nutjobs were swarming out of the woodwork.

One group in Arkansas had announced that the Apocalypse was right around the corner and only the faithful who renounced all worldly possessions and met at the group's compound in the Ozarks (accommodations available for a modest fee) would be spared the Almighty's righteous judgment. Another group seemed to have cornered the market on generators and freeze-dried food left over from Y2K and COVID-19 and was offering it up for sale on eBay at exorbitant prices. All the proceeds went to further the Lord's work, of course, although the website was vague about exactly what that work was.

Gold for their leader, I bet, Unes thought.

Crazies, yes, but were they murderous crazies? Unes wasn't so sure. The Bureau had pulled out its own Y2K survivor, the Project Megiddo report, and it was the official starting point for this investigation. Someone in D.C. was convinced that the threat of a global war centered in the Middle East had pushed a fundamentalist group over the edge. The media, not surprisingly, was all on board with that narrative.

Shaking his head, Joe opened another folder and began reading the background report on the Liberty Bible Church just outside Saint Louis, which might have inspired Conrad Reston to kill himself and thirty-six others, including Unes' partner, Friday night at Grandy's. Sighing, he scanned the file, looking for any hint that these people might throw something more dangerous at their neighbors than gospel tracts.

At first, Gruner was nervous about touching anything in Stauffer's apartment. Fingerprints, forensic evidence, and all that. Bad enough Stauffer had been snatched, but somebody had to stay on the outside to keep track of what was really happening.

Gruner was sure the government was responsible. It was the Grandy's bombing. Maybe the FBI agent they drove home wanted them for questioning. But why? They told him everything they knew, which was nothing. They came to the fire from five miles away. Besides, Agent Unes seemed like a nice guy. No, that wasn't it.

Then it hit him: *It was the computer.* The computer was the key. *Stupid, stupid, stupid!* Gruner cursed himself for not taking a few extra minutes to hide his hack Friday night.

Of course, if the NSA had ID'd Stauffer's computer, almost nothing Gruner could have done would have prevented the them from knowing about it.

With a start, Gruner realized they probably had the apartment under surveillance right now. A cold sweat broke out on his forehead, and his stomach wrenched at the thought.

Easy, boy, Gruner thought, looking around. *No need for panic. You're just a concerned friend who stopped in as a favor to his office.*

Slowly, with a nonchalant air, he walked over to the kitchen sink that looked out onto the parking lot and the building across the way. Wait—was that someone looking back at him from the apartment directly across?

Gruner dropped to the floor—but he failed to gauge the distance from the kitchen counter. His forehead caught the edge on the way down. Hard.

"Ow! Man, for crying out…nuts!" Blood dripped from his forehead onto the dated green and gold linoleum. More forensic evidence to tie him to the scene of Stauffer's disappearance. He started to sweat harder. *Be cool! There was no crime, but—well, how will I explain to the—even if I wipe it all up, that stuff they spray that fluoresces under black light—*

Gruner sighed. This was stupid. He didn't have time to be stupid.

First things first. Find where Stauffer kept paper towels. Then call Norlock and Vijay.

He wasn't normally one to hold a grudge, but Sheriff Ted Thornton was going to make sure that somebody paid a hell of a price. He'd lost track of the number of civil rights violations he'd suffered in the last twenty-four hours. Ted knew a few defense attorneys who'd been thorns in his side over the years, and he'd see which of them was up for a run at the feds when this was over.

The presence of Pastor Schiebold kept a lid on his temper. Thornton wasn't proud of his hair trigger, and he knew full well the Bible commanded the faithful to turn the other cheek and forgive their enemies. It was one thing to hear it on Sunday morning, but *living it* when the government, whose laws he'd sworn to uphold, was trampling on those laws in the pursuit of he didn't even know what—it made it hard to think straight.

He'd been too angry to sleep much, and Thornton's mood always grew worse when he was tired. The rough copter ride kept him from drifting off, but Thornton knew he was only one or two smart remarks away from doing something he'd regret.

"You okay, Ted?" Pastor Schiebold asked, leaning toward him from the other side of the chopper to make himself heard above the rotor.

Thornton just nodded, not really in the mood for conversation. He looked at Bob Moore, who seemed lost in his thoughts. Probably thinking about his wife and son. Thornton scowled and his mood soured even further. It was bad enough that his wife and kids were waiting and worrying, but to see his friends, good men, dragged away from their families, too, was almost unbearable.

Somebody will answer for this.

The ride in the copter gave him time to think. With no windows and too much noise to talk, Thornton had nothing else to occupy his mind.

The whole sequence of events had to tie together. Someone sent the team. Who? They wanted Bob Moore. Why? Somehow Bob was connected to Ed Belcher. How?

First things first. These punks in black were pros. Special Forces, but on American soil? And with unconditional immunity? Could that be?

Okay, Thornton thought, start with that assumption: Somebody ordered an A-team into the middle of Iowa to grab Bob Moore. Two of Bob's friends interfered with the grab so the team took them, too. And now they were in a black helicopter going—where?

Wherever they were going, it must be designed to hold prisoners and equipped with a helipad. He frowned. Could be anywhere.

One thing was sure: Whoever did this had a lot of juice.

That just made Ted Thornton more determined. Someone would pay, he had no doubt about that. It would just take a little more work.

FIFTEEN

Not too bad a shape for seventy-three, he thought. Congressman Harold Benson liked to start each workday with a brisk mile walk. Twenty minutes, just enough to get the blood moving without making him sweat so hard that he needed another shower. Benson knew he ought to set aside more time and stretch the walk to two miles, but the extra twenty or twenty-five minutes ate into precious time.

Besides, with all the concrete barricades around government buildings lately, walking the last mile to the Hill was almost as fast as driving.

Even though he'd represented Iowa's Sixth Congressional District for thirty-three years, he still enjoyed getting to his office in the Capitol when the building was still nearly empty. It was a habit he learned early, rising with the chickens as a boy on the farm eighteen miles west of Mayfield.

The dark brown hair of his youth was pure white, but it was still as thick as it was the day he enlisted for the Marine Corps during the Vietnam War. His six-foot frame was still lean, and his sharply angled face still had the proud, weathered look of the farmers in his home state. Harold Benson looked more at home in overalls and a seed corn cap than in the suit he wore through the halls of power most of the year.

He reached the Capitol at the usual time, seven-thirty, and exchanged a friendly greeting with the security team. "Good morning, boys." At his age, nearly everyone qualified as a boy or girl.

"Morning, Congressman," the senior guard replied. "Shouldn't be out walking alone, not in times like this."

"If they want me, they know where to find me," Benson said, grinning.

He enjoyed this time of the day, early enough to catch up on the news, scan his correspondence, and lay out the game plan for his day without interruptions. Benson unlocked the outer door to his office, walked through the reception area and into his private office. He slipped out of his conservative, navy-blue suit coat, which he unceremoniously draped over the back of an office chair, and then he sat down to peruse the Washington dailies.

The domestic terror over the weekend would set the legislative agenda for the next couple of weeks. There would be demands for broader powers from Justice, Homeland Security, and the FBI, CIA, and NSA.

That would generate protests against the expansion of police powers. Nothing new there; that had been going on since the first Patriot Act. Benson mused that this might be the only issue that made allies out of the far right—limited government, strict constitutionalists—and the anarchists on the far left.

The opposition would demand an inquiry into the weekend's terror spree, allegedly to assign responsibility. Inside the Beltway, of course, everyone knew the real goal would be to hamstring President Bell's reelection campaign. He would agree, reluctantly, and then his staff would work like the devil behind the scenes to tilt the investigation in his favor.

Harold Benson was all in favor of national security. Through the years, he'd consistently pushed for more funding for America's fighting men and women as he gradually worked his way up to the chairmanship of the House Armed Services Committee. But he was not inclined to give the government more power to spy on Americans when it still hadn't sealed off the borders. Plug the holes in the boat, *then* bail.

As Benson finished scanning the world news in the *Washington Post*, the phone rang in the outer office. Seven forty-five was a little early for a call, but Benson decided to pick up instead of letting it go to voice mail.

"Hello," he said. "Congressman Benson."

"Oh, thank God I got right through," a woman said. "I was going to wait until eight—I mean nine, your time, but I just couldn't. This is Susie Thornton back in Mayfield."

It took Benson a second to shift mental gears. Susie—Ted Thornton's wife. Lovely lady, two fine children. "Yes, yes, Susie. It's good to hear you. How are you? It's awfully early in Iowa for a social call."

"Well, I'm not good, Congressman," Susie said, "But I hope you can help."

Benson frowned. "Sounds important. Anything I can do, young lady, you just name it."

"Thank you, Congressman."

"Please, it's Harold. Now how can I help?"

Susie proceeded to relate the affairs of the weekend in detail, beginning with the arrival of the men in black at Ted's office Friday night through the sight of her husband twitching helplessly on the floor. Her voice broke as she relived the moment. Congressman Benson retrieved an empty legal pad and a pen from a desk drawer and started taking notes.

"Now, Susie," he said, "Did you notice any patches or insignia on the clothing of these men?"

"No, not that I remember."

"Was anyone wearing a windbreaker with any lettering on it? FBI, or ATF, maybe?"

"No," she said. "Just black clothing with no identification. In fact, they never even told us who they were. When Ted told me about them, he said he thought they were Special Forces."

"Hmm," Benson said. "And these men wanted this Bob Moore for something?"

"Yes," Susie said, "But Ted thought that was all nonsense."

"I guess so, since he told this fella to run." Benson rubbed his chin with his free hand. "Well, Susie, I know a few people who can start the ball rolling. And there are one or two people I can get in touch with who might have a clue as to where they took your husband."

"Oh, thank you so much, Congressman. You don't know how much we appreciate this."

"It's Harold, please. And don't you worry, Susie, we'll get this straightened out," Benson said. "Give me your number so I can call you back later today. Meanwhile, you just keep Ted and his friends in your prayers."

"I will." Susie recited her telephone number. "Thank you again, Congress—I mean, Harold. Goodbye."

"Bye for now." Benson frowned again. *Pray for me, too, young lady,* he thought. *Special Forces on home soil? Good God. Somebody in our government just crossed the Rubicon.*

The concrete block building was identifiable as a church only by a plain white cross mounted on its roof. Liberty Bible Church sat on a lonely stretch of I-44's south outer road in far western Saint Louis County. The building itself was perpendicular to the outer road, a long, rectangular, beige structure with a simple peaked roof that, except for the cross, might have been an office or a small factory.

It was just after noon when Joe Unes pulled his burgundy Chevy Traverse into the lot. The pastor, one Edward L. Harper, waited for Joe at the front door.

Pastor Harper practically defined "average appearance," Unes thought: about five-eleven, maybe two hundred pounds, neatly combed short, light brown hair, wire framed glasses, fair complexion, and a rounded chin. Wearing dress pants and a short-sleeved white shirt with a conservative, striped tie, he looked more like a grade school principal than a man who'd inspire violence.

Harper's attitude when Joe called this morning had been hard to gauge. He was polite, even cordial, but Joe sensed a reluctance— or was it resentment?—to talk about his former church member, Conrad Reston.

"Good morning, pastor," Unes said, extending his hand.

"Good morning, Agent Unes," Harper said, gripping his hand firmly. "I trust you had no trouble finding us."

"No, not at all, thanks," Unes said. "GPS makes it easy these days."

"Are you all right?" Harper asked, frowning.

Unes touched the oversized bandage Cathy had forced him to wear on his cheek this morning. "Fine," he said. "Scraped it on the parking lot at the Grandy's bombing the other night. But my ears have mostly stopped ringing."

"Praise God for that, anyway. Won't you come in? We can talk in my office," Harper said, opening the door.

"Thank you, that will be fine."

The entrance was on the left side of the building as one looked at it from the front. The two men made an immediate left inside the door and walked down a hallway that took them into the sanctuary. The church was plain but neat. The pastor, or whoever made such decisions, clearly did not go for ostentatious displays.

The pews were basic varnished wood benches, and the floor was covered with a generic, blue level-loop carpet found in schools or offices all over Saint Louis. The walls were a flat off-white, and the only religious symbol in the entire church was a simple wooden cross on the front wall over the baptismal.

It was very different from the traditional formal decor of the parish Unes attended as a boy, St. Mark's, and the modern architecture of St. John's, the parish he and Cathy belonged to now. To Unes, a building didn't feel like a church unless it had stained glass.

Harper led him along the back of the sanctuary through a set of open doors into another hallway which, after another left turn, brought them to the pastor's office.

Harper offered Unes a seat in a straight-backed wooden chair set next to his desk. The room was small, no more than ten feet square, and the walls were lined with bookcases filled with an intimidating array of reading material. Unes looked closer and saw that most of the books were related to the Bible in some way—concordances, commentaries, encyclopedias, and lexicons. He hadn't realized that so much had been written about the words between the cover of the Bible.

Ed Harper smiled as he settled into the creaky office chair. "Eunice, eh? I had a grandmother named Eunice."

Unes nodded. "Same pronunciation but spelled different," he said. "U-n-e-s. It's Lebanese. Originally Y-o-u-n-e-s, but my grandfather shortened it."

"Lebanese? From Peoria?"

"That's right. How'd you guess that?"

"I have relatives in Peoria," Harper said. "There's a big Lebanese community there. We make it a point to stop at a little place downtown for gyros every time we visit." He pronounced it *GEE-rows*, with a hard "G."

"You even say it the right way," Unes noted with a smile. "Greeks never got it right. They stole the gyro from Lebanon, you know."

Harper laughed, obviously at ease. "So I hear, so I hear. Of course, they say the Lebanese stole ouzo and called it arak."

Now, it was Joe's turn to laugh. "My father would fight anyone who said so. He made his own. It would dissolve the paint off a car."

Harper settled back in his chair, smiling. "What can I do for you, Agent Unes?"

"Well," Unes began, "You're aware of the incident Friday night in Valley Park."

"Very much so," Harper said.

"When did you learn about the bombing?"

"We heard it on the radio Saturday morning."

"The radio?"

"Yes," Harper admitted. "My wife and I rarely watch television. Not much worth watching any more, except football. And I try not to spend too much time on the Internet. Too easy to get pulled into distractions."

"When did you learn of Mister Reston's involvement in the bombing?"

"Some time on Saturday. I think that afternoon. A news report said that Brother Reston was responsible. And then he didn't come to church yesterday morning, of course. As far as I know, Agent Unes, no one in our congregation had heard from him since last week. I presume the FBI isn't mistaken—I mean, the body is Brother Reston's?"

"No mistake," Unes said. "Did you have any hint that Reston was depressed or under some kind of stress?"

"No, sir," Harper said. "To tell you the truth, Brother Reston was not very regular in his attendance."

"Really?" Unes asked. "So, he wasn't a regular member of your congregation?"

Pursing his lips, Harper said, "Well, I'd say when he came to church, he came here. We would like to have seen more of him."

"What kind of a man was he?"

"Well, who can truly know the heart except the Lord?" Pastor Harper replied. "He was friendly enough. He professed a faith in the Lord Jesus Christ. Conservative in his politics, but that's probably true of most of us here. But I have to tell you honestly, I don't think I ever got past his defenses, if you know what I mean."

Unes nodded and made a note in the small pad he used for interviews. "Did he show an interest in the end times? Apocalyptic prophecy, that sort of thing?"

A small smile crossed Harper's face. "We all have an interest in the future, don't we?"

"I suppose so," Unes said, "But what was Mister Reston's level of interest?"

"Well, now, he was at a couple of our prophecy workshops and our Revelation conference," the pastor said. "But so were most members of our congregation, and many folks from other churches. End-times seminars are very popular. Biggest crowds we draw here, actually."

"You hold conferences on the book of Revelations?"

"Revelation, singular," Harper corrected. "The Revelation of John—or more accurately, the Revelation of Jesus Christ as told by Saint John. It's 'revelation' as in 'unveiling.' But it wasn't just about the last book of the Bible. There are many other prophecies about the second coming of Jesus. Daniel, Ezekiel, Isaiah, Jeremiah, Amos, Zephaniah, Peter, Paul, and even Jesus—all of them had something to say about it."

"I guess it's a hot topic right now," Unes said. "A lot of books about the Rapture are top sellers at Amazon."

"It's an important topic, Agent Unes. Too important to get your theology from fiction."

"Do you recru—I mean, evangelize at these conferences?"

Harper raised an eyebrow. "We give an invitation for those who want to accept Jesus as Lord and Savior to come forward, yes. We do that every Sunday and Wednesday, too."

"Mm," Unes said. "How many are in your congregation?"

"About seventy-five families and a handful of singles. About two hundred people altogether."

"Not a big church."

"No, not by some standards," Harper said. "But the Lord provides, and we have been blessed."

"So," Unes said, looking at the books around the walls, "Do you preach on the Apocalypse often?"

"As often as the Holy Spirit leads," Harper said. "The Apocalypse—*apokalypsis* is the Greek word for 'unveiling,' and the Latin is *revelatio* as in 'revelation'—well, it's all about the return of our Lord to the Earth. That's a pretty big deal to a Christian, don't you think? Jesus commanded us to watch and be ready. I want my congregation to be prepared. I'd love for the whole world to be prepared—but that won't happen, of course."

"Why not?"

"There are those with ears who will not listen, those with eyes who will not see. We're in the days of the great falling away. The Greek word is *apostasia*, apostasy. We try to reach as many as we can. The harvest is plenty, but the workers are few."

"How do you reach out to the world, Reverend, to spread your message, I mean?"

"Just pastor, please," Harper corrected, "And it's not *my* message. It's the message Jesus preached two thousand years ago. 'I am the way, the truth, and the life, and no man cometh unto the Father but by Me.'"

"Not very politically correct."

Harper chuckled. "No, I guess not. But Jesus told the Apostles, 'If the world hate you, ye know that it hated me before it hated you. If ye were of the world, the world would love his own: but because ye are not of the world, but I have chosen you out of the world, therefore the world hateth you.' In plain English, if you follow Jesus, you lose a lot of friends. But to answer your question, we try to talk about Jesus with everyone we meet. Our church has a bus ministry that gives free rides to our services for folks who can't get here on their own. We spend a lot of our church budget on missionaries overseas. And we have a website. I podcast my sermons. One of the young fellas takes care of that techie stuff."

"I see," Unes answered. He clicked his pen closed and looked up from the notebook. "Rev—Pastor Harper, when do you think the Second Coming will be?"

Shrugging, Harper said, "I have no idea."

"You don't?" Unes was a bit surprised. With as much literature as he saw in this room, Unes assumed Harper would at least have an opinion.

"Oh, make no mistake, we are in the end times," the preacher said. "But the exact day and hour? Jesus said even He didn't know. 'But of that day and that hour knoweth no man, no, not the angels which are in heaven, neither the Son, but the Father.' In fact, some of His last words on this Earth, just before He was taken up into heaven, were very clear on this point: 'It is not for you to know the times or the seasons, which the Father hath put in his own power.' Acts, chapter one. No, Agent Unes, anyone who says he's figured out the precise date is probably selling something."

Unes tapped the barrel of his pen against the note pad. These weren't quite the answers he'd expected. "So, what are your plans to get ready for the Second Coming?"

Smiling again, Ed Harper leaned forward, his eyes filled with honest concern. "I should ask you that question."

Cindy Moore drummed her fingers on the kitchen table in frustration. Susie Thornton's line had been busy since Eric told her about the missing computer. Cindy hoped the busy signal meant she'd reached Congressman Benson.

She decided to give Susie a few minutes before trying again, shooing Eric upstairs to get dressed while she took a quick shower. The warm water helped to relax muscles aching from a night of tossing and turning. It helped, too, knowing that *something* was finally happening, even if events were still out of her control.

Maybe that was the message God had in all of this: *Trust, and lean on Me.* There wasn't much else to do.

She dressed quickly, throwing on a sweatshirt and jeans, although she took the time to dry and style her hair as usual. It was a routine and sticking to routine brought some comfort. Cindy realized that her ten-year-old son was looking to her for cues on how to react. If she fell apart, he would assume that things were really bad. They were bad enough without frightening Eric even more.

Thirty minutes later, Cindy emerged from the bedroom just as Eric came out of his. She smiled inside. There was no way on Earth that just getting dressed and making a bed required thirty minutes, but Cindy wasn't going to complain. If the process required a twenty-minute break for reading his latest science fiction novel from the library, so what? That Eric actually made his bed every morning was a victory in itself.

As she entered the kitchen, she noted that it was nearly seven-thirty. Eight-thirty out east. She decided to try the Thorntons again, and this time it rang through.

Susie answered on the second ring. "Hello?"

"Hi, Susie, it's Cindy."

"Cindy, hi. You'll never believe it. I got through to Congressman Benson already."

"Wow," Cindy said. "That was quick."

"I know. I guess he likes to get to the office early. Anyway, he said he would definitely help us. He's going to call some people at the Defense and Justice Departments to get some answers."

"Praise God!" Cindy felt a load lifted from her shoulders. No, Bob wasn't on his way home, but they had an ally looking for him now. "Susie, I need your advice."

"Sure," Susie said. "How can I help?"

"Well," Cindy said, "We discovered this morning that our computer is missing."

"That's strange," Susie said. "Is anything else in the house missing?"

"No. Just the computer."

"How weird!"

"I know. But that's not the only weird part." Cindy took a deep breath before continuing. "Eric tells me that he received a very strange email Friday. Something about being one of *the chosen*, and the time being *now*, or coming soon, or something. And it was signed, 'God'."

"God?"

"I know it sounds crazy, and it's probably just spam. Eric thought it was a joke one of the kids at school was playing, so he forwarded the note to three boys in his class to see if he could figure out which one sent it."

"Oh," Susie said. "Cindy, I don't see what a spam email has to do with—."

"One of the boys Eric sent it to was Mike Belcher."

There was a long pause on the other end of the line. Finally, Susie said, "Oh my gosh. Cindy—quick!—who were the other two?"

JoAnne Fisher's phone rang eight times. Susie Thornton waited, counting the rings, her stomach tightening with each electronic chirp.

At the ninth ring, Susie started to pull the phone away from her ear. Just before her thumb touched the "off" button, she heard a frantic voice.

Susie lifted the phone back to her ear. "Hello? JoAnne?" In the background, she heard the crash of breaking glass. There was shouting and the sounds of a struggle.

"Hello? JoAnne? This is Susie Thornton. Is everything all right?"

Another crash. "Jason—I…Jason, stop! Drop it! No! No! Ja—"

Silence. She immediately hit the speed dial for the police line at the county building. Ann Jurasik picked up.

"Sheriff's office, Chief Deputy Jurasik."

"Ann? Susie Thornton."

"Susie! How is Ted? We're just sick. Is there any—"

Susie cut her off. "Ann, there's no time. Get somebody over to the Fishers' house. 114 South Second in Mayfield. Something's going on. Something bad."

"What?"

"Just go. Please! Hurry!" Susie hung up. She'd found the Fisher listing in the Mayfield Elementary School student phone directory. She quickly flipped pages until she found the listing for John Allen, the third boy who was sent the email by Eric Moore.

The Allens didn't answer. *This is not good*, she thought, jamming her phone into her purse.

Unnerved, Susie quickly checked her children's rooms. Steve and Jenny were still asleep, exhausted from the long night. She went back to the kitchen and scribbled a note on a yellow sticky note and left it on the handle of the fridge, the one place the kids wouldn't miss it. Then she grabbed a coat and ran to her car, praying she wouldn't find the Allens the way her husband found the Belchers Friday night.

A muted ring announced a call on the private line in Green's office. This particular line bypassed the normal connections that routed miles of fiber-optic cable into the heart of Raven Rock Mountain. Its only connection inside the mountain ended at a black telephone, hidden inside the upper left-hand drawer of Green's mahogany desk.

"Green."

"Why, Mister Green. It's your old friend, Ryder. Are you ready to begin the games?"

Green shut his eyes, imagining the face on the other end of the call. What would it be this time? "We begin tomorrow," he replied. "There aren't enough prisoners in the camps yet to make large-scale inoculations practical."

"Yes. Well, let's hope you haven't overreached. You are an ambitious little devil."

"Your experiment in New Mexico didn't go as you'd hoped."

"Now, now, let's not be petty." Ryder's voice was smooth as silk. "Mistakes were made, lessons were learned. But that operation was carried out with the advice and consent of the council. Not to put too fine a point on it, but the key word there is *consent*."

Green gritted his teeth and said nothing.

"Keep us informed," Ryder continued. "We are a team, after all. Aren't we?"

"Of course." Green replaced the phone in the drawer and retrieved his cigarette case. *A team. For now. By the end of the week, the world will change forever.*

SIXTEEN

The camp was somehow just what Bob Moore expected. The helicopter had put down at an airfield that seemed to be used mostly by smaller jets, the kind favored by business executives. Most of the aircraft bore military insignia, but the planes were parked too far away to make them out clearly.

Bob, Pastor Schiebold, and Sheriff Thornton followed their captors into a waiting truck painted in a green camouflage pattern, where they were herded into the covered cargo area in the back. After a short ride on uncomfortable benches, they were dropped off at a long, low cinder-block building and escorted inside to a detention area. The room was windowless, about fifteen feet on a side, with benches bolted to the floor along opposite walls.

After half an hour, a soldier unlocked and opened the door. He was shorter than Bob by a couple of inches, but powerfully built and sporting a close-cropped goatee. He introduced himself as Lieutenant Harris. The lieutenant and two others in military gear escorted the three men outside, through two gates in a double row of ten-foot-high chain-link fence topped with razor wire, and into a barracks-like building nearby.

"This will be your home for a while, gentlemen," Harris said. "Cooperate with us, and we'll do what we can to make you as comfortable as possible."

"How about telling us why we're here?" Ted Thornton said.

"Sir, I don't have that information," Lieutenant Harris replied. "My orders are to see to your needs and make sure you don't go anywhere."

"We have a right to know why we're here," Thornton said, his jaw set. He'd been in a bad mood all morning.

"Sir, I just don't have that information."

"Ted," Pastor Schiebold said, "He's just doing his job."

"Right," Thornton said. "Like the guards at Auschwitz."

Harris stiffened. "Showers and toilet are at the end of the building. You're welcome to go outside any time you like except after lights out. Meals will be brought to you at eight, noon, and five. If you have questions, address them to one of the guards, and he will contact a superior officer." With that, the lieutenant and his men left Bob, Pastor Schiebold, and Ted Thornton alone in the barracks.

"This stinks," Thornton said.

"You know it," a voice said from somewhere along the row of bunk beds, near the end of the building with the showers.

The three men looked at one another, and then a young man stepped into the center aisle between the rows of beds.

Their new companion was short with dark hair combed straight and black plastic-frame glasses that Bob thought had gone out of style in the late sixties. Maybe they'd come back in while he wasn't paying attention—but then, style was always about five years late getting to Mayfield, Iowa. "My name's Scott. Scott Stauffer. They dragged me here yesterday. They still haven't told me why."

Schiebold was the first to introduce himself. "Hi, I'm Dave Schiebold. This here's Ted Thornton, and that's Bob Moore." He shook the young man's hand. Bob followed, as did Ted, who only grunted a greeting.

"So, what're you in for?" the young man said with a chuckle. "I've always wanted to say that."

"We're not sure," Bob said, and then he corrected himself. "Well, that's not entirely true. I'm not sure why *I'm* here. Ted and Pastor Schiebold are only here because they tried to hide me and my family."

"Whoa, daddy," Scott said. "They went after you and caught you, but they pulled you guys in anyway?"

"Yeah," Thornton said.

"Bob here saw them arresting us, and he gave himself up," Schiebold added.

"Like they'd trade us for him," Thornton said. "Bob, you should have stayed put."

"I couldn't," Bob said. "It wouldn't have been right."

"We knew what we were doing."

"Sorry, Ted. I just couldn't have looked at myself in the mirror."

"And you guys have no idea why?" Scott asked again.

"No, but I'll tell you what," Thornton said. "We'd better hear some charges soon. Somebody's got a reckoning coming."

"Now, remember, Ted," Pastor Schiebold said, "Getting even is the Lord's prerogative. 'Vengeance is mine; I will repay, saith the Lord. Therefore if thine enemy hunger, feed him; if he thirst, give him drink: for in so doing thou shalt heap coals of fire on his head. Be not overcome of evil, but overcome evil with good.'"

"Wait—you're a preacher?" Stauffer said, pushing his glasses up onto his nose nervously. "They arrested a *preacher?*"

Schiebold nodded and Thornton shook his head. "And I'm an officer of the law. It's *Sheriff* Thornton. He took a deep breath and gestured toward Schiebold. "And the good pastor here better keep reminding me about the Word of God so I don't do something stupid."

Midday Monday, and so far there were only four men in the barracks. As near as Tony Harris could figure, the camp was designed to hold about two thousand. Did the government really expect to arrest that many? Were there that many terrorists walking the streets of America?

Colonel Hostler had said there were a couple dozen of these camps. Was this one for the entire Midwest? Harris shuddered.

The four they had seemed cooperative enough, but the big county sheriff, Thornton, might be trouble. He was angry. They'd have to watch him.

This was some kind of business, when pastors and policemen were plotting against the government.

Eric had finished his breakfast and Cindy was tidying up, getting ready to open the store. She hoped for a light day, even though they needed the business. Reliving the weekend with every customer wasn't worth the sales. And she wanted to talk to Susie Thornton as soon as there was news, which would be harder to do with curious ears listening in. Living in a rural community was a two-edged sword—pretty much everybody had your back, but they all knew your business, too.

Other thoughts ran through her mind, things to attend to as soon as the day's business commenced. They needed an attorney, for sure. She'd have to call Mayfield State Bank and tell them about the missing computer. All of the data for their home and business accounts were on that hard drive. Cindy didn't like it one bit that all their personal, private information was in the hands of someone she didn't know, password protected or not.

She hoped Bob had remembered to back up the store's information. She checked under the desk where Bob kept the external hard drive.

No luck. It was gone, too.

An unusual noise from outside caught her attention. A sharp crack, like a whip. Or a rifle?

Two more followed in quick succession. "E.J.! Come in here, now!"

Eric dashed in from the kitchen. "What, Mom?" he huffed, catching his breath.

"Come here! Quick now!" Cindy grabbed his shoulders and pulled him under the desk with her. "Somebody is shooting outside!" Two more shots echoed through the neighborhood.

Behind his glasses, Eric's eyes widened with fear. Cindy's heart went out to her son. Could this really be happening? Bob gone, taken at gunpoint, and now they were hiding in their own home from *gunfire?* It felt like the whole world had spun off its axis.

As she huddled under the desk with her son, Cindy closed her eyes and prayed, *Lord, please keep us safe so we can welcome Bob back home.*

"Hello, Eloise. Would you please put me through to Sam Wilmer?" Congressman Harold Benson sat at his desk with a list of names arrayed on a yellow legal pad in front of him. He planned to talk with every one of them before the end of the day. Wilmer's name was at the top.

"Sam Wilmer speaking." The voice was a relaxed Texan drawl, an accent that belied a sharp, educated mind and keen memory. Many had underestimated Sam Wilmer to their regret.

"Sam. Harold Benson."

"Harold," Wilmer said, his deep voice full of warmth. "How's my favorite Hawkeye?"

"Just fine, you old cowboy," Benson said. "Sam, I need a favor."

"Gee, I don't know, Congressman," Wilmer said, laughing. "You gave us a pretty rough time at your committee's hearing last week."

"Just business, Sam, you know that. You tell your boss to come better prepared for those hearings, and he won't take such a drumming. Just because the president is from my party doesn't mean his cabinet members can skate through without explaining what they're doing when they want to reorganize the whole darn military. What is all this about expanding the domestic intelligence gathering powers of NORTHCOM? With drones?"

Benson heard a sigh. "I tried to warn him, Harold, I truly did, but he wouldn't listen. You know, you're not exactly on the administration's list of most favored congressmen right now."

"Don't care. The president doesn't vote in my district."

Wilmer laughed. "Okay, okay. We'll chew on that another day. What can I do for you, Harold?"

"Sam, I got a very disturbing phone call from a woman back home this morning," Benson said. "The wife of the sheriff in Kiowa County, next county over from mine. She tells me three men—her husband, a friend of the family, and their pastor—were hauled out of church yesterday morning at gunpoint by a team of military men dressed in black."

"What? Ah, it's too early for pranks, Hal. Pull the other one."

"I've never been more serious, Sam. This is on the level. It sounded like an FBI hostage rescue team, except the men never identified themselves, and they wore no insignia. Think you can find out what's going on?"

"Why don't you ask Justice?"

"Oh, I plan to cover all bases," Benson said. "Quietly, of course. You just happen to have the honor of being first on my list."

"Am I now? Well, Hal, I am humbled, sir."

"That'll be the day!"

Wilmer laughed again. "What are you trying to find, Congressman?"

"The FBI's Hostage Rescue Teams share training and weapons with Special Forces, do they not?"

"I reckon they do. Sometimes. Are you implying that Special Forces arrested those men?"

"I don't know. Maybe. That's what I'd like you to find out," Benson said.

"Hmm. Gimme a few hours on that," Wilmer said. "I'll kick a few stones and see what kind of snakes slide out."

"Thanks, Sam," Benson said. "I owe you one."

"That you do, Congressman, that you do."

The Thorntons lived about five minutes from the Allens if one obeyed posted speed limits. Susie Thornton made it in three.

She pulled to a stop in front of the house, a small, two-bedroom cottage on a street that ran alongside a cornfield on the edge of Mayfield. As she opened the door, she heard a gunshot not far away. Susie knew enough about guns to recognize the sound of a hunting rifle.

She hesitated. She couldn't tell where the shot came from, and she certainly didn't want to step into somebody's field of fire.

Crack! Crack!

From the sound, the shooter was at least two or three blocks away, she judged. Susie got out of the car and ran to the Allens' front door, hoping she was right.

There was no answer to the doorbell. Susie rang again and leaned against the wobbly metal porch railing as far as she dared, trying to see through the picture window into the Allens' front room. The television was on, but she didn't see any movement.

She quickly glanced at the rows of nearly identical homes lining the street. No neighbors in sight. Susie hoped at least one of them was busy calling in the gunshots. She turned the knob on the front door, at the same time trying to come up with a quick and believable excuse for breaking in—just in case she found somebody in the shower or otherwise unable to answer a doorbell.

Locked.

She jumped down two steps to the front walk and cut around the left side of the house. The side door off the driveway was partly open. Susie hesitated only a moment before going in.

It was one step up into the kitchen. The television in the front room was tuned to one of the morning news shows, and the volume was turned up loud.

"Hello?" Susie called. "Is anyone home?" She waited a few seconds for an answer. None came. She moved slowly through the kitchen, and she was nearly into the dining room when she heard running water—running water and a soft splashing noise. *Not from a sink*, Cindy thought. It was a lot of water.

The bathtub.

"Hello? Mrs. Allen? It's Susie Thornton. No one answered the doorbell." *As if that's an excuse to walk into your house uninvited.*

She stepped from the kitchen's black and white checkered linoleum onto the blue pile carpeting of the dining room. Her shoe squished. Susie looked down and saw that a quarter of the dining room carpet was soaked in an arc radiating out from a doorway on her left, the entrance to the bathroom and the two bedrooms.

Foregoing all pretense of an excuse, Susie rushed to the bathroom and shoved the door open. The floor ran with water that surged from an old clawfoot tub against the far wall. Her eyes went instantly to the tub, and her hands flew to her mouth to contain a scream.

Verna Allen, Johnny's mother, lay fully dressed and with open, unseeing eyes beneath the water.

"What do you see, little lady?" asked a man's voice, eerily calm, right behind her.

Susie whirled, swallowing a scream as her feet slipped on the slick, ceramic tile. She fell sideways, hitting the tile with a splash. The cold water soaked through her clothes, but she barely noticed. She rolled to her side and looked up into the eyes of Verna's husband, Frank. The sleeves of the big man's plaid flannel shirt were rolled up—wet at the ends, and water dripped from his powerful fingers.

"Ain't you the sheriff's wife?" he asked calmly.

"Y-yes," Susie said, scuttling away from him across the cold bathroom floor, trying to find enough room to stand up out of his reach.

"Good." He took a step forward, grabbed Susie's jacket with his right hand and yanked her to her feet. With a face so serene that he seemed filled with an unearthly glow, Allen held her fast and said simply, "It's time to be baptized."

SEVENTEEN

"Mom, shouldn't we call the police?"

Huddled under the desk with Eric, Cindy had completely forgotten the phone in her hand. "Yes, yes. Good idea."

She hit the speed dial number in her contacts list for the sheriff's department. A woman answered on the second ring.

"Sheriff's department, Chief Deputy Jurasik speaking."

"Yes, this is Cindy Moore calling. I hear gunshots outside."

"Where are you, ma'am?"

"In Mayfield," Cindy said. "One-twelve Main Street. The Mayfield Family Market."

"Oh, right. Mrs. Moore," Deputy Jurasik said. "Your husband was arrested with Sheriff Thornton."

"Yes, that's right."

"I'm sorry—it's been a circus here," Jurasik said. "Can you tell what kind of shots they were? Handgun? Shotgun?"

"I—I don't know. A rifle maybe. I'm not much on guns," Cindy said.

"Were they close to the house?"

"No, I don't think so. They sounded a little ways away." She hesitated a moment, and then added, "But I think I know where they are."

"Where?"

"Either the—Eric, what were your friends' names again?"

"John Allen and Jason Fisher," the boy said tightly.

"The last names would be Allen and Fisher."

There was a moment's pause. "Susie Thornton just called and asked me to send a car to the Fisher place. It should be there by now."

Cindy felt a chill run the length of her neck. "Deputy, I have a strong feeling that you should send another car to the Allens' home right away."

"Can you tell me why?"

"Not exactly, but I think it has to do with our computer. It's missing, and we think those men in black took it."

"Your computer?"

"Yes. My son forwarded a strange email he got to friends at the Allens and Fishers."

"And Mike Belcher, Mom," Eric added.

"And the Belchers," Cindy repeated.

"I—I don't understand how…"

"Neither do I, but please—it might be nothing, but please send someone to the Allens."

"Okay, Mrs. Moore," the deputy said. "I'm on it."

Sipping a Styrofoam cup of bad coffee, Ann Jurasik tried to make sense of what was going on. With Sheriff Thornton gone, she was in charge. This was not the way she wanted to inherit the sheriff's office.

Jurasik set down the phone, and then changed her mind and picked it back up again. She dialed the Thorntons. She couldn't call the sheriff, but maybe he told Susie something about the computer connection.

After nine rings, a sleepy voice answered, "Hello?"

"Hello," Jurasik said. "Is this Jennifer?"

"Yes."

"Jen, this is Deputy Jurasik. Is your mom there?"

"Just a minute." Jurasik heard the sound of feet padding on the floor, silence, and then Jennifer lifted the phone to her ear again. "No, she's not. She left a note."

"What does it say, Jen?"

"Um, 'Going to the Allens, Two twenty-three South Third. Back soon. Love, Mom.'"

Jurasik started. "What was that address?"

"Two twenty-three South Third in Mayfield."

"Thanks, hon. Gotta go." Jurasik burst from Thornton's office, looking for someone to take over the phones. There was no one. Jurasik quickly doubled back, set the sheriff's phone to ring through to the front desk in the county office building. Then she bolted out of the building and ran for her prowler.

It had already been a long morning for Congressman Harold Benson and it was only ten o'clock.

The day began on a strange note with the call from Susie Thornton back in Iowa. As soon as he'd been able, he contacted people who could help, men and women he'd grown to trust in his years on the Hill. None of them had quick answers, of course—no one in Washington ever had quick answers—so he was forced to set the problem aside. He'd get back to it after lunch.

For now, Benson faced another grueling session of the Armed Services Committee and its ongoing discussion of the changes proposed by the Secretaries of Defense and Homeland Security.

Then there was the ugly situation in the Middle East. Because the earthquake that devastated Damascus earlier in the year had been centered on the fault line that ran through the Bekaa Valley, the Israelis had met little organized resistance in Syria and Lebanon. When they did, though, some of the weapons hitting their tanks shouldn't have been in the arsenal of any terror group in the world. A state-level entity, maybe the Turks, were supplying the forces encountered by the IDF. The Israelis might be angry enough about their losses to consider small tactical nukes. Benson shuddered at the thought. A nuclear exchange would almost surely draw the rest of the Muslim world into the fight.

Against that backdrop, the committee session seemed unimportant. Maybe that was what the administration hoped; Benson was under a lot of pressure from the White House to push through a package of broad domestic surveillance powers for NORTHCOM, the U.S. Northern Command.

Benson was not inclined to push or be pushed. NORTHCOM already had access to the FBI database called eGuardian, which had replaced the old TALON system in 2007. Threat And Local Observation Notices that had been cataloged by the defunct Counterintelligence Field Activities office in Washington. TALON itself had been folded into a new office called DCHC, the Defense Counterintelligence and Human Intelligence Center. It was supposed to be a clearinghouse of intel on domestic threats to DoD and key infrastructure sites.

But like too many government programs, it had turned into one more trough where corporate hogs fed at taxpayers' expense. Obviously, that hadn't solved the problem, which was the need for *useful* data to prevent terror attacks. Four thousand dead made that point painfully clear. A culture of corruption, regardless of which party held the White House, was inevitable when up to seventy percent of the country's intelligence budget went to private contractors. They were often more worried about shareholder value than national security.

Now, with the weekend terror attacks and the new Middle East war as cover, the White House wanted NORTHCOM to go data mining, sifting through virtual mountains of intercepted communications, credit card records, and social media posts for actionable intelligence against possible domestic terror groups. To Benson, this sounded like the Information Awareness Office that the House shot down in 2003.

IAO had been closed, but development of the Total Information Awareness technology continued. Funding was shifted to classified sections of the annual defense and intelligence appropriations bills, although it was supposed to only be used against foreigners. Edward Snowden blew the lid off that ruse in 2013. The National Security Agency's PRISM program essentially tapped the Internet. Although the NSA wasn't supposed to spy on Americans, well, there were ways to stay within the letter of the law while ignoring its intent.

Even though the surveillance tools exposed by Snowden had been unpopular with lawmakers, Ten-Thirteen threatened to bring them back in a big way. Even though the government's spying on Americans hadn't made the country much safer after 9/11, politicians would always do something, even something stupid, after a major event, just so they could tell the voters back home why they deserved another term in office.

And there was never a shortage of lobbyists and political action committees with bills already written, just waiting for opportunities like this. It's how two-thousand-page emergency spending bills seemed to magically appear just days after a crisis.

At long last, after the members of his committee wasted most of the morning pontificating for the record, Benson adjourned it for the day. Not much accomplished except the onset of a headache. He was caught in a political vise between the opposition party and the White House. He'd served thirty-three years in office, earning the clout that came with knowing how and where to make good, trustworthy friends that allowed him to stand his ground.

Benson returned to his office a little after eleven-thirty to find several messages waiting for him. Ellen DiStefano at Justice; Mark Andourian, a reporter with the *Washington Times*; and Sam Wilmer, God love him.

There was also a pink slip with no name on it. His receptionist said a man had called and asked for the congressman. When he'd been told that Benson was out, the man instructed her to leave the word *Mayfield* as his message. There was no callback number.

"He said he'd contact you," his receptionist said.

Benson frowned. "Thank you, Cheryl."

The congressman closed the door to his private office and settled into the creaky chair behind his desk. Knowing that Sam Wilmer always took a late lunch, he dialed Ellen DiStefano first.

"Hello?" The attorney at the Justice Department was a good thirty-five years his junior, but she impressed Benson with an analytical mind and the ability to get things done. He'd have been proud to have her for a daughter.

"Hello, young lady. It's Harold Benson."

"Oh, hello, Congressman. Can you give me a second?"

"You bet." He heard a *bump* as Ellen put the handset down on her desk, and a few seconds later he heard a door close.

"I'm back," she said. "I wanted a little privacy."

"I understand. Were you able to learn anything?"

"Congressman, what are you trying to do?"

"Do? Why, I'm investigating what seems to be a violation of the civil rights of several fine, upstanding men in my home district."

A pause. "Is that all?"

"Isn't that enough?"

Another pause. "Ordinarily, yes. Let's just say my sources were unusually reluctant to talk this morning," Ellen said.

"Reluctant," Benson said warily. "As in they didn't know, or were afraid to say?"

"I honestly don't know," Ellen replied, her voice a soft whisper. "Everyone is on edge after this weekend. Some of the higher-ups want to know why we didn't see this coming. Heads may roll at the FBI. Again."

"That's the American way. Somebody attacks us, it's our fault. Just like the ancient Hebrews—pick a scapegoat and kick it out into the desert. So, did you get anything at all?"

"According to what little I heard—and that is very little, I assure you—we are not aware of any FBI operation in progress that would require the use of a Hostage Rescue Team—assuming what you've described to me really *is* an HRT."

"None at all?"

"Not one," Ellen said, "But I have to advise you that there may be operations that I haven't heard about. I don't know everything."

"You get close enough for me," Benson said. "Tell me this, Ellen: What are the odds a twelve-man HRT would drop down in the middle of Iowa without your knowing about it?"

"Pretty slim."

"As I suspected. Thank you for your help, young lady."

"Anytime, you sweet talker."

The three-minute trip from one side of Mayfield to the other seemed to take forever. Deputy Jurasik realized that sometimes not knowing what waited at the scene was worse than knowing you'd find a worst-case scenario. At least then you had time to prepare yourself.

She squealed the wheels of the prowler as she turned off Main Street onto South Third. The big Ford SUV covered the last two blocks to the Allen home in about ten seconds. Jurasik brought the car to a stop behind Susie Thornton's Bronco.

No sign of movement inside or out. Jurasik climbed out of the car and sprinted to the front door, drawing her gun as she ran. Ignoring the bell, she pounded on the wooden front door with the side of her fist.

"Open up! Police!" She stood to one side, not wanting to present an easy target if the first thing through the door was a shotgun.

She waited five seconds and pounded again. Another five seconds crawled by, and just as Deputy Jurasik prepared to kick in the door, it opened.

It was Susie Thornton. She looked dazed and mussed, but unhurt.

"Susie! Are you all right?"

A shadow passed across Susie Thornton's face. She nodded. "I'm okay," she said. "But I'm really glad you're here." Her words were slow, dreamy. *Shock,* Jurasik thought.

Susie stepped out of the doorway to allow Jurasik room to enter. "He's in here," Thornton said, leading the way through the living room.

"Who's here?"

"Frank Allen. He tried to—he wanted to drown me."

"What? Here, stay back. Let me go in." Jurasik moved toward the doorway off the dining room. The water-soaked carpeting squished beneath her boots.

"It's safe," Susie explained, following the deputy. "He's unconscious."

Jurasik peered through the doorway, directly into the bathroom. Frank Allen lay face down on the floor, head toward the bathtub. The deputy quickly checked his carotid for a pulse—weak, but there. "He's alive," she said, mostly to herself. Frank Allen's nose and mouth were just out of the water that dripped from the edge of the tub onto the white tile floor of the bathroom. A thin stream of blood from Frank's nose mixed with the water on the floor. In the tub—

"Susie? Is someone in the bathtub?"

Deputy Jurasik turned to see Susie Thornton, hands pressed together in front of her mouth as she fought to hold back tears.

Susie nodded, her eyes round, a little glassy.

Jurasik slowly stepped forward, keeping one eye on Frank Allen. Verna Allen lay motionless beneath the water—eyes wide open—her face pale, mouth slack.

"Dear God!" Jurasik whispered tightly. The deputy took a deep breath to recover her composure. "Sue, what happened?"

Thornton wiped a tear from her cheek. "I got no answer when I called over here. I don't know why I came over instead of calling you back, but it was the only thing I could think of. The front door was locked, but the side door was open. I came in. The water was running. It was all over the floor out here. I opened the bathroom door to look, and—and there she was." Her voice trailed off as a sob caught in her throat. Jurasik lowered her weapon and put a free hand on Thornton's shoulder. Susie shuddered and tried to force a smile.

"And Frank?" Jurasik prompted.

"He came from nowhere," the stunned woman continued. "He looked crazy, talked crazy. Said it was time to be *baptized*, and then he grabbed me and wouldn't let go! He pushed me toward the tub, so I hit him in the nose—with my palm, I think. Ted taught me that. His head jerked back, and he let go. Then I kicked him in the—the crotch, and when he bent over his head hit the sink."

Jurasik holstered the weapon and retrieved the radio handset velcroed to her left shoulder. "Dispatch, we need an ambulance and backup at the Allen place. One dead. One injured. It looks like a homicide. Better notify the coroner."

Thornton felt sick. "Poor Verna."

Jurasik shook her head, forcing herself to remain detached. "You're lucky, Susie."

Thornton shut her eyes and turned back into the hallway. She wanted to vomit but couldn't bear the thought of doing so with Verna's corpse watching from the trickling water. *Frank. He said he wanted to baptize me. What in God's name is going on? Lucky? Me? No, God spared me—but not Verna. Why, Lord, why?*

The call with the *Times* reporter had been fruitless, but at least now a reporter who'd shown some initiative in the past had a story that might get some attention. Harold Benson picked up the phone again and dialed Sam Wilmer's office.

Two rings in, a voice answered. "Sam Wilmer."

"Sam? Harold Benson. Tell me what you've got."

"Whoa, there, Congressman! You sound as rushed as our New York friends."

"Sorry, Sam," Benson said. "Busy day today. The White House is all over me about the domestic intelligence bill."

"Everybody's in high gear in this town," Wilmer said. "We got our hands full, too, trying to make folks in the Middle East see reason. But they're just hell-bent on killing each other, so what are you going to do?"

"Is the President going to intervene?"

"Don't know. I'm too far down the food chain to hear that kind of talk. Somebody better do something, though, before somebody launches a nuke. That happens and only God knows what'll follow."

"Well, you got that part right, young man," Benson agreed. "Let me start again. Do you have anything for me?"

Wilmer, who was fifty-three, laughed. "Young man," he said. "Don't I wish I was young again. I feel like Methuselah himself today. Yeah, I got something for you. Not much, though. Pretty much straight from the press release that'll come out around one o'clock."

"Let's hear it."

Wilmer cleared his throat. "At the request of Homeland Security, NORTHCOM has deployed an undisclosed number of teams from its base at Peterson AFB in Colorado. NORTHCOM's orders are to apprehend and detain suspected domestic terrorists in connection with the terror attacks last Friday night."

"That's it?" Benson was incredulous. "No real specifics?"

"Told you it wasn't much."

"What kind of teams? Special ops?"

"Don't know yet."

"How did they determine their targets? What's the intel source?"

"Don't know that, either," Wilmer said. "You're really going to have to hit up Justice or DHS for that, Hal. NORTHCOM doesn't initiate—it only acts at the request of another agency. Gotta stay within the law, you know."

"I know, the rule of law," Benson said dryly. "That's what the White House keeps telling me. Thanks, Sam. I appreciate it. Will you let me know the minute you have anything further?"

"You bet." The line clicked, switching to a dial tone. Benson set down the receiver, wondering for a moment if his line was tapped. *They wouldn't dare. Would they?*

Benson picked up a toothpick and settled the slender wood into the side of his mouth, a habit inherited from his father. He stared at the yellow legal pad, thinking through what little he'd learned.

Justice had nothing. Neither did Defense. He still had calls out, and a few more cards to play. By the end of the day he'd either have the information he wanted or he'd know just how much clout he was dealing with.

Sucking on the toothpick, Harold Benson leaned back in his chair and closed his eyes. Scenes from a favorite movie played in his head—*Seven Days in May*, the Kirk Douglas-Burt Lancaster film about an attempted coup by the Joint Chiefs of Staff. At least in the movie, Douglas' character knew about the plot. Benson didn't even have that, much less who was behind it or what they wanted.

This would be a very long day.

EIGHTEEN

"I'm telling you, this is Crisis Level Alpha!"

"Cool it, Grunes," Terry Norlock said. "Bogus military jargon doesn't help."

Gruner sighed and ran his hand through his disorganized crop of hair, carefully avoiding the oversized bandage stuck to the middle of his forehead. "Okay, okay. But I'm telling you, man, it's the government. They snatched him, right from his apartment in broad daylight. And we've got to get him back."

Vijay and Norlock had agreed to meet at Gruner's house after work to brainstorm. Stauffer's parents had to be called, that was a given. But beyond that, what to do?

"This is all my fault, man. All my freakin' fault!" Gruner moaned. "I never should have hacked a DOD server without an anonymizer. Stupid! Stupid! Amateur night!"

Vijay blinked. "That is not much of a hack, if you ask me."

Gruner's pride rose up automatically. "Okay, like you could do better."

Vijay shrugged his shoulders. "Perhaps."

Gruner slammed a hand against a wall, rattling its sole decoration, an oil painting of four dogs huddled around a computer monitor, a gift from his cousin the previous Christmas. "I left tracks. Must have. Stupid, stupid!"

"There is no way to resolve that now," Vijay replied evenly, carefully straightening the painting. "The bulldog looks a bit like you, I think." The modest Indian could have gotten in without leaving tracks, but he wouldn't have done it. Vijay's code of ethics was more rigid than a Baptist's on Sunday morning.

"Look," Norlock said, "I don't see why waiting for the police to call back is a bad idea. They're pretty busy right now, in case you haven't noticed."

It hit Gruner all at once. "I see it now! How could I have been so stupid? The terror attacks are the excuse the government's been waiting for to start locking up everyone who's a threat! It's Main Core! Rex Eighty-Four! They're probably looking for *us* right now!"

Norlock raised an eyebrow. "What the hell are you talking about?"

"Readiness Exercise Nineteen Eighty-Four! It's a plan they drew up in the early Eighties to round up large groups of refugees coming across the Mexican border—or at least that's what the press reported. It was supposed to get us ready for a revolution down south, or a hurricane or a killer earthquake or something. FEMA and the DOD would use old military bases like concentration camps—you know, to house everybody. But the full plans, see, were never really made public. It was all a smokescreen to cover the *real* plan—to lock up domestic troublemakers. And that's where Main Core comes in."

Gruner took a breath. He was rolling. "Main Core is a secret database kept by the government since the Eighties. Records on millions of Americans who might be a national security threat—personal information, financial data, scooped up by the FBI, CIA, NSA, DIA, and God knows who else. None of it with warrants. And—get this—they use PROMIS to search through it."

"What?" Norlock asked.

"How can you not *know* this? Main Core has been public knowledge since about oh-seven. PROMIS a lot longer than that."

"Dude, we were in high school," Norlock said. "I had other priorities. Like girls."

Gruner rolled his eyes. "Okay. PROMIS. Developed in the Eighties for law enforcement. Helps prosecutors search through case files and find everything from the arresting officers to the phone numbers of witnesses. But here's the thing: The company that developed it claims the Reagan administration stole it and gave it to the NSA and CIA. They adapted it for intelligence ops and tracking money. The NSA built back doors into PROMIS and then sold it to banks around the world so they could tap into those banks and see whose money was going where without anybody knowing about it. Man, that was more than thirty years ago. Think about what they can do with the changes in tech since then! Email, texts, smart phones… Holy crap, they could be listening to us through our phones right now!"

Vijay and Norlock stared at him. Vijay's eyebrows were raised. After a long pause, Vijay asked, "Jared, are you well?"

Gruner sighed. "Okay. Maybe it's not a government takeover. But Stauffer's gone and the local cops say they don't know anything about it. That's bad. Veej, look—one of the fundamental rights of an American citizen is the writ of *habeas corpus*. That's basically a piece of paper that says the cops have to have a reason for arresting somebody. According to the Constitution, anybody can demand one. Convicts sometimes use it if they think their rights were violated. Guys, if the government's suspended *habeas corpus*, they can arrest anybody and not have to show one single reason for it."

"You think?" Norlock asked.

"It's been done before," Gruner said. "Lincoln, during the Civil War."

"Extreme circumstances," Norlock said. "Enemies and collaborators on home soil."

"Which is what they're calling this," Gruner countered. "More likely a monster-sized setup. Know what the media is calling it? Ten-Thirteen. That's got Illuminati written all over it! Ten-Thirteen? Knights Templar? The attacks were on Friday the thirteenth, just like the day the Templars were rounded up by King Philip the Fair in 1307! That's why Friday the thirteenth is supposed to be unlucky. I don't like it one bit. Stofe's disappearance is a bad sign. I mean, it's bad for him, obviously, but the way it happened is bad news. Why hasn't he called anybody? Yeah, he's a goof, we all know that—but he's never just vanished before."

"I'm not sure what temples have to do with it, but if Scott's computer needed repair, he would have brought it with him to work," Vijay added.

"And his van wouldn't be outside," Gruner said. "Okay. Norlock, check out some patriot groups at Facebook. Maybe somebody out there saw something."

"All right, you win." Norlock opened his laptop and checked to make sure it was getting a signal.

"Not here! Don't use my router! For all we know, we're being followed! They might be monitoring my IP!"

Norlock pulled a face. "Chill, Groaner. I've got my 4G card. And I'm using a VPN."

Gruner relaxed. "Sorry. I'm just freaked. And hungry." He was still upset about Homeland Security disrupting pizza deliveries.

"Hungry. There's a surprise," Norlock said as his opened a web browser.

Gruner fingered the bandage on his forehead. "Cut me some slack, man. I'm injured."

"What are patriot groups?" Vijay asked.

"You might have something there," Norlock agreed. "The government could be monitoring electronic communications, but at least they haven't shut down the web yet. It seems pretty fast, considering."

"A few posts describing the situation should stir up some action," Gruner suggested.

"You think? Why would anybody in their right mind post anything incriminating to Facebook?"

"People share a lot of personal stuff they shouldn't," Gruner answered. "We're just looking for anybody who's seen something. I'll search Twitter and some of the other social sites."

"Please!" Vijay was indignant. "What are you talking about?"

Gruner drummed his fingers impatiently. "We're talking about patriot groups," he said. "Conspiracy hunters. Kindred spirits, resisting the encroachment of the global plot to enslave us into serving the New World Order."

Norlock tried to translate. "What he means is—"

Gruner cut him off. "Never mind what I mean! Vijay, can you hack into the Justice Department's criminal database and see if Stauffer's in there?"

"What?" Aghast, Vijay stopped with his laptop half-opened.

Gruner rolled his eyes and sighed. "Kidding. I'm kidding. How about you search the web to see if anybody else is missing."

"Like temples?"

Gruner started to answer, but then he saw the sly smile on the Indian's face. "Remind me to sic a dragon on you next time we play."

The appointment would have eaten up more of Unes' day, but traffic on I-44 was still light. The rain had ended, and the clear weather pushed speeds back up to normal, clearing out the slowdowns he'd faced all morning. Getting in and out of downtown without a headache might have been the only good thing about the situation.

The interview with Pastor Harper was informative, but not in the way that would satisfy a Special Agent in Charge. Steve Clay was waiting for Unes when he returned to the FBI's downtown office.

"What's the word on Harper and his bunch?" Clay asked, intercepting Unes halfway to his desk.

Unes shook his head. "I don't think there's anything there."

Clay frowned. "You make that conclusion on the basis of one interview? You got anything to back that up?"

"No, not yet," Unes admitted. "But this guy wears his faith on his sleeve. Like he's compelled to talk about it. I didn't get the sense that he was hiding anything."

His boss folded his arms. "I see. And what did he say that was so persuasive?"

Here we go, Unes thought. It wasn't unusual for Clay to challenge his agents to dig deeper, but sometimes it was hard to tell when he was convinced that his agent was off track or just playing devil's advocate. Unes was just achy enough to be irritated by the questions.

"We talked theology."

"Theology?"

"That's what this is supposed to be about, right?" Unes took off his jacket and flung it carelessly across the back of his chair. A couple of other agents in the office looked up from their desks to see what was going on. Joe Unes never treated a suit jacket that way.

"Right-wing Christian extremists," he continued, "That's what Project Megiddo says, right?"

Clay remained silent, lips pursed.

"I don't buy it," Unes continued. "It's too simple. Maybe there are some crazies out there, but I don't think this church is run by one of them. Know what his take is on the Apocalypse?"

"Tell me."

"That no one knows when it's coming. In fact, no one *can* know when it's coming," Unes said. "Jesus didn't even know when he was on Earth. Only God the Father knows, and He's not telling. The bottom line is there's nothing man can do to change the timetable."

"Is that so?"

Unes shrugged. "It's what Harper believes. Whether it true or not, he's not one of those—what did you call them? Dominionists? Here," he said, grabbing his jacket off the chair and digging into the pocket, "Some of his propaganda." He handed Clay about half a dozen small tracts, printed on pulp. They looked like miniature comic books.

"What are these?" Clay asked as he flipped through them. "'How to Know if You're Saved,' 'The Romans Road,' 'This Was Your Life'—what is this stuff?"

"Recruiting pamphlets," Unes said. "He wants soldiers in the war against evil."

"Ah," Clay said, nodding. "And evil is…?"

Unes shook his head. "He's not trying to overthrow the government. Where is that—" He opened his notebook and flipped through a few pages. "Here, this one says, 'For we wrestle not against flesh and blood, but against principalities, against powers, against the rulers of the darkness of this world, against spiritual wickedness in high places.'"

Clay folded his arms. "Rulers of darkness? What is this? Sounds like the name of a bad movie."

"It means the battle's not physical, it's spiritual," Unes said. "Satan is the enemy, and Harper's teaching his people to fight this war on their knees." He closed the notebook. "If Conrad Reston had the idea that he was blowing up a supermarket for God, I don't think he got it from Ed Harper."

Kiowa County Sheriff's Deputy Scott Farnsworth was three steps from the prowler when a gunshot cracked and a bullet whistled over his head.

One second later, Farnsworth was on the ground, reaching for his revolver and searching for the shooter. He was still new to the department, but he'd been around guns as long as he could remember.

At six-four, Farnsworth was a big target even to a bad shot. He didn't intend to give the gunman a second chance.

No one was outside that he could see. The proximity of the shot meant the most likely location was—

A flash and another shot.

Farnsworth's hunch had been right. The shooter was in the house. He took a deep breath. In Kiowa County, police rarely faced the decision of whether discharging a firearm was appropriate. Being shot at made it easier.

Caught between his car and the house, Farnsworth quickly rolled to his right and lined up a shot on an open front window, most likely one of the bedrooms. The deputy saw movement in the shadow of the room and the glint of something metallic. He pulled the trigger.

Farnsworth thought he hit something, but he waited, lying still for what felt like an eternity with all his senses trained on that open window.

Minutes ticked by with no sound or movement inside; Deputy Farnsworth rolled to his feet and moved quick and low to the front of the house, next to the window. He waited a few seconds more until he was sure he heard no sounds of life inside, and then, after a deep breath, he peered through the open window, holding his gun in front of him.

Nothing could have prepared him for what he saw there.

"Oh, God. Oh, God!" Farnsworth said out loud. His arms fell limply to his sides, and he dropped his handgun.

Inside the white clapboard rental, sprawled across a twin bed topped with a bloodstained, Iowa Hawkeyes comforter was the shooter. A Browning A-bolt rifle lay on the floor between the bed and the window. Farnsworth's single shot had found its mark. The shooter was clearly dead.

Deputy Scott Farnsworth began to tremble uncontrollably as he tried and failed to hold back tears for the first time since grammar school.

Through the open window, he stared in horror at a bloodstained bed and the lifeless body of a boy who couldn't be more than eleven years old.

All through the morning, helicopters and C-21 transport jets kept coming. Each time another craft landed, it disgorged more men. And each time, Lieutenant Harris and the third platoon of the 369th Military Police Company escorted the new group from the airfield to the barracks inside the double line of chain-link and barbed wire.

"Sergeant Williams, our latest guests settled in?" Harris looked up from the desk he'd appropriated in the headquarters building for the avalanche of paperwork he expected any minute.

Sergeant Kendall Williams nodded, his usual smile absent. "Yes, sir."

Harris indicated a vacant chair next to the desk. "What's up? Something bothering you?"

"Sir—I uh…"

"Speak freely, Sergeant. Just you and me here."

"Thank you, sir." Settling into the seat, Williams said, "Have you noticed that none of these detainees fit the profile?"

"What profile is that, Sergeant?"

"Terrorist, sir," Williams said.

"Okay. What about them doesn't fit?" Harris had his own ideas, but he wanted to hear what Williams thought.

"Sir, these guys look like they should be home cutting grass or putting up storm windows. Ain't one of them looks like he ever picked up a gun."

"Somebody who wants to blow you up isn't going to wear a T-shirt telling you who he is," Harris said.

"I know, I know. But you know what they're doing over there? In the barracks?"

"What?"

"Praying. On-their-knees kind of praying. You know?"

Harris wrinkled his eyebrows as a question. "Fanatics pray, too, Sergeant. Remember Iraq?"

"No, no. Not like that. Not that kind of praying," Williams repeated. "And not, 'God, please kill all these wicked evil-doers,' either. Just praying."

"So?"

"So, have you counted how many preachers they brung in here?" Williams leaned forward, his eyes wide. "We put nearly three hundred men in that barracks so far today, and I'll be danged if at least a quarter of 'em ain't men of God."

"So they say," Harris said simply. "Terrorists been known to lie, Sergeant."

"Yeah, well, it's making me nervous," Williams admitted. "Even if a few of them deserve to be here, some of them are closer to the Big Man than me or you, and that don't seem right. Not right at all."

It was awkward at best. Deputy Farnsworth sat across the desk from Ann Jurasik in the office that should have been occupied by Sheriff Thornton. But the sheriff was gone and Jurasik still didn't know where he was.

The small office wasn't very private, even with the door closed. The county hadn't had much money when the addition to the County Administration Building was put up twenty-five years earlier, and the thin walls weren't much of a sound barrier.

Consequently, the whole department now listened to the agonized sobs of Deputy Scott Farnsworth.

"Farns," Jurasik said in a low voice, "It's okay. The boy fired at least two shots at you from that room. There was no way you could know who was pulling the trigger."

Farnsworth stared at the floor, his chest heaving with the effort of trying to contain his emotions. Jurasik's heart ached for him. *First time he pulls his gun on the job and it's a ten-year-old boy. What got into that kid?*

For that matter, what got into Frank Allen? Jurasik took him into custody after Doctor Kuehne checked out the bump on his head. When Allen woke up, Doc had to put him under again, which had been tough to do.

He'd gone wild, the kind of uncontrolled rage police in big cities see when they run into somebody on PCP. Kuehne finally got a sedative into Allen with Jurasik and Farnsworth holding him down. And poor Farnsworth had been so distraught that he was only half aware of what was going on.

Ordinarily a quiet man, Frank Allen had nearly thrown all three of them through the walls of Doc Kuehne's office.

Then there was Allen's son, John. Jurasik had notified the county's child welfare agency. They were now tracking down a relative of Verna's in Des Moines to notify her and to find somebody who could take in Johnny.

If that was even necessary. Maybe Johnny was staying at a friend's house for the night, taking advantage of the day off from school.

Or maybe we just haven't found where Frank Allen left him. Jurasik took a deep breath and tried to put that thought out of her mind.

Her problem at the moment was to keep Farnsworth from falling apart. The force was undermanned to start with. Losing the sheriff made things worse.

On the other hand, she had no idea of what it felt like to shoot a ten-year-old boy dead. She prayed she never would.

"Look, Scott," she said in as soothing a voice as she could muster, "take a couple days off. There's a guy the state police recommend that you can talk to about this, over in Cedar Rapids. I can call him, if you want. County'll pay."

Still shaking, Farnsworth barely nodded, stood, and slowly left the office. Jurasik heard the outer door open and close. Through the one window in the sheriff's office, she watched the young deputy drift across the gravel lot to his car. He moved like he was pushing through chest-high molasses.

Jurasik sighed. It was a long week, and Monday wasn't even over yet.

The phone beeped. It was Rob Vitale, the other deputy on duty.

"Ann? Got a reporter from a Quad Cities paper on the line, making the usual cop shop calls. You want to tell him what's been going on or should we keep it quiet?"

Jurasik thought for a moment. *Would the sheriff sit on this or get it out? Are there other families in the area who might be affected? Lord, is there something in the water?* "Put him through, Rob. I'll talk to him."

NINETEEN

He had to do something. His dad was missing. His mom, even though she tried to hide it, was really worried.

Eric decided he couldn't just sit around and wait any more. But what *could* he do?

He thought about it for a long time, sitting on his bed with his back against the wall, knees pulled to his chin. He'd have to get a message out to the world, but how? His parents still wouldn't let him have his own phone or tablet, and Eric didn't like his odds of getting away with stealing his mom's phone or iPad.

And then he remembered the old computer in the attic.

It was a crazy idea, but this was a crazy situation. He wasn't sure it would work. He wasn't even sure they still had the old machine.

Eric hopped from his bed and walked quietly down the hall. The door to the storage space was next to the stairs that led down to the kitchen. His mom was still at the table with a mug of decaf coffee. Turning the knob slowly, Eric eased the door open without making a sound. *No need to bother Mom with this.*

The air in the unfinished part of the attic was cool but not unpleasant. At different times of the year, opening that door could hit you with a fifty-degree temperature swing one way or the other. In winter, cold air flowed from the attic and down the stairs to the kitchen like water spilled from a cup.

He switched on the light, an old seventy-five-watt incandescent bulb screwed into a plain fixture hanging from a joist in the middle of the room. Walking on the balls of his feet and shifting his weight slowly from foot to foot, Eric crossed the rough plywood flooring with only a few soft creaks to give him away. Sure enough, the old PC was still there, waiting for his parents to figure out something to do with it. The church hadn't needed it and his parents weren't too keen on selling stuff over the Internet, so there it was.

It was one of those all-in-one computers. Good. One piece meant less stuff to carry. He could make it to his room in two trips—one with the computer, and one with the keyboard, mouse, and power cable.

He examined the computer carefully. It worked the last time they'd used it, about seven months ago. The machine was about four years old, almost ancient in computer terms. *Computers must be like dogs*, Eric thought. *Seven years for every people year.*

He turned and silently crept back across the plywood to the door, carefully closing it behind him as he returned to his room. Later tonight, when his mother was asleep, he'd come back for the computer and put his plan into effect. Then the world would hear about his dad. Something would happen then for sure.

Congressman Harold Benson drummed his fingers on his desk as he waited for someone to answer at the Thornton house back in Mayfield, Iowa. He'd put in a full day on the Hill watching the preening and posturing by his committee colleagues, who pretended to offer serious debate when everyone knew each vote was already decided.

Every year, it got a little harder to play the game. Benson grew less and less patient with the childish power plays that passed for representing the will of the people. He really needed a trip back home to Iowa.

Someone picked up on the sixth ring. "Yes? Is that you, Deputy?" Her voice was hoarse. Benson hadn't noticed that this morning.

"No. Not the deputy. It's Harold Benson. Are you all right? You sound a little froggy there."

"I'm sorry—oh, Congressman!" she said. "I'm sorry. Oh—please, no, I'm all right, I guess. It's been a tough day."

"I can only imagine."

"Oh, that's right! You don't know. Congressman, the town's gone mad. It's more than Ted. A neighbor drowned his wife in their bathtub this morning, and I discovered her body."

"Good Lord."

"And then—" She sniffed. "Then a ten-year-old boy got hold of his father's hunting rifle and shot his own mother! A sheriff's deputy went to the house and the boy shot at him, and the deputy— oh, I can't believe it. The deputy—he…"

Benson waited a moment while Susie Thornton tried to bring her emotions under control. "The deputy returned fire?"

"Y—yes," she said, her voice cracking.

"How is the boy?"

"I'm afraid he's dead."

Benson heard a muffled sob on the other end of the line. He took a deep breath and exhaled. There probably hadn't been five murders total in Kiowa County since the Kennedy administration, and now there were seven dead since Friday night. What in hell was going on?

"Susie, I am terribly sorry," he finally said. "No one should have to go through that."

"Thank you," she said, her voice stronger. *Tough woman*, Benson thought.

"Look, I won't keep you," he said. "I just wanted to report back to you about Ted. Unfortunately, so far I don't have any information for you."

"Oh," she said simply.

Benson could feel her disappointment from a thousand miles away.

"Now, don't get discouraged just yet," he continued. "I have a number of people checking into this. I'd be very surprised if I don't have something for you by tomorrow."

"Thank you, Congress—"

"Harold."

"That's right. Harold. Thank you, Harold."

"You get yourself a good night's rest and we'll talk again tomorrow."

"I'll try," she said. "Good night."

After he hung up the phone, Harold Benson sat back in his office chair with his hands folded behind his head. The pieces of the puzzle didn't fit. Not at all.

Getting to his feet, the congressman decided to head home. Maybe a walk would help him think.

The sour feeling in Joe Unes' stomach made for a long drive home. He normally felt good at the end of the day, especially on days when he'd made progress on a case. Today, he just felt—well, he wasn't sure yet. Irritated, but not entirely sure why. Talking to Cathy would help him sort things out.

He pulled into the driveway at the usual time, a little before six. Still light outside. That would change in a couple of weeks when the clocks were set back an hour. That started his least favorite time of the year, when he drove to work and back in the dark.

The spicy scent of a tomato-based sauce washed over him as he opened the front door. Unes announced his arrival as he always did: "Hi, honey!" Setting his briefcase in the foyer, he followed his nose back to the kitchen.

"Hi, sweetheart," Cathy said.

Unes took a deep breath of the tangy aroma filling the air. That was all it took to set his stomach right, and it growled with anticipation. "Smells good," he said as he sidled up behind his wife, putting his face next to hers to inspect her handiwork over her shoulder.

A big stainless steel pot sat on a back burner with something tantalizing simmering beneath the shining silver lid. His glasses fogged over from the steam in the air. Chicken cacciatore, if his larger-than-average nose was any judge.

Cathy, busy with a pot full of boiling pasta, couldn't turn around and face him, but Unes felt her smile. "So, how was your day?" she asked.

"Not as exciting as Friday, thank God," he said.

"One of those per career is exciting enough for me," Cathy said.

"Me, too."

"Back up."

"Huh?"

"Back up," Cathy said. "I have to drain the pasta."

"Ah." Unes followed orders, giving Cathy room to shift the pot to the sink, where she poured the contents into a green plastic colander. A great cloud of steam erupted from the ceramic sink, clouding the window that looked out over their backyard.

Unes took a chair at the kitchen table and cleaned his glasses by undoing a bottom button and wiping them with his shirttail. He still needed to call their optometrist to get a replacement for the scratched left lens.

"So, nothing exciting today?" Cathy asked.

"I interviewed a preacher," Unes said, settling the cleaned spectacles on his nose. "I guess you'd call him one of those Bible-thumping, fire-breathing types. The man who blew up the Grandy's was an off-and-on member of his church. Steve Clay thinks it was religion that made him strap on the bomb belt."

Cathy turned from the sink with a puzzled expression. "Why would he think that?"

Unes shrugged. "I'm not sure. End times stuff, trying to bring on the Apocalypse, maybe. That's the theory in Washington, anyway."

"Yeah, but—why? Was this man you interviewed preaching violence?"

"Not as far as I can tell," Unes admitted. "The preacher seems on the level. Pretty conservative, but unless he's a great liar, and the church secretary is uploading bogus sermon notes to the Internet, he's sticking to the Bible. But it seemed like that wasn't what Steve Clay wanted to hear when I got back to the office."

Cathy finished with the noodles and set the colander in the sink again to drain. "I don't follow you. Why does Clay assume religion has anything to do with the bombing?"

Shaking his head, Joe said, "The evidence is thin but compelling, I guess. The man was shouting verses from the Bible before he detonated the bomb, but that doesn't necessarily mean motive. As far as I know, nobody's put one out there that makes any sense. And that goes for everything that happened over the weekend. A couple of whackos have claimed credit, but their stories don't make sense. We get fake confessions all the time. Mostly sickos trying to get famous on other peoples' misery."

He sighed, took off his glasses and rubbed his eyes. "All the stuff that happened over the weekend was either the most bizarre series of unconnected events in history, or whoever planned it is the most brilliant terrorist that ever walked the earth."

"You just haven't found the common thread yet," Cathy said, wiping her hands on a terry-cloth dishtowel. "You will."

Unes smiled ruefully. It was nice that one of them thought so.

The computer was slow, but it still worked. Fast enough for Internet work, anyway.

Eric Moore sat on the floor of his darkened room, a blanket over both the computer and himself to keep the monitor's glow from seeping through the crack underneath his bedroom door. He didn't want his mom to find out what he was doing, not yet.

This was one of those times when Eric thought the ends justified risking his mother's disapproval, but after the fact, if possible. If he asked, she'd probably say no. If he did it first and *then* she said no—well, she hadn't exactly told him *not* to do it, so he wasn't *technically* breaking any rules.

Besides, he had to do something.

It only took Eric fifteen minutes to set up accounts on Facebook and Twitter. His parents hadn't wanted him on social media at his age, but this was a special circumstance. He needed to get word out to the world. Once people saw how unfair this whole thing was, somebody was bound to help.

Eric spent another ten minutes trying to figure out what to write. It had to be short. Two hundred and forty characters didn't give him a lot of room for details.

Half an hour later, he was done.

PLEASE HELP MY DAD! shouted the first posts at his new accounts, both with the username @EricInMayfield. Below that, several more gave a summary of his adventurous weekend, especially the arrest at church Sunday morning. He made sure to give descriptions of the guns carried by the men who took his dad away.

His final posts included contact information for anyone with an idea about where his dad might be and who could be responsible for his arrest. Eric bit his lip, trying to decide whether he should include their home phone number on the web page. He decided that might tip off his mom sooner than he wanted, so he settled for just giving his email address.

Satisfied, he logged out and shut down the computer. He thought about stashing it in his closet, but then changed his mind. If his mother asked why it was in his room, he'd tell her he was testing it out to see if it was okay to use as a backup to the one that got stolen. She'd believe that.

Tomorrow, he'd set it up in the office, so he wouldn't be telling her a lie. Besides, he'd need to start checking his email again so he'd know when someone answered.

Email. Eric closed his eyes and leaned back against the side of his bed to rest. He just hoped there wasn't another message from God in his Inbox.

They'd been at it for hours. Three men with determined faces reflecting the eerie glow of computer screens, three sets of bleary eyes searching for clues.

Jared Gruner sighed in frustration. His eyelids itched, his stomach screamed for carbs, and social media had nothing—nothing he was looking for, anyway. Twitter was swamped by news of protests in dozens of cities. Alleged anti-fascists were marching to protest religious extremism, or something. Anarchists and opportunists were taking advantage of the crowds to smash windows and loot.

Gruner had just decided to try another search for hashtags like #FEMA, #NewWorldOrder, #militia, and so on, when Vijay interrupted his thoughts.

"Jared? Terry? Please look at this." The little guy had a look of profound concentration pressed into his forehead, as though the weight of his thoughts had pulled his eyebrows down on top of his eyes.

Norlock set his laptop on the dining room table and scooted his chair around to where Vijay sat. Gruner got up from his desk in the living room and trundled over to look.

Vijay had the browser on the website of an online newspaper. *Des Moines, Iowa*, read the dateline, with the headline: *Iowa Pastor, Two Others Taken From Church at Gunpoint.*

"What is this?" Norlock asked.

Gruner scanned the story over Vijay's shoulder, leaning in closer, his eyebrows rising higher as he got deeper into the copy.

"Scroll down, Veej. Men in black hauled three guys, including the pastor and the county sheriff, out of church at gunpoint, during the service…no charges filed…seven others dead…all in one weekend in the middle of Nowhere, Iowa."

Gruner straightened up, rubbing his ample chin in thought. This was too much. The odds against random chance were a mathematical impossibility.

"Holy Toledo," he said at last. "We got something here. Something…big."

"What?" Norlock asked again.

"Gentlemen," Gruner continued, "It's time to make a phone call."

TWENTY

He heard the bell of an old wind-up alarm clock ringing somewhere. But somehow, as Joe Unes tried to find it in the elastic landscape of his dreams, the sound morphed into an annoying electronic bleat.

It was a full sixty seconds before Unes realized it was his cell phone on the nightstand. He slowly reached over and picked it up.

"Hello?"

"I'm sorry to call you so late, Agent Unes, but we think it's important." The voice sounded vaguely familiar, but at the moment, it could have belonged to his own mother and Unes wouldn't have recognized it.

"Uh, that's okay. What's going on?" He sat up in bed and took a couple of deep breaths, trying to force some oxygen to his brain.

"That's just it. See, we've been trying to figure out what's been going on since Friday, so we've been on the web since about two-thirty, and we think this is bigger than just one guy—well, bigger than three guys anyway."

Unes waited while his brain caught up and processed that statement. He came to the conclusion that he had no idea what the caller was talking about.

"Okay. First of all, I don't know who you are. Second—uh," He paused as he squinted to make out the glowing numbers of the alarm clock on his dresser. "Second, it's two-ten in the morning. You have until two-eleven to explain who you are and why this couldn't wait or I'm hanging up."

"Joe?" Cathy rolled over to face him. He shrugged and shook his head.

The caller's voice rose in pitch. "Wait, don't hang up! This is Jared Gruner, and I'm really sorry, but we don't know who else to call."

"Tick tock," Unes said impatiently while trying to recall anyone named Gruner.

"Somebody kidnapped our friend, Scott—the guy who was with us Friday at Grandy's."

Unes sighed. *Friday at Grandy's. Gruner. One of the Nerdsmen?*

"Yeah, yeah. Friday. Okay, I'm with you. Wait, what did you say? Kidnapped? Are you sure? Did you call the police?"

"Well, yes and no," Gruner said, speaking rapidly. "We think it *was* the police, or some covert branch of it anyway. The local cops say they don't know anything, but maybe they wouldn't tell us anyway. Then we thought maybe *you* had him arrested, but that didn't make sense either, cause if you'd done it, then *we'd* probably be in jail, too, and besides, it's a lot bigger than that."

Unes rubbed his eyes and fumbled for his glasses. "What are you talking about?" he asked.

"Man, I hope this line isn't tapped. It looks like people all over the country are disappearing, usually in places close to where the terror attacks happened. Scott's just one of them. There's not much in the news about it, but on social media it looks like a lot of people are being rounded up by what sound like SWAT teams."

"Mm hmm, SWAT teams," Unes said, sitting up. "You do realize that the nation is at Threat Level Red?"

"Of course!" Gruner said excitedly. "But that doesn't explain why in a small town in Iowa, a preacher and two other men including the county sheriff, were dragged out of church Sunday morning by men in black with automatic weapons! That's according to the sheriff's deputy who said they don't have any official word as to why or where they were taken."

Unes was more alert now and pushed himself up to a sitting position. "Okay, let's say you're right. How does this relate to your friend?"

"We don't know," Gruner said. "That's why we called you."

Unes sighed wearily. "Mister Gruner. I have to be at the office in less than six hours. Do me a favor. Pull this into a coherent narrative and call me at the office tomorrow morning, when I might actually be able to do something for you."

"Tomorrow morning. Got it! First thing. Thanks!"

"You're welcome." Unes set his phone back on the nightstand.

"Who was that, Joe?" Cathy asked sleepily.

"The Three Stooges of conspiracy theorists," he said, settling back into bed. "That was Curly. Sounds like Moe is missing."

"What?"

"Never mind. I'm still mostly asleep."

Harold Benson walked with a spring in his step. It wasn't that he felt especially cheerful. He didn't. It was habit, part of his morning routine. Walking was good for you, but walking briskly was better. Kept you young.

The morning was humid, and the muggy D.C. air promised another uncomfortable day.

While his legs pushed him along, Benson's mind tried to make sense of the last four days. Bad things were happening all over, not just in his home state. A madness was spreading, and people were dying in horrible, senseless ways in places that rarely saw violent crime. The tragedies in Mayfield, Iowa, had been repeated in at least a dozen other places across the country.

Thus preoccupied, he almost walked into the two young men who emerged from a black sedan at the curb. They wore dark suits and sunglasses, and they had the thick, broad-shouldered look of football players.

"Oh. Excuse me." Benson tried to step around the nearest of the two, but he moved to block Benson's path.

"Congressman Benson, we have a message for you."

Benson immediately shifted gears and focused on the men in front of him. Close-cropped hair meant military or one of the intelligence services. Judging by the fit of their suit jackets, they were probably armed.

The near one had dark hair and was a little shorter and leaner than the other. His partner's hair was blond and cut in an old-fashioned crew cut; his face showed a bit of roundness, a tendency to carry more body fat. He looked like an offensive lineman. The shorter one was more like a linebacker.

The congressman stood straight and tall, refusing to give them the satisfaction of seeing him sweat. "You do, do you? Well, young man, what is it?"

The near one answered. "Discontinue all inquiries into the incident in Iowa."

"What? Really? Who sent you?"

"It doesn't matter," the other said.

"Does to me," Benson said. "I like to know whose toes I'm stepping on."

The two goons glanced at one another. The near one said, "It's a matter of national security."

"Don't jerk me around, son. I've been dealing with national security longer than you've been alive. Probably longer than your daddies have been alive."

"You don't know what you're getting into here."

"And I suppose you do." Benson said it not as a question, but as a challenge.

"Enough to know when to quit asking questions."

"Well, then, I guess you win. You're smarter than me. Now let me by. I have a meeting."

"This is the only warning you get," the linebacker said.

"Warning? Threat, you mean," Benson said. "You know, it's usually cowards who hide behind national security."

The linebacker's jaw tightened.

Good, Benson thought. *Score one for the old man.*

The linebacker stepped closer. "Congressman, it's a shame how often men your age suddenly die with no warning. And in ways that arouse no suspicions whatsoever."

"Is that a fact?" Benson hit back without blinking. "Son, I'm too old to scare with death."

"Maybe. But your grandkids aren't."

Now it was Benson's jaw that clenched, and he felt his blood pressure spike. The ex-Marine in him wanted to take these two punks to the mat right there on the street, but common sense kept that impulse in check. He knew some handy tricks from his days in the Corps, but this wasn't the movies. Youth and strength would win out.

"You'd threaten children?" he said.

"Whatever it takes," the lineman replied evenly. "Just forget about Iowa."

"No dice. My district's in Iowa."

"Drop it, Congressman. This is your only warning."

"Good," Benson said. "Then your boss won't waste any more of your time."

The linebacker glanced at his partner. "Our boss doesn't waste time, Congressman."

"And I don't play games," Benson whispered, glaring into the man's cold eyes. "You tell your boss that. Good day."

For a Tuesday, it felt suspiciously like another Monday. Bruised and sore, Joe Unes' ears still sang a high-pitched whine, and his sleep had been interrupted by that phone call. Traffic was slow because police had been out in force again, but doubly agitated because of looting downtown the night before that looked suspiciously less than random. And now, he discovered that his colleagues had let the coffee boil away in the bottom of the pot the night before. Beautiful.

"Uh, Agent Unes?" Janice, the department secretary, poked her head into the coffee room. "There are some men here to see you."

Unes closed his eyes and took a deep breath. *Say it isn't so. Not this early.* "Are there three of them?" he asked, praying the answer was no.

"Yes, there are," the secretary said with a smile. "Either you're a mind reader, or they were telling the truth about having an appointment. I told them to wait in Conference Room A."

Joe sighed. "Tell them I'll be with them in a minute. Thank you, Janice."

Unes washed out the carafe as best he could and started a new pot brewing before heading down the long hallway that led to the conference rooms.

"Agent Unes," the big one said, getting out of the chair at the head of the long table as Unes entered the room. "Thanks for meeting with us. We flashed your business card and they, uh, said we could wait here. They gave us these badges. Security is tight, huh?"

"You could say that. Jared Gruner, right?" The big guy nodded, smiling nervously. He sported a bandage across the middle of his forehead, which Unes found odd. He didn't remember Gruner getting hurt at Grandy's.

Gruner's two friends, the tall, blond guy and the short Indian—Norlock and Sampurnan-something, Unes remembered—stood off to the side, apparently content to let Gruner talk. "To be honest, guys, I didn't expect you today," Unes said. "At least not so early."

"I know we said we'd call, but we figured face to face would be better. And we were still up. Energy drinks, you know? Is this a bad time? I mean, we can come back," Gruner said.

Unes weighed his options. While he really liked to take the first twenty minutes or so at the office to plan his day over a cup of coffee, putting these guys off meant he'd have to slot them in later. No. Better to bite the bullet and get it over with.

"No, no, that's fine," he said. "Let me grab some coffee. You guys need any?"

Gruner looked at his friends who shook their heads. Turning back to Unes, Gruner said, "Sure, thanks. Black, please."

Unes dropped a legal pad and pen on the conference table. "Back in a minute."

He smelled the pot brewing as he turned the corner into the office's tiny coffee room. Two minutes later, Unes carried two mugs of hot coffee into the conference room where his three guests waited. "Here you go," he said, setting a mug emblazoned with the FBI logo in front of Gruner.

"Hey, thanks," Gruner said. "Say, do you think we'll be able to keep these badges?"

"No," Unes said as he settled into the chair at the head of the table. "Security requires all badges be accounted for. Smart guy like you should know that."

"Sure, that makes sense. They're just kinda cool, you know?"

Unes had never thought of FBI security badges as *cool*. "Maybe I can get you a coffee mug. No promises. Now, what was so urgent that you had to call me at two in the morning?"

"Well," Gruner said, "you probably noticed our friend, Scott, isn't here with us."

"I remember that much of our conversation."

Gruner, seated to Unes' right, ran a hand through his unkempt hair. "Yeah. Sorry about that. Anyway, uh, we think he's been abducted."

Unes sipped his coffee while considering Gruner's statement. "Uh huh. Abducted by whom?"

A nervous glance passed between Gruner and his friends. "Well, we're not sure, but we think it's the government."

"And why would you think that?"

"Um, well, it might be my fault." Gruner said. He stared at the oak veneer of the conference table. "We were over at Scott's Friday night before the—you know—the thing at Grandy's."

"Yes?" Unes prompted.

"Well, we were at his apartment, and I used Scott's computer to, uh, access a Defense Department server so I could download some current satellite images of Israel, Lebanon, and Syria."

"Wait. You did what?" Unes wasn't intimate with DOD security, but he didn't have to be to guess that Gruner had committed a serious bit of illicit electronic snooping.

"Yeah. Stupid, huh?"

"Stupid, yes," Unes said. "And illegal, in all probability. So why do you only think Scott was arrested?"

"Abducted," Norlock said.

Unes frowned. "The government isn't in the habit of abducting people. We still have a Constitution."

Gruner looked up, incredulous. "Are you serious? You think the Constitution still matters?"

"Of course, it does. And I'm sworn to uphold it." Unes was annoyed. Gruner seemed oblivious to the fact that he was talking to a government employee.

"Sure, but the document may as well be in the shredder. It's a fact that in a national emergency, our constitutional rights don't mean squat," Gruner said.

"Says who?" Unes demanded.

"Says anyone who's paying attention to the man behind the curtain," Gruner said slowly, "You can't—I mean, do you really believe the government worries about civil rights at a time like this?"

Unes had seen good investigations derailed more than once by civil rights complaints. He just stared at Gruner.

Sighing, Gruner continued, "Okay, look. In a national emergency, federal law gives the president power to take over transportation, food distribution, even banks. A series of Executive Orders over the last forty years authorize the director of FEMA to take over during times of civil unrest, like—well, like now. They've got these camps set up just waiting to be used. FEMA hired three contractors for, like, three hundred million each just to stand by, ready to put up temporary cities for millions of people on short notice."

"Jared, that's all Internet propaganda. It's just not true." Unes felt the day beginning to slip away.

"Is it? You can look up the Executive Orders yourself. I can give you the numbers. I can email you links to the news articles that list the companies with the construction contracts," Gruner said earnestly. "It's all out there in the open—hidden in plain sight!"

Unes took a sip of coffee while evaluating Gruner's eyes and mannerisms. The three men struck him as sincere. Gruner believed what he was saying. Didn't mean he was right, but he wasn't obviously crazy.

"Go on," he prompted.

Gruner took a breath and continued. "Okay. You see, everybody knows about the Japanese-Americans who were sent to camps during World War Two, but there have been other times in history when American citizens were rounded up without warrants or *habeas corpus*. Like when Woodrow Wilson sent the army to Colorado in 1914. Ordered them to disarm police, militia, and anybody else who resisted, and to refuse to honor any writs of *habeas corpus*. McKinley sent the army to Idaho in 1899. Grant used troops in South Carolina during Reconstruction, and Lincoln—well, during the Civil War, it was like the Constitution didn't exist. Look, under the United States Code, the President can basically suspend the Constitution any time he wants just by declaring a national emergency."

"There are reasons for that," Unes argued. "Martial Law is the only way to restore order in times of chaos. And right now, given all that has happened, it seems to me we have a national emergency on our hands." He pointedly rubbed the bandage on his cheek.

"Sure. President Bell could declare a National Emergency any minute. And he probably will," Gruner said, leaning in closer. "But did you know that the United States has been under official states of emergency ever since Roosevelt's bank holiday in 1933?"

Unes set down his coffee. "Really," he said flatly. Joe had heard this before. It was tiresome.

"No, it is true," said the Indian, coming to life suddenly.

Vijay, Unes thought to himself.

Sampurnananda continued. "I did not believe him myself until I searched the archives at the website of the White House." He smiled with the sincere satisfaction of a Boy Scout helping an old lady across the street.

"You take this conspiracy theory stuff way too seriously," Unes said with a sigh. He pulled his legal pad into reach. "Look, with the weekend we just had, I've got a lot to do today. Let's get to why you're here."

"It's all connected," Gruner said. "Scott's missing and so's his computer."

Unes made a note on his legal pad. "Maybe Scott interrupted a robbery."

"Nothing else is missing."

"Car accident?"

"His van is outside his apartment. No new dents or scratches."

"And you haven't heard from him since when?"

"Sunday night."

"Anyone else hear from Scott?"

"No, not at all."

Another note. "Okay," Unes said. "Guys, why aren't you talking to the police? This sounds like a missing persons case."

Gruner looked directly into his eyes. "Like I said, we called them. The county cops say they don't know anything," he said. "They've got jurisdiction over the part of West County where he lives. We figured—well, I figured we needed to go to somebody we could trust at the federal level. And, uh, you're the only FBI agent we know." His friends nodded. "Besides, this is a whole lot bigger than just Scott."

Unes started to speak, but Gruner held up a hand. "Please, Agent Unes, hear me out. Vijay, give me that file."

The Indian produced a manila folder stuffed with pages from an ink jet printer. Gruner took it and rifled through it until he found what he wanted.

"Here." He handed several pages to Unes. "Take a look at this stuff from Iowa." The top page looked the printout of a Twitter feed, headlined with *PLEASE HELP MY DAD!*

As Unes scanned the pages, his frown gradually deepened into a scowl. *What in the world are these guys trying to get me into?*

The place was getting busy. Normally, Lieutenant Tony Harris would have been glad for something to do besides drill and weapons maintenance. He hadn't expected this.

Since the 369th arrived at the camp yesterday morning, over four hundred men, potential terrorists, had been deposited with the company for safekeeping. Harris wondered if the other camps Colonel Hostler mentioned were as big or as busy as this one. He hadn't been able to ask Poverello yet—the captain had been busy getting the men and women of the 369th settled and organized, establishing duty rosters, coordinating meals with cooks on loan from Scott Air Force Base, and making sure the new arrivals were processed in.

What bothered Harris was the fact that this camp, so new that it was still waiting for a name, had sprung out of Illinois farmland almost overnight, ready to hold a couple thousand prisoners. Had somebody expected this?

He'd been thinking about what Williams said, too. Strange that so many of the people dragged in were preachers. Not all of them, but more than you'd expect in a random sample of the population. A whole lot more than you'd expect to find hanging out with terrorists.

Captain P was still nowhere around. Harris checked his clipboard—nothing pressing for the rest of the morning. The rain had stopped last night and the sun was out, so he decided to take a walk. Harris and his men weren't supposed to question any of the prisoners; the FBI or somebody would be in later for that. But maybe some of the men behind the barbed wire felt like a friendly chat.

There was nothing like a good five-mile jog over hilly terrain to get the blood moving in the morning. Thiel sprinted the last hundred yards to the barracks at Fort Campbell, his temporary home. He planned a quick shower, breakfast at the mess, and then a phone call to Malthus for his team's next assignment.

They'd spent too long at that podunk town in Iowa, and Thiel still chafed at the interference from the county sheriff. He should have expected it. Everyone   in flyover farm towns knew everybody else, like sickly, inbred ants. He wouldn't make such a rookie tactical error again.

His team had returned from Iowa with the computers Malthus wanted, but they'd attracted more attention than they should have.

More than anything else, Thiel wanted another shot to prove that he deserved the confidence Malthus placed in him. He looked forward to getting his team back in the air.

Back inside the top-secret unit's barracks, long rows of sterile bunks greeted him in the gloomy lighting, looking for a moment like the ghosts of soldiers standing at review. Thiel paused, startled by the eerie vision. Everyone was out, either on assignment or tending to personal matters. He stood alone in the long, concrete and metal building.

A thin voice called to him from a distant past—*Lieutenant! They're all over us! Forgodssake—push the button!*

Thiel shivered, physically shaking off the memory. *Live the moment or die in time.* Thiel had no intention of dying. Not then, not now, not ever. Not if Malthus had the power he claimed.

Snap to, soldier!

Thiel jumped. A flash at the corner of his eye had engaged his reflexes. Thiel hit the wooden floor of the barracks as a round from an M4 whistled over his head.

"What the—"

"It's all going to hell, man! It's all going to hell!" The words cracked with emotion. *Real. This is real. Snap to!*

It took Thiel several seconds to identify the voice, because it was a voice he almost never heard charged with any emotion at all. Raymond Bako, his tech sergeant.

Thiel twisted around on the floor to locate the voice's owner. He spotted a pair of spit-shined boots underneath a row of bunks down at the far end of the barracks. The boots began to move slowly toward him. Early morning sunlight filtered through the cloud cover outside and glinted off something on the floor; something *wet.*

"Bako, what the hell are you doing?" Thiel demanded.

"That's right! That's right! It's hell! We're all going to hell!"

Thiel jumped as another shot ricocheted off the frame of the bunk next to Thiel.

"Armageddon is here! The battle to end the world! Hell on Earth has come!" Another blast as a 5.56 millimeter round dug a furrow in the floor two feet from Thiel's head. Splinters and microscopic metal fragments sprayed across his forehead, just missing his eyes.

The boots continued their slow progression. Step...step. Each beat in the ominous cadence brought death a yard closer to Captain Alan Thiel.

Think! Thiel cursed. No weapon. Bako's field of fire covered the space between Thiel and the closest open door. Bako would have a clear shot if he tried to get to it.

"What the hell's the matter with you, Bako? Put down that weapon—now!" Though his ears rang from the near miss, Thiel could hear the drumming of boots on the dirt outside, coming fast. Would they get here in time? Somebody was close to dead if things broke wrong.

"Hell *is* the matter!" Bako shouted hoarsely, close to tears. "It's the end of all things. War, war, Armageddon. It's happening! We're all dead! And we're—"

The second barracks door was yanked open from outside. Somebody, most likely an MP, yelled, "What the—"

The man's voice was cut off by a sharp burst from the M4. Bako had switched the gun to automatic. The roar of a dozen M9 and .45 Heckler & Koch pistols answered from outside: dozens of rounds, firing blind.

Thiel cursed again and started crawling under the bunks, making for Bako. He hoped the fire from outside would distract Bako long enough to let him get close.

Spidering under the bunks, Thiel kept his eyes on Bako's boots, the slow, deliberate march forward never slowing, never wavering. Step…step. Tech Sergeant Raymond Bako advanced steadily forward, firing short bursts from his carbine at the MPs outside the barracks door.

"Armageddon!" he wailed, his voice cracking. "The end of all things!"

Thiel edged closer, closer, desperately hoping Bako hadn't noticed that he'd moved. He pulled himself along the floor, gauging the distance and calculating where best to emerge from underneath a bunk—hopefully just *behind* Bako.

Except that Bako took a step back when he should have stepped forward.

Suddenly exposed, half under the bunk and unable to stand, Captain Thiel looked up at the square, sharply angled face of a man he'd worked and trained with for nearly three years. Bako's dark eyes were fixed on his, but Thiel could see no trace of the man he knew behind them.

Sweat ran down the sergeant's face, and spatters of blood stained his white T-shirt.

"Bako—"

"That's right, Cap," Bako said in a quiet voice. "Time to get baptized."

Bako pointed the M4 at his captain's face. Thiel lay on the cold concrete, frozen in place, his eyes locked on the black steel of the carbine's muzzle.

The M4 jerked and flashed. Thunder roared and lightning lit up the floor. Heat flared for an instant across Thiel's scalp, just above his left ear.

And then—in horrific slow motion, like a grisly action movie scene—blood sprayed the bunks a bright red as Tech Sergeant Raymond Bako buckled and collapsed to the barracks floor.

TWENTY-ONE

"I really ought to know better," Joe Unes muttered to himself. He'd debated whether to follow up the so-called leads the Three Stooges had dropped into his lap. After twenty minutes of reading stories pulled from various news sites on the web, posts to social media, and the semi-literate ravings of a few conspiracy nuts, Unes decided to call the sheriff in Iowa, or whoever was covering for him, assuming the web story was true.

"Chief Deputy Jurasik."

Unes paused. He hadn't expected a woman. "Yes, Deputy, this is Special Agent Joe Unes at the FBI field office in Saint Louis. Do you have a minute?"

"Only just, Agent." Jurasik said. "Things are a little hectic around here."

Unes could hear noises in the background. It sounded like the office there was crowded.

"I'll be brief," he said, wondering where to start. He still had no idea how to explain any possible connection between the disappearance of Scott Stauffer and the three men in Mayfield. Worse, he had no way to justify spending time on this to SAC Clay. He was supposed to be working on links between the bombing at Grandy's and the other terror attacks Friday night.

"We have a case here that involves a possible kidnapping," Unes began. "There's a slight chance the man who's gone missing was actually taken into custody by a federal agency. I understand you had an incident there over the weekend."

"Which one, Agent?" Jurasik sounded wary. "We had several incidents, as you call it."

Several? Unes cleared his throat. "Is there any reason federal marshals would be interested in Sheriff Thornton?"

A pause. On the other end, Jurasik double-checked the caller ID on her desk phone. "How do you know they were marshals, sir? What was your name again?"

"Well, I assumed—I mean. Sorry, Deputy. The name again is Unes. U-n-e-s. Are you saying the men were *not* marshals?"

"The descriptions I got sounded like an FBI hostage rescue team," Jurasik said. "Maybe you can tell me why they were here."

"I don't think—"

"Look, Agent Unes. I don't have any more information than you do. All I know is what the witnesses told me: Men in black with automatic weapons busted into a church service and hauled out three men who are well respected around here. One's the church's pastor, one's an elder, and the third is my boss, Sheriff Thornton. Not only that, these same men interfered with an official investigation of a murder-suicide by removing evidence from the scene. Claimed Homeland Security authorized it. So, if I'm less than—"

"Wait a minute," Unes interrupted, shuffling through the papers on his desk. "Interfered with a crime scene? The, uh, hold on—the Belcher case?"

"Yes. The Belcher case. You're aware of that much, at least." Jurasik said. "Your team told us to forget they were there."

"*My* team? I assure you, the men did not represent the Bureau. But—wait—didn't the Belcher murders happen Friday night?"

"Yes, they did. Is that relevant?"

"And you were there Friday night?"

Another pause. "I was. I hope you're going somewhere with this." Jurasik's voice had taken on a very unpleasant edge.

"Bear with me, Deputy, please," Unes said as politely as he could muster. "This team remained in or around Mayfield until Sunday morning?"

"Yes," Jurasik said tightly. "The lead man told the sheriff they were after Bob Moore, one of the three they arrested at the church. Which reminds me," Jurasik continued, as the background noise grew louder. "Ssh! Please, Mister Atkins, I'll be with you in just a minute. *Please!* I am on the phone with the FBI."

"FBI?" a man's voice echoed in the background. "Hear that? I knew it! It's the goldanged FBI! Told ya!"

"Sorry," Jurasik said. "It's a zoo here. I don't know if it's relevant, but somebody stole a computer from the Moores' house sometime between Friday night and Sunday afternoon. We think it was the Hostage Rescue Team."

"Deputy, are you sure it was an HRT? Wait—oh, wait a minute. What did you say about a computer?" Something tickled at the back of Unes' mind.

Jurasik sighed and repeated herself. "A computer was stolen from the Moore home over the weekend."

"And Moore was the guy the team was after."

"Affirmative."

"Was anything missing besides the computer? Or just the computer?"

"Just the computer!" Jurasik yelled over the rising sea of voices in her front office.

Unes blinked, pulling the phone away from his head for a moment.

"Sorry!" he heard her say as he returned the handset to his right ear. "Sorry," she repeated, this time quieter. "I shut my office door. I only have a minute, Agent Unes."

"Understood," Joe said. "What evidence, if any, did this team remove from the Belcher home?"

"A…a computer."

"Hold on." Unes dug through the stack of manila folders until he found the file on Conrad Reston. He opened it and quickly scanned the reports filed by the investigators who'd checked into Reston's background—family, work, hobbies—and searched his apartment. After a few seconds, Unes found what he was looking for.

"Deputy, I see you had a couple of other incidents yesterday," Unes said. "Were any computers missing from those homes? Have you looked?"

A pause. "What are you thinking?"

"A computer was taken from the apartment of the guy down here who's missing. Nothing else."

Seconds passed. Unes could almost hear the light bulb pop on over Jurasik's head. "Gotcha. I see where you're heading with this," the deputy said at last. "Give me a sec."

"And the guy who blew himself up here Friday night," Unes said as Jurasik searched her files. "When our man searched his home, there was an empty spot on the computer desk."

After a moment, Jurasik returned, "Okay, see how this fits: The boy at the Moore home received an unusual email Friday that he said he passed on to three friends. Each one of these three friends' homes became the site of a violent incident over the weekend."

Unes did some quick math. "Deputy, I can be in Mayfield by—" He checked his watch. "Four-thirty this afternoon. Can I meet with you and compare notes? Maybe see if we can find a couple of computers?"

Jurasik sighed. Unes could almost hear her thoughts: *As if my day isn't long enough.* "Okay. Four-thirty."

"Five at the latest, if I don't stop for lunch. Where is your office?"

Several minutes later, Unes had directions to Mayfield, and from there to the Kiowa County administration building. He straightened his desk, ordered the notes in the file from Jared Gruner, and was just getting ready to tell SAC Clay about his plan for the day when he heard Clay's voice behind him.

"Joe, who were those guys you talked to this morning?"

Unes swung his chair around to face Clay, grunting at the stiffness in his lower back. "Witnesses to the bombing at Grandy's. Just having them in for a chat."

Clay nodded. "They showed you some papers."

"Yeah," Unes said. *I knew I should have closed the blinds.* "Conspiracy theorists. They thought they had some ideas for me."

"Did they?"

"Nah, nothing relevant. They blame the government."

"Mph." Clay nodded, apparently thinking about something else. "Like my brother-in-law. He blames the government for his migraines. So, what's next?"

"I've got a lead," Unes said, "But I have to take a road trip."

"Where to? There are no flights out of Lambert for at least another day or two."

"I can drive. A little town in southeast Iowa called Mayfield."

Clay raised an eyebrow. "Iowa?"

"There's a connection to a group there that was pulled in by Homeland Security over the weekend."

"Can't somebody in the Des Moines office run down there?"

Unes stood and picked his jacket off his chair—and made a quick gut decision to lie. "No. Nobody's available and this is time sensitive. It's five or six hours up there. I'll get a cheap motel tonight and be back by lunch tomorrow."

"That hot, eh?"

"Maybe. If I don't check it out, I'll never know."

"You want somebody with you?"

Pulling on his jacket, Unes said, "No, I'm good. I'm meeting with the sheriff's department there this afternoon."

Clay nodded. "All right. Call me when you get there."

"Wilmer."

"Sam. Harold Benson." The congressman's blood pounded in his ears, only partly from his morning walk. He'd stormed past the security team with an expression they hadn't seen since the last time the White House ignored one of his committee's subpoenas.

"Hey, big dog, what's new on the Hill?" Wilmer asked cheerily.

Benson had no time for pleasantries. "Sam, I really need to know what's going on."

"What do you mean, Hal?"

Benson took a deep breath before answering. "I was accosted on my way to the office this morning by two very large men who made it quite clear that I should stop asking questions about what happened back home."

"Accosted? You all right?"

"Yeah, but I'm about to punch out some lights—I just have to learn whose porch they're on first."

"Ever the diplomat," Wilmer said. "I reckon you're all right at that. So, you don't know who these men represent, I take it."

"I do not, not yet," Benson said. "They carried themselves like military. Intelligence, maybe."

It was a moment before Wilmer responded. "Hal, I wish I could help, but I can't imagine who would dare such a thing. Maybe it was a misunderstanding. Are we still on for lunch, or is that out?"

"I don't know about today, Sam, I—"

"That's a shame, Hal. I wanted to show you my new fishing lure. It's a beauty."

A light bulb went on for Benson. Wilmer was a hunter, but you couldn't pay enough to get him out on a boat. *Hell's bells. My line is being monitored.*

"Sure, you bet. Can't wait to see it," Benson said at last. "I could use some fresh air after this morning, anyway. How about the place we went after I was made chair of the committee?"

"Sounds fine. How's twelve-thirty?"

"Perfect."

The gunfire still echoed in his ears. Captain Alan Thiel finished reading a typed transcript of his statement, signed it, and handed it back to the MP sitting across the desk. It was late morning and Thiel still hadn't eaten breakfast, but he wasn't hungry anymore. He wanted a shower before calling his team together. They needed to talk over what happened, find out if anyone had seen this coming.

He rubbed his eyes and asked the MP, "Am I done?"

"Yes, sir. Hell of a way to lose a man, isn't it, sir?"

The young MP across from Thiel couldn't have been much more than legal drinking age. Big kid, probably good in a fight. Good reflexes, too; he and the other MPs saved Thiel's life that morning. The kid's shot was golden, especially firing on the move the way he had.

But doubt lurked in the shadows just behind the young man's eyes, and the meaning was plain: today was the first time he'd used his sidearm on another man.

"Thank you, Sergeant," Thiel said. "If you'd missed that shot, there'd be more than two dead in the barracks. I'd be one of them."

Following the gun battle, the MPs discovered that the wet spot on the floor was from another victim of Bako's deadly madness—a comm sergeant from another unit whose throat Bako had slit his throat from behind minutes before Thiel entered the building.

"Yes, sir. Thank you, Captain Thiel, sir." The MP went back to assembling the paperwork needed to explain the death of Sergeant Raymond Bako. "I guess you're right, sir."

The captain slowly made his way out of the building and once again pointed himself toward the barracks. He really needed that shower.

Halfway there, the satellite phone in his pocket beeped. Only one man had the number. He answered before the third ring.

"Thiel."

"We have unfinished business in Iowa." Malthus' voice was dry and emotionless as usual. He might have been reading updates of corn futures.

"What business is that, sir?"

"There have been two more incidents. We need you to retrieve the computers."

The captain stopped in his tracks, in the middle of an open area between the rows of barracks, like a village square.

"More computers? Sir, what do the computers have to do with this?" Thiel asked.

"You need only retrieve them," Malthus said. "Don't concern yourself with anything else."

"It'll take a day at least before we can leave. We have to replace a team member."

"Oh?"

"Bako," Thiel said. "Tech sergeant. He snapped or something. Tried to kill me a couple of hours ago. One of the MPs had to shoot him. Dead."

"I see. You'll have to make do," Malthus said. "Leave today. Get in and out tonight. Your transport has been arranged and will be ready at sixteen hundred. Is that understood?"

"Yes, sir. Completely."

"And captain?"

"Yes, sir?"

"Avoid contact with the locals this time."

Thiel gritted his teeth. "Yes, sir. We'll complete the mission without local interaction." The phone clicked and Malthus was gone.

"Come on!" Gruner slammed his hand onto his computer desk in frustration.

"Is something wrong, Jared?" Vijay Sampurnananda appeared over his shoulder, squinting at the computer screen.

"Ah, the ISP is slow," Gruner huffed. He stood and stretched.

After leaving the FBI offices that morning, Vijay and Terry Norlock had come back to Gruner's house, their base of operations for finding Scott Stauffer. It was nominally bigger than Stauffer's apartment, but Gruner's habit of leaving laundry, electronics, and discarded pizza boxes strewn across every horizontal surface created a less desirable ambiance, so their Underground Kingdom games were usually held elsewhere.

But Gruner had the best Internet connection besides Stauffer, so Norlock and Vijay had agreed to put up with the debris piled in the corners of the living room. But soon after they got back to the house, the web connection started acting strange: sites that normally loaded in a few seconds now took minutes, if they rendered at all. Gruner was sick of the little spinning disc marking time on his screen.

Vijay watched the glowing, multicolored disc intently, stroking his chin as he thought. "Did you—"

"Yes, I tried everything," Gruner interrupted. "Cleared the cache, restarted the browser, restarted the system, reset the cable modem. Parted my hair on the opposite side—even stood on one leg and clucked like a chicken! Nothing. The problem's not here."

"Funny," Norlock said, emerging from the kitchen with a can of Blast Cola. "You think maybe it's a DDoS?"

"Possible," Gruner said.

"But unlikely," Vijay said. "A denial of service attack of this magnitude would surely be noticed. I believe we would have heard of it."

"Yeah, you're probably right," Norlock said. "Virus?"

"Nope."

Norlock took a long pull on his soda while he thought, and then he nodded. "I don't like this."

Vijay sat down at the computer and began tapping away at the keys. "Jared," he said, "Do you think maybe this is not a coincidence?"

Gruner exchanged a look with Norlock. "You're coming along," he said. "We'll have you thinking right yet."

"What do you mean?" Vijay asked.

"Okay," Gruner said. "Think about this: What if the government, or some element inside the government, is responsible for all the stuff that happened? Would they benefit from tying up the Internet?"

Norlock said, "You think?"

"Doesn't the timing seem really convenient?"

"How?" Vijay asked.

"Look, the Internet is like the ham radio of the twenty-first century," Gruner said as he plunked his bulky frame into the overstuffed couch in front of the living room window. "If the deep state decides that the news getting out isn't what they want us to know, they start pulling plugs."

"Okay," Norlock said. "But how would they do that?"

"Not too hard," Gruner said. "They just shut down the routers carrying traffic to sites they want to block. A guy in Milwaukee figured out a way to do it years ago. He found a flaw in the TCP. Threw everybody into a panic. Homeland Security even issued a warning. Don't think for a minute they didn't keep a back door open for themselves."

Vijay turned from the computer screen. "Jared may be right."

Gruner pointed at Norlock. "Ha! See?"

"It is the most probable explanation for this curious delay in opening websites," Vijay agreed. "Do not forget, Terry, that the Internet was originally a project of the United States military. ARPAnet, named for the Advanced Research Projects Agency, which—"

"Which became DARPA, the *Defense* Advanced Research Projects Agency," Gruner finished.

"Yes. Well," Vijay continued, annoyed, "only later was ARPAnet made available to major universities for research, and then finally opened up to the public."

"Yeah, yeah, we all know that," Norlock said. "Okay, so they probably know where all the connections are. I guess all they really need is a targeted DoS anyway, not one that takes down the whole web. Hit the news and social media sites that are spreading information they want kept under wraps."

"Or the ISPs serving a lot of troublemakers," Gruner said.

Norlock raised his eyebrows. "Say you're right. What now?"

"We need to find Stofe," Gruner said.

"Duh," Norlock said. "Where?"

"Okay, where would the feds take large groups of prisoners in wartime?"

"We are not technically at war," Vijay said.

"Threat Level Red? Come on," Gruner said. "Two dozen terror attacks? The whole Middle East ready to swap weapons of mass destruction? And then there are those so-called anti-fascists getting ready to protest again. No mistake—we're at war."

"FEMA camps," Norlock said. "Remember those? Maybe they've been activated."

"Wait," Vijay said. "I found something earlier that may be of interest."

He got up from Gruner's computer desk and retrieved his laptop from the dining room table. Taking a seat next to Gruner on the couch, he tapped a few keys and opened a document file. "This is a map based on a list of possible sites to be used by the government as internment camps in the event of a crisis. I paid little attention because it seemed unlikely that the government would actually use such things. But perhaps—"

"Crush my cans!" Gruner shouted. "REX Eighty-Four! Now is when they'd finally need them. Let's see." He took the laptop from Vijay and scrolled down the page. "Hello…?"

"What have you got?" Norlock left the table and leaned over the side of the couch to look in over Gruner's shoulder.

"Okay, gentlemen, let's see," Gruner said. "We have two choices that are pretty close: Fort Leonard Wood or Scott Air Force Base. Pick one."

"What about the air base near Kansas City?" Vijay asked, pointing to the list on the screen. "That is also a possible site."

"Too far for us to check out," Gruner admitted. "I mean, we can at least hit the closer sites and rule them out. See if they're in use. You know, as a favor to Agent Unes."

"Favor," Norlock said. "To the FBI?"

Gruner speared him with a look. "You got a better idea?"

Norlock shrugged. "Guess not."

Cindy Moore couldn't believe her ears. The President of the United States was on television telling the whole world that her husband was a terrorist.

She'd turned on the old analog set in their upstairs sitting room to drown out the thoughts in her head and found the President about to address the nation.

Forty-seven-year-old Adam Bell had aged considerably since taking office nearly three years earlier—streaks of prematurely gray hair salted his temples and lines had appeared at the corners of his eyes. Dealing with an unsteady economy, a potential bird flu pandemic, and the threat of an imminent Middle East war had robbed the handsome, dark-haired politician of some of the luster that made him a natural for campaigning in the video age. Now, as he gazed into the cameras of the oval office, the expression on his face was grave, reflecting the content of his speech and the mood of the nation.

"Good evening. Forces bent on destroying the freedoms we enjoy have struck at the very heart of our nation. As you know, since Friday evening, some four thousand American men, women, and children have been killed in violent acts of terrorism. I say to you now, these cowardly attacks will not go unpunished.

"Every resource at our disposal has been brought to bear in the few short hours since the first attack. A task force, combining resources from the FBI, our intelligence agencies, and local law enforcement, under the coordination of the Department of

Homeland Security, is even now assembling a picture of the enemy we face.

"It is an enemy we have confronted before. We have seen their handiwork in the death and destruction caused by bombs placed at abortion clinics, and in the carnage of violent attacks across our nation over the last thirty years. This is an enemy that seeks to bring about what they call 'the end of all things'—the apocalypse written of in the Book of Revelation.

"I am not speaking of all Christians—let me make that perfectly clear. This is a splinter group, a cult, a loosely organized collection of cells consisting of pseudo-religious zealots who call themselves the Maranatha Militia. This group has carried on a low-level campaign of terror against innocent Americans for years. They use God's name as a weapon, and it is their hope to advance not just a twisted religious agenda, but to bring down the government of the United States. Their acts of terrorism are intended to force a swift and terrible governmental response, a response that would trigger the final confrontation between good and evil—Armageddon.

"It is not a coincidence that this group, the Maranatha Militia, chose this time to implement their plan. The spread of avian influenza and the outbreak of war in the Middle East are considered triggering events in their twisted interpretation of the Bible. They see these events as the work of the Four Horsemen of the Apocalypse, and they believe they can somehow usher in the End of Days through their cowardly acts. Rather than peace, this group seeks war. The United States cannot—we will not—tolerate such a cancer.

"My fellow Americans, I understand your concern at the events taking place in the Middle East. It is a delicate and dangerous situation, and we are fully engaged with our partners and allies to bring the conflict between Syria and Israel to a quick and peaceful end. Tonight, I can report to you that I have had conversations today with the Prime Minister of Great Britain, the President of Russia, the Secretary General of the United Nations, and the leaders of Israel, Jordan, Iraq, Egypt, and Palestine. All parties are willing to talk, to listen, and to resolve the very difficult

obstacles to peace. And the United States, as the leader of the free world, stands ready to offer every assistance to the peace process.

"Meanwhile, here at home, rest assured that the Department of Homeland Security, using the various branches of law enforcement at its command, is quickly identifying and apprehending the suspected members of the Maranatha Militia, wherever they hide, for their roles in this planned Armageddon. Let me be perfectly clear: We will never submit to terrorists, we will—"

Cindy shut off the TV. This made no sense. Maranatha Militia? What was that? Why had she never heard of it? Were there really people that evil in the world?

The ringing of her phone broke Cindy's concentration. She reached over and picked it up from the nightstand.

"Hello?"

"Cynthia Moore?" It was a man with a deep, raspy voice, with perfect diction and a vaguely European accent.

"Yes?"

"It would be wise to keep matters concerning your husband to yourself."

"What? Who is this? How did you get this number?"

"That does not matter. What should matter is the safety of your son. Eric, I believe?"

Cindy felt as though she'd been punched in the stomach. Her mouth went dry and her voice came out in a dry croak. "What do you mean?"

"Simply this. Talk to the media, post to the Internet, or even discuss with your friends what happened in Mayfield this weekend, and I will hear of it. Should that happen, Eric will disappear on his way home from school one day. And you will never see him again."

TWENTY-TWO

Something smelled wrong about the mission. Thiel didn't know what yet, but he was going to find out. A nagging feeling in his gut told him he was being used. He didn't like it.

What made Bako snap? He was always cool, a guy who did his job without breaking a sweat under any circumstances. There was no trace of that man in the tormented eyes of his would-be killer this morning.

There wasn't much time. The Night Rangers would be ready to go in a few hours. Thiel wanted at least a couple of answers before they took off. There might just be time to trace Bako's last hours before flying back to Iowa.

The barracks were quiet, eerie after the frenzied moments of gunfire, splintered wood, and blood just a few hours ago. The entire area had been cordoned off until investigators could verify what Thiel and others had witnessed. The air was still heavy with cordite and the dark stink of blood.

Bako's personal possessions were untouched under the bunk he'd been assigned for their stay at Fort Campbell. There'd be an official investigation, but Thiel wanted his own answers. He had a strong hunch that when he and his team returned to Iowa, retrieving sensitive items for Malthus, another team would be here sifting through the remnants of Raymond Bako's life.

There wasn't much to go on. Thiel scanned the contents of Bako's duffel: typical soldier's gear, and only the bare essentials at that. It paid to travel light, especially when you move quickly and often.

One item stood out. A small Bible was tucked into the bag. Bako never mentioned a belief in God. If Thiel remembered right, Bako was more of a Buddhist than anything.

Thiel removed the small, soft cover book. It appeared almost new. He opened it and looked inside the cover. No wonder—it was from the base chapel.

He was about to drop it back into the bag when Thiel noticed a couple of pages dog-eared near the back. Frowning, he opened the Bible to the first marked page. It was the sixth chapter of Revelation.

Thiel was familiar with it. Everyone in Special Forces was. The Night Stalkers, the crazy SOBs who flew the helicopters that carried Thiel's men into action, used part of verse eight as a motto: *And I looked, and behold a pale horse: and his name that sat on him was Death, and Hell followed with him.*

But that wasn't what Bako had marked.

Further down a page as thin as tissue paper, he'd underlined verses fifteen and following:

> *And the kings of the earth, and the great men, and the rich men, and the chief captains, and the mighty men, and every bondman, and every free man, hid themselves in the dens and in the rocks of the mountains; and said to the mountains and rocks, Fall on us, and hide us from the face of him that sitteth on the throne, and from the wrath of the Lamb: For the great day of his wrath is come; and who shall be able to stand?*

Thiel stared at the verses for several minutes. Why these? Did they mean anything? Underneath his cool exterior, maybe Bako had been spooked about the fighting in Israel, Syria, and Lebanon. It was possible. There were more than enough Bible thumpers in southwest Kentucky who read prophecy into every headline. Maybe Bako caught some of that and let it get to him.

He shook his head. Thiel was no psychologist, but that theory had no legs.

The captain closed the Bible returned it to its place. He decided to check out the computers they'd brought back from Iowa. Computers seemed to be at the heart of this.

As he turned, he noticed that the pillow on Bako's bunk seemed to be oddly shaped. Sitting funny, too, like it was heavier than it looked. Thiel reached and touched it, gently.

Hard. Not a pillow.

Slowly, he pulled back the pillowcase. Hidden under a thin, Army-issue pillow, Thiel saw rectangular blocks wrapped in olive-colored plastic, about one inch by two inches by ten inches. Neatly stacked, six across and two high. Bako was always one for order.

"Holy hell," Thiel muttered.

C4. Plastic explosive, about two-dozen blocks. Thirty pounds. Enough to make a very big bang.

Thiel searched gingerly but thoroughly, making sure there wasn't a detonator attached somewhere. By itself, C4 is stable. It takes a small explosion from an ignition fuse or a blasting cap to set it off.

Thirty pounds of C4 could do some damage. If it were used to ignite something else, like gasoline or jet fuel, it would do *serious* damage.

Thiel quickly opened Bako's duffel again. Nothing out of the ordinary. Then he got down on the floor, uneasily remembering his close escape while in this position earlier.

Sure enough, under Bako's bunk, duct-taped to the underside of the bed frame, were a couple of detonating fuses.

You were on your way to making a hell of a bomb. But why?

Thiel decided he really needed to see those computers.

Congressman Benson was on time, as always, waiting at the small cafeteria in Georgetown where he and Sam Wilmer met when they wanted to talk without prying ears listening in. The Red, White, and Blue Café was a throwback to the white tile and stainless steel diners of the fifties, and every now and then Benson needed a jolt of grease from their one-third-pound Betsy Burger and the restaurant's signature, thin-sliced Paul Revere fries.

Twelve-forty, and Wilmer hadn't arrived. Benson checked his watch, although he knew clocking Sam wouldn't bring him any faster. The congressman had a busy afternoon, and he didn't have time to spare. This was one of the few times in recent years when Benson almost wished he'd let himself get caught up in the wave of modern technology.

Harold Benson was a throwback to the previous century. He refused to carry a mobile phone. The hateful things had overrun the world. You couldn't move in public without running into people who were too busy talking or texting to watch where they were going, as if the very fabric of the universe would rend in two if a message had to wait an hour or two before you picked it up. He figured that was why you never reached a live body when you called an office anymore.

Twelve-fifty. Benson decided Wilmer must have run into a snag. Benson signaled a waitress and ordered a chocolate milk shake to go. On his way out, he tipped her five dollars and asked her to keep an eye out for Sam Wilmer in case he finally showed up.

Back to the office. Benson had a full plate for the afternoon. Talk was circulating on the Hill about a possible request from the White House for authority to send another ten thousand troops to the Middle East, possibly to secure Lebanon. As if the Pentagon wasn't busy enough already in Afghanistan and Iraq, where the Marines were just holding their own because of the flare-up over the Army's expedition into Iran.

If the surge rumors proved true, there would be a street brawl in the House. Some of the members across the aisle had sworn they'd pull out every trick in the book to block any attempt by Bell to expand the power of the presidency any further. Of course, that was for the voters—they just wanted to get their own hands on that power.

Benson stepped out of the diner and back into the warm D.C. afternoon, thinking of the political dog and pony show that lay ahead. Maybe he could short-circuit some of the nonsense with a few quiet hallway conversations. Before he made it halfway to his car at the end of the block, working on a mental list of colleagues to search out at the Capitol, something heavy met the back of his head.

For a moment, Benson stopped dead, suspended in space and time. Then he pitched forward, drifting down into a long black tunnel with a brightly lit exit that kept moving farther away. Suddenly it blinked out, and he remembered nothing more.

Mayfield, Iowa, was far, far away. That's how it felt, anyway. Bob Moore had begun to wonder when he'd see Cindy and E.J. again. The sun was setting on what had been an overcast day, and the damp, gray chill of the early evening matched the emptiness in Bob's heart. The scent of a wood fire somewhere reached him and brought with it another pang of homesickness.

On a night like this, he and Cindy would have a fire going in the fire pit out on the patio, a welcome connection to a simpler age long past. A time without modern conveniences, sure, but a time when the government was there mostly to protect you from other governments, not to break into your home to drag you off God knows where.

Or was that just an illusion carried forward from a more naive time? Had the good old days ever been that good?

Pastor Schiebold said to "count it all joy," a reference to James' advice to endure trials patiently. Easier said than done.

How long, O Lord?

A voice to his right snapped Bob from his thoughts as he gazed through the double row of chain-link at the empty fields beyond.

"Not much of a game, is it?"

"Huh?" Bob turned to see a uniformed man outside the fences, one of the military police guarding the compound. It was athletic lieutenant who greeted them when they arrived. Harris, Bob remembered.

"Sorry," the soldier said. "Bad joke. You been staring at that empty field for a while. Most guys I know only pay that much attention to football."

"Oh," Bob said. "No. I was thinking about my family."

Lieutenant Harris nodded. The two of them were the only ones at the far end of the compound, away from the main body of the camp. Another C-21 whined overhead, getting into position for its approach. A small group of new arrivals clustered together just outside the nearest barracks, agitated, talking non-stop, trying to get a handle on their situation. Bob had wandered out to the fence because it was quieter.

The soldier cleared his throat and tried to restart the conversation. "Where you from?"

"Mayfield," Bob said. "A little town in east central Iowa."

"Sounds nice. I'm from Baltimore. Live in Chicago now. Name's Harris, Lieutenant Tony Harris."

"Hi," Bob said, without enthusiasm. "Bob Moore."

"Are you being treated okay, Bob? Is there anything you need?"

"Yeah," Bob said. "A phone would be nice. Unless you or one of the other guards called my wife, she doesn't know where I am."

"I'll see what I can do about that," Harris said. "I think security's still pretty tight on this place, though."

"Why is it so tight?"

"What do you mean?"

"I mean, what do you think we'll do? Why are we here, really?" Bob turned to face Lieutenant Harris. Although he was normally even-tempered to the point of blandness, his gut churned and he felt his face grow warm.

"You really don't know? I thought you guys were charged before you got here," Harris said, frowning. "That's why we—"

"Nope," Bob said forcefully. "No charges. Nothing. Some crap about being involved in the murder of a family in our church, which I could not possibly have done. Any rookie police officer could take a look at the evidence and clear this all up, but nobody will talk to us. Meanwhile, my wife and son are sitting at home worrying, and I don't think they even know where I am!"

"We were told you were here as a suspected terrorist."

Bob's eyes nearly popped. "Terrorist? *Terrorist?* I can't believe this! This is a bad dream! On what grounds?"

Harris shook his head. "I don't know."

Bob took a deep breath and tried to calm himself. This lieutenant wasn't being confrontational. He was just doing his job.

"Okay," Bob said. "I'm sorry. This will all get straightened out. I just wish somebody would at least talk to us and let us know what's happening."

The lieutenant seemed to be studying him, evaluating him. Bob didn't care. He resumed looking at the trees in the distance.

"How old is your boy?"

"Hmm—what?"

"How old is your son?" Harris repeated. "Me, I've got an eight-year-old. Name's Demetrius. Gonna grow up to be a football player someday."

Bob turned back to the lieutenant, his face softer. "Eric is ten. He'll probably be a—well, I don't know what he'll be. Not football, probably."

"Why not?"

"He's like me. He doesn't like getting hit." Bob smiled ruefully, and Lieutenant Harris laughed.

"I didn't either, but I ran fast," Harris said, "so I wouldn't get hit."

"You played in college?" Bob asked.

"Towson, just outside Baltimore," Harris said. "Four-year starter. Thought I'd be an All-Pro in the NFL, but I found out there are lots of fast guys in the pros. Played a few years with the Bears. Special teams, mostly."

"Wait," Bob said. "Tony Harris?"

"Yeah, that's right," Harris said, smiling. "You a Bears fan?"

"Since I was a kid," Bob said. "Unfortunately, I was too young to remember the Ditka years. I came of age when Harbaugh was the quarterback."

Harris laughed. "You are a true fan if you stuck with the team since then."

"I always thought they should have given you more of a shot," Bob said.

"Well, thanks. But like I said, there are a lot of fast guys in the NFL. I was just one more."

"So," Bob said, "If you don't mind my asking, how did you wind up here?"

"Tore up my knee. Found out I wasn't ready for life after football. Finally got my degree in Phys Ed, went into teaching, and joined the National Guard for some discipline. They called us up a few days ago, no warning, and here I am."

Bob smiled. "Small world. Well, that makes this a little easier to handle. Being guarded by a former Bear." He looked out at the trees again. "That has to be tough, getting called up without notice, leaving your family and all."

Harris sighed. "Demetrius lives with his momma. I'm not exactly her favorite person."

"I'm sorry."

"Me, too," Harris said. "It was my fault. And she makes sure I know it."

"How often do you see him?" Bob asked.

"One weekend a month. She's got custody. I wasn't ready to be a father eight years ago. I'm trying to get the visitation schedule changed, but she's fighting me." Harris shook his head. "A boy needs his daddy. I was too busy feeling sorry for myself. So now my boy's growing up without me."

The pain in the lieutenant's voice echoed the ache in Bob's heart, and he'd only been separated from E.J. and Cindy for two and a half days. "I think I know how you feel," Bob said.

"Well," Harris said. "I didn't mean to burden you. You got enough to worry about. Let me know if there's anything you need, and I'll see what I can do."

Bob thought for a moment, and then said, "How about some Bibles?"

Harris cocked his head. "Bibles?"

"Yeah. We don't have anything else to do. Bible study would at least be constructive. That would probably help morale, too."

Harris nodded. "Okay, Bibles. I'll see if I can't round up a few."

"Thank you," Bob said. He watched the guardsman as he walked back to the main gate and wondered if his brief meeting with Lieutenant Harris was really as random as it seemed. *Lord, You brought us together out here for a reason. I just wish You'd let me in on the plan.*

"Computers? The ones your team brought in?"

Captain Thiel waited impatiently while his simple request percolated through the brain of the squat sergeant parked at the desk in front of him. "Sorry, Captain," the sergeant said. "No can do."

"Excuse me, Sergeant? Would you care to rephrase that?" Thiel's tone made it clear he wasn't in a friendly mood.

"Just what I said, sir," the sergeant said, stiffly. "Sergeant Bako was here before he—uh, well, before he lost it. He was looking at 'em in back. I heard something break, like he dropped something, but then I heard it again and again. I went back to see what was going on, and the sergeant's smashing all of the computers with a fire extinguisher. I tried to stop him, but he just threw the extinguisher at me and ran out the back. Sir."

Thiel mentally digested the information. "Show me."

The sergeant pried himself out of the undersized office chair and led Thiel back into a large storage area. The room was filled with rows of metal shelving that reached to the ceiling. Buzzing fluorescent shop lights suspended between the shelves cast a blue white light without warmth.

"Right here, sir," the sergeant said. "I haven't cleaned it up yet because I didn't know if the MPs wanted a look at it first."

Thiel pursed his lips in distaste. Maybe, or maybe the sergeant didn't want to put in the effort to clean up unless he was specifically ordered.

Shards of plastic, metal, and glass lay scattered over a six-foot diameter at the end of a row of shelves. Whatever had been stored on the computers might be lost forever. The cases were thoroughly smashed. The hard drives were probably toast.

What now? What could have been in the computers that Malthus wanted?

Or wanted destroyed, Thiel thought suddenly.

"Sir?" The sergeant interrupted his thoughts, a nervous set to the NCO's eyes.

"Yes, Sergeant?"

"Whaddya want done with these others?"

"Others?" Thiel looked in amazement as the sergeant pointed to a row of shelving units, stacked end to end with computer equipment—desktops, towers, notebooks, all makes and models. There were at least two, maybe three dozen. Someone had been busy while Thiel was in Iowa. *Just how many teams does Malthus have out there?*

"Secure them behind locked cabinets for now. My eyes only, you got that?" Thiel said. "When I get new orders from upstream, you'll be the first to know."

Thiel had a new plan: get the machines out of those houses in Mayfield, just as Malthus ordered, only this time, Thiel would inspect the computers himself.

If only Harold Benson carried a phone. Sam Wilmer cursed under his breath. A cab had slammed into the left rear quarter panel of Wilmer's government issue Chevy Impala almost as soon as he'd pulled out of the Pentagon's ZIP-code-sized parking lot.

It was a clear day, no rain to slick up the streets, and Wilmer hadn't stopped, turned, or changed lanes suddenly. It was like the cabbie hadn't been paying attention to the road at all.

So much for meeting Benson on time. Since Wilmer didn't have the restaurant's phone number, and Benson was too stubborn to move past the 1980s when it came to electronics, there was no way to let the congressman know he'd be late.

Wilmer unlocked his door to begin the process of exchanging information with the cab driver.

Before Wilmer could set both feet on the asphalt, the driver was beside his car.

"Well, now—" Wilmer began in his Texas drawl—and then he noticed that the driver wore latex gloves.

He didn't see the hypodermic in the driver's right hand until it was too late to get out of the way.

The drive from Saint Louis had been uneventful. Dull, actually. Miles of farmland, stretching as far as the eye could see, occasionally broken by a farmhouse, a barn, or a clump of trees.

If Joe Unes' mind hadn't been wrestling with a problem, the five-hour drive might have lulled him to sleep. Distracted as he was, he stayed awake for the entire trip, but he noticed very little of the scenery.

The playlist of Bobby Darin's greatest hits on his phone had just started to play through for the eighth time when he reached the outskirts of Mayfield, Iowa. *Population: 1,035* announced the white-on-green sign at the edge of the property owned by G & R Small Engine Repair.

Unes followed the directions Deputy Jurasik had given him: North on Iowa Route 3 through to the other side of town, a journey of about two minutes. It would have been faster except for the town square, a two-block detour around the gracefully aging county courthouse.

The county administration building sat at the north edge of town, a few blocks farther on. It was a low brick structure—brick facade, more likely—with a 1970s modern look that was out of sync with the organic backdrop of tall, golden-brown corn in the field beyond, waiting its turn for harvest. A green and yellow combine idled near the field's dirt road entrance next to an old grain wagon, while the driver shared a cup of coffee and a sandwich with a younger man, possibly the farmer's son.

Unes smiled at the picture-perfect setting. *Like something out of a Stephen King novel, just before things go horribly wrong. A Hollywood movie set.*

The agent laughed out loud as he turned into the gravel parking lot and pulled around the side of the building, Unes saw that the brick façade he'd noticed on the way in was just for show for those passing through on Route 3. The sides and back were simple, painted cinder block.

Unes checked the dashboard clock before shutting down the engine of his Traverse. Four-thirty on the nose.

Once inside the building, a fresh-faced deputy with big shoulders and an Iowa grin showed Unes back to the sheriff's office. "Uh, Chief Deputy?" The young man leaned into the room. "There's an FBI agent here for you."

"Thanks, Robbie. Send him in."

Unes entered an office that couldn't have been more than ten by ten. Two walls were lined with shelving units, each one filled with books. A cluttered desk dominated most of the back third of the room, making it feel even smaller. Apparently, Sheriff Thornton made do with what the county could afford, which clearly wasn't much.

"Chief Deputy Jurasik, I take it," Joe said as he entered the room and moved to the chair Jurasik had indicated, facing the desk. "I'm Special Agent Joe Unes. I really appreciate your seeing me on such short notice."

"Yeah, well, it sounds like we have a mutual interest," Jurasik said. "How was the drive?"

"Dusty," Unes admitted. "Looks like the farmers will have a bumper crop this year. I saw lots of tractors and trucks."

Annie Jurasik smiled. "Yeah, well, Iowa's known for its corn. Take your coffee black?" she asked. "Or would you prefer a can of pop? We've got a machine in the back."

"I'm full up on caffeine, thanks. I had enough coffee to float a battleship on the drive up."

"So, Agent Unes, how can the Sheriff's Department of Kiowa County help the FBI?"

The chief deputy sat, hands folded, eyebrows raised. She had short dark hair, a minimum of makeup over a lean, angular face Unes would have called attractive rather than pretty, and a no-nonsense manner that he appreciated—even if she was a bit cool. Probably from years of dealing with men and bigger law enforcement agencies that didn't treat her or her department as equals.

"Well," he said, searching for the right words, "Let me say first of all that I have no doubt that you and your department have done everything at your—"

"Yes, we have," Jurasik interrupted. "Contrary to what the Bureau might think, our little eight-person department knows procedure."

Unes paused for a moment and cleared his throat before continuing. "I assumed as much, or I wouldn't be here asking for your help." He lowered his voice. "Contrary to what *you* might think, Chief Deputy, not everybody at the Bureau has an attitude problem. Most of us hold local law enforcement in high esteem."

Jurasik relaxed a little. "Sorry. It's been a long couple of days."

"Tell me about it. I was nearly blown up Friday."

Jurasik frowned. "Excuse me?"

"The supermarket explosion in Saint Louis. I was there. It's where I got this." Unes pointed to his bandaged cheek.

"Oh." She seemed to soften a bit. "Bad scene?"

"Yeah," Unes said. "Besides the dead in the store, my partner was killed by flying debris. I was lucky." He decided not to derail the conversation by sharing the story about his phone.

Jurasik's lips tightened. "I'm sorry."

"Thank you," Unes said. "But that's not why I'm here. At least, I don't think it is. I'm supposed to be chasing the group who blew up the store, but my hunch is that the Bureau is going after the wrong guys."

"You mean this—what did that DHS memo call them—the Maranatha Militia?"

"I hadn't heard that yet. That must have come across while I was on the road. I kept the radio off. Talk radio drives me nuts anymore."

"The President had a special announcement from the Oval Office. He practically declared war on this group. Washington says they're right-wing religious nuts, trying to start Armageddon."

"What?"

"According to the memo, somebody in Washington's been convinced for years that this group's been waiting for the right moment to start a war with the government—something about forcing the hand of God to bring on the end times." Jurasik tapped at the keyboard on the desktop computer and a printer on top of a file cabinet against the wall whirred to life.

Unes sat in silence for a moment, then leaned forward, his mind whirling through years' worth of briefings. "Yeah. It's starting to make a weird sort of sense. And it explains why my boss sent me down the religion trail."

Jurasik scooted her office chair over to the printer and grabbed the pages as they emerged. "Maranatha Militia. That's what they're called. Here, take a look."

She handed Unes the three-page report. He quickly scanned the contents, whistling low and shaking his head. "This is worse than I thought. If this bunch is for real, they must be celebrating. They've got a real war breaking out over in Israel, almost on top of the Valley of Megiddo—Armageddon."

Jurasik leaned forward. "What timing," she said.

"Not coincidental," Unes said. "Funny. It's like the Bureau expected it. We were told to dust off the Project Megiddo report from Y2K. It was a threat analysis of apocalyptic nutjobs. I never took it seriously, but somebody upstairs does."

"So, maybe…"

"Maybe that's why these men in black grabbed the pastor when they came to get the sheriff."

"Maybe," Jurasik said, "Maybe not. I think they found out the Moores were hiding at the parsonage."

"Ah." Unes nodded. "So, they hung around for the weekend until they caught wind of the Moores' hiding place. They grabbed the pastor because he was harboring a man they wanted."

"Looks that way."

"All right," Unes said. "But a lot of other church leaders disappeared over the weekend. Mostly what you'd call fundamentalists. My guess is they've been pulled in, either by the FBI or Homeland Security."

"Homeland Security has its own agents?" Jurasik asked. "These weren't ATF? That's disturbing."

"I don't know," Unes admitted. "I thought *we* were the enforcement arm of DHS. But a lot of people haven't been seen in the last twenty-four to forty-eight hours, most of them aren't showing up in the Bureau's system, and more than you'd expect are conservative pastors or evangelists."

"How does this tie in with the guy you're looking for?"

Unes scratched his head and smiled. "Honestly, I don't know that, either. Stauffer's not religious, as far as I know. He's a computer programmer who turned up just after the supermarket explosion on Friday night. In fact, he and his buddies pulled me away from the fire and got me to an EMT. They might have saved my life. I owe 'em one."

"And now this guy Stauffer—he's disappeared."

"Yep."

"What about his friends?"

"They're looking for him," Unes said. "They came to me. In fact, if it wasn't for them, I might not have heard of Mayfield, Iowa. What caught my attention about your cases here were the missing computers."

"Yeah, we haven't figured that out, either. And you're right. Nobody I talk to in the Justice Department knows anything about this. Nobody knows about any arrests here that we haven't made ourselves. It's like the earth just swallowed the three of them up whole."

Unes leaned back in the cheap, understuffed office chair. "You know, I'm almost surprised *you're* still here, Chief Deputy."

Jurasik's eyes snapped fully open. "Why?"

"You know about the missing computers," Unes said. "That seems to be the common denominator. And I assume it was you who released the information about the arrests at the church to the press."

Jurasik nodded, lips pursed. "Guess I'll have to start looking over my shoulder. Want to go find some computers?"

Eric Moore sat on the floor of his bedroom, staring dejectedly at the computer screen. His social media posts had been up for almost a full day, and still no emails. What was going on out there? Was something wrong?

Eric had been really careful to make sure everything was right. He'd even created a new webmail account so his mom wouldn't find out about his secret plan too soon.

He decided to check the email account one more time, even though he knew that every minute he spent out in the open with the computer he risked being discovered, even with his door closed.

Eric adjusted his glasses and clicked the bookmark he'd created for the webmail account. There was a message—the first one.

Leaning closer to the screen, Eric clicked to open it, his stomach tingling with excitement. As he read the message, his mouth fell open. He was too excited to breathe.

Finally, he thought. *Now something's gonna happen.*

TWENTY-THREE

This was exactly the kind of mission for which Jared Gruner had prepared ever since he read *America's Phoenix* by K. C. Adamson and learned that FEMA was just a cover for the deep state's shadow government and that ancient, secretive group called Redwing. They made the Bilderbergers look like Cub Scouts.

Gruner sat behind the wheel of his beige Protegé, using high-powered binoculars to peer through a concealing row of brush at the expanse of Scott Air Force Base. It was one of the first air bases built for the American military, so old that it once had hangar space for dirigibles, America's answer to Germany's zeppelin fleet.

He was dressed entirely in black—black sneakers, black sweats, and a black sweatshirt. Actually, it was an Oakland Raiders sweatshirt, but Gruner had put it on inside out to hide the logo. Unfortunately, after a brisk morning, the Indian summer day had grown uncomfortably warm for his choice of stealth wear, and he perspired freely even with his window rolled down.

"Are you sure about this?" Terry Norlock sat next to him, his lanky frame folded into the passenger seat. It was pulled as far forward as he could stand to allow Vijay a little breathing room in the back.

"Yes, please, what are we looking for, Jared?" Vijay, although not tall, sat with his back against the door to keep his knees from bumping Norlock's seat.

"Unusual activity." Gruner's voice was grave, his eyes fixed on the airfield across the two-lane road.

Norlock looked sideways at Jared. "And you know what *usual* activity is, right?"

Jared responded with an icy glare, not even deigning to put his contempt for such a question into words. That Norlock's suspicion was mostly correct was irrelevant.

"Ooh," Vijay said from the back. "What type of aircraft is that?"

Following the line of Vijay's gaze, Jared and Norlock looked off to the northwest, squinting into the setting sun. A sleek, modern-looking twin-engine jet descended, wheels down, on final approach to one of the base's runways.

"C-21," Gruner said. "Military version of the Learjet 35-A. It's the main bird the 375th Airlift Wing flies out of here. Seats eight plus two crew. Powered by two turbofans with thirty-five hundred pounds of thrust each. Cruising speed, five hundred thirty miles per hour; ceiling, forty-five thousand feet; range, about twenty-three hundred miles. Used for light cargo or medevac."

Norlock stared at him for a moment before asking, "Is that the air speed velocity when fully laden?"

"What do you mean?" Vijay asked.

"*Monty Python and the Holy Grail*," Gruner explained.

"Oh, that again," Vijay said, still sounding confused. "So that is not unusual activity?"

"No," Gruner grunted. "Just wait. There's got to be something here."

Minutes stretched into an hour as the sun gracefully settled behind the line of trees fronting the Mississippi River, and beyond that, the famous St. Louis Arch. A few more C-21s came in to land, but even with binoculars, Jared couldn't see anything on the ground that looked out of the ordinary.

Nightfall colored the sky a deep violet. They'd been sitting in the car for over two hours when a strange noise, like a sudden rush of wind, swept over them.

"Holy moley, Batman! What was that?" Norlock sat up so quickly that he banged his head against the roof of the car.

Gruner nodded as though he'd expected it. "Black helicopter. Night Stalkers. Bringing prisoners in after dark, I bet."

"Maybe it is simply a training flight," Vijay offered from the back seat.

"Not likely, Veej," Gruner said. "Those choppers fly out of Fort Campbell in south Kentucky."

Norlock rubbed the top of his head where he'd hit the roof. "So? Maybe they've got a reason to be here."

"Right," Gruner said, opening his door. "And we need to get close enough to see what it is."

"What? What are you talking about?"

"Come on," Gruner said, prying himself out of the driver's seat and pulling a black knit cap onto his head. "Time for some perimeter reconnaissance."

Harris had just returned to the headquarters building when Captain Poverello called to him from his office. "Harris, got a minute?"

"Yes, sir." Harris changed directions and navigated the maze of desks between the front door and Captain P's office.

"Harris," Poverello said, "I was just notified by Colonel Hostler that a medical team is flying in tonight from the CDC. We need to get the detainees together around twenty-thirty."

"Examinations?"

"Flu shots."

Harris asked, "Flu shots? Why?"

Poverello shrugged. "I guess this bird flu's got somebody worried. The Chinese had a lot of people die because they didn't get after it right away. And the CCP made sure it spread to the rest of us by keeping it quiet until it was too late."

"And somebody here's got it?" Harris didn't like that at all. This strain was supposed to be nasty. Thirty percent kill rate, or something like that, if what he'd seen on the web was right. Hard to know what was true and what was spin anymore. Even science was politics these days. But the Spanish flu in 1919 only killed about five percent of its victims and more than fifty million people died before it burned out.

"Don't think so," Poverello said. "I think they just want to keep it that way."

It gradually came to Cindy Moore that she hadn't heard Eric moving around for nearly twenty minutes. While she appreciated some time to herself this evening to sit with a cup of decaf, watch the news, and think, her instincts triggered an alert. Sighing, Cindy got up to look in on him and make sure he was all right.

A lot of things seemed wrong tonight. Understandable, considering what she'd been through the last four days. But the news tonight had been anything but calming.

The war in the Middle East had gone all Israel's way today, with armored units within sight of the ruins of Damascus. But that had triggered ominous warnings from Russia and Pakistan, which prompted counter-warnings from the United States, Britain, and India. India's involvement brought an official response from China, and within twelve hours, all of the members of the world's nuclear club found themselves staring at one another with fingers poised over their versions of The Button.

Lord, deliver us from evil, she thought as she climbed the stairs, the wood creaking reassuringly with each step like an old friend saying hello.

The light was on in Eric's room—a good sign, she supposed. Cindy tapped lightly on the door, and then turned the knob and pushed the door open.

Eric sat in the middle of the floor in front of the old family computer. As the door opened, he spun around so quickly that his glasses flew off and landed across the room, against the wall. The look on his face was that universal expression of shock displayed by children who discover that their parents aren't as easily fooled as they'd hoped.

"Eric," Cindy said, frowning, "What are you doing?" Judging by his startled reaction, she half expected to see a picture of a nude woman on the monitor.

But no, it was—a picture of Bob.

She leaned in closer as Eric scrambled to retrieve his glasses. "Mom, I can explain. I was just—"

"Hush." It was Twitter. A tweet featured a picture of Bob above big, bold text: *PLEASE HELP MY DAD!* Cindy closed her eyes as her stomach turned to ice and tears filled her eyes. "Oh, Eric. What have you done?"

"I was trying—"

"Is this out on the Internet?"

"Well, uh—"

"Yes or no?"

"Yes, but I—"

"Get rid of it!" The memory of the sinister voice in her ear was still fresh, and she wondered if it was already too late. "Delete it, get rid of it, erase it, do you understand me? Do it now!"

Kneeling on the floor where his glasses had come to rest, Eric stared at her, stunned.

"Now!" Her voice cracked, and Cindy rushed from the room. Moments later, in her room, Cindy Moore collapsed to her knees against the side of her bed. As she pulled the flowered comforter to her face with clenched fists, trying to muffle her sobs, she silently cried out to God: *Please, please, please, don't let them take my little boy, too!*

"So, what was the story here again?"

The cool October air vibrated with the evening songs of crickets and frogs as Joe Unes and Ann Jurasik made their way to the front door of the Fisher home in Mayfield. The last rays of the setting sun cast long, orange-hued shadows across the front lawn of the now empty home.

"A ten-year-old kid found his father's rifle and used it on his parents," Jurasik said, trying hard to mask her emotions. "The boy took a shot at our deputy who answered the call from a neighbor. The officer returned fire, and—it didn't end well."

"The boy was shot?" Joe asked.

"The deputy had no choice. He didn't realize the shooter was a kid until it was all over. The boy's dead."

"Wow. How's the deputy holding up?"

Jurasik sighed. "Not good, at least not when I saw him yesterday. I recommended a counselor—yeah, I know, it's SOP, but I doubt it would help *me* sleep at night. I can count on one hand the number of times I've discharged my weapon in the line of duty. I served three years in Iraq. Mostly in the Green Zone, but I spent five months in Mosul. That was hard. I've seen way too much blood for one lifetime. When I got home, I wanted to serve my hometown—keep a real peace, you know? Mayfield just doesn't normally deal with stuff like this."

"Be glad."

The front entry of the Fisher home was still criss-crossed by yellow crime scene tape fixed to the doorframe. Jurasik lifted the tape from the left side of the jamb and unlocked the door with a key she'd brought from the office.

The air inside was as cool as it was outside. The thermostat had been turned down to fifty. No point in heating the house just for police.

Jurasik entered first, flicking a switch next to the door to turn on the living room light. The small one-story home, built during the post-World War II construction boom, was modestly furnished with mismatched hand-me-downs and carpeting that was clean but about fifteen years out of style.

A plaid couch and flowered love seat claimed two sides of the cozy living room. A small coal-grate fireplace anchored the right-hand wall, and an ancient, pre-LCD twenty-five inch Zenith topped white laminated fiberboard TV stand in the far left corner of the room.

The dining room was behind the living room, separated by a half wall that extended three feet into the room on both sides. A wooden, five-piece dinette set occupied the middle of the dining room, and the white-tiled walls of the kitchen were visible beyond.

Unes took a few steps into the living room, the floor creaking under his weight. It was a disturbing sound, given what had happened in the empty house less than thirty-six hours ago.

"The boy shot his mother in the kitchen," Jurasik said. "She was at the stove, making bacon and eggs. The father came running from the bedroom, through that doorway off the dining room, and the boy turned and shot him before he got around the table."

"What a world," Unes said. He could picture the scene in his mind, playing it like a flickering 16 mm film: a Mayberry scene genetically altered with *Twilight Zone* DNA. Twisted American

Gothic. *Keep your mind on why you're here*, he reminded himself. He turned to Jurasik. "So, where do you think the computer would be?"

"It's not in the living room, so one of the bedrooms, probably," Jurasik said. "I'll go right, you go left."

The bedroom to the left of the doorway from the dining room was the son's. Joe switched on the light to reveal posters of rock bands and football players lining the walls. The bed was stripped, and a bullet hole scarred the window facing the street. *Scene of the crime. The boy died here.*

A cramped wooden desk sat against the wall next to the door. Clutter littered the desktop, as you'd expect from a ten-year-old boy—except right in the middle. An empty space about the size of a desktop PC glared back at him.

Unes looked more closely at the desk—pulling it away from the wall. Sure enough, hurriedly disconnected cables lay coiled underneath, and a printer sat on one side of the desk, nearly buried by well-thumbed comic books.

"Score one for the other guys," Unes called, "We're too late."

Susie Thornton had expected a return call from Congressman Benson long before now. Darkness had come and it was well past the dinner hour on the east coast. A call just before five Eastern Time found the congressman away from his office. Not unusual, his secretary had said, with the new developments in the Middle East.

Still, he was a man of his word, and he'd promised to call with an update today. Instead, there was no news at all.

Susie sat on the overstuffed couch in their living room holding a pillow to her chest, her mood sinking like a stone in a stagnant pond. What was happening? Where was Ted? Why hadn't someone, *anyone* from the government been able to let her know what was happening?

Steve and Jennifer were downstairs in the family room, subdued, and lost in their own thoughts. Voices from the television floated up the stairway from the lower level of the tri-level home.

The telephone rang. Susie started, her stomach fluttering as she wondered whether this call would finally bring word of Ted.

"Hello?"

"Hello, Susie? It's Michelle." Michelle Schiebold, the pastor's wife.

"Hi, Michelle, how are you holding up?" Susie's aching heart was pelted by a pang of disappointment laced with guilt that she hadn't thought to call and check on her friend.

"Ok, I guess. What about you?"

Susie sighed. "I've been better."

"No word from Congressman Benson, I take it?"

"No, nothing. I was sure he'd call back by now."

"Well…" the pastor's wife began. Susie waited for a moment while Michelle chose her words. "Sue, I had to call because Cindy is really on my mind."

"Me, too. Have you talked to her today?"

"No. I tried her phone a couple of times, but it always rang busy," Michelle said. "I have a very strong sense that she needs some help right now."

"With the store you mean?"

"Well, she might need that, too. No, I mean prayer. I just really feel she can use some prayer."

"Okay," Susie said. "I'll remember her when—"

"No," Michelle interrupted. An unusual intensity hardened her normally cheerful voice. "I think we should go over there and pray with her. I think she needs us *right now*."

Susie frowned. "Okay."

"I'm sorry, Susie," Michelle said. "I didn't mean to cut you off. You—I can't really explain it. But I really think we should go right now."

"It's okay," Susie said. "Give me a couple minutes to secure the kids and get some shoes on, and I'll meet you over there."

A sliver of a moon guided their movements as they circled the tall chain-link fence along the southern perimeter of the air base. Gruner and his companions edged through the tall grass alongside the barrier, undeterred by the low light. Their night vision goggles came from a source in Singapore that Gruner had found online. They worked fine, but Gruner had to admit that he and his friends looked like refugees from a low-budget 1950s science fiction movie.

Through his goggles, the terrain ahead was bathed in a soft green and silver glow. No one in sight. Gruner motioned for the others to follow.

The area south of the Scott Air Base seemed the most likely place to shield a new government installation from prying eyes. The north side more or less fronted onto Interstate 64. New buildings and activity would be noticed. Less than twenty miles from the Arch and downtown Saint Louis, traffic along that stretch of the highway was heavy during rush hour. Too risky.

The south side was bounded by Illinois Routes 158 and 161. Southwest of the main base was a large tract of land with a good buffer between the road and the fence line they followed. With at least four miles between the base and the subdivisions along the edge of Belleville, a bedroom community just close enough to Saint Louis to be called a suburb, neighbors weren't likely to notice a large number of new guests, especially during an official Threat Level Red when such curiosity would be discouraged, and if such guests were carried by Night Stalkers coming in over the farmland to the southeast.

"Ow!" Behind Gruner, Norlock cursed under his breath.

Gruner wheeled and motioned for quiet. "Shh! Button it! There's no telling how the base is guarded."

Norlock's face glowed white at the cheeks through Gruner's goggles. "Are you sure this is the right place? We've been out here for forty-five minutes and all we're finding is ticks."

"Ticks? There are ticks here?" Vijay's voice was strained. He had a thing about bugs.

"No," Gruner said. "No ticks. Terry, I oughta—"

"Gruner, I'm tired," Norlock interrupted. "Let's call it a night."

"Wait," Vijay said.

"What is it?" Gruner held his breath and listened. Nothing but crickets and the sound of distant tires on pavement.

"Look here," Vijay said, pointing up. "If this fence is to stop intruders from breaking in, why does the barbed wire at the top angle inward?"

Gruner and Norlock turned their eyes upward. Sure enough, the barbed wire on top of the chain-link fence was to keep people *in,* not out.

"Zounds," Norlock said.

"This is it," Gruner hissed. "Vijay, you're right! This is it! There's got to be some barracks here or some—"

Suddenly, a white-hot light speared them with the intensity of a solar flare. Through their night vision goggles, it might as well have been a high-powered laser aimed directly into their eyes.

"Aaaah! My eyes!" Gruner ripped the goggles from his head, eyelids squeezed shut. He heard Norlock and Vijay wailing and thrashing as they ripped off their own goggles.

The afterimage blazed an angry purple slash across his field of vision. Gruner realized he was effectively blind. "Vijay? Norlock? Can you see?"

"No! I'm blind!"

"The light was so bright!"

A deep voice from above, impossibly loud, surrounded them. "STAY WHERE YOU ARE. DON'T MOVE OR WE WILL SHOOT."

A rush of air washed over them, tall grasses near the fence line swirled like green and yellow tornadoes, and for the first time the trio heard the rotor of an MH-60 Blackhawk helicopter.

A thud.

Norlock yelled, "Ah, jeez!" He had tripped over something, stumbling around blind.

"What do we do? I cannot see!" Vijay cried out.

Gruner fumbled through the pocket of his sweatpants for his phone. By memory, blinking hard to try to clear his eyes, he tried to press the sequence of virtual buttons to call a specific number stored in his contacts. He only hoped he had enough time before the men in the black helicopter came and took them away.

Unes and Jurasik closed up the Fisher house and jogged to Jurasik's prowler. Sixty seconds later and three blocks away, Unes waited impatiently as Ann Jurasik worked the lock in the front door of the home where Susie Thornton encountered Frank and Verna Allen the day before. Icy fingers brushed the back of his neck, a tingle of anticipation he usually felt when he was about to discover that one of his hunches was right.

Unes wasn't sure whether he wanted to find a computer inside or not. If the computer was still here and had nothing of interest on the hard drive, his theory of a connection between the violence in Mayfield, the Grandy's bombing, and possibly Scott Stauffer's disappearance was no further along than when he left Saint Louis this morning. The theory was flimsy, he knew. Probably not solid enough to justify the drive up here.

On the other hand, if he and Jurasik found that the Allens' computer had been taken, then it was a pretty sure bet somebody was cleaning up. But what? And for whom?

And if there *was* a computer with something of interest on the hard drive, how far would the interested parties go to get it back?

With a creak and a bump, the front door swung open. The sun had set, leaving barely enough light to see inside. Jurasik had just reached for the light switch when they heard a thump from the back of the house. *A footstep?*

"Hello?" Jurasik called. Instinctively, Unes reached toward his sidearm, a nine-millimeter Glock holstered under his left arm. Jurasik's hand rested on the grip of the pistol on her hip.

"Hello? This is Chief Deputy Jurasik of the Kiowa County Sheriff's Department. This is a crime scene, and you are trespassing. Step out into the room where I can see you."

Unes held his breath, listening. Silence. Even the crickets outside had hushed. Jurasik eased forward, quietly. A floorboard creaked as Unes shifted his weight to follow.

Two steps. Three. Unes risked a breath as he followed Jurasik into the dining room. The floor plan of the house was a mirror image of the Fisher home.

Another step. A thump in the darkness, off to his right. One of the bedrooms. Unes signaled Jurasik with his left hand while drawing the pistol from his shoulder holster with his right. He moved quietly toward the doorway that led to the bedrooms. His chest was tight and his mouth dry. Unes thought briefly of Cathy, Emily, and Molly at home. *What in the world am I doing here?*

"Freeze! Drop it! Drop it! Put it down!" The voice was male, loud, and sounded like someone who'd been in situations like this before. It came from the bedroom to Unes' left. The shadows were too deep. He couldn't see anyone.

He spun right, out of the doorway, heart racing. Jurasik pressed herself against the wall on the other side of the doorway, pistol raised.

Unes' mind churned through possibilities: *Who are we dealing with? Will he shoot? What's he carrying? How big a round will these plaster walls stop?* "FBI," he shouted back. "Identify yourself!"

"No one you need to know," answered the voice. "Now set your weapons down and let us be on our way."

"You're disturbing a crime scene," Jurasik shouted. "You are trespassing—"

"You don't know who you're dealing with," the voice shouted back. "We don't want a firefight. Put down your weapons. Go back out the front door. We'll leave by the back, and we'll all pretend this never happened."

Unes thought furiously. These guys had to be just as surprised as he and Jurasik. He played a hunch: "Okay, you can go, but leave the computer!"

Silence. He'd guessed right. It was the cleanup crew.

It suddenly occurred to Unes that proving his theory correct maybe wasn't a good thing. How far would this crew go to erase the evidence? Jurasik glared at him from the other side of the doorway. She'd thought of that, too.

Joe Unes closed his eyes and leaned his head against the hard, cool plaster. If only it were brick. Or steel.

If only I'd kept my big mouth shut.

"What do you know about the computers?"

Unes opened his eyes. Jurasik stared back at him, eyes wide. If these guys were the men she ran into at the Belcher farm, he and the deputy were outgunned and outnumbered. Had he already said enough to get them killed?

"Some connection to what happened here yesterday," Unes said. "Maybe some other things, too."

His breathing was a giant bellows in his ears. A floorboard creaked in one of the bedrooms, and he tensed. Jurasik crouched lower, hugging the wall.

A whispered hiss from the back bedroom was followed by another. Another creak as somebody's weight shifted. Unes waited, alert for movement in the dark.

Jurasik moved, a small motion with her head, and Unes saw she was grinning—no, trying to hold in laughter! He gaped, wondering what she could possibly find amusing just now.

"Can't get the window open, can you?" she called.

She was answered by a muttered curse from the bedroom.

"Yep, I noticed that yesterday. Painted shut."

More curses, just loud enough to hear.

"You could break it, you know," she continued. "But I should warn you, the storm's jammed, too. So, you got two windows to break if you wanna get out that way. Small town like this, though, the neighbors are gonna hear. They'll probably call the cops. Oh, wait—that's me." She giggled. Unes stared. The chief deputy had an odd sense of humor, and an odder sense of timing.

An electronic chirp, obscenely loud, knifed the air and stabbed Unes in the gut. He jumped, his mind so focused on the unseen men in the other room that it took him a moment to identify the noise. *My phone!*

It chirped again, demanding attention.

Gritting his teeth, Unes used his left hand to pull the phone from the pocket of his sport coat on the third ring. "Yeah, Unes."

A voice shouted into the phone. Other sounds muddied the background, raised voices—a megaphone? Machinery, a motor, rushing wind, so painfully loud that Unes had to pull the phone away from his ear.

"Agent Unes," the voice cried, so loud Unes was sure everyone in the house could hear it. "It's Jared Gruner! We found a prison camp! Scott Air Base! Do you hear me? Come quickly! Scott Air—"

Then the phone was jostled, it hit something with a *click*, and the connection died.

TWENTY-FOUR

The pounding in his skull was worse than the shelling he'd suffered in Vietnam when a spotter relayed the wrong coordinates to a friendly artillery unit. But Harold Benson doubted he'd feel anything at all if he were dead, so he chose to take the pain as a good sign.

He opened one eye and then the other, slowly. The room was dimly lit, but even so, it was agonizing. A burning cigarette fouled the air. Benson had never tolerated smoke well.

"Ah, good. You're awake." The voice had cultured overtones, deep, and gruff mixed with aristocratic superiority. *Like a James Bond villain*, Benson's brain signaled.

The congressman gradually became aware of the duct tape that bound his wrists and ankles. His clothing had been removed, except for his white T-undershirt and boxers. He was seated on a simple wooden chair, held in place by a webbed belt that passed around his chest and under his arms. The room appeared no bigger than a child's bedroom. His captor stood between Benson and the door.

"Where, where—?" That was all Benson managed. He was dizzy, and a sudden wave of nausea choked off his words.

"Where are you? Why, you are in the belly of the beast, Congressman Benson."

Benson's eyes slowly focused on a trim, dark-haired man who could have been anywhere from thirty-five to fifty. His sharp features, dark eyes, and thin lips gave him the appearance of a predatory bird.

"Who are you?"

"If it helps you to focus, you may call me Green."

"Why am I here?"

"Careful. Curiosity had a deleterious effect on the fabled cat, you know," Green said. He paused to take a pull on his cigarette. "But since you ask, I shall oblige. Simply put, Congressman, you were ahead of the curve. The questions you asked were bound to surface sooner or later, but I couldn't afford to let you rush things. Another couple of days and it wouldn't have mattered."

"The situation in Iowa. You're behind it."

Green smiled. "You're a clever cat, Congressman. You may prove useful."

Benson said nothing.

"Now, I know that you're a stubborn man," Green continued. "It is why you're a successful politician. So I've arranged a little demonstration of what happens to stubborn people."

He opened the door and called outside. "Sergeant Jenkins. Come in here, please." A young man in fatigues with a military buzz cut atop a round, boyish face entered the room and stood at attention.

"No doubt you are aware of the threat posed to the health of Americans by the strain of avian flu that resurfaced in China recently." Green paused to draw on his cigarette. "Nasty bug. You might remember it from about fifteen years ago. Some of the characteristics of the deadlier hemorrhagic fevers, like Marburg and Ebola, but much faster and more deadly."

Benson watched Green intently. He didn't like where this was going.

As he spoke, Green casually reached into an inner pocket of his tailored suit coat and produced a small, thin metallic box. "What isn't well known—well, actually," he said with a thin smile, "with the three of us, now, fewer than two dozen people in the world know about this—is that *we* created this little devil to go with it." With his thumb, Green casually depressed a red button set into the top of the box.

The young soldier didn't move, but his eyes widened as he grasped the weight of Green's words. Benson could almost hear the young man's thoughts because they mirrored his own. *Why is he telling me this?*

"That's why all of our men here have been vaccinated. Isn't that right, Jenkins?" Green returned the box to his jacket and took another pull on his cigarette.

As he lifted the Bentley to his lips, Green glanced at his wristwatch, holding the pose as though waiting for something. After several seconds, he lowered his arm and smiled.

"I have a small confession," he continued. "The inoculation we gave the soldiers here offers no real protection against the avian flu. It is merely a means to an end. The so-called 'vaccine' is nothing more than a point five-milliliter dose of saline, useless against any biological threat. Ah, but within that innocuous saline is a most remarkable example of nanotechnology—the BioStrain chip. Third generation, of course. Nothing but the best for my men."

The soldier's eyes grew wider.

"I thought BioStrain went under," Benson said. "Shut down years ago."

"Yes, I know," said Green. "The chip is an incredible thing—as alive as an actual virus. Which is interesting, since viruses are not, technically speaking, alive. They have no metabolic process. They do one thing, and one thing only—commandeer cells and force them to make more copies of the virus. In a sense, they are simply biological machines. But the BioStrain chip is a vast improvement. You see, it transmits and receives data on a low-power radio frequency. And it not only receives, it executes commands."

Sergeant Jenkins was trembling. Beads of sweat had appeared on the young man's forehead and upper lip.

"You see, Congressman," Green continued, "the BioStrain chip gives us a means of controlling the herd more effectively than any method we've used to date."

"What did you do to him?" Benson demanded.

Angry blotches of red appeared on the soldier's face, and Jenkins blinked rapidly—either to clear his vision or because of the sweat now streaming into his eyes. He swayed slightly, and Benson thought the young man would be sick.

"The button activated a command within the chip," Green said. "It has released a recombinant virus tailored especially for Sergeant Jenkins. His primitive immune system is hopelessly overmatched."

"It did what?" Benson began, but he was unable to continue, watching in mute horror as the young soldier began to shake violently. The soldier moaned, his eyes rolled up in his head, and he collapsed to the floor, writhing in agony. A trickle of dark blood leaked from his mouth onto the floor.

"Right about now," Green said, as calmly as if he were ordering breakfast, "the custom-made virus is shredding our toy soldier's blood vessels. He should bleed out at any moment."

A coppery stench filled the room as the helpless sergeant thrashed, gurgling thickly as his lungs bloated with blood. Crimson flowed freely from his nose, eyes, and ears, and a horrifying pink foam bubbled from his lips. Jenkins wheezed and coughed, fighting for his life, overwhelmed by the microscopic assassin that attacked with surgical precision from within his own cells.

"You're a monster!" Benson croaked, struggling against the tape that held him fast.

"Am I? Monstrosity is in the eye of the beholder, Congressman," Green replied airily. He brushed his hands as if wiping off dirt. "Blame yourself for making it necessary. That demonstration was for your benefit. And now you know the price of disobedience."

From his jacket, Green produced a hypodermic filled with a clear fluid.

"You're a man with some power, Congressman," Green said as he advanced. "You will be useful to me. But I must make certain I can depend on your cooperation."

"No! Dear God in heaven, no!" Benson strained, but the tape held fast.

"Oh, let's not bother Him with our little problems. Trust me, He's busy with weightier matters. Now, hold still," Green said, smiling slightly as Benson continued to struggle. "You may feel a little sting."

Joe Unes stared at the cell phone in his left hand, trying to process what he'd just heard. He found it hard to focus with men carrying automatic weapons in the next room who might want him dead.

Unes decided to play another hunch. "Okay," he called into the bedroom. "Here's one for you: What's going on at Scott Air Force Base?"

Silence.

Hit or miss? Unes wondered as seconds ticked by. He figured it must be a miss, and started to speak, but the voice interrupted.

"Prison camp. It's a prison camp. Terror suspects."

What do you know—the geeks were right! "Homeland Security—FEMA?" Unes asked.

Slight pause. "Yes."

It made a sideways kind of sense. The attacks were nationwide. There could be hundreds—maybe thousands of suspects in this Maranatha Militia. "How many camps are there?"

"Not sure. Couple dozen, I think."

Now, how far do I trust these guys? Unes took a deep breath to steady himself.

"We're going to back away from the doorway," he said at last while looking at Jurasik. "The deputy here will back into the kitchen, and I'll move into the living room. Then we're going to lower our weapons and wait while you come out, where we can all see each other so we can talk."

Another long pause. Whispers in the bedroom. A conference. Joe glanced nervously at Jurasik. She looked just as worried as he felt. Would they decide to come out, or to come out shooting?

"If we start talking," the voice said, "your lives won't be worth spit. Ours, either."

Unes thought for a moment. "What's your worth now, huh? How do you feel about what's going on?" Jurasik looked at him from across the darkened dining room like he'd lost his mind.

A pause. "What do you mean?" the voice asked, softer now, uncertain.

"I mean, is this the America you wanted it to be when you grew up? Breaking into houses to cover up murder? Is that why you volunteered?"

There was a long pause. The crickets outside had started up their evening serenade again.

"Okay," the voice said at last. "All right. We're coming out. Let's talk."

Susie Thornton pulled up in front of the Mayfield Family Market just as Michelle Schiebold was getting out of her small SUV. Susie parked the Bronco behind Michelle and jumped out without bothering to lock the doors.

"Okay, I'm here," Susie said. "What's going on? Is Cindy all right?"

Michelle's small face was drawn with worry. "We'll know in a minute. It's a feeling in the pit of my stomach that I just can't get rid of," she said. "I really think Cindy needs some company. And some prayer." She smiled weakly. "Maybe I do, too."

"That makes three of us," Susie said. "Let's go 'round the back."

The two women walked side by side, past Cindy Moore's herb garden, to the green and white kitchen door that opened onto a long, cedar deck. Michelle pushed a dragonfly doorbell and was rewarded with a muffled, two-toned chime from somewhere inside.

They could see Cindy through the top window of the door as she descended the back staircase. She crossed the kitchen floorboards, wiping her eyes with the back of her hands as she approached the door. She looked terrible. Her eyes were swollen and her nose was red. She'd been crying hard, and for some time.

As Cindy opened the door, Michelle extended her arms and, without a word, pulled her into a warm hug. Cindy, caught off guard, looked down in surprise at the top of the shorter woman's head.

Susie said, "Michelle thought you might need some friends right about now. We all do."

Cindy Moore could only nod, and she began to sob.

"Well, well," the lieutenant said. "You boys were so curious to see what was going on in here. Looks like you get to find out."

Gruner sat on one of the hard benches in the windowless, white-walled room and did a slow burn. Every item they'd brought with them had been confiscated. Plus he, Norlock, and Vijay had been required to trade their clothes for orange jumpsuits. They looked like convicts in one of those 'True Crimes' reenactments.

Worst of all was knowing that he'd gotten Stauffer arrested, and now he'd managed to get Vijay and Norlock busted, too.

"Yeah," Gruner said at last. "I heard the food was to die for."

The lieutenant, a muscular black man named Harris, chuckled. Norlock snorted in disgust.

"You're just in time, too," Lieutenant Harris said. "About half an hour from now, everybody's getting flu shots. On the house." The lieutenant closed the door of the detention cell. The cold, metallic snap of the lock sliding into place made the hair on the back of Gruner's neck stand on end.

"Flu shots?" he said, looking at his companions with wide-open eyes. "Did he say flu shots?"

"Yeah," Norlock replied, "Why? Are you afraid of needles?"

"No—well, maybe, but more to the point, I'm afraid of what's in them," Gruner said, his stomach clenching. "And if it's what I think it is, we've just landed in Westeros, and it's feeding time for the dragons."

Thiel had cursed his bad luck when the FBI agent and the sheriff's deputy had shown up. Now the only way to get out of town without leaving witnesses was to shoot them.

His team had numbers in its favor—five against two inside the house, with the other four members of Thiel's team outside. They might be able to cover up taking out the sheriff's deputy, especially since her boss was officially a national security threat, but taking down an FBI agent might cause problems even Malthus couldn't sweep under the rug.

And then Alan Thiel realized with a shock that he'd been weighing the pros and cons of killing these two people in cold blood—people working for the same government, trying to uncover the ones responsible for these senseless deaths. Just as he was.

And his first thought hadn't been whether killing them was right or wrong—only whether he could get away with it.

The realization hit him like a fist in the gut: *What kind of man have I become?*

Thiel quickly weighed his options. Being caught in the house might be the best thing that could have happened to him and his men. Exposure could be their one guarantee of long-term security. If this FBI agent had any smarts, he could let enough people know what was happening to stop it—whatever *it* was—and provide the protection of 'sunlight' for Thiel's men.

Or maybe they were already dead—Thiel's men and anyone else who knew too much—when this operation was over. That would guarantee Malthus and anyone above him absolute security. Dead men don't talk. In which case, talking to the FBI now wouldn't make any difference.

Getting away clean was no longer an option. Thiel felt Bako's blood was already on his hands, and he was going to find out who put it there.

"Okay," Thiel said at last. "We're coming out. Let's talk."

Burgos grabbed Thiel's shoulder as he tried to stand. "Captain, are you nuts? Our orders!"

Thiel shook free and turned to face his warrant officer. In the dark, only Burgos' eyes were clearly visible. Thiel had kept his suspicions about Bako's death to himself. It was time to share with the team, and fast.

"What's your plan, Mister Burgos? Shoot your way out? Attract attention from the neighbors? Kill them, too? How many civilians have to die before we get back to the chopper?"

"We can do it quietly," Burgos said.

"No," Thiel said. "What are we cleaning up here? And for who? Why is Bako dead? What set him off? What made the people here lose it? Why are we collecting evidence from crime scenes? What does this have to do with national security?"

Burgos thought for a moment. "Terror cells."

Thiel hissed, "In the middle of Corntown, USA? Think, Burgos! We were sent here to get a computer, one computer.

Suddenly, people start dying and our orders change. What's the connection between the computers and the killings?"

The warrant officer just shook his head.

Thiel glanced around at the other three in the room: Grevey, Santos, and Evers. "Something is very wrong here. Whatever caused Bako to snap might be responsible for the mayhem here. *Capice?* It all goes back to the computers. Bako was looking at the computers we pulled out of here before he tried to kill me. I'm telling you, somebody's using us to cover up a major PSYOP, and I don't like it. We need to find out what's going on and who set it loose."

His team looked at one another and nodded agreement. Thiel turned to the doorway of the darkened room. "Okay," he said. "We're coming out slowly, one at a time, and with our hands where you can see them."

Thiel set his weapon on the floor, raised his hands in front of him, palms out, and stepped into the hallway between the two bedrooms. Despite the gloom, he could see through the doorway and a few feet into the dining room. There, behind the wide arched doorway that separated the dining room from the living room, he could make out a shape in the darkness. Too big to be a woman— the FBI agent.

"My name's Captain Alan Thiel of the U.S. Army," Thiel said with a loud voice, advancing slowly. "There are five of us in the house, and four more outside." He hoped the team outside was listening.

"Special Agent Joe Unes," the figure in the dark said. "I'm lowering my weapon." He holstered his sidearm and then extended his hands to show that they were empty.

"Mister Burgos," Thiel called over his shoulder. "You and the other men come out into the room, weapons down and hands out."

Thiel stood against the edge of the dining room table. The floor creaked behind him as Burgos entered the room. The lieutenant made space for Sergeant Grevey, followed by Sergeants Santos and Evers.

"Now what, Agent?" Thiel said. "We're here. What do we talk about?"

"How about some light first?" the agent asked.

"Hold it," Thiel said. "Santos, talk to the team outside and let them know what's happening in here. I don't want a rescue attempt. No misunderstandings."

Sergeant Santos spoke briefly into a headset mic. He listened for a moment, and then nodded at Captain Thiel.

"Okay," Thiel said. "Lights, but keep them low. You know we're here, but the neighbors shouldn't see us."

"I understand," the agent said. A few seconds later, the room was bathed in a soft glow from a lamp atop an end table in the living room. "That's better," he said.

Thiel assessed Unes silently. An old habit. The FBI agent was a big guy, maybe six-two and thickly built. He looked like a guy who probably played high school football but let himself get a little soft with age, marriage, and kids. His thick dark hair and eyebrows had a sprinkling of gray mixed in. He'd probably be steel gray before he was fifty.

"Where's your partner?" Thiel asked.

A female voice answered from behind. "Right here, you bastard. I should have figured it'd be you."

He turned to face the female deputy who'd been at that slaughterhouse Friday night. "Yeah. Me."

"You kidnapped my boss!" The woman walked up and took a swing at him.

Thiel had trained in hand-to-hand combat for too many years to let her connect. He blocked her punch with a swipe of his left arm.

He didn't expect her to have martial arts training, too. Before he finished his blocking move, she struck his nose with the palm of her left hand. *Hard.*

"Augh!" He grabbed his nose and bent over in pain.

"Hey!" Burgos and Santos jumped in and grabbed the deputy before she could hit him again.

"Easy! Easy! Take it easy!" Unes rushed into the room and was met by Grevey, who blocked his path menacingly.

"It's okay. I'm okay! Stand down!" Thiel said. He blinked to clear his watering eyes, and tears streamed down his face. It wasn't broken, but the deputy had bloodied him and it hurt like hell.

Burgos and Santos had the deputy under control. She still fumed, but at least she wouldn't do any more damage. Grevey stared up at Unes, daring him to take another step. The agent waited, watching Thiel.

"Okay, you get that one," Thiel said. "Yes, we took the sheriff. Now, if you want to get him back, we should work together."

"You know where he is?" the deputy asked.

"I do. Shall we all play nice?"

She glared at Thiel and his men. "Sure. For now. Let me go and we can get started."

Michelle Schiebold and Susie Thornton had taken Cindy Moore by complete surprise. She hadn't expected their visit, but it was good that they'd come. Cindy needed to share the burden of the threatening phone call she'd received, and only Susie and Michelle could possibly understand how she felt.

"You have no idea who this man is?" Michelle asked.

"No," Cindy said, pouring coffee for her friends, seated at the round kitchen table.

"What will you do?" Susie asked.

"I don't know. I don't know what I should do." Cindy set steaming mugs of freshly ground decaf in front of Susie and Michelle, and then went to retrieve a sugar bowl from the counter and vanilla creamer from the fridge.

"It has to be somebody connected to what's happened," Susie decided. "There's been so little news coverage that it almost has to be someone involved, don't you think?"

Cindy returned to the table with the creamer. "Have you heard anything more from Congressman Benson?"

Susie frowned and shook her head. "No. It's very strange. He said he'd call today, but he never did."

"Maybe he was busy," Michelle suggested. "I'm sure Congress is swamped with all the fighting in the Middle East."

"That's possible," Susie said, "but Harold Benson's good about keeping his word."

"What strange days," Michelle said. "David said we could expect trials and tests of our faith, but I never really expected to see it during my lifetime, not in America anyway. I wonder if this is what he meant."

The three women grew quiet as they sipped their coffee, lost in thought.

"Mm. Good coffee, Cindy," Susie said after several moments passed.

"Thanks. Bob just got it in."

A sudden glow outside drew their attention. A pair of headlights splashed a flood of light over the walls of the kitchen as a car—no, three—pulled into the driveway outside.

Cindy stood up, fear catching in her throat. *I wasn't to talk about this. The man on the phone! Oh, dear Lord! He knows!* Her panicked heart drummed inside her ears as a group of people climbed out of the vehicles, nearly a dozen in all. They came up the sidewalk toward the deck behind the kitchen.

Cindy had gone pale—she turned to look at Michelle and Susie, her throat dry. *Are they be coming for Eric?* "Who—what's this?"

Her friends were frozen in place, eyes wide.

There was a tap at the door.

Cindy turned. It was Ann Jurasik from the Sheriff's Police. A tall, stocky, dark-haired man with wire-framed glasses stood just behind her, squinting against the light over the door.

Relieved to see a familiar face leading the group outside, Cindy crossed the kitchen and opened the door. "Ann! Thank God it's you!"

"Cindy, this is Special Agent Joe Unes of the FBI. And these men here," she said, indicating the group behind her with her thumb, "are the ones who kidnapped your husband."

TWENTY-FIVE

Even with a hundred-watt floodlight right in Joe Unes' eyes, the tall woman in the doorway struck the agent as a bit disheveled—no, make that terrified. Understandable, he thought, from what he'd learned about the last few days.

Coming here had been Chief Deputy Jurasik's idea, and it seemed the logical next step in their new partnership. There'd been some tense moments when Captain Thiel and his men emerged from the bedrooms at the Fisher home—especially when Jurasik slugged Thiel. But Unes judged the captain sincere when he insisted that he wanted to find out what was going on, too.

Somebody, somewhere, was pulling strings that left innocent people imprisoned or dead, and Unes believed they'd uncovered one of those strings. The big question now: where would it lead?

"May we come in?" Jurasik asked Cindy Moore. Mrs. Moore didn't look very happy about bringing Thiel's team into her kitchen, but she stood politely aside and let them enter. Her bloodshot eyes made it clear that she'd been crying.

The soldiers, with Unes and Jurasik, nearly filled the country kitchen. They stood awkwardly and ill at ease, forming a rough circle around the outside of the room.

"Mrs. Moore, I'm Special Agent Joe Unes, FBI," he said, stepping forward and extending his hand. "I'm here—well, I'm investigating another disappearance, one in Saint Louis that may be connected to your husband's case. You may recognize these men here from the incident at the church Sunday morning."

Cindy Moore shook Joe's hand warmly but glared at the soldiers, apparently too shaken to speak.

One of the women at the kitchen table rose, a blonde of medium height and build, wearing a sweatshirt and jeans. Her hair was pulled back into a ponytail. "I'm Susie Thornton. My husband is Sheriff Ted Thornton. These men took him, too, Agent Unes. As well as Michelle's husband, Pastor David Schiebold."

Unes saw Captain Thiel take a deep breath. What were the odds of finding all three women together?

"Ma'am," Thiel said, removing his black baseball cap. "I am sorry. We were under—"

"Where are they?" Susie demanded. "Where are our husbands?" Her had reddened, and she advanced on Thiel, fists clenched.

Not again, Unes thought. "Mrs. Thornton, please! Captain Thiel and his team want to help us."

Susie paused, unsure. She stared daggers into Thiel's eyes.

"Ma'am, please," Thiel said, quietly. "My men and I were under orders to retrieve a computer from the Moore's home here, and to bring in Mister Moore for questioning. We were told it was connected to the terror attacks over the weekend. When your husband tried to interfere—and your husband, Mrs. Schiebold, was found harboring Mister Moore—well, we were ordered to bring them in also."

"Where did you take them? Are they all right?" Susie Thornton said through clenched teeth.

"I believe they've been delivered to a camp just outside Saint Louis," Thiel said. "A new addition to Scott Air Force Base."

"You didn't hurt them, did you?" Cindy Moore asked.

"No, ma'am," Thiel said honestly. "They were fine when we dropped them off. That was yesterday morning."

Cindy Moore looked ready to burst into tears again.

"Mrs. Moore," Unes said gently, "can you think of any reason why someone in the government would want your computer? Is there some connection between your computer and those owned by the Fishers and the Allens?"

Her eyes grew wide. Unes had hit a nerve. Cindy Moore walked over to the stairway and called, "Eric? Could you come down here, please?"

A few moments later, a shy-looking boy of ten or eleven with rumpled orange-red hair slowly made his way down the stairs. He blinked behind his glasses, trying to adjust to the brightly lit kitchen. He wore a T-shirt and gym shorts; his Iowa Hawkeyes T-shirt bore a sea of wrinkles as though he'd been in bed asleep.

Cindy Moore took her son's hand. "Eric, this man is an agent from the FBI. He's trying to find out why these other men were after your father. Can you tell them about the strange email you got on Friday?"

Eric took a deep breath before answering. "You're the guys that took my dad?"

Thiel nodded. "Yes, but we want to make it right. Can you help us?"

"Maybe," Eric said softly, and he told them about the email from 'God.' As the young boy described the cryptic message, Unes glanced at Jurasik and Thiel. They were just as confused as he was. *This is about spam from God?*

"Eric, tell Agent Unes what you did after you read the note," his mother prompted.

"I, uh, I sent it to some friends."

Thiel and Unes exchanged glances. "What friends, Eric?" the captain asked.

Eric gulped, his eyes wide with fear and guilt. "Mike Belcher, Jason Fisher, and—and John Allen."

Belcher, Fisher, and Allen.

Thiel had been ordered to retrieve computers from each of those homes. And people had died in each of those homes. "Eric," Thiel said, "I'm sorry we took your dad away. My boss gave me an order, and now I see it was a mistake. We'll do our best to sort this out." A few of Thiel's team nodded; a couple of them looked lost, as though they were caught in somebody else's bad dream.

"Eric," Thiel continued, "tell me something, will you? It's important, so be precise in your answer, okay? When you read this email from 'God,' how did you open the note?"

Eric's forehead wrinkled. "What do you mean?"

"What app did you use?" Unes interjected. The agent understood what Thiel was really asking: *Why didn't you become psychotic after reading it like your friends and their parents?*

"None of them. I use webmail," Eric said.

Thiel thought for a few seconds. "You opened it with the web browser—online?"

The boy nodded. "Yeah."

Unes jumped in again, "Does your webmail automatically show attachments, like pictures or movies, when you read your mail? Did you open an attachment to that email?"

"No. No way!" Eric said. "My dad says attachments sometimes have viruses, so I have to ask permission before I open anything."

"He's right," Unes said. "That's smart. Thank you, Eric. That's what we needed to know." Thiel looked at Unes, and his expression was easy to read: *The kid's father might have saved his life. Maybe the lives of everyone in the family.*

"Why did you ask about image files?" Thiel asked, looking at Unes.

The agent shrugged. "I guessed. Saw an *X-Files* episode like that once."

"Well played, Mulder," Thiel said.

Unes smiled for a second but then shook his head, trying to come to terms with the evidence. An email from 'God'? It sounded like science fiction. Mind control by email that turned ordinary people into murderers? Was that even possible?

And yet he felt certain that whoever had ordered Thiel's team to Iowa knew exactly what was in that email and the effect it would have on unsuspecting recipients.

If he was right, that hellish email could still kill, like a cancer cell waiting to metastasize all across the Internet. This virtual monster lived on inside the hard drives of the computers in the back of Chief Deputy Jurasik's Tahoe.

And was it still circulating around the web?

Gruner, Norlock, and Vijay sat on wall-mounted benches in the small, windowless holding room. "Now what? Do we play cards? Pass the time by playing a little solitaire?" Norlock grumbled.

Gruner noted the reference to *The Manchurian Candidate*, but he was too stressed to acknowledge it or its potential relevance to the deadly events of Ten-Thirteen. "We wait," he answered simply. "I got a message out. We wait."

"Who is it we are waiting for?" Vijay asked his friends.

"Our federal buddy," Gruner said. "I called Agent Unes."

"A fed!" Norlock groused. "Right. Like he's going to take on the government. Man, he *is* the government."

Gruner's eyes narrowed. "Maybe. I have a hunch."

The click of the lock drawing back surprised the three friends, and they jumped as if pulled by the same string. The door opened, and a tall, beefy sergeant flanked by two MPs filled the doorway. Their trigger hands hovered near their sidearms.

"Okay, boys, time for your medicine," the sergeant said. "We're all lining up over at the barracks for a flu shot, courtesy of Uncle Sam."

"What if I don't want it?" Gruner asked.

"You got no choice," said the sergeant. "Now come on."

Thiel's stomach tightened as he considered their next move. It was bizarre. Here he was, the epitome of American military training, standing in a cheerfully decorated country kitchen in the middle of Iowa, apologizing to a woman whose husband he'd kidnapped—on orders from someone inside the shadow government. A government of, by, and for whom?

Turning to his team, he said flatly, "We've been used."

Burgos said, "Sir?"

"We're a cleanup crew," Thiel explained. "Someone made a mess, and we're being used to wipe it up."

"Whose mess?" Burgos asked.

"Not here," Thiel said. "These people don't need to know." He turned to the three women, their expressions a mixture of anger, relief, and frustration. "I'm sorry, but the less you know, the less likely somebody's going to come back. Unless you hear differently from us, we were never here."

"Here's my card," Agent Unes said, offering one to Cindy Moore. "I'll be back in Saint Louis tomorrow afternoon. I promise,

I'll do everything I can do find out where your husbands are and how soon they can be released."

"Maybe you can coordinate with Harold," Susie Thornton suggested. "He's our congressman, and he's been working on it, too. Though, he hasn't gotten much so far."

"Harold—what's his last name?" Unes asked, pulling a pen from his jacket pocket.

"Benson. Chairman of the House Armed Services Committee," Thornton replied. "B-e-n-s-o-n."

Unes scrounged another business card, made a note on the back, and stuck it in the pocket of his shirt. "Got it. I'll call him first thing in the morning."

"We'll be leaving, ladies," Thiel said, turning to his team. "We have some planning to do."

Thiel thought of the unholy deal he'd struck with the man who called himself 'Malthus.' *I can give you eternal life, captain. But you must follow me without question.*

Eternal life? At what ungodly price? Thiel felt clean for the first time in years. Funny, how Bako's death had brought life, but that's how the captain felt. Alive. At long last—*alive. This may not last,* he thought, *but it feels good for now.*

Captain Alan Thiel followed his men out of the bright kitchen and into the night's chill. They were about to take on the real power behind the mightiest nation in the history of the world—the puppet masters who'd been running the show for over two hundred years.

Overhead, the Harvest Moon cast silver shadows across their path. Thiel glanced up, relishing the cool, clean night air on his face. *Show's over, Malthus, or whatever the hell your real name is. And I get to bring down the curtain.*

"Hey! What are you doing here?"

Jared Gruner whirled around and faced the man they'd come to find. He'd expected the question, but he hadn't looked forward to answering it.

"Hey, Stofe," he said, waving. "We're here to rescue you."

Scott Stauffer wore an orange jumpsuit like everyone else. He stood halfway back in a line that stretched the length of the barracks. At the head of the line, men in white lab coats fussed with equipment as they prepared to administer the flu shots.

Stauffer looked all right, considering. The barracks were clean but spartan. Rows of bunks on a concrete slab, really. Stauffer smiled weakly. "Great rescue. Thanks a lot."

Norlock snorted. "No kidding. They caught us outside the fence."

"Come on," Gruner said. "How was I supposed to know they'd have drones?"

Vijay seemed to be the only one happy that the four were reunited. "It is good to see you, Scott."

"How are they treating you?" Norlock asked.

"Okay," Stauffer said. "No computer access, though. I feel like part of my brain's ripped out."

"Uh, Stofe," Gruner said, sheepishly, "I need to tell you something. I think it's my fault you're here."

"How's that?" he asked, moving one step forward in the line.

"Uh, that satellite photo I downloaded Friday night? It—well—it came off a secure DOD server."

Stauffer stared for a moment, then—unexpectedly—shrugged off his friend's confession. "Yeah, I figured it was something like that."

Gruner was stunned by Stauffer's reaction. "You're not mad?"

Stauffer shook his head. "Not now. Not anymore. Probably would have been before, but at least there's a reason they grabbed me. Most of these other guys have no idea why they're here. It's like the cops are just snatching people at random and planning to sort them out later."

Gruner pointed to the men in the lab coats. "You know what they're gonna give us, don't you?"

"Some kind of vaccine," Stauffer said. "They came in here after dinner and told us they'd be giving us these shots tonight. It's that bird flu, I guess. It makes sense. If it's like the one about fifteen years ago…"

Gruner waved him quiet and turned toward the front of the line. The doctors—or whatever they were—were still unpacking gear on a folding card table near the outer door, the biggest patch of open floor space in the barracks. An unfamiliar piece of equipment on the table caught his attention. It looked wrong. His stomach twisted into a knot.

"I think I know what that is."

"What?" Norlock asked. "What are you talking about?"

"That thing. It's like… Oh, crap. It's that thing K. C. Adamson wrote about. That thing from the last outbreak."

"What thing?" Stauffer asked. "What's he talking about, Terry?" Norlock shrugged.

Gruner stared at it for a long moment, and then stepped out of line and pushed his way up to the front.

"Excuse me," Gruner said to the nearest lab coat, "What's really in these shots? RFID tags? Nanoscale chips?"

"Huh?" A man with thinning hair and a pinched, ferret-like face looked up from a plastic tray full of syringes filled with clear liquid.

"I said, what's in the syringes?"

"Gruner, what are you doing?" Norlock was right behind him. Gruner hushed him.

"It's a vaccine against the strain of influenza virus that's…"

"Yeah," Gruner interrupted, "What *strain*, huh? That BioStrain thing? I do not consent!"

"Gruner," Norlock hissed, "Cut it out! We're in enough trouble already!" His normally fair skin glowed splotchy red across his face and neck.

"What do you mean?" the lab coat asked.

Gruner raised his voice. "Is this a real vaccine or an injectable computer chip? That one you almost got away with during the last bird flu?"

"I don't have to, uh—" The lab coat glanced around nervously, looking for backup. Some of the jumpsuited men in line began to take notice. Nervous chatter coursed through the line.

"Well? Is it?" Gruner practically shouted. He planted his feet and folded his arms. He wasn't a fighter, but he knew from experience that his bulk could be intimidating.

"It's—uh, just a vaccine that was prepared to inoculate you against the influenza virus."

"Prepared to mark us for life!" Gruner shouted. Most of the men in line stared at him now, not sure of how to process the confrontation. "So you'll always know where we are, right? Little ID chips, floating around inside us for the rest of our lives. Tiny silicon spies!"

"No, no, that's not it," the man in the lab coat said.

"Gruner, knock it off!" Norlock tried to grab his arm, but Gruner shook him loose.

"What's going on here?" The sergeant who'd escorted them to the barracks wandered up to the table, assessing the situation.

"Just a vaccine?" Gruner said to the medical tech. "Tell us what *that* thing does!" He pointed to the device on the table, a charcoal gray box the size of a laptop computer. A power cord extended from one side, and a handheld attachment like the scanner used by department store cashiers attached by a cable to the other.

"That, uh, codifies—"

"Encodes, that's what you mean! That's how you download ID numbers from the chips, isn't it? How you set up the freakin' database!"

"Sir?" The sergeant interrupted. "You need to get back in line now."

"Uh, yeah. Back in line," the tech stammered.

"What's in that shot?" Gruner demanded, standing his ground.

"Sir," the sergeant began, but a broad-shouldered man at the front of the line interrupted him.

"Sergeant, I think we have a right to know." A murmur of agreement from the men behind him echoed his opinion.

"Sir," the sergeant said, addressing the man in line, "I'm just following my orders. You are all to receive the vaccine. You do not have a constitutional right to refuse."

"Him first!" Gruner pointed at the tech. "If he takes one, I'll take one."

The thin man in the lab coat blanched and took an involuntary step backward.

Gruner smiled triumphantly. He'd guessed right. He *really* didn't want that shot.

Eric Moore stood in his pajamas—well, what passed for sleepwear, anyway, now that he'd outgrown animal print jammies. The adults kept talking about what happened to his dad, but he still didn't hear any plans for getting him back. The army men were gone, but maybe with the sheriff's police and the FBI here, it was time to tell his mom about *his* plan.

"Mom?" he said, tugging on her sleeve.

"Just a minute, Eric," Cindy Moore said.

"Mom? I need to tell you something."

"Just a minute, Eric."

"It's kind of important, Mom."

"Eric, I said—"

"Mom!" he shouted, seeing no other way to make her listen. "Somebody's coming!"

His mother's face flashed anger then bewilderment as his words hit home. "What do you mean, Eric? Who's coming?"

"This man who saw my tweet," Eric said. "The one about Dad. He saw it, and he sent me a note. He wants to help us."

The room went very quiet, and Eric became aware that all of the adults in the room were looking at him. His face grew hot, and he suddenly wished he could hide.

"What man?" Cindy Moore asked, her voice tight.

A pair of mismatched headlights slowed and stopped outside, just across the street from their kitchen window.

Eric pointed toward the lights. "I think that's him."

Everyone in the kitchen turned to look out the window. The FBI agent went to the glass and peered out, his sober face an odd juxtaposition against the cheerful begonias on the windowsill.

Unes was on alert, and so was Ann Jurasik.

The agent's trained eyes assessed the new arrival. "One man, coming alone. Civilian. He looks okay."

Eric heard heavy footsteps out on the deck, and a very tall man stepped into the beam of light from the floodlight over the door. He looked both ways and peeked into the house before he knocked. He seemed surprised to find so many people in the Moore's kitchen.

Cindy Moore went to the door and opened it. "May I help you?" she asked.

"Yes, ma'am. I am Barney Ison," he said. He stood at least a full head taller than Eric's mom, with thinning light brown hair combed over the top, a round face, and eyes that moved constantly. Eric thought he looked as old as his grandpa, but he wore a green T-shirt decorated with a cartoon of an almond-eyed, inhuman face behind a red circle with a diagonal slash. Below the 'no aliens' symbol were the words *Alien Resistance HQ - Roswell, New Mexico*. Over his shoulder, the tall man carried a battered black leather bag about the size of a briefcase.

Eric's mother didn't move. She turned to look at Eric, eyebrows raised. He stage-whispered, "That's him, Mom, that's *him*."

Ison looked past Eric's mom. "Well, then. You must be Eric Moore."

Eric nodded.

"And you're Mrs. Moore."

Cindy nodded.

"I'm Barney Ison," the big man said with a grin.

"Nice to meet you, Mister Ison," Cindy said automatically. "Can I help you?"

Ison smiled, a twitch of his lips that disappeared in a blink. "Actually, Mrs. Moore, I think I can help *you*."

"Harris, come in here. Now!"

Harris froze, dreading what would likely be a very unpleasant encounter. It was plain from Captain Poverello's voice that he wasn't happy.

"What the hell is going on in the barracks?"

"Sir," Harris began as he stepped into the captain's office. "Well, sir, the men refuse to take the flu shot."

"I can hear that." A muffled three-syllable chant, "No consent!" repeated over and over, drifted through the thin walls of Poverello's office. The captain took a deep breath, frustrated. "Why?"

"Sergeant Keloski said it's something about that biochip that was in the news a few years back."

"What about it?"

"Somebody wanted to know if we were injecting the biochip without telling them."

"What? It's just a flu shot! We are *not* going to start a pandemic here, with prisoners in close quarters!"

"But is it, sir? Just a flu shot?"

Poverello stared at Harris as though he'd sprouted a second head. "What are you saying?"

Harris thought for a moment and decided to share his suspicions. "Sir, why would the DOD fly doctors up here from CDC just to pass out flu shots? The base medics can do that. If it's just a flu shot, why not just overnight the vaccine and let them give the shots?"

Poverello thought for a moment. "Okay, for the sake of argument, let's say it's this biochip thing. What's the problem?"

"Some of them think it's a tracking device."

"So? Major terror event. Maybe tracking them is a good idea."

"I don't know, sir," Harris said. "Now, they been putting RFID chips in dogs and cats for years. But Keloski says he read that BioStrain chip could send *and* receive."

The captain rubbed his chin, thinking. "Can they update the information on those chips?"

"I'm not sure. I guess they'd have to, if they can update medical records after the chip's inside your body."

"So, theoretically, these things transmit and receive." Poverello's chin rubbing gathered steam as he considered the implications of that thought.

Harris swallowed as he suddenly realized how a device like this might be used—like an electronic branding iron. As the descendant of several slaves freed by the American Civil War, that was a startling and uncomfortable thought. This technology was more subtle and potentially more powerful than a mark on the skin. "Permission to speak freely, sir?"

Poverello nodded. "Of course."

"Sir, what are we really doing here?"

The captain frowned, his dark, bushy eyebrows meeting in the center of his forehead like two caterpillars holding a conference. "We're doing our jobs, Harris. Following orders."

"Sir," Harris said, "I get that. But if these men haven't been charged, tagging them with a tracking chip just isn't right. With all due respect, sir, *somebody* better start asking questions before we wake up and find out this isn't our country anymore."

Poverello sighed. "All right, Lieutenant. Point taken. Tell the docs to hold off the injections for tonight. I'll talk to Colonel Hostler before we stick a needle in anybody."

The barracks were quiet but for the murmur of a few voices talking or deep in prayer. Bob Moore sighed as he sat on the edge of the bunk. Another full day without his wife and son; another day that they had no word of his whereabouts or well-being.

"Count it all joy, brother," Pastor Schiebold said as he joined Moore on the bunk. "How are you doing, Bob?"

"Okay, I guess. I miss my family pretty bad. How about you?"

"Well enough," Schiebold answered, his voice heavy. "I'm trying to leave it in the Lord's hands, since there's not much for ours to do."

Bob nodded. "It's tough. Hey, Ted."

Sheriff Thornton sat down on the bunk opposite his friends. "Lord, it's been a long day."

Schiebold nodded. "Not much to do but watch and pray. And wait."

"Yeah. The waiting is driving me nuts," Thornton admitted, his face slack and his voice hollow.

"We mustn't despair, men," Schiebold said. "Maybe we need to follow the example of Paul and Silas."

"What do you mean?" Bob asked, looking up. "You mean—sing?"

"Sure!" said Schiebold, cheerfully. "Why not? Bob, you're a fine tenor. And, Ted, I've heard that baritone of yours sail past the front row more than once. Come on!"

Thornton almost blushed. "Maybe—ah, but some of these fellas are sleeping for Godsake!" Thornton pointed out.

"Exactly! For God's sake, and for ours. And maybe it's for the sakes of all the soldiers as well," Schiebold exclaimed as he sprang to his feet. "Who's with me?"

Bob nodded. "Sure, I'm in. Why not?"

He followed Pastor Schiebold to the far corner of the barracks. It wasn't exactly private, but it was the closest thing in the confined space. As they arrived, Bob noticed that Ted Thornton had followed them after all.

"Maybe we should, uh, move into the men's room over there," Thornton said. "Just to give the sleeping guys a break."

Schiebold smiled. "All right, we'll try not to wake the sleepers, but I can't guarantee God won't shake them up! Besides, you can't beat a men's room for acoustics. Nothing like ceramic and stainless to amplify harmony."

Once inside the rectangular white and green men's room, Schiebold thought for a moment. "How about 'Leaning on the Everlasting Arms?' he asked. "We all should know that one."

The others nodded, and the makeshift trio began to sing: *"What a fellowship, what a joy divine, leaning on the everlasting arms! What a blessedness, what a peace is mine, leaning on the everlasting arms!"*

As they reached the second verse, a curious face peeked through the swinging door that separated the sleeping quarters from the latrine. The man entered and joined in on the chorus, anchoring the chords with a rich bass. A moment later, two others appeared, one man smiling as he wiped sleep from his eyes.

By the time they finished and started in on '*I'll Fly Away*,' their number had swelled to fourteen, covering both tenor parts, baritone, and bass, and their voices grew louder with each measure.

When they reached the line, *"like a bird from prison bars has flown,"* it sounded like a full-blown gospel choir had stuffed itself into the cramped latrine, and not one of them cared if they woke the entire camp.

TWENTY-SIX

Joe Unes stared in amazement at the man, nearly seven feet tall if he was an inch, standing at the Moores' kitchen door. Who in the hell was Barney Ison? And why was he here?

"Mom," Eric Moore said, "That's him. He's the one."

"One *what?*" Cindy Moore asked. "Eric, how do you know this man?"

"Please, Mrs. Moore, let me explain," Ison interrupted. "I was directed to your son's online plea about twenty-four hours ago by a colleague of mine who's been tracking the government roundup of so-called suspected terrorists. What happened to your husband isn't an isolated event, I'm sorry to say. Men and women are being swept up all over the country in the name of security and peace. Pardon my French, but that's a load o' granola. The terrorist events have all the earmarks of a major false flag event to neutralize some of the more troublesome elements of our society."

"Troublesome?" Cindy asked.

"Patriots," Ison answered back. "True lovers of freedom. And most of all—outspoken, Bible-believing Christians. Those who understand that no earthly government, no matter how powerful, is the ultimate authority over our lives. May I sit?"

"Well, uh, certainly," Cindy replied wearily. "I'm so sorry—where are my manners? You can have a seat here, Mister—"

"Call me Barney," Ison said, setting the heavy leather satchel on the table. "My viewers do."

Unes' internal radar beeped a warning. "Viewers? Who are you, Mister Ison?"

Ison fixed Unes with an icy stare through narrowed eyes. "I should ask you the same."

"Special Agent Joseph Unes from the Saint Louis field office, FBI."

"And you?" Ison asked Jurasik.

"Chief Deputy Ann Jurasik, Kiowa County Sheriff's Police," she replied. "Why are you here, Mister Ison?"

Ison flashed a grin and pulled out one of the kitchen chairs. There was something magnetic about him. He was clearly used to being the center of attention.

"You might say I'm the cavalry," he answered with a wink in Eric's direction. "Thanks to your son's quick thinking in getting out the word. Eric put out a distress call—a distress call so powerful and so poignant that it lured me from a very safe, undisclosed location, from which I broadcast my daily program. Deputy, I've spent years dodging unique and very powerful forces that would love to shut me up. Forces I daresay that you, Special Agent Joseph Unes, would not comprehend, unless I'm pleasantly mistaken. I came because a young boy's father had been snatched away at *gunpoint* right in front of his eyes! That, fellow slaves, is a sight no one should see and a pain no heart should bear. You might say I'm here to shine the avenging light of truth on the face of the beast, to force it back into the shadows whence it came." As if punctuating his final word, Ison plopped into the chair with a thud.

Unes pursed his lips and glanced at Jurasik. "Interesting," he said. "So, can you put all that into English? What exactly are you talking about?"

Ison rearranged the sparse hairs on top his head. "Very funny, Agent. Simply put, I learned of the plight of these poor families here in Mayfield, and I am here to add my voice to the fight against the vicious hydra our government has become." Turning to Cindy Moore, he asked, "May I assume that these ladies are Mrs. Schiebold and Mrs. Thornton?"

Cindy nodded, speechless. Eric crossed the kitchen and closed the door to keep out the moths careening around the security light.

Ison stood up and bowed slightly. "Ladies, I am honored—no, humbled—to offer my assistance. I've been in hiding for too long.

Oh, I've kept my fingers on the pulse of the news, you can be sure of that. Every day, I send reports to the outside world through video broadcasts, kindly uploaded to the World Wide Web by a network of trusted friends who wisely use secure methods to hide our virtual trail. This has allowed my whereabouts to remain hidden from those who wish to do me harm. But your plight demanded my return to the light of day, to take up arms once again in the age-old battle between good and evil, to add my voice to the chorus of the oppressed who defiantly sing, 'We shall overcome!'"

Ison stared ahead as if gazing into eternity, his eyes filled with righteous fire. The performance couldn't have been better, Unes thought, even if the big man had been accompanied by an orchestra softly playing *The Battle Hymn of the Republic*.

"Very nice, Mister Ison," Unes said. "Now, how exactly are you going to shine this light of truth?"

"Hmm. I can see you need convincing. No matter. To answer your question, I've already begun," Ison said. "Through my daily broadcast, the word has already begun to spread across America, and, though I blush to say it, the entire globe. If you don't believe me, Agent Unes, then look for yourself!" Ison's long arm pointed toward the kitchen window and the darkness outside.

All eyes turned and followed—and saw not one beam of light, but dozens, like beacons of hope piercing the darkness.

At a noise from the front of the store, Eric ran excitedly through the office to the closed storefront. "Mom! There are more out here!"

Joe Unes looked through the kitchen window, astonished, at the glittering stream of headlights—cars, pickups, motorcycles, campers, seemingly anything with wheels and an engine, dozens of them strung together in a long, incandescent line, winding through the streets of Mayfield, Iowa, and converging on the Mayfield Family Market.

The mood in the bunker was all caffeine and raw nerves. Captain Tom Wetzel didn't know why, but a palpable sense of urgency grew stronger with each passing hour.

Wetzel's desk was strewn with reports on the security situation across the country. Thousands of suspects had been rounded up and shuttled to detention centers with blinding speed. This surprised Wetzel. In his experience, military operations rarely proceeded as quickly or as smoothly as planned.

Especially since a new stream of chaos was flooding America's streets. Since President Bell had publicly blamed a fundamentalist Christian group for Ten-Thirteen, anti-fascists were defacing and destroying churches in literally hundreds of cities, taking advantage of the police preoccupation with tracking down anyone who might be linked to the Maranatha Militia.

Wetzel wondered how so many suspects—over nine thousand, if his math was right—could have been identified, located, and arrested within forty-eight hours of the attacks. How could that many be involved? And when were the detention camps built? They didn't appear overnight like mushrooms after rain. Somebody had put a lot of planning into this. Who?

His gut told him he already knew the answer. Maybe the others in the office had the same feeling, and maybe that was the source of the tension, the cognitive dissonance of a dozen men wrestling with information that conflicted with an inner sense of right and wrong.

Who'd be the first to say something?

The intercom on his desk telephone beeped. "Wetzel?"

It was Green.

Wetzel picked up the handset. "Yes, sir?"

"Mister Wetzel, National Guard units were called up to contain prisoners at a number of detention centers. Some of these citizen soldiers are too close to their day jobs to be trusted with guarding American civilians. We not only have a security problem, we may have a national health crisis on our hands. Do you see the difficulty?"

Wetzel, unsure of how to respond, chose the safest answer when talking to Green: "Yes, sir."

"Get me General Wilkinson at NORTHCOM," Green said. "We must replace these soft-hearted, weekend soldiers with professionals."

"Burgos," Captain Thiel said, raising his voice to make himself heard over the whine of the Blackhawk's rotors. "We need to find the man behind all this. Where would you locate yourself, if you wanted to direct a covert campaign inside the U.S. with at least a dozen independent A-teams?"

Warrant Officer Burgos sat next to Thiel on the chopper's bench seat. He deliberated before answering. "Not Bragg. How would you cover up the incoming intel? Need a lot of guys just to handle communications."

"Right. How about Campbell?"

"Same problem."

Thiel thought for a moment. "Pentagon?"

"You kidding? Too many leaks."

"Langley?"

"Maybe," Burgos said, "but that's risky, too. A lot of civilians around. Plus, think of the turf war if it got out that the CIA was directing Special Forces. If this is as big as you think, it'd be hard to keep the lid on it."

"Where, then?"

"Someplace tied into comms for all branches of the military."

The steady thrum of the rotors filled time while Thiel calculated the necessary logistics. He turned to Burgos and asked, "Raven Rock?"

Burgos nodded slowly. "That would work. Comm center for the entire military. Away from the Beltway, easy to hide guys coming and going."

"Hell, they'd live there," Thiel added. "It's an underground base."

"Raven Rock. Site R. That would work."

"Okay," Thiel decided. "That's where we go."

"Cap, are you sure about this? Security will be tight. Especially now."

"Remember who we are," Thiel shot back without hesitation. "Nothing is impossible. A few things are slightly more difficult."

Burgos nodded, mentally walking through the steps. "Not easy, but we might—you know, we're talking about maybe shooting fellow soldiers. And we don't even know if it's the right place."

"That's right. But you and I have to figure it out," Thiel said. "Look—somebody's hijacked the government and used it to *kill* American citizens. You and I are being used to cover it up. Do you want civilian blood on your hands?"

"No, sir!"

"Me, neither. So, let's figure out how we stop this."

"They're doing what?" Tony Harris sat up in his bunk, groggy at being pulled from a deep sleep.

Sergeant Ortiz crouched next to the bunk. "I'm sorry, sir, but I didn't know what to do. They're singing."

"Singing?"

"Singing. Hymns," Ortiz said. "Like in church."

Harris blinked, clearing his brain. "Singing, huh? How many?"

"Sounds like the whole barracks, sir."

"The whole—what time is it, Ortiz?"

"Twenty-three thirty, sir."

Harris took a deep breath as he sat up. "Well," he said, "If they're not hurting anyone, then let 'em sing."

"Sir," Ortiz said, "They might disturb some of the other prisoners."

"Detainees, Sergeant. They are not prisoners," Harris corrected, clearly annoyed. "Any of them complaining?"

"Not yet, sir."

"Then leave them be," Harris decided. "And if anyone does complain, move them to another barracks. Or give them cotton balls for their ears and tell them to deal with it."

"Yes, sir." The sergeant stood and left. Harris lay back down on the hard bunk, awake in the dark, thinking.

Asking for Bibles and singing hymns in the middle of the night. And these men are supposed to be a clear and present danger to the country? What in God's name am I involved in? – Then again, maybe God has nothing to do with it, he thought gloomily.

Outside, over the southwesterly breeze, he could the faint sounds of men's voices, and for the first time in years, Tony Harris began to talk to God.

The sight outside her kitchen window was beyond belief. Cindy Moore stood with her mouth open, speechless, as headlights, like so many fireflies, came to roost near her family's home. Finally, she turned to address her self-appointed champion.

"Mister I—Barney," she began, "why have you brought these people here?"

"Strength in numbers, Mrs. Moore," he said proudly. "United we stand. With dozens, hundreds rallying to your cause, the shadow government won't be able to sweep your little problem under the rug."

"But our congressman—" Susie Thornton began, but she was cut off with a wave of Barney Ison's massive hand.

"Harold Benson? I'm sorry to report that your congressman is missing, ladies," he said somberly. "Congressman Benson disappeared today around thirteen hundred Eastern Daylight Time and has not been seen since. I don't think he will be able to help."

His words hit Cindy like a hammer blow. Susie and Michelle looked sick.

Agent Unes appeared equally stunned. "Are you telling us that whoever's behind this has the *cajones* to take out a member of the United States Congress?"

"And no ordinary congressman, the Chair of the Armed Services Committee," Ison said matter-of-factly. "It's good to see your brain working, Agent Unes. The men and women of the DS—that's Deep State, ladies—believe themselves invulnerable. This is why I have to be so careful. And you should be, too."

"What should we do?" Cindy asked, exasperated.

Ison looked back and forth at the group in Cindy's kitchen, sizing them up like a basketball coach addressing his team before a big game. "Listen, fellow slaves, I have certain allies in the media— those who, like me, believe that the power of the DS is growing like a cancer. Worse, it's controlled by certain—*invisible*—forces, whose nature we don't entirely understand. However, exposing their actions, even a bit at a time, frustrates their ultimate plan to extinguish the torch of freedom on this planet, however dim and unsteady the flame."

"So, you want us to hold a press conference here?" Cindy asked. She shuddered, remembering the threatening phone call the previous night.

"All those headlights out there? That's just a taste of what the capital-T-Truth can accomplish. You give me a few hours, Mrs. Moore, and the press will beat a path to your door."

"I don't know if I want that," Cindy said.

"Why not?"

She weighed her words carefully. Eric was still in the room and she didn't want to scare him. "I received a threatening phone call last night," she said. "He didn't give me a name, but he said if I told anyone about Bob, we'd be in danger."

Agent Unes frowned. "Any clues at all? Caller ID?"

"No," Cindy said. "The number was blocked. He sounded sort of foreign. He had a slight accent, but I can't place it. That sounds horrible, I know. His English was excellent, but I got the sense that it's not his first language."

Jurasik said, "We might not be able to track him, but we can keep a deputy here for a while, until we're sure it's safe."

"Good idea," Agent Unes said. "I have another one. If it works, it might just reunite these ladies with their husbands. And soon."

"Hmm?" Ison turned, his amber eyes round, eyebrows arched high—he looked for all the world like a seven-foot owl.

Unes smiled. "First things first. Mrs. Moore, could we impose on you for some coffee?"

In his office, Green's eyes smoldered in anger at the unexpected delay. He was so close. So close! And to have his designs stalled by a few paranoid imbeciles was nearly more than he could bear.

The phone inside his desk beeped. Green ground his teeth in frustration. He yanked open the drawer, picked up the phone and spat, "Green."

"My, but we're testy today, aren't we?" It was an all too familiar voice, and one he particular did not want to hear at this moment. *Ryder.* "Apparently, the rumors are true. We have a problem. Or at least, you do."

"Now, why would you think that?" Green bluffed.

"Don't play games, Herr Grün," Ryder replied. "You loathe the Lessers, especially the followers of the Nameless Weakling. That shaped your so-called plan. The camps were unnecessary. Too complicated. Too many links in the chain."

Green's fingernails began to dig grooves into the dark wooden surface of his desk. "I have a contingency."

"Oh, you do? Good for you," Ryder said, his voice as smooth as glass. "I needn't remind you of the stakes, Señor Verde. Don't forget that the Lessers have an annoying habit of exercising free will in unpredictable ways. And those who pray—well, He has an inconsiderate tendency to dispatch our brothers to intervene in response to their prayers."

It was a superhuman effort to keep his voice under control. "I know what you think, Ryder," Green spit into the phone. "You would betray me for your own ambition. Don't try it. I am not your inferior—not like Grayson in New Mexico. Your deceit will not deter me."

A long pause. Green's heart pounded in his chest—a heart liberated years before from the chest of an unfortunate young man in London.

At last, Ryder spoke, his voice even, but dripping with menace. "You have exposed the Watchers to a great deal of risk. A reckless gamble for one of your rank."

"Great reward requires risk," Green replied, hoping his fear didn't translate through the ether.

"The risk is all yours, Green. Mister One has never responded well to failure." Ryder disconnected without another word.

As Green replaced the phone in his desk drawer, his face contorted involuntarily into a rictus of hate. *Ryder!* How he longed to destroy the ageless firebreather!

But Ryder was right. The fault was with Green's plan. The camps should have been guarded by outsiders, soldiers with no emotional connection to the prisoners. Ryder would be watching every step and misstep. It wasn't too late—not yet!—but Green needed to move quickly.

And then, soon—soon he would unleash a terror on this land that would make all that had come before as nothing. There would be a wailing and gnashing of teeth such as had not been heard since the days of Nebuchadnezzar.

And there would be blood. Oh, yes—there would be rivers of blood. Mister One would be very pleased.

TWENTY-SEVEN

Barney Ison stepped out of the Moores' kitchen and onto the deck, grateful for the chance to light up a Lucky. It had been almost two hours since the last one and he was starting to feel it.

Ison gratefully exhaled a cumulus of smoke before continuing out to his base of operations, an ancient Winnebago motor home that had been a gift from a generous supporter. It was the video studio and nerve center of *The Barney Ison Show*, two hours each weekday, mainly shared through social media. Even though he'd been banned from the largest video sharing sites long ago, he'd built a large and loyal following over the years.

The show had changed with new technology. It began on local radio in the 1980s and moved to shortwave in the '90s when Ison felt compelled to speak about national and world issues. When the Internet revolution took hold at the dawn of the twenty-first century, he shifted from shortwave to podcasting in as soon as the code was developed, recognizing the Internet as the future.

But his life changed forever when he spoke once too often about the links between government biowarfare research and the mysterious deaths of dozens of biologists and genetic scientists. He'd gone underground just in time. All police ever found of his good friend, Dave Hitchins, were charred bits of clothing and part of a leg.

After more than fifteen years, Ison still hadn't figured out what kind of weapon could incinerate a body like that.

But now someone inside the government had gone too far, and he had to risk exposure. It felt good to be back in the game. He'd been in hiding for far too long.

Crossing the street, Ison waved a grateful acknowledgment to the line of vehicles that had traveled to Mayfield in response to his call for help. He pulled open the driver's door of the Winnebago, which protested with a metallic groan. Folding his six-foot-ten frame into the driver's seat, he said, "Popeye, my boy, we've got some work to do."

A thin man in his early thirties with a shock of unkempt red hair roused himself from a fitful nap in the passenger seat. "Hmm? What?"

"We have a target in sight," Ison said. "Let's bring our weapons systems online. How many do we have with us?"

Theodore "Popeye" Bailey did a quick mental calculation. "Thirty-six, including the converted school bus from Ottumwa."

"There's been a change of plan," Ison said. "We need more. A lot more."

"The Alliance?"

"The Alliance." Ison checked his watch while he took a drag on his Lucky. "We need to move quick. Hand me that map and I'll give you the route. We need a communique in the air in less than fifteen minutes."

It had been a long, long day, and the end still wasn't in sight. Captain Tom Wetzel's eyes were gummy and a dull, throbbing ache threatened to grind through the center of his forehead. But Green said things were breaking, and his team was on the job until further notice.

"How long is he going to keep us here?" Larry Martin, an Army intelligence officer, sat at his desk and rubbed his eyes.

"Until frost warnings are issued for hell."

Martin grinned. "At least we'll be the first to know about that."

"Yeah." Wetzel stretched. "What's happening in Syria?"

"Stalemate. Israelis could take what's left of Damascus tomorrow, but if they do, they'll have to fight the entire Middle East. Plus that would be a bear to hold. Urban warfare in a ruined city that big? What a nightmare."

"What about Iraq?"

"No telling," Martin said. "We probably have enough boots there to keep the Iraqis in line, but who knows? With that second front in Iran, we might be spread too thin."

"Russia? China?"

"Tough call. If the Israelis don't back down, maybe they come in, too."

"And then we jump in."

"That's what the President said."

Rolling his eyes, Wetzel whistled softly. "Talk about Apocalypse Now."

Martin shrugged. "Maybe the Bible thumpers are right."

Wetzel massaged his temples, trying to push the ache from behind his eyes. "I'm gonna make some more coffee."

"Make it strong enough to slice."

Before he stood, the intercom buzzed. "Wetzel." It was Green. His gravel voice was as pleasant as a metal file on a broken tooth.

"Yes, sir?"

"Have those new units arrived yet, Captain?"

"Arrived where, sir?"

"Everywhere! Everywhere!"

Wetzel paused for a deep breath, capping his anger before responding. "I don't know, sir. I'll find out."

"Do it now! Now!" The line went dead.

Martin looked over with sympathy. "Sorry, man. I'll get the coffee."

Rubbing his eyes, Wetzel reached for a telephone earpiece and a list of phone numbers that existed only in this office and started dialing.

Green was losing it. Wetzel wondered what was really going on out there.

Harris woke with a start. Someone had called his name. The captain, yelling for his lieutenants: Morgan, Long, Shoemaker, and Harris. Poverello wanted them, and he wanted them *now*.

Harris rolled out and dressed in record time. Less than two minutes later, Harris joined the other platoon leaders of the 369th MPs in the captain's office. As he settled into his desk chair,

Poverello nodded at four Styrofoam cups filled with steaming black coffee. "Help yourself, gentlemen."

Harris and his fellow platoon leaders took the cups gratefully. Captain Poverello was clearly stressed about something, and it was more than just getting hauled out of the rack at oh-three-hundred.

"We have a situation," Poverello said quietly. He stared at his desk, and the silence stretched so long that Harris felt the need to prompt the captain.

"Sir?" he said.

Poverello sipped his coffee before he continued. "I was notified about thirty minutes ago that a company of troops is in the air, coming by transport helicopter. They will touch down in about an hour with orders to relieve us."

Harris exchanged glances with the other platoon leaders. This didn't make sense. They'd only been at the base a couple of days.

Lieutenant Shoemaker, a police officer in the south Chicago suburbs, spoke up. "Is this bad news? I mean, we can go home then, right?"

"I don't know," the captain admitted, his eyes still fixed on his desk. "I wasn't notified through proper channels. The colonel and I were told by somebody working air traffic in the tower who thought we should know."

"Sir? What unit?" Harris asked.

Poverello finished the coffee and crumpled the cup. "I don't know," he said. "Tower doesn't, either. The colonel is trying to chase down somebody who knows what's going on. If somebody in the tower hadn't sent a runner to pull me out of bed, they'd have had our places at mess in the morning before we knew they were coming."

"So, what are you going to do, captain?" Lieutenant Long, a writer for technical journals by trade, liked things cut and dried.

Poverello sighed. "Wake your men. Get them up, and have them ready. We're going to wait for official orders. Until we get them, we're not going anywhere."

The world returned to Jared Gruner slowly.

Hungry.

He tried to ignore the pangs, but his stomach's demands slowly intensified until he finally couldn't stand it any longer.

Gruner opened his eyes and suffered a moment of panic when he didn't recognize his surroundings. Then it came back to him, and he shut his eyes again with a groan.

What have I gotten us into?

Gradually, he realized that it wasn't just hunger that pulled him from sleep—there was a noise. Not loud, but loud enough to cut through the combined sniffles and snorts of over a hundred sleeping men.

There it was again. Muffled shouts. Movement. Somewhere outside.

Gruner opened his eyes. All he could see were shapes in the darkness, silhouetted by a dim light from the latrine at the end of the barracks. The guards had taken his wristwatch when he was processed so he had no way to know the time, but it looked pretty dark for so much activity. There was no way they hustled the guards out at this hour of the day.

He hoped they weren't coming to get the prisoners up. The gospel sing-along had been entertaining, but it lasted way too long. He needed a few more hours at least.

More shouts in the distance. Gruner sighed and sat up. He couldn't sleep, not when he was this hungry. Might as well slip on the shoes he'd been issued and take a look around. Maybe he'd learn something useful. Or at least find a snack.

Barney Ison was fairly sure they'd gotten in and out of Mayfield without giving away their location. Just to be sure, he had Popeye Bailey keeping a sharp eye out the rear window of the creaky Winnebago—in addition to his regular job, which was overseeing an impressive collection of radar and radio detecting equipment, computers, and video gear stowed in racks and cabinets along the length of the motor home.

To their relief, so far the road had been empty.

Ison punched the cigarette lighter on the dash to heat it up for another Lucky.

"You ought to quit," Bailey commented from the back. "Secondhand smoke kills."

"So does being a smart aleck. I'll quit when this pack is done."

Popeye flipped a switch on the police band radio. "You said that about fourteen hundred packs ago. Boy, it's quiet around here."

"Yeah," Ison muttered. "Be grateful for it. You know, Pop, you gotta give the Alliance credit. A few coded messages uploaded to the web, and the Mayfield story spread across the Midwest like ripples on a virtual pond. Good folks out here. Good people."

Three dozen cars and trucks, and one converted school bus, responded to Ison's first call and followed him to Mayfield. Like Ison, these brave warriors had also taken to back roads, traveling by different routes. A convoy traveling together could be stopped by a single roadblock.

Homeland Security still had the official Threat Level at "red." The hope was that even if some of them were detained en route to the rendezvous, police wouldn't catch them all.

There'd been a hasty conference back in Mayfield—thirty-seven vehicles, and nearly that many different ways plotted from Point A to Point B. How many more joined them at the rendezvous was in the hands of the Alliance.

No, Ison reminded himself. *Not the Alliance. The Almighty. Lord, if it's Your will, please hide us from the Enemy's sight.*

The lighter popped out. Ison pulled it from the dash, held its glowing orange coil to the end of his Lucky and inhaled deeply. A few hours without being seen. That's all they needed, just a few short hours. And then the enemy would get a wakeup call it couldn't ignore.

From the moment he'd decided on this course of action, Captain Thiel knew the key would be getting the right pilot. Frank Marvin was the best Thiel knew, and being the best in the 160th SOAR was saying a lot.

It hadn't taken much to persuade Marvin that the mission was valid. Career soldiers are always skeptical about the politicians who pull their strings. A quick visit with the supply sergeant to verify Thiel's computer story was all it took to convince Frank Marvin that something was very wrong at a senior level of the United States government.

They were prepping Marvin's MH-60 for flight less than an hour later.

"How long until we get there?" Thiel asked through the headset. The eight remaining members of his team sat on two benches behind him in the Blackhawk. Most of them were sleeping or trying to.

"Couple of hours," Marvin answered from the pilot's seat. "Relax, Captain. This isn't my first dance.'"

Thiel settled back and closed his eyes, letting the vibration of the Blackhawk's dual engines relax him as the helicopter sped almost silently through the dark night. Maybe Burgos was right. Maybe this was a fool's mission. It was suicide, one way or another. Even if they lived, their careers were dead.

He just hoped he'd guessed right about where Malthus was holed up.

No. It was too late for doubts. They'd been used as the sharp edge of somebody's knife. That was their job, what they'd trained for, but the one wielding the knife had violated the sacred trust that went with that responsibility.

It had happened too many times in the last half century: good men lost in secret wars, disowned by the country they loved because well-groomed men in tailored suits deemed their hold on power more precious than the lives poured out in southeast Asia, Africa, Central America, and the Middle East.

And now the deadly skills of these elite warriors had been turned against the very people and the way of life they were sworn to protect. It was wrong. It had all been wrong.

No more expendable elites. It was time to put an end to it.

His high beams painted a glowing pool across the two-lane asphalt ribbon of US Highway 61, illuminating the yellow center stripes that flashed by with hypnotic regularity. Joe Unes blinked and reached for the travel mug he'd bought at the Mayfield Family Market and filled with Cindy Moore's freshly brewed coffee.

Driving back to Saint Louis tonight, after a long and stressful day, was probably not the wisest thing he'd ever done, but Unes sensed that things were about to break loose and he wanted evidence to back up the wild theories spinning in his mind. With luck, he might even have time to stop at home to shower and spend a few minutes with Cathy and the girls. Then he'd head down to the office early and deliver the computers to Fred Schuler, the Saint Louis field office's topnotch IT guru and cryptology expert.

More important, Schuler was a man Unes trusted.

Joe turned up the volume on the car stereo. He was glad his youngest daughter, Molly, had turned him onto the Basin Street Rapscallions. The swing band wasn't exactly Bobby Darin, but Molly had discovered them during her first year of playing trumpet in junior high and now Unes was hooked. Nice to know his daughter could appreciate music without screaming guitars and guaranteed-to-make-you-blush lyrics.

As he reached for his coffee, Unes knocked his phone from the other cup holder to the floor of the car with a plasticky clatter. He didn't want to step on it and crack the screen. It's hard enough to teach kids responsibility when you can't even keep track of your own stuff.

Sneaking quick glances between his knees, Unes gauged the approximate position of the phone. He looked up—the road ahead was straight and clear. He decided to risk it.

As he leaned over to reach for the phone, his windshield exploded in a shower of pebbled glass.

"Holy—!" Unes fought to control the Traverse as a gale-force wind hammered his face. His foot was off the accelerator, but he'd jerked the wheel when the windshield shattered, and the car swerved left and then right before he stabilized and straightened out.

"What the…?" Was it a rock? A deer? Unes looked back over his shoulder. A pair of headlights switched on alongside the road.

Suddenly, he knew all too well what it was.

A gun.

Cold sweat chilled him to the bone, made colder by the brisk October air roaring through the hole in his windshield. Unes punched the gas and tried to think. The shooter had to know he'd missed.

Unes was just south of Hannibal. It was another hour and a half to Wentzville and Interstate 64. He didn't think he'd make it that far with this wind in his face.

There!

Unes locked the brakes and jerked the wheel hard left, aiming for a dirt lane on the side of the road. The dual tracks led into a field of corn waiting for harvest. His tires screamed as they slid across the asphalt, finally gaining enough purchase to launch the SUV into the field.

His body jerked painfully as the Traverse danced along the track, jittering along ruts and potholes gouged into the earth by tractors and half-ton trucks.

Unes shut off the headlights and gradually slowed the car to a stop. He killed the engine, alone in total darkness.

He sat for a moment, trying to clear his head while he listened for the shooter's car. The only sound in his ears was his own heavy breathing.

A quick check of his sidearm to make sure it was still loaded— good. Unes switched off the dome light, opened the door, and jumped into the cornfield.

The rich scent of earth and the rustling of leaves all around him unexpectedly triggered a memory of the long, hot summer thirty years earlier when Unes endured that Midwestern rite of passage, detasseling. He'd hated corn for years afterward.

Unes moved a few paces into the field and then circled back toward the highway, parallel with the dirt track. Had the shooter seen where he'd turned? If not, would he—or maybe *they*—just set up another ambush farther down the road?

Joe considered using his phone—no go. It was still on the floor of the car.

Great. Just bleeping great.

And he hadn't called Cathy to let her know his plans had changed. She thought he was asleep at a motel somewhere near Mayfield.

Standing in the middle of the long rows of yellowing stalks, God only knew where, shaking from nerves and the brisk night air, and chased by someone who wanted him dead, Special Agent Joe Unes experienced an epiphany: No matter how well you organize your life, you're always just one heartbeat away from discovering that you wasted far too much time on things that, in the end, don't really matter at all.

TWENTY-EIGHT

The miles clicked by at a steady rate of one per minute. No faster—Ison didn't want to attract the attention of the police. Couldn't trust them. Besides, the old Winnebago developed a nasty shudder over sixty.

Popeye Bailey sat on a bench seat they'd installed in the back when they converted the mobile home into a rolling electronic surveillance lab and media production studio. His freckled face was constantly in motion, a model of nervous energy as he scanned several computer screens, a radar detector, and an infrared scanner.

"Anything?" Barney called back from the driver's seat.

"Nope. Nothing so far," Popeye yelled back, his high voice nearly lost in the bone-numbing buzz of the motor home's engine.

Better than halfway there. Another hundred miles or so to the interstate. Ison would have preferred a less-traveled route, but there were few options. There just weren't that many bridges across the Missouri River, so I-64 would have to do. Besides, he couldn't trust the Winnebago on some of the back roads between Mayfield and I-64.

Once across the Missouri River bridge and into Saint Louis County, he could get off the highway and pass for local traffic. The Missouri tags he and Popeye had swapped onto the bumpers after leaving Iowa helped. Less conspicuous than out of state plates, especially with the Terror Threat Level at Red. As inconspicuous, that is, as one could be in a thirty-four-foot Winnebago.

Ahead on US 61, Ison could just make out the dim red glow of the FBI agent's taillights. Good thing Agent Unes wasn't speeding.

Ison hadn't told Unes that he planned to follow. It was better Unes didn't know.

Ison wanted to keep an eye on the agent. He wasn't sure he could trust Unes, not yet. Unes didn't strike him as stupid, so either the agent was a plant or he really didn't understand the danger.

In the trunk of the agent's car, wedged between a suitcase, a briefcase, and a box of emergency supplies, was the key to the terror outbreak and Homeland Security's roundup of "suspects." Ison felt it in his gut. He just needed to get his hands on the computers so Popeye could pull out the data.

If Unes was one of *them*, then the evidence was already as good as lost. Ison wrestled with the problem as he drove. As far as Agent Unes knew, Ison was alone in the motor home. Maybe Ison could catch the agent at a gas station or rest stop before Saint Louis and delay him for just a little while—long enough for Popeye to break into the agent's trunk and copy the hard drives to one of the portable five-terabyte drives they kept in the back of the Winnebago.

Ison blinked. Was that a flash of lightning ahead? No, the skies were clear. It looked more like—

The taillights ahead careened from one side of the road to the other like lanterns in a hurricane. Ison caught his breath, stunned. The lights stabilized and then accelerated.

Headlights flared alongside the road, and a second car pulled onto the highway maybe half a mile ahead, following the agent. Ison instantly slapped a knob on the dashboard and killed the Winnebago's lights.

"Hey! What's up?" Popeye yelled, looking up from his iPad.

"Night goggles, Pop! Looks like our G-man is one of the good guys!"

Bob Moore hadn't slept well the last few nights. He was too used to being next to Cindy in the dark to relax. Others might prefer silence at night, but the sound of his wife's breathing in the stillness was his lullaby.

The sounds he heard now were disturbing. A commotion outside, in the distance. Voices shouting orders, the impression of boots hitting the turf at a run. It wasn't loud, but the noise was growing.

Bob rolled to his side, the lower bunk on which he lay creaking in protest. Pastor Dave Schiebold lay on the next bunk. His eyes were open.

"Do you hear that?" Bob asked.

"Yes," Schiebold answered.

"What do you think?"

"I don't know," Schiebold said. "Maybe 'the end of all things is at hand.'"

Bob smiled ruefully. "I thought scripture was supposed to make you feel better."

A glow like the beam of a searchlight swept across the cornfield where Joe Unes stood, shaking. They'd found him.

Over the chirp of crickets and the occasional peep of small frogs, Unes heard the idling engine of his attackers' car creeping along the dirt path. There had to be at least two, he reasoned, a spotter and a gunman.

Unes moved to his right, back toward the highway, three or four yards into the standing corn. Maybe he could circle behind the car and get the drop on his would-be assassins.

Light suddenly stabbed into the corn like a giant pitchfork trying to impale him and drag him out into the open. Flashlights. One of the beams caught Unes for a moment. He jumped to the side and began to run deeper into the field. Behind him, a roar was followed by a spray of buckshot tearing through the corn where Unes had been a moment before.

Car doors opened, voices shouted, footsteps, rustling as his pursuers dove into the field after him. Fingers of light pierced the darkness around him, forcing Unes ever deeper into the uneven, grasping sea of corn.

To the right—Unes pushed through several rows of stalks, hoping again to circle behind his enemies. A flash; another shotgun blast behind him. Running, stumbling, panting, a growing pain in his ribs. Unes wished he'd been more regular on the treadmill he and Cathy bought last Christmas.

A bright light flashed ahead. Unes was startled—he hadn't expected anyone there. Had he lost his bearings? No, they'd probably split up to search for him. Were there more than two?

Trying to change direction, a clod of earth caught his foot and Unes fell heavily to the ground. A moment later, someone in black pants and spotless, gleaming dress shoes stood just out of reach, dazzling Unes with a powerful flashlight aimed directly into his eyes.

"Sorry, agent," a deep voice said. "You just stuck your nose where it didn't belong."

Unes squinted, trying to make out a face, but the glare was nearly blinding. A metallic glint caught his eye, and it was then he noticed that his pursuer also held a large-caliber pistol with a laser sight.

As the barrel of the revolver and its thin beam of green laser light centered on his forehead, Joe Unes offered a silent, desperate prayer: *Please, God, if it has to be this way, please take care of my girls.*

His entire world compressed to a single point. The future, his daughters, grandchildren, retirement with Cathy—all crushed into a singularity, the impossibly black hole at the end of the pistol aimed at his forehead.

Unes closed his eyes and waited for the gunshot and whatever would follow the moment after.

Instead he heard a growl, the mechanical bellow of an engine pushed far beyond its design specifications. He opened his eyes just in time to see a pair of glowing orbs leap from the cornfield in front of him and tackle the man with the gun. A huge boxy mass crashed through the corn and stopped a few yards away.

A motor home. In the cornfield.

Barney Ison's Winnebago.

From the darkness, a voice cried out, "Agent Unes! Get in! We need to go!"

The first glow of pre-dawn sunlight crept over the horizon in the east. The helicopter continued on, nearly invisible against the pitch-black sky.

Frank Marvin was a master. Weaving and dodging through the mountains of southeast Pennsylvania, hugging the trees to avoid radar, Marvin controlled his bird with the grace and skill of a ballerina. Not that Thiel would ever say it that way to Marvin's face.

A surge of adrenaline coursed through Captain Thiel's blood, the rush he always felt just before action. There, ahead, was the looming granite mound of Raven Rock Mountain. Buried six hundred feet beneath its peak was the communications nexus of the United States government. Site R: the entire complex of American civil and military operations could be controlled from the small city under this mountain.

Thiel was betting he knew who sat at the center of the web. And they were flying right into the spider's lair.

But this fly packed a sting of his own.

"Sir," Sergeant Williams huffed, out of breath, "The captain wants rifles issued?"

"Yeah, yeah," Lieutenant Harris said. "He was clear. Get the men up, out, and ready. And by ready, he means armed. Are we clear?"

"Yes, sir," Williams said, turning his attention back to their platoon. "McSorley, pick it up! We ain't got all day!"

"Sir," Sergeant Keloski said, jogging up, "Squad Two is just about ready."

"Good," Harris said. "Williams, Keloski, get your squads over to headquarters. Tell Ortiz. We'll find out what the captain needs from us."

"Sir," Keloski said, "Is this some kind of drill?"

"Don't think so, sergeant."

"What's going on, sir? Are we under attack?"

"I don't know," Harris said. "Just get your men together and do it quick."

"Yes, sir!"

Harris jogged toward the headquarters building through the growing uproar swirling around the company's barracks, thankful for good sergeants. Made his job a lot easier. He just wished he knew what in hell was going on.

Whatever it was had to be big. Jared Gruner crouched in the shadows and watched the guards swarm out of their barracks like angry bees.

Gruner looked at the sky—still dark. Couldn't be any later than four or four-thirty. What could possibly get them out and running at this hour? A big load of prisoners coming in? Why would they need the whole company? How many was that, a hundred and twenty men?

Something was up. He decided to head back inside. He needed to wake the guys. They'd want to see what happened next.

TWENTY-NINE

"Don't stand there, Agent Unes! Get in!"

Stunned, Joe Unes stared at a blurry, moonlit Winnebago in the middle of a cornfield where, seconds before, he'd expected to die. The sudden change of fortune was just beginning to register.

Feeling around on the ground for his glasses, Unes picked up the wire frames and blew the dirt off the lenses before replacing them on his face. Broken stalks bit into his hands as he pushed himself up. With his glasses in place, Unes instantly recognized the unmistakable outline of the RV and ran to the driver's door where Barney Ison leaned out of the open window. The night-vision goggles on top of Ison's head were perfectly appropriate for the situation, which could not have been more surreal.

"How did you find me?" Unes managed to ask, his breath coming in gasps.

"Followed you," Ison said. "I'll explain after you get in! Or would you prefer to stay out here with a target painted on your back?"

"But—wait. The shooter is still out there!"

"Ran him over on the way. Now, *get in!*"

"Okay. I need to get—"

"The stuff in your trunk, I know," Ison said. "Get in, I'll take you."

Unes stumbled around to the passenger side of the big motor home in a fog, detached, as though he'd actually been shot and this was all a dream. Behind the Winnebago, Unes nearly tripped over the victim of Barney Ison's road rage, who lay face down in the dirt, twisted into an unnatural position. Unes stopped, and with two fingers he picked up the man's gun, knocked loose when the motor home plowed into him. Unes' own pistol lay somewhere in the field nearby. It would have to stay there. No time to look.

The agent climbed into the passenger seat, holding the shooter's MP5. Ison whistled. "Nice piece," he said. "Yours?" He shifted into gear and eased the Winnebago forward.

"No," Unes answered. "It was his. I dropped mine when I fell."

"Too bad. They'll find it and trace it back to you. You'll catch hell for it."

"Mind if I look at that?" The voice from the back seat made Unes jump. He thought Ison was alone.

"Sorry, Agent Unes," Ison said. "Meet Popeye Bailey. He's the technical wizard who keeps *The Barney Ison Show* on the air. Well, on the web, to be precise. We didn't have an opportunity to introduce him earlier."

"Hi," Unes said. "Uh, no, I want to take this back to—"

"You won't find any prints or registration," Ison said. "These guys are über careful."

"What do you mean?"

"You're in deep, Agent Unes. Through the looking glass. Welcome to the dark side. Here's your car."

The Winnebago parted the corn just behind the rear bumper of the abandoned SUV. Unes jumped out of the motor home and opened the driver's door of his car, sending broken pieces of glass tinkling to the ground. Leaning in, Unes retrieved his phone and suit jacket and pulled the trunk release. With Popeye's help, he carried his overnight bag, briefcase, and the two computers to the Winnebago and set them in the back with Popeye.

It only took twenty minutes from the time his sergeants rousted their squads to fall in outside the headquarters building. Most of them looked dazed, still trying to wake up.

Sergeants Ortiz, Williams, and Keloski had herded them through Supply, where Master Sergeant Podowsky issued rifles and ammunition to everyone. Captain Poverello had insisted on everybody being rated for nearly all of the weapons used by standard infantry units. Harris wondered who the captain expected his men to shoot.

"Sir," Sergeant Williams said, "all present and ready, sir."

"Good job, Sergeant," Harris said. Podowsky was still equipping the other three squads of the 369th. They were quick, but his Third Platoon was first.

"Sir," Williams continued, "Do we know what we're doing yet?"

"Not yet," Harris said. "Captain's coming, though. We'll find out in a minute."

Huddled in the cool predawn air, four men squinted through the pink-hued darkness at a clump of soldiers gathered outside what had to be the headquarters building for their guards. Jared Gruner had led his three friends outside, quietly, careful to avoid illuminated areas that might expose them to the eyes of the guards in the watch towers posted on opposite sides of the perimeter.

"See? What did I tell you?" Gruner's voice rasped as he tried to whisper. "The whole freakin' company's out there!"

"And they've got rifles," Scott Stauffer said. "None of them carried rifles before, except for the guards in the towers."

"Right," Gruner said. "And usually the MPs just wear a sidearm."

"Sidearm?" Vijay asked.

"Pistol," Norlock said. "Sidearm is just another word for handgun."

The four watched in silence for a few minutes. Gruner wished he had some of the electronic listening devices he and Stauffer had read about in a recent issue of *Popular Mechanics.*

Snippets of the commanding officer's voice drifted to them on a light breeze as the captain addressed his troops. Whatever he said, it was obvious the men were surprised. Several of the soldiers turned to look at one another as if to confirm that they really heard what their captain had just said.

"What do you think? Bad news?" Norlock asked.

"Not sure," Stauffer said.

"Could it be they are preparing for the arrival of many new prisoners?" Vijay asked.

"Look at them, for cripe's sake!" Gruner said. "They're a little overdressed to escort prisoners."

The captain finished his speech or his orders, whatever they were, and one by one, the platoons turned and began marching double-quick toward the air base.

"Do you think—?" Stauffer started.

"Yeah," Gruner cut in. "It looks like they're going to secure the airfield."

"Against whom?" Vijay asked.

"That, my friend," Gruner said, "is the big freakin' question."

The FBI agent sitting next to him looked terrible—sweating, breathing hard, dirt everywhere, and a deer-in-the-headlights look. Made sense, considering that he'd been about a second away from being shot in the head. Maybe now Agent Unes understood the stakes.

Barney Ison took another draw on his Lucky and prepared to get back on the road. Every minute counted.

As he eased the big vehicle back onto US 61, thankful they hadn't gotten stuck in the cornfield, the screen on Agent Unes' phone lit up. "What are you doing?" Ison asked.

"I need to call my wife," Unes explained. "Let her know I'm all right."

Ison put his size sixteen boot back down on the brake pedal and extended a long right arm. "Let me see that a minute."

"What?"

"Let me see your phone."

Frowning, Unes placed the phone in Ison's oversized hand. Ison looked at it for a moment, and then hurled it out of his open window.

"Hey! What the hell are you doing?"

Ison turned to the agent, his voice low and intense. "Agent Unes? Do you not yet understand the nature of the threat we face?"

"What are you talking about?"

"Tell him, Pop." Ison hit the gas and willed the Winnebago out of the corn and back onto the highway.

"Every phone's got a unique ID GPS transmitter," Bailey said from the back. "It's probably how the hit team found you."

Joe's mouth went slack. "I hadn't thought of that."

"All phones have 'em," Bailey said, occupied with the computers they'd rescued from the agent's car. "Safety feature, they call it. But it also makes it simple for the government to track anybody, anywhere."

Ison exhaled a cloud of smoke. "Clever, eh? Who doesn't want to be safe? Alone on the road at night, tire blows, the GPS tracker saves your life, no? Helps the police pinpoint you. But even when you don't know it, the phone sends a signal. Finding it is a snap. Very sophisticated and not cheap. Have you never wondered why phone companies practically give smart phones away?"

The agent looked like he was in shock. Good. Maybe it was starting to sink in.

"Whoever wants you dead is now tracking a phone that's stopped by the side of the road." Ison took another drag on his cigarette. "Isn't that better than having them chase us down? I've got a cache of old analog phones, courtesy of an Alliance member. Pop, give the man one of the burners. We use 'em once and toss 'em. You can call your wife with that."

The Blackhawk swung around a curve as it followed Pennsylvania Route 58. "Almost there," Marvin called over the intercom. "Get ready."

Using the helipad at the site had been ruled out. While it would have been safer to land, it also would have triggered the intruder detection system. Thiel and his team would have had to fight through nearly a quarter mile of security detail before reaching the first portal into Site R, on the west side of Raven Rock Mountain. They agreed their best chance was to drop onto the guard post just outside Portal A from above.

None of Thiel's team had been inside Site R. Their only intel was a hand-drawn map Burgos pulled from an old DOD database.

They'd find out how accurate it was when they were inside the mountain.

"We're here," Marvin announced. "Have fun at the dance, ladies."

Thiel took a couple of deep breaths to clear his head as Marvin's crew lowered ropes toward a tiny clearing just a hundred yards east of the unsuspecting MPs in the guard post.

This was it. What happened from here on in would depend on their training. And luck.

"You tailed me all the way from Mayfield?"

Barney Ison nodded as he took a drag on his Lucky, concentrating on the road ahead. "Had to be sure I could trust you. That assassination attempt answered my questions."

Unes stared at the tall man behind the wheel of the creaky motor home. "I can't believe I didn't notice."

"You're tired and you didn't expect to be followed, but you gotta be alert twenty-four seven," Ison said with a smile. "I hope you realize that now. I hope the truth is sinking in."

"What is the truth, Barney?"

"Our duly elected government is a front," Ison said. "It's a shell game, a puppet show scripted and produced to distract the average, pleasure-seeking American from the real game behind the scenes. The average slave in the street thinks he has the right to vote, the right to a trial by his peers, the rights to life, liberty, and property, but those rights were sold to the highest bidder years ago. We have no rights in the eyes of the real power behind the throne, only privileges. And there's a big difference between rights and privileges, Agent Unes."

"Uh huh," Unes said. "Somebody else told me the same thing yesterday."

Ison took a final drag on his Lucky and snubbed the remains in the ashtray. "This time I'm quitting," he declared as he tapped the empty pack and handed it to Bailey. "File that where it belongs, Pop. No more, I promise."

Bailey laughed and threw the white and red pack into the Winnebago's kitchen garbage can. "Believe it when I see it."

Ison shrugged and adjusted his rear view mirror. "You see, agent," he continued, "rights are guaranteed. Not open for discussion. Not to be abridged, abused, or abrogated by any man or any government. A privilege—well, now that's just permission, to be granted or denied as the masters please. We can vote, but for the candidates they select. We can speak freely, but anyone who crosses the party line never gets on the air. Our press is free, but it's in the hands of a few media conglomerates with a vested interest in preserving the status quo."

"Don't tell me you're one of the tinfoil crowd, Barney. You think the Trilateral Commission runs everything? Council on Foreign Relations? The Fed?"

Ison laughed. "A tinfoil hat has its place, but we'll discuss that another time. Would it surprise you, agent, to learn that a hundred and twenty of the wealthiest and most powerful people in the world meet every spring for a weekend getaway, out of the media's sight? People who spend the rest of the year accusing each other of the most hideous crimes gather to break bread and discuss how to run the world."

Joe's head hurt. "What are you talking about?"

"The Bilderberg Group, Agent Unes. Bankers, politicians, journalists, oilmen, industrialists, educators—even some of the royal houses of Europe. *Créme de la créme.* It's all very incestuous. Bill Clinton and Tony Blair both came from nowhere to lead the most powerful nations on Earth after being invited to Bilderberg meetings in the early Nineties."

Unes sighed. "So you're saying the world is run by a group with a name that sounds like a fast-food restaurant."

"Far from it," Ison explained. "Bilderberg is a red herring. A decoy. Just like the CFR, the CIA, the Fed, the Trilaterals, the Freemasons, the Jesuits, or any other favorite conspiracy target."

"I'm too tired for this. You're confusing me." Unes longed to be home, in his own bed, snoring happily next to his wife.

"Think about it, Agent Unes. If you wanted to secretly rule the world, would you call an annual meeting of the most powerful and visible people on the planet? People who can't go for a hot dog without getting their picture in the paper?"

Unes stared out of the passenger window of the Winnebago. This wasn't going anywhere he could follow at the moment. "I don't know. I guess not."

"They're pawns. Useful idiots. Most of them probably don't even realize it."

"Pawns for whom?"

Ison glanced at Unes, one eyebrow raised. "Who is man's oldest enemy?"

"Hey!" Unes turned around to see Popeye's boyish face illuminated by the glow of a flat-panel computer monitor.

"Got something, Pop?" Ison called.

"Yeah," Bailey said. "There's a hidden attachment on these emails. I—"

Unes jolted upright in his seat. "You're not looking at it, are you?"

"Oh, hey, no," Bailey said, raising his hands. "Not after what we heard happened! I'm opening up the files to see what they got in 'em. And this attachment here is an animated GIF. Most email software opens it automatically. What's weird is it looks like it's designed not to even register at the conscious level."

"What are you saying, Pop? Subliminal insertion?" Ison asked.

"Yeah, but very sophisticated. Looks like it's supposed to display like a normal email," Bailey said. "But when you open the file and examine it frame by frame, instead of letting it loop, it looks like it displays some weird flashing pattern in the background so quick you wouldn't consciously 'see' it, you know?"

"But your subconscious brain does," Ison said, with an ominous tone to his voice.

"Plain English, please," Unes said. "I'm tired."

Ison hit his turn signal, aiming for a filling station at the next exit. "Simple. Some saboteur in the shadowland we call a government may have figured out how to trigger psychotic episodes in unsuspecting people," he said. "Through their email."

THIRTY

Lieutenant Tony Harris and his Third Platoon of the 369th MPs crouched behind a line of cargo boxes near the south end of Scott Air Force Base's main runway. The blinking lights of the radio tower behind them cast an intermittent eerie red glow over the scene. He felt a little silly; probably all that was going to happen was a quick transfer of responsibility for the detainees to the new unit. It was strange that they were being reassigned so quickly, but he'd overlook it if it meant sleeping in his own bed again.

Most of all, he looked forward to seeing his son. Maybe he wouldn't have to miss his weekend with Demetrius after all.

The morning was cool, just enough to chill his fingers. Harris blew through his cupped hands to bring back some feeling. The glow of predawn painted the eastern sky with a hint of orange and pink.

Captain Poverello walked up, making the rounds of the platoons he'd positioned around the airfield. It was a lot of real estate to guard with a single company of military police, but the captain had chosen their ground well. Not great cover, but decent, and with overlapping fields of fire.

Poverello quickly scanned their position. "All set, Harris?"

"Yes, sir," Harris said. "Sir? If I can ask—what's Colonel Hostler say about this?"

"He's the one gave me the go," Poverello said. "He'd be out here with us, but he's trying to raise somebody at the Pentagon who can give us a straight answer. Something about this stinks."

The distinctive sound of dual helicopter rotors echoed between the hangars alongside the runway. "Sounds like the replacements are here, captain," Harris said.

"I see it," Poverello said. "Keep your men down. Don't let them know you're here until I tell you. I'll check it out and keep in touch." The captain turned and started toward the runway, speaking into his radio.

Harris walked along the line to check on his three squads. "Keep your heads down until we find out what's going on," he said. "Be ready. And pray this is all a big mistake."

The noise of the rotors grew steadily louder. Overhead, the first bird slid into view—a dual-rotor Chinook, primary transport and cargo carrier for the U.S. Army and the armed forces of about a dozen other countries.

Behind the Chinook came five—no, seven other helicopters in rapid order. Harris did some quick math: eight birds would hold almost two hundred and fifty men. About two companies.

Great. If something does *happen, we're outnumbered two to one.*

The eastern sky was lighter now, the black of night shaded from azure to crimson along the horizon. The first Chinook slowly settled to ground, like a giant, prehistoric nightmare of a bird floating gently to Earth. The others followed, each staking out a piece of the main runway.

"Listen up." It was Captain Poverello on the radio. "I'm going out to meet the first chopper. There are no markings that I can see. I don't like this one bit."

No markings? Who owns these things? Harris peered over the top of a cargo container, trying to get a glimpse of what was happening.

The flashing white and red landing lights silhouetted Captain Poverello as he approached the Chinook. He stopped halfway to the helicopter and waited as a set of cargo doors on the side of the craft slowly opened.

"Can't see anything yet," Poverello said, the tinny speaker squeezing the emotion from the captain's voice. "If we're lucky, this is some idiot mistake, and we'll all be home by the weekend."

The copter's door opened fully. Harris glimpsed movement inside the black maw of the helicopter's door and the first man hopped down to the runway.

"What the—?" Captain Poverello let the question hang as he took three steps toward the Chinook. A few more men jumped out of the transport copter. Poverello waved his hand to get the attention of the commander of the replacement unit. Suddenly, he stopped. His voice crackled through the radio again, nearly lost in the noise of the big engines of the helicopters.

"These guys have blue helmets! Blue helmets! Repeat—blue hats!"

Blue helmets? Harris tried to remember which unit wore blue helmets.

Harris looked back at the runway. Captain Poverello was shouting into the radio and coming back at a dead run. "Do not let these men leave the runway! Is that clear? Repeat, do not let these men leave the runway!"

It finally hit Harris.

"What's he talking about, Lieutenant?" Sergeant Ortiz looked at him quizically. "Blue helmets?"

"Blue helmets," Harris shouted. "They're UN! Squad One, spread out down there! Get a clear shot at those chopper doors!"

His stomach knotted. United Nations troops. Deployed on American soil, to stand guard over American citizens.

Harris sighted down the length of his pistol at the unmarked Chinook. *Hell, no!*

First obstacle: The guard post outside Portal A, manned by two MPs. Good thing the official DOD security procedures for Site R assumed that threats to the base would approach on the ground. Thiel glanced at the six-foot chain-link intended to protect the perimeter—it might have been built to MIL-T specifications, but it was useless against a Special Forces team dropped from a helicopter.

Thiel's crack team moved silently, like jungle cats with guns, each movement timed to the second. The stunned MPs surrendered on the spot and, better yet, had no time to sound an alarm. It took exactly forty-one seconds to bind and gag the guards with duct tape and zip ties.

"Don't worry, boys, it's only a drill," he told the MPs with a wink and a smile. "It'll be over before you can wish for breakfast."

Burgos pulled the magnetic-strip ID cards that hung around the bound guards' necks. "Bingo," he said, pocketing both cards. "These should come in handy."

"Too easy," Thiel said. "Don't get cocky, ladies."

Site R had been designed to keep an emergency government alive and in contact with military units in the field if Washington, D.C. were taken out by a nuke. If Thiel's team hit a door they couldn't bypass or blast, it was over. Then it was just a matter of time until reinforcements from Fort Detrick trapped them inside. Thiel hadn't decided what to do if things played that way.

And there was still the very real possibility that he and Burgos had guessed wrong, that Malthus was nowhere near Raven Rock. If Malthus wasn't here—well, Thiel didn't even want to think about tomorrow.

Focus on now. Get inside so fast that nobody has time to bar the doors.

One obstacle down. Thiel steeled his nerve and gave the hand signal to move ahead. It was time to storm the hall of the mountain king.

"What's going on?" Norlock stretched to his full six foot five, staring across the open area of the compound, trying to catch a glimpse of what was happening at the air base.

"Get down," Gruner said. "They'll see you."

"Don't think so, my lad," Norlock replied. "The guards in the towers are looking over that way, too."

He was right. Gruner scanned both towers, and the darkened shapes of the troops on duty were on the north side, facing the air base.

"What can they be so interested in?" Stauffer said, rising from a crouch and stretching.

Vijay stared at the east tower. "Would they be so concerned about the arrival of prisoners?"

"Not likely," Gruner said, standing. "There's only one way to find out." He walked out into the field and headed for the nearest guard tower.

"Say again?" Captain Wetzel didn't understand the message relayed to him over the secure line. "Scott is being occupied by who?" Wetzel scribbled a note on a legal pad, all the while thinking the caller had to be wrong. *Had* to be.

Wetzel set the receiver back into its cradle and stared with gritty eyes at the paper in front of him. "This can't be right," he said.

"What is it?" Martin asked, yawning.

"Scott Air Base in Illinois," Wetzel said. "They say United Nations troops just landed."

"UN? Here?" Martin looked as stupefied as Wetzel felt.

Wetzel scratched his head, and then punched the three-digit extension for the boss.

"Green," came a gravelly answer.

"Sir, I have an unconfirmed report that United Nations troops have landed at Scott Air Force Base."

"Good," the voice said. The line went dead.

Wetzel stared at the handset with his mouth hanging open. *So these are the professionals he called in—blue helmets?*

"You okay?" Martin asked.

"Green," Wetzel said, tasting bile in his mouth. "I think he ordered them in."

Now it was Martin's turn to sit with his mouth open.

Wetzel pushed himself away from his desk. "I need air."

"Sir? Orders, sir?" Lieutenant Harris met Captain Poverello as he returned to their position.

"Give me the radio," Poverello snapped. Master Sergeant Podowsky passed the mic to the captain.

"Tower, this is Captain Poverello of the Three Sixty-Ninth MPs. Can you get me through to the commander of the unit that just landed?"

A woman's voice crackled through the speaker. "Sir, the colonel is trying to reach them now. They are not responding."

"They flew through American air space," Poverello shouted. "They have to be listening to you!"

"Yes, sir," the woman responded. "Sir, Colonel Hostler is here."

"Colonel," Poverello said. "I've instructed my men to contain the unit to the airfield for now. Your orders, sir?"

"Captain, I still can't get anybody to tell me what's going on here. Until we know more, you and your men hold your positions."

Poverello paused for a second. He didn't like this one bit. "Rules of engagement, sir?"

"I have made it clear to the UN troops," Hostler said, "that they will be fired upon if they attempt to leave the airfield. Do you understand?"

"Yes, sir. I understand." Poverello turned to Harris. "Get your men ready. Check their fields of fire, make sure they're covered." Keying the mic again, the captain said, "Morgan? Shoemaker? Long? You copy?"

The officers in charge of the other three platoons of the 369th acknowledged. And from their concealed positions, one hundred and twenty young men stared at eight helicopters on a long black tarmac and wondered if they'd actually have to use the weapons cradled in their arms.

So far, so good. Thiel and his team hurried into a tunnel wide enough for two lanes of vehicle traffic, fully committed now. They quickly covered the hundred and fifty yards from the mouth of the portal to a point where the entryway curved to the left. It joined another tunnel that doubled back out to the side of the mountain, forming a giant "U" under the west side of Raven Rock.

There was no one in the tunnel at this early hour, and after a quick look inside, the team followed Thiel into the heart of Site R, turning right and passing through a set of immense double doors that served as a barrier against the feared nuclear holocaust that had motivated Harry Truman to build the place.

"Where to, Cap?" Burgos jogged alongside Thiel as they moved into the complex.

"Bear left up here," Thiel said, indicating a bend in the tunnel ahead. "And just pray that map you found is halfway right."

Bob Moore had taken Pastor Schiebold's advice and prayed, but it was hard to concentrate. His mind wandered, and every sound, no matter how small, set his nerves on edge. A hush of wind, the creak of a mattress, a sudden gasp from a man with sleep apnea a dozen yards away—all drew his focus and his attention away from what he wanted to say to God.

He finally gave up, trusting in the Bible verse that said God knew what he needed even before he asked.

A sharp noise, like the crack of a whip, brought Bob's eyes fully open. He listened, fully alert, his stomach tensed. Another *crack,* and then another. Bob rolled over and reached for his glasses on the floor, just under the bunk. He fixed them on his face and looked around the room to see if anyone else had noticed. Dave Schiebold lay awake in the next bunk.

"Did you hear that?" Bob asked.

"Yeah," Schiebold said. "Gunshots."

Other men began to stir and murmur; two more gunshots, and then a flurry, like firecrackers on the Fourth of July.

"Are we under attack?" Bob asked.

Another voice called, "Did somebody try to escape?"

From the bunk above Bob, Ted Thornton answered, "Too many guns. It's more than a possible escape."

Thornton's legs dropped over the side of the top bunk. The sheriff lowered himself down and sat on the edge of Bob's bed. "Sounds like answering fire. They're shooting at each other," Thornton said. "Two different sounds, two different weapons. I don't think the guards are shooting at somebody who got out. It sounds like they're shooting at somebody trying to get in."

At the first shot, Jared Gruner was nearly underneath the tower on the east side of the compound. The report echoed through the little clump of buildings, hitting Gruner like a backhanded slap on a cold day. He stopped in his tracks and began to sweat, wondering if the shot was meant for him.

Then came an answering shot, and then another, and then dozens. With a shock, Gruner realized that a full-blown battle was developing at the airfield. But who in the world would invade an Air Force base in the middle of the United States? A fringe militia group? Not likely. But what foreign power could penetrate so far into American airspace?

Those helicopters that landed up at the airfield—they had to have clearance, or they'd have been forced down long before they got here. Threat Level Red. There was nothing in the air the military didn't know about.

In fact, no foreign-based helicopter had the range to make it halfway across the United States.

A light dawned. *That means—*

"Hey! Hey! You up there! What's going on?"

The guards, focused on the airfield, hadn't seen Gruner cross the field. One of them started so violently that Gruner thought he would fall out of the tower.

The guard who leaned over to answer wore a very unpleasant expression. "Get back inside!"

"What's going on at the airfield?"

Even in the dim morning light, Gruner could see the guard wasn't in the mood for questions. "Get your ass inside! Now!"

Gruner tried again. "Come on! Who are they shooting at?"

The guard raised his rifle. "You have five seconds to make it back to the barracks. One…"

Gruner didn't stop running until he nearly flattened Scott Stauffer at the corner of the nearest barracks. He didn't hear anything after *two*.

THIRTY-ONE

When he got back to Saint Louis, Joe Unes determined he would never ride in another motor home as long as he lived. He was cold, dirty, and bone weary, and the obnoxious rattle and buzz of Barney Ison's Winnebago made everything worse. It was only slightly better than the ambulance ride to Saint Christopher's Friday, but that ride had only lasted four miles. This one was going to take another hour.

Something had nagged at Unes since he first saw Barney Ison earlier in the evening. There was something very familiar about the taller man, and Unes found himself watching Ison as the miles slid by, trying to figure out what it was.

"Does something interest you, Agent Unes?"

Unes grimaced. He thought he'd been discreet. "Now that you mention it, I was just thinking that you look very familiar."

"I get that a lot. I host a daily video program."

Unes tried to picture a younger Ison—more hair, less paunch. Then it hit him. "No, that's not it. Did you play basketball?"

"Yes. Indiana, back in the seventies."

"I knew it," Unes said. "I went to Illinois. Later than that, but I've followed the Illini since I was a little kid. You guys used to beat us up pretty good."

Ison nodded. "Coach Knight didn't lose too many back then."

"Not against us, anyway. You played a pretty physical game."

"Making up for a lack of athletic ability," Ison said. "I set picks and drew charging fouls. Grunt work."

"Did you ever think about going pro?"

"Surprisingly, there is very little demand in the NBA for slow guys who can't jump. Just because I'm freakishly tall doesn't mean I'm a natural athlete."

Unes stared out into the night for several minutes. "So why do you do this, Barney?" he finally asked.

Ison popped a stick of spearmint gum into his mouth. It was a poor substitute for a Lucky, but it would have to do. "What exactly do you mean?"

"This whole conspiracy theory thing," Unes said. "How did you get from there to here?"

"It started as a knee-jerk reaction to the government encroaching on basic freedom," Ison said. "After reconciling myself to the harsh reality of my athletic limitations, I started a coffee shop in Bloomington near the IU campus. Every time I turned around, I had to go back to the city council for a permit. One day, I'm explaining my frustration with the city council with a customer who turns out to be the new general manager of a local radio station. Next thing I know, I've got my own show."

"Every afternoon at four," Popeye chimed in from the back of the Winnebago. "Best show in town."

"You said it, Pop," Ison called back with a grin. "As the show caught on, I was introduced to a group of like-minded people who helped me focus on the critical issue."

"Which is?" Unes asked.

"'We hold these truths to be self-evident, that all men are created equal, that they are endowed by their Creator with certain unalienable rights.'"

"The Declaration of Independence?"

"No, the justification *for* independence." Ison grew more animated, steering the Winnebago with his left hand while he gestured with his right.

"The bedrock of this republic, the basis of the Constitution, the grounds for asserting that humans have rights that are unalienable— it all stems from one simple fact: those rights were granted to us at the dawn of time by the Creator of the universe—God himself. He created us in His image. Did you ever wonder what that means?"

Unes started to answer, but Ison paused only long enough to take a breath. "I'll tell you this: It does *not* mean that Yahweh or Jehovah or whatever you want to call the God of the Hebrews stood about six foot tall, give or take, with two eyes, two ears, a nose, and a mouth. No, the original Hebrew, taken in context, means that we were created to rule over Earth in the same way that God rules over the universe. We are His regents on the planet, His moral agents. *That's* why no government—no king, no president, no *man*—has the right to take them away. And *that's* why the Pilgrims sailed across the ocean in a leaky boat to get here in the first place."

Ison paused to unwrap a second stick of gum and cram it into his mouth. "Did you know," he continued as he chewed, "the one hundred and twenty people on the *Mayflower* were packed into a space the size of a volleyball court for seven weeks? No fresh food, no fresh water, no sanitation. Stuck below decks most of the time because of the weather, rocking and rolling a few feet above the bilge. And knowing they'd get to the New World just in time for winter. No shelter waiting for them, no crops, no fast food restaurants or discount superstores. Keep in mind, now, these were professional people—educated, good careers. They weren't craftsmen, farmers, or hunters. They probably didn't even know how to fish! But they trusted that God wasn't going to let them fail as long as they stayed faithful. Many of them died that first winter, but they stuck it out. They persevered. *That* is how seriously they took their freedom. They knew it was the way God meant for men to live—as free men and women with free will."

Ison paused, letting the tension build. "Today, most Americans won't even bother to vote if it rains on Election Day." He snorted in disgust.

Unes shifted in his seat, trying to get comfortable. "So you really believe the country is controlled by a shadow government? The deep state?"

Ison glanced at Unes with one eyebrow raised. "Long before the birth of this nation, forces conspired to deprive men of their freedom."

"Mm hmm." Unes rubbed at his burning eyes, longing for his bed and the sound of Cathy's breathing instead of the numbing drone of the Winnebago's tires.

Ison took a sip of coffee from a thermos marked *Barney's Café*. "Better brew up another pot, Pop," he called toward the back where Bailey sat puzzling over the computers. "I'm out. Agent, you want some coffee?"

Unes shrugged. "Sure. And you can call me Joe. Anyone who rescues me from an assassin has the right to call me by my first name."

Ison laughed and handed the empty thermos to Bailey. "Yes, I suppose so. I'm thankful we were in the right place at the right time. Barney. Call me Barney."

Unes smiled. "Okay. Barney. You were saying about freedom?"

"That's right. Freedom!" Ison continued, happy to return to his favorite subject. "While the typical American stuffs his face and stares at his idiot box of light and shadows, distracted by what the Roman poet Juvenal called bread and circuses, the freedoms our fathers fought and died to protect are being taken away. The men who hide in the shadows—the Bilderbergers, Freemasons, CFR, Trilateral Commission, whoever—they think they're pulling the strings. Ha! Idiots! They're just puppets. The real masterminds are far more clever and infinitely more dangerous than they could ever hope to be."

"Okay," Unes said. "And who would that be?"

"Look," Ison said. "Consider the last four days. Thousands of Americans dead and dying; many thousands more arrested without warrants; and in the pursuit of an investigation into those events, a prominent congressman is missing and must be presumed dead. And you, sir, spent your evening dodging bullets in a cornfield. Now, besides your wife, who knew where you were tonight, and why?"

"Just my—" Unes stopped, stunned. Only SAC Clay—his boss. That was a very ugly thought.

A minute passed before Ison spoke again. "Are you a praying man, Agent Unes?"

"What?"

"Do you pray? To God?"

"Uh, not usually."

"You should start," Ison said. "That is unquestionably the best and, at the same time, most underused weapon against the enemy we're fighting."

The blue helmets were halfway across the runway before Lieutenant Tony Harris got over his surprise. Soldiers poured out of the transport helicopters like sand from a broken hourglass. And they all came straight at the 3rd Platoon of the 369th MPs.

Harris shouted down the line to his men, "You heard the captain! Keep 'em on the runway! Keloski—give 'em a warning shot! If they don't stop, everyone open fire!"

Sergeant Keloski fired first, the report from his rifle piercing the sustained rumble of the helicopters idling on the runway. A blue helmet stopped and returned fire, the bullet hitting the cargo container directly in front of Keloski.

That jarred the rest of the 369th to action, and the company opened fire as one on the swarm of UN troops charging across the tarmac. In the dim glow of the early morning, Harris couldn't make out the faces of their attackers. He raised his pistol, sighted on a moving figure not fifty feet away, and fired.

His man fell, clutching at his leg. The whole sequence was straight out of a nightmare. *What the hell's going on here?*

No time to think. At least a dozen UN troops had fallen, but twenty times their number still rushed them at a dead run.

Captain Poverello had positioned his four platoons in a U around the southern end of the field, assuming the camp would be the objective of the UN force. He was right. But the UN force was professional enough to know that concentrating their attack gave them the best chance of overwhelming their enemy.

Lieutenant Harris and his Third Platoon were the base of the U. These thirty men faced over two hundred running right at them with guns ablaze.

"What's happening? What's going on?" Stauffer grabbed Gruner as he rounded the corner to keep both of them from falling over.

"I don't know," Gruner panted. "Shots…from the airfield. Sounds like…firefight."

The others waited for Gruner to catch his breath after his mad scramble across the field.

"I think," Gruner said, "the guards in the tower don't know what's happening, either."

"Those helicopters we heard—" Norlock began.

"Brought whoever the guards are shooting at, right," Gruner finished. "And since the copters—"

"Landed here," Stauffer picked up, "somebody with clout knew they were in the air. Oh, man, this is big."

"Really big," Norlock said. "We gotta tell somebody."

"Who?" Gruner asked, bent over with his hands on his knees.

"Excuse me," Vijay interrupted, his hand raised.

"The news," Norlock said. "Radio, TV, somebody. This is big!"

"A coup?" Stauffer asked.

"Excuse me," Vijay said, a little louder, waving his hand in the air.

"Could be," Gruner said. "How else do you get military units fighting each other?"

"Excuse me, please."

"I don't know," Norlock continued. "Maybe they're not American."

"What?" Stauffer said, incredulous.

"Nah," Gruner said. "They'd have never made it through our airspace."

"Would they be shooting at Americans?" Stauffer said.

"Excuse me!" Vijay shouted. The other three turned to him as if noticing his presence for the first time. "Please! The noise of the shooting is getting closer. Do you think we should perhaps move inside, away from the bullets?"

That hadn't occurred to Gruner. "Uh, yeah. That would make sense."

Norlock nodded. "You guys go ahead. I'm going to get us some publicity."

"What?"

Norlock drew himself up to his full height. "Now, in our hour of need, men of valor must rise to the challenge. The tower guards are distracted. Get me some pillows or blankets to cushion that barbed wire at the top of the fence and I can make it over. I'll get to a phone and call the all-news station's tip line."

"You're crazy!" Stauffer said.

Norlock grinned. "Nope," he said. "Just wanna be outside looking in, like always."

Bob Moore expected the firing to stop after the first few shots. A misunderstanding in the dark, probably. It had to be. He hoped.

But it didn't stop. It was getting closer.

"Ted? What do you think?"

"Getting closer," Thornton grunted.

Most of the men in the barracks were sitting up in bed now, trying to make sense of the rapid exchanges of gunfire less than half a mile away.

Bob asked, "Should we get down or something?"

"I don't know," Thornton said. "It's hard to tell where they're aiming."

Among the shots rose the sound of voices again, shouting. The words were unclear, but the stress in the voices cut right through the walls of the barracks.

A *thunk* against the wall facing the airfield caused Bob to jump.

"Spent bullet, I think," Thornton said. "They're coming this way."

Dave Schiebold leaned forward. "Hey, fellas, why don't we pray?"

That seemed like the only sensible thing to do. Actually, it was about all they could do, given their circumstances. The three men leaned forward.

As they did, a man with light brown hair and wire frame glasses leaned in between the bunks from the aisle.

"Excuse me, fellas, I don't mean to horn in," he said. "But would you mind if I prayed with you?"

"Not at all," Schiebold said, moving aside to make room on the bunk. "I'm Dave Schiebold. This is Bob Moore and Ted Thornton."

The stranger smiled and extended his hand. "Pleased to meet you. I'm Ed Harper."

Fluorescent lights cast a pale, soulless light on the asphalt surface of the wide passageway. Captain Thiel kept his team moving double time, aware that they'd probably been spotted on a camera somewhere. Where was security? Somebody inside had to be watching the tunnel. Surely the MPs weren't depending on the concrete barriers and chain-link fence to keep intruders away.

Don't think about it. Be glad you haven't had to shoot another American soldier.

"Sir," Burgos said, jogging alongside, "Blast doors should be just ahead."

"Right. Look sharp." Thiel signaled the team to hug the right-hand wall. Quietly, a line of nine black-clad, heavily armed merchants of death crept forward into the heart of one of America's most secure underground bunkers.

Ahead, on the right stood the massive blast doors and the inner guard post. *Decision time*, Thiel thought to himself. *Do I really want to kill some kid for trying to do his job?*

He had an idea.

"Jackson, Minelli, come with me," Thiel whispered. "Burgos, stay here. Anything goes wrong, it's your show." He signaled the rest of the team to stay put.

Stepping out into the middle of the wide passageway, Thiel let his M-4 hang by its shoulder strap and advanced purposefully on the guard post. Jackson, Thiel's remaining engineering sergeant after Bako's death, and Minelli, one of his two weapons sergeants, followed a couple of paces behind.

"Stop where you are!" A young MP, barely old enough to drink legally, emerged from the security shack, his sidearm aimed squarely at Thiel's head.

Thiel obeyed, raising his arms to display his empty hands. "Lieutenant," he said, "I am Captain Alan Thiel. We are here on a mission from Homeland Security. We need your help."

As bizarre as it was to encounter a team of heavily armed men dressed in black at oh-five-thirty, Thiel's response was even more confusing to the guard.

"Say again?"

"We are here on a mission for Homeland Security," Thiel repeated. "A man inside has been identified as a threat to the United States. My men and I are here to take him."

A second MP emerged from the post, another square-jawed kid from somewhere in the heartland. "What the—"

"Call the captain," the first guard said, keeping his pistol trained on Thiel. The second MP froze, staring at the Special Forces soldiers arrayed against them. Thiel could almost hear the kid calculating the odds of surviving a shootout.

"I am going to say this one time," Thiel said, advancing again, slowly. "My team has been tracking the men behind the terror attacks. We believe one of them is inside. A mole. Now let me be clear: We would not be breaking into a secure government compound unless it was a matter of national security. Second, if we were here for any other reason, you men would already be dead. We are on the same side, and I don't want to kill you. But I will if you make me. Now, please—open the blast doors and let us in."

The first MP swallowed, trying to hide his fear behind a nine-millimeter semiautomatic. The second guard slowly, finally, reached for his own sidearm.

Thiel watched the first one's eyes and tried to guess how long it would take to bring his M4 to bear on the kid. *This must be what Wyatt Earp felt like,* he thought. *Great. Shootout at the Site R Corral.*

The blue helmets were way too close. Harris could barely believe his eyes. *This is insane!*

The UN troops charged right at his platoon's guns, taking their hits, counting on surprise and superior numbers to overrun his position.

It was going to work. And Harris didn't know what to do.

"Sir? Sir?" Sergeant Williams finally grabbed Harris' shoulder to shake him out of his stupor. "Sir?"

Harris blinked. Only one option. "Fall back! Fall Back!"

His troops heard and obeyed, making for the cover of a radio tower behind them and the maintenance buildings underneath. Where was Captain Poverello? What were they supposed to do next?

Harris fired a couple more rounds into the ranks of advancing troops, not knowing if he hit anyone, and then he turned and followed his men. His sergeants—Williams over there, Keloski behind the shed—shouted orders, trying to regroup the platoon into a new defensive line. Was that smart? Should they keep running?

Was battle always this confused?

Harris made it to a maintenance building at the far side of the tower. He had no idea if any of his men were down. He couldn't see any, but in the dim light he couldn't see much of anything.

The UN troops made the line of containers that Harris and his men had just abandoned, but now they took heavy fire from their flanks, the sides of the U that Poverello set up when he deployed the company. Harris realized if his platoon could hold its position long enough to stop the blue hats for even a minute, the rest of the 369th could put some serious hurt on the invaders.

Off to his left, Harris saw Sanchez call a couple of the men to him, a position with good cover. Keloski was beyond Sanchez, with half a dozen spread out behind buildings and trees keeping a steady fire on the UN troops.

Twenty or thirty yards behind Keloski's squad, a small trailer park housed some of the employees at the base. Lights popped on one after another as the sleepy residents gradually realized that something bad was happening right outside their windows.

Harris scanned right and spotted a problem if he didn't move. A gap had opened between his unit and Lieutenant Long's. That was disaster if it wasn't filled in a hurry. And it looked like the UN force had seen it because they were moving that way.

Where was Williams? There—behind the next building, trying to move some of his boys around the side of a storage shed for a clear shot at the Blue Hats. Harris covered the twenty feet between buildings in about a second.

"Williams! Take three men and come with me! Let's go!" Harris didn't wait for a response, but took off at a dead run to beat the advancing UN soldiers to the gap. He darted and weaved through the complex of small equipment sheds and maintenance buildings, determined to extend his line to link up with Long's platoon.

This is a lot like football, Harris realized. His men ran toward new positions like linebackers and defensive backs scrambling to fill a gap in the line before an opposing running back could break through for a big gain.

Except that this game really was decided by sudden death.

The kid was so nervous Thiel almost felt sorry for him. He was probably near the end of his shift, wired on coffee to stay awake, and wanting nothing more than to go home and get into bed. Then Thiel shows up with his A-team, and now the kid had to be wondering if his next nap would be inside a pine box.

"I'm telling you," Thiel said, "we don't have to do it this way. This is a mission for Homeland Security."

"Shut up!" The guard's pistol was remarkably steady, even though he was sweating freely now. "You're going to slowly take your weapons and place them on the ground in front of you."

"No, we are not," Thiel said calmly. "We are—"

"I'm not telling you again! Take your weapons—"

Behind the guard, the blast door began to open. Thiel calculated the odds of covering the distance to the guard without getting shot if the kid turned his head to look. Not good, but it might be their only chance to get inside that door.

From inside the bunker, a man in the uniform of an Army captain stepped out. He was tall, with dark hair and a movie actor's looks, even with the military buzz cut. His eyes were weary, he needed a shave, and he looked ready to spit nails. "What the hell is this?"

The first guard glanced over his shoulder. "Captain Wetzel. We caught these men trying to break in."

The captain looked over Thiel and his men with a practiced eye. "Who caught who?"

The guard didn't respond, but he seemed less sure of his position.

"Why are you here?" Wetzel demanded.

"There is a man inside who poses a clear and present danger to the United States," Thiel said. "We're here to take him in."

"Who are you after?"

"A man named Malthus."

Wetzel's eyes narrowed. "There's no one inside by that name."

Thiel cursed under his breath. It was all for nothing. He and his men were truly and officially done, toast. He'd be court-martialed, if he was lucky. And for what? The man responsible for the deaths of Bako, those people in Iowa, and who knew how many others, was still free.

"Are you sure?" Thiel asked. "Someone with the brass to command Delta Force A-teams on home soil. Deep, raspy voice—"

"Wait." Captain Wetzel's eyebrows lifted slightly. His eyes searched Thiel's, as if hunting for something to confirm his words. Finally, he said, "Stand down, Lieutenant."

The guard protested. "But sir—"

"I said stand down, Lieutenant. Is that clear?" The young man nodded and slowly holstered his pistol.

Wetzel turned back to Thiel and said, "Come with me."

THIRTY-TWO

The last twenty-four hours had knocked Joe Unes well out of his comfort zone, leaving him adrift on an ocean of doubt. He had evidence that might tie someone in government to the deaths of thousands of people. Someone had tried to kill him, probably to keep him from sharing that evidence. Thousands had been herded into detention camps he never knew existed before today. A prominent United States congressman had been abducted and possibly killed, and a senior assistant at the Department of Defense, a known associate of the congressman, had been found dead in his car. Heart attack, officially, but was it really?

What chance did he have of staying alive? Or protecting his family?

"It's sinking in, isn't it?" The weathered face of Barney Ison was more visible now as the pre-dawn glow began to lighten the eastern horizon.

Unes could only nod.

"Like scales falling from the eyes of Saul," Ison said. "I remember my epiphany. A dark and lonely time. But like the hours before dawn, necessary to pass through into the light of understanding."

"To understand what?"

"That you need to question everything, Joe. Very little of what you see or hear in the mainstream media is unfiltered. It's what you don't see that you need to believe."

"Hey, Barn?" Popeye Bailey, still sitting in the back, had a strange quality to his voice. "You might want to turn on the radio."

"What's up?" Ison asked.

"Something on the web here about Scott Air Force Base."

Ison reached over to the dashboard and switched on the AM radio, twisting the tuner until he found a news station.

"...*forty-seven degrees at Lambert, forty-five downtown. It's five forty-five, normally a little early to go to our eye in the sky, but we're getting word of a situation over on the east side. Let's go to Captain Bo Arnold in Jet Chopper One. Bo?*"

"*Thanks, Mike. Yeah, there's usually not much traffic out on the roads this early, but we're seeing a line of vehicles tying up the approaches to Scott Air Force Base. Illinois Routes 158, 161, and 4, and I-64 leading to the exits near the base, all heavily traveled at this hour for some reason. Now, we had a report of a disturbance in the area of Scott that came in to the All News 670 News Tip Line this morning. We can't say if this traffic is connected in any way, and—well, we're taking a chance getting this close because it's restricted air space, and security will be especially tight after the terror events over the weekend. But we're circling around to the south side of the base, and I can tell you, Mike and Margie, there are regular, repeating flashes of light on the ground. I don't know what we're seeing, but the flashes are like—like fireworks, or— and I hate to speculate, but it might be gunfire.*"

"*Bo? Did you say gunfire?*"

"*Well, Mike, I can't say for sure. It's still too dark on the ground to see what's causing those flashes, but it doesn't look like—wait. Oh, God! God! They're shoot—*"

The traffic report ended in a sudden burst of static, a loud crackle, and several moments of silence. After seconds that felt like hours, the female half of the morning news team opened her mic, obviously shaken.

"*We, uh, seem to have lost contact with Captain Bo Arnold. He was...was reporting on a disturbance at Scott Air Base near Belleville, and—*"

She choked up and the silence stretched ominously. Her partner finally jumped in.

"*Uh, we'll take a break and be back in a minute on All News 670.*"

Ison punched the radio off. "Well, Agent Unes?"

Unes rubbed his eyes, shock written all over his face. "That—well, that just doesn't make any sense. Gunfire? And what the hell happened to that copter? What's really going on out there?"

The motor home rumbled under a green highway sign indicating the exit from I-70 to US 40. "We'll find out in another hour or so."

"Wetzel," Thiel said, following their guide through the blast doors and into the heart of Site R, "you don't have to do this. We could be walking dead." Their footsteps on the concrete floor echoed off the cinder block walls of the passage.

"I know," Wetzel said. "But Green, or Malthus, whatever his name is, he's selling out the country. He brought in UN troops to take over at least some of the camps. On our turf. That can't happen."

"What?"

"It has something to do with flu shots," Wetzel said. "All the detainees were supposed to get them. At some of the bases, the detainees refused the shots. The Guard units wouldn't push the issue. I guess too many people remember that BioShield fiasco about fifteen years back. So Gr—Malthus called in UN troops to replace the Guards."

"Over flu shots?"

Wetzel stopped and turned around. "Look, Thiel, whatever it's about, I didn't sign up to sell out American citizens to the UN. It's gotta be stopped. I hope to God you can do it."

"That's why we're here," Thiel said, grasping Wetzel by the shoulder. "Come on. Let's take out the trash."

Harris, Williams, and three men from Williams' squad gained a small rise southeast of the landing strip, placing them more or less between the main body of advancing UN soldiers and the detainees' camp. In the confused retreat from the airfield, Harris had lost contact with his radioman, and he had no idea what was happening on either flank.

"Here!" Harris shouted. The higher ground gave them a slight advantage, and there were some sizable trees for cover. Harris pulled up behind a grand old oak and listened. Sure enough, the thud of boots announced the advancing troops, once again coming double-quick as they pushed through the hole in the 369th's line.

"Now!" Harris stepped from behind the tree and fired at the first movement he saw. Williams and his men followed suit with their M16s. Startled, the UN troops stopped and scuttled for cover. They didn't pause for long; return fire erupted from at least a dozen UN rifles, and Harris found himself pressed against the back of the oak, wishing he had more light to see what was going on. And a bigger gun.

But at least they'd stopped the UN unit for the moment. Harris hoped Captain Poverello would figure out what was going on. Quick.

He gradually became aware of a helicopter hovering somewhere behind their position. It didn't sound like another Chinook, which could be good or bad. They could sure use some reinforcements. Soldiers with some experience. *How did I get into this, anyway?*

It had to be a friendly. The UN troops were aiming a few long-distance shots at it. Harris risked a look around the tree and squeezed off another shot in the direction of a muzzle flash.

Then a flare blasted into the reddening dawn sky from somewhere close to the airfield. Without thinking, Harris tracked the flare—no, a missile!—as it streaked overhead, toward the detainees' barracks.

A second later, an explosion rocked the early predawn sky, and Harris gaped in horror as the small helicopter exploded in mid-air, scattering thousands of pieces over the camp.

The shooting was definitely closer. Gruner, Stauffer, and Vijay huddled together outside the barracks. They could see muzzle flashes through the trees beyond the fence.

"So, what do you think, Stofe," Gruner asked. "Are they coming to rescue us or kill us?"

"Kill?" Vijay was definitely uncomfortable with the idea.

"Relax," Stauffer said, more bravely than he felt. "This is still America. They can't just come in here and shoot us."

"You think?" Gruner said.

"I hope that Terry is all right," Vijay said.

"Yeah," Stauffer agreed.

Gruner was silent. Fifteen minutes had passed since Norlock insisted on going over the fence to get to a phone. He'd been right about the tower guards being distracted. Gruner hoped he'd been smart and made for the headquarters building near the guards' barracks. If Norlock tried to go all the way to the main part of the base, he'd be right in the middle of the firefight. No amount of practice sword fighting with medieval re-enactors gets you ready to face an AK-47.

"Look!" Vijay said, pointing toward the sky.

A small helicopter floated over the camp. They could just make it out in the dim light, but it was clearly not a Blackhawk. It stopped and hovered maybe five hundred feet above their heads. The passengers seemed very interested in what was happening at the air base.

"Who is that?" Stauffer said.

"Not military," Gruner answered. "Maybe—hey, maybe Norlock got to a phone and that's a news helicopter."

"Do you think so?" Vijay asked.

"Worth a shot," Gruner said. "Come on!" He lunged out into the open field, shouting and waving his arms, trying to get the attention of whoever was inside the helicopter overhead. Stauffer and Vijay followed him, yelling and jumping.

Suddenly, a bright yellow streak from the north caught their attention and froze them in place. Too quickly to react, but so slowly that it seemed to crawl across the early morning sky, Gruner and the others watched in horror as a deadly finger reached up from the ground and speared the helicopter.

A fireball ripped the air apart with a deafening roar and the angry glare of a dozen suns.

Gruner suddenly realized what had to follow. "Move! Move! Move!"

Jolted to action, the three friends ran for the barracks as a deadly rain of hot, shredded metal from the shattered helicopter pelted the ground around them.

"Joe? Is that you?" Cathy Unes stood at the top of the stairs in her robe, eyes filled with sleep.

"Hi, honey." Unes' heart swelled to nearly bursting. He dropped his briefcase and jacket to the floor, rushed up the stairs, and wrapped his arms around his wife.

"Are you all right?" Cathy pushed him back and looked him up and down. "What happened? Are you hurt?"

He didn't want to keep anything from her, but Unes had to get the computers out of his hands as soon as possible. Every minute that passed was another minute closer to whoever ordered the botched hit finding out that he was still alive. Once the computers were in forensics, he would be safe. His family would be safe. Then he'd tell Cathy everything.

"No, babe, I'm okay," he said, brushing her cheek with his hand. "Meeting went late and then I had car trouble in Iowa. I didn't want to wake you. I got a ride back with a couple of guys heading this way. I hope I didn't scare you."

"Why didn't you call?" She wasn't accusing, just worried that he wasn't feeling as well as he said he was.

"I didn't want to wake you," Unes lied. "I need to take some evidence downtown, honey. Right now. It's very time-sensitive. Related to the terror investigation. Could you make some coffee while I take a quick shower?"

"Now?"

Unes nodded. "Please. And then I promise I'll come straight home and take the rest of the day off."

He hated driving right through the heart of the city, but there wasn't much choice. Six bridges cross the Mississippi River at Saint Louis, and three of them were too small for the Winnebago. Barney Ison chose the most direct route, the fastest at this time of day: I-64 straight across into East Saint Louis, and then on to

Belleville and the air base. He prayed that God would keep the police from spotting them for just a little while longer.

Ison opened a fresh pack of gum. "Any more news, Pop?"

"Couple of other stations picked up what's going on," Popeye called from the back. "Looks like a firefight on the ground, but nobody knows who's fighting who."

Ison's eyes tracked a dark sedan in the rear view mirror. "I don't know, Pop. Jailbreak? A military unit refusing to hold Americans prisoner without due process? I just don't know." Ison maneuvered the Winnebago into the center lane of the Poplar Street Bridge. Below, the muddy waters of the Mississippi lapped lazily at the bridge supports—a brief pause on the river's winding journey southward to Cairo, Memphis, and New Orleans.

"I just don't know," Ison repeated as they crossed into Illinois. "I only hope we get there before they seal off the area."

They took turns at prayer. Dave Schiebold had begun, Bob Moore picked up when Schiebold stopped, and now the newcomer, Ed Harper, petitioned the Lord.

An explosion that sounded as though it happened right outside the barracks interrupted them. Pastor Harper only let the noise distract him for a moment, even when the blast was followed seconds later by loud *clunks* as bits of metal hit the roof.

Bob's concentration was jarred by the bang of the barracks door being thrown open followed by the sound of hurried footsteps across the barracks floor. He looked up to see three, wide-eyed young men, pale and winded. Pastor Harper stopped in mid-sentence and opened his eyes.

"You boys all right?" he asked, concerned.

The largest of the three said breathlessly, "They just shot down a helicopter. Think it was a news copter."

Other men around the room, their attention drawn to the three when they burst into the barracks, began to murmur. Fear clouded the room like fog over the Missouri River on a cool morning.

"Well, boys," Pastor Harper said, "crowd in here with us. We may not know what's going on out there, but in here we're armed with the strongest weapon known to man."

Wetzel led Thiel and his team deep into the complex of tunnels carved from the green granite of Raven Rock Mountain. Thiel was probably right—they were dead men. Somebody in security must have seen them on a closed-circuit monitor by now. Wetzel doubted anyone inside could put up much of a fight against Thiel's men, but they'd probably find a hot reception waiting outside the mountain.

He hadn't asked Thiel what they planned to do with Green once they got him. Best not to. Men like Green never stood trial. Justice for spooks was usually administered quietly, out of sight.

What amounted to five three-story buildings had been scooped out of the heart of the mountain. Wetzel led the team off the corridor and down a staircase to the lowest level. They crossed another wide corridor into an office filled with metal desks, each with a desktop computer. They were all dark.

"Quiet here this morning," Thiel observed dryly.

"It's early," Wetzel said. "Besides, these offices are for when the government needs to keep enough politicians alive to run a war."

He led them through several more empty offices before emerging into another concrete-floored corridor. "Hold it." Wetzel pointed across the passageway to a gray steel door. "Through that door and down two offices on the left. There's probably a guard outside his door. Outer offices should be empty now."

"Thanks," Thiel said. "We would have never found him without your help."

"Glad I went outside when I did," Wetzel said. "Good luck. You'll get one shot. Make it good."

THIRTY-THREE

It didn't take the Blue Hats long to figure out that only five men stood between them and the camp. They started coming again a couple of minutes after taking out the helicopter. Slower this time, more carefully, moving from tree to tree, staying down and putting up good covering fire. Harris wondered where these UN guys had been when they might have been useful, like Iraq after the war. This unit had some skills.

The situation was bad. Harris looked over at Williams, pinned down behind a big maple. He signaled for Williams to get himself and the men out of there. Williams acknowledged and began withdrawing in the direction of the detainees' camp, followed by the three men from his squad.

Harris peered around the tree, aimed a couple more shots in the direction of the UN troops, and then quickly reloaded his pistol. They were close now, close enough that he could hear them talking to one another, although he couldn't make out the language. Russian?

Didn't matter. Too close. Time to leave.

He bolted from the tree, running a zigzag course through the lightly wooded area. Shots echoed behind him, and bullets whistled past as he ran.

Ahead, the woods thinned and ended at the clearing that surrounded the camp. A funeral pyre marked the wrecked heap of the helicopter inside the fenced compound, a pall of black smoke rising into the sky. An acid scent of death poisoned the morning breeze. No survivors.

Where to go? If he tried to cross the field, Harris doubted he'd get to cover before his pursuers caught up and had a clear shot at his back.

Without warning, his foot hit a small depression, causing his left knee to buckle and cave. Searing pain sliced through his leg, a white-hot knife under the kneecap. Harris pitched forward, momentum carrying him headlong to the turf as his body suddenly found nothing to bear its weight.

Just like that preseason game against the Packers nine years earlier.

Harris rolled on the ground, clutching his leg, trying not to cry out and give himself away. Maybe, he thought through his agony, just maybe he could hide himself somehow and be rescued later. Gritting his teeth, he rolled over, pushed himself up, balanced on his right leg, and began to hop.

Keeping his weight off the damaged left leg, Harris searched the ground frantically for a hollow, a culvert, even a big pile of leaves, something he could use as cover.

A shot whistled past, close—too close. Harris jumped back in surprise. As he planted his right foot, he hit another patch of uneven ground. The radical change in direction was too much for his ankle. It gave with an unnatural twist, and once again Harris tumbled to the ground.

Now what? Harris tried to ignore the torment in his legs long enough to think. About four yards to his left, the leaf litter looked like it might be thick enough to cover him. He began crawling, pulling himself forward with his elbows, his traitorous knee and ankle screaming in unison.

Never in his football career had four yards looked so unreachable.

Leaves crunched just behind him. Harris spun and saw a tall man in khakis, wearing the blue helmet of a UN soldier. Harris raised his pistol to fire, but the other man was too quick, lashing out with a kick that launched the weapon into the underbrush.

He looked young, Harris thought, not much more than a teenager. The kid's face was blank, no expression, just a cold determination to follow orders.

In this case, that meant killing Lieutenant Tony Harris.

The UN soldier raised his AK-47 and pointed the barrel at Harris' forehead. He realized with a chill that he'd never see his son again, and his heart nearly drowned in icy regret.

But before the soldier could pull the trigger, a blond-haired giant in orange burst from nowhere and swatted the gun with a club, deflecting the shot upward through the canopy of leaves.

Surprised, the UN soldier turned to deal with the intruder. The man in orange expertly spun a length of branch as long as he was tall and knocked the gun aside, forcing the soldier to waste a second shot into the brush.

Before the soldier could recover, the giant spun completely around, swinging his makeshift staff in an arc. His movements were fluid, graceful, and effective. The branch connected with the side of the UN soldier's head below the helmet with a wicked *crack*.

The soldier collapsed to the leaf-covered sod.

Harris stared at his savior, wide-eyed, too stunned to speak.

"Greetings, brave sir," the blond giant said, extending an arm. "Guallac Lauhir. Wallace Long-Hand in English. But normal people call me Terry Norlock."

Harris grunted as Terry pulled him to his feet. "Ah! Watch the legs. Left knee, right ankle."

"I know. I saw."

"How did—"

"Association for Renaissance Martial Arts."

"Huh?"

"Medieval MMA," Norlock said, grinning. "I specialize in the quarterstaff." A shot echoed through the morning air. The sound of UN troops moving through the wood was getting close.

Norlock dropped his branch, lifted Harris' left arm and placed it over his shoulders. "Come on, lieutenant. Let's get out of here."

It was hard to leave home again so soon, especially because he was sure he'd never see it again just a few hours ago. Joe Unes sipped hot coffee from his new travel mug as he maneuvered his wife's white minivan through the morning rush.

News on the radio was all about whatever was happening at Scott. A traffic helicopter had indeed been shot down, but nobody knew who was responsible. There was no new information about the situation on the ground. The prevailing theory was a terrorist takeover, but local police wouldn't confirm or deny anything. It wasn't sure that the cops could get close enough to know what was going on. There was a rumor that fighters had been scrambled by the Air Force in case unauthorized craft tried to take off from Scott.

Even more disturbing, similar reports of unexplained gunfire were coming in from Fort Drum, New York and the former Reese Air Force Base outside of Lubbock, Texas. If Barney Ison was right, those sites, Scott, and maybe others he didn't know about had been turned into detention camps almost overnight.

The problem was things like that just don't happen overnight. Which meant—Unes didn't like where his thoughts were leading.

And who was fighting who for control of the camps?

Unes pulled the van into the parking lot outside the FBI building on Market Street. He wasn't surprised to see a fair number of cars there already. The workload dumped on them by Ten-Thirteen, now complicated by a wave of vandalism and violence directed at churches, would keep the Bureau busy for months. He'd expected it, but this morning Unes wondered if they were looking for leads in the wrong places.

Carrying the computers inside, Unes headed downstairs to the basement of the building, where the forensics team worked their magic. He secured the electronic equipment in an evidence locker, scribbled a note that he dropped on Fred Schuler's desk, and quietly slipped back outside.

He debated whether to leave a note telling SAC Clay not to expect him today, but he decided against it. Unes wanted to hear Clay's reaction when he called in. He considered staying at the office long enough to confront Clay as he arrived, but Unes was exhausted. That meeting would have to wait.

Joe climbed back into the van and turned the ignition, wanting nothing more than a nice long session with his mattress and pillow. On the radio, a female reporter on the scene announced that a growing crowd of protesters, hundreds, had gathered outside the stately brick headquarters building at Scott Air Force Base, despite the sounds of sporadic gunfire. Cars and vans had lined up along Illinois Route 158 trying to get into the base.

Unes laughed out loud for the first time in days. "Go, Barney."

Wetzel was right. A single guard dressed in black stood outside the office door of Malthus/Green. To call him big would be understatement. The soldier was a mountain with legs.

Thiel, Jackson, and Minelli crept forward through the darkened outer office. About a dozen feet from the gigantic guard, Thiel signaled the other two to wait and be ready.

Thiel advanced confidently and addressed the guard. "Good morning, soldier. Is Green in the office?"

Frowning, 'Goliath' reached for his sidearm. "I don't think—"

"I have to see Green," Thiel insisted. "Is he in?"

"You need to stop right where you are," the guard said, deciding that this wasn't an authorized visit.

"Oh, I think Mister Green will be very interested in what I have to say."

Thiel walked past the guard, turning his back to the giant. He pretended to be interested in a piece of mediocre artwork on the wall, trying to draw the guard's attention away from his sergeants.

It worked. Thiel heard the electric discharge of a taser, and the guard flopped to the deck, overwhelmed by the powerful current. Minelli stood over the massive guard with the stun gun at the ready to make sure he didn't get back up.

Thiel rushed the door. They'd given Malthus too much warning already.

It was locked.

Thiel aimed his M4 at the doorjamb and shattered the lock with a shot. One step back, then a kick, and the door flew open with a crash. He jumped through the doorway and scanned the room.

There, seated behind a richly carved wooden desk, nearly hidden by a blue-gray haze of cigarette smoke, sat a man, unmoving, watching Thiel intently through eyes that glittered like diamonds.

"Congratulations," the man said, flicking cigarette ash into a marble tray on the desk. "Come in, Captain Thiel. I've been expecting you."

They somehow managed to avoid traffic after crossing the Poplar Street Bridge into Illinois. Popeye had plotted a back route to the air base that took them through some of the rougher parts of the East Side, the term Saint Louisans use for towns on the Illinois side of the river. After some of the things Barney Ison had seen, depressed neighborhoods didn't scare him.

The sun peeked over the eastern horizon as Ison and Popeye eased through the crowd outside the main headquarters at Scott. The clear sky and brisk morning air were refreshing, especially after a long day and night in the confines of the motor home. It might have been a beautiful autumn day but for the column of rising black smoke to the south.

More ominously, the sounds of sporadic gunfire rattled nearby. *Somebody's dying back there,* Ison thought grimly. *We need to get this show on the road.*

He carried a megaphone that he'd picked up at a flea market in Wisconsin a few weeks earlier. He'd had a feeling it would come in handy someday.

Today was that day.

He quickly found a spot where he could address the uneasy crowd. Ison surveyed the faces, a group of at least two hundred with more on the way. The Alliance had done well on short notice. Most were unfamiliar, though he recognized a few from his travels in recent weeks, fellow operatives in the underground resistance against the age-old plot to destroy God's prized creations—Earth, and humanity.

Shifting his attention to half a dozen vans bristling with antennae and satellite dishes, Ison smiled grimly. Good. The media was already here. It would mean his face on local news, and probably national, too.

Scanning the crowd again, he noted a few smart phones pointed in his direction. Good. Social media would send it around the world within the hour.

Of course, that also meant whoever torched Dave Hitchins fifteen years ago would undoubtedly spot him and the chase would get hot for a while.

So be it. God had brought them this far; they'd keep going as long as He willed it.

Ison turned to Popeye Bailey, who looked back through the viewfinder of an action camera. They needed to document this day.

"Ready, Pop?" The redhead gave him a thumbs up.

Lifting the megaphone to his lips, Ison said, "May I have your attention, please? Thank you. I am Barney Ison." He paused to wait for a groundswell of applause to die down.

"Thank you. Thank you all for coming on such short notice, and at such an ungodly hour. And thank you most of all for exposing yourselves to identification and the persecution that comes from standing up to the beast."

Ison paused for a moment, collecting his thoughts. "What we have inside this base, fellow slaves, is evidence of the most dangerous threat to our freedom we have faced since the founding of this great nation. Inside this base is a concentration camp. A camp built to house American citizens—something that hasn't happened on our soil since World War Two, and something that should never happen again.

"You see, fellow slaves," he continued, "the people held here have been arrested, and in some cases literally dragged away from their families, without warrants, or even any evidence of guilt by association with the perpetrators of the terror attacks of the last few days. In fact, *we* have evidence—concrete proof!—that the terror attacks of Ten-Thirteen were triggered by elements *inside our own government* as an excuse to round up freedom-loving Americans, those who believe it is not in the power of any man to deny our fundamental rights. That evidence will be posted to the Internet through the usual channels before the end of the day.

"I say again, these crimes against American citizens, the violence and the arrests, were planned and executed by elements within the United States government. Elements that work to weaken this nation from within, to break our will to resist, and to reduce us to a mob of frightened, angry people, desperate for security at any cost. That security will be offered for a dear price—and that price, fellow slaves, will be your God-given rights to life, liberty, and property.

"But we will not buy! Not at their price! Not today! Today, we call their bluff! Today, we march! We march—to the sound of *their* guns!" With that, Ison turned and stormed up the asphalt roadway into the base proper. His ragged mob of followers cheered and began to fall in behind him.

Ison thought, *Too bad we couldn't pass out torches and pitchforks.*

"Barney, where are we going?" Popeye Bailey appeared at his side, back from checking the edges of the crowd for suspicious guests.

"The detainment camp."

"You know where it is?"

Ison glanced around to be sure no one overheard. "The smoke," he said. "That's as good a guess as any."

The kid was tall, at least six-five, and surprisingly strong. Harris was amazed that the beanpole could drag him along so quickly. Harris felt like his arm was about to pull out of its socket, but considering the alternative, he didn't complain.

They maneuvered back to their left, where Harris still heard some M16s firing at the UN troops. It sounded like the UN force had made it off the runway and were on their way to securing the camp. Harris hoped they could link up with the rest of his unit and fall back, regroup, and wait for reinforcements. This had to be a huge mistake.

But how many were dead because of this mistake? The thought made Harris so angry he nearly forgot his tortured knee, until he applied a little weight to it without thinking.

"Ah! Son of a—"

"Whoa, sorry." The blond kid stopped and steadied him, and for the first time Harris realized that his rescuer was dressed in the coveralls they gave all the detainees.

"Hey. How'd you get out?" Harris asked.

"I used some pillows and blankets to get over the barbed wire when the guards weren't looking."

"Not that I'm not grateful, but what were you thinking?"

"I wanted to find somebody with a phone," Norlock said. "Somebody needs to know what's going on here."

"Did you?"

"Yeah. Cook for the air base. I think a couple of the TV and radio stations are on their way."

"Good."

Norlock looked toward the column of oily smoke that reached toward the sky. "Jeez, I hope that wasn't a news helicopter they shot down."

"Nothing you could do about it," Harris said. "Now let's you and me stay alive, son. This way."

He looked just as Thiel had imagined: crisp white shirt and a power tie; closely cropped black hair; hard, humorless eyes that anchored sharp, predatory features; and thin, bloodless lips set in a line. He sat behind a designer desk decorated with odd carvings, strange symbols of some kind.

"You," Thiel said. "Malthus. Or Green. Whatever. You're through."

Malthus' smile stopped just below his eyes. He replied with a voice that was very familiar to Thiel—deep, raspy, vaguely European. "Really?"

"You're a traitor."

Still smiling, Malthus shook his head almost sadly. "Captain Thiel, you have no concept of what you're doing."

"That's funny. I think I do."

Malthus' smile disappeared altogether. "No, you do not. You're a child, Captain Thiel. An infant! With what will you bring me to justice?"

"The computers. That email. The FBI has it."

That annoying smile returned. "You must do better than that," Malthus said. "What else?"

"I'll testify."

Malthus laughed, a harsh sound, like fingernails on a chalkboard. "Allow me to enlighten you. You have no recourse with me."

Thiel flushed. He wasn't used to being patronized. A sick feeling hardened in his stomach. Even though he held the weapon, Thiel felt the situation slipping through his fingers.

"You went too far, Malthus," Thiel bluffed, trying to sound confident. "People won't stand for foreign troops on American soil. Wetzel told me about that."

"They will stand for anything they think guarantees their security," Malthus said, eyes glittering. "Like the Hebrews who cried for the meat pots of Egypt after a few weeks in the desert. The masses are sheep, Captain Thiel. Threaten the flock and they bleat for a shepherd, but most are too stupid to know one when they see him. So, remove the troublemakers and the rest will be led wherever I want them to go."

"I don't believe it."

"As I said, you are a child." Malthus inhaled deeply on his cigarette and then stubbed it out in the ashtray. "All of your kind are children. Squalling, filthy infants who deserve none of what you've been given. In His image. And *you* will judge *us* someday? Bah! This is tiresome."

Malthus casually rolled his chair back from the desk and stood, adjusting his tie, apparently unconcerned that a highly trained American soldier aimed a deadly weapon at his heart. "Unfortunately, Captain Thiel, enough threads have been pulled loose that I must regroup elsewhere. Killing you and your team solves my immediate problem, but I have no time for the questions that will follow. I am patient, more patient than you can know, but my time here grows short."

"Stay right there." Thiel kept his M4 trained on Malthus' midsection.

Malthus ignored him. He removed a tailored suit jacket from a coat rack behind his desk and slipped it on as though preparing for a business meeting. "I've invested a lot of time here," he said. "Congratulate yourself for this much: You've inconvenienced me more than anyone—well, any *human*—in a very long time."

"I said, stay where you are."

Malthus turned to Thiel, his dark eyes full of disdain. "Really, Thiel. You are trying my patience. Get out of my way."

"Stop, damn you!"

Malthus' face twitched, a tic at the corner of his left eye. Then he started for the door.

Thiel gave him two steps before pulling the trigger. The carbine barked twice, shell casings pinged to the floor, and biting smoke from the powder swirled into the air to mix with the haze from Malthus' cigarettes.

And yet he stood.

Thiel refused to believe his eyes. Two shots, point-blank, and Malthus stood in the center of the room, unmoved.

Pounding reverberated through the room. Thiel's men outside, trying to get in, found it impossible to open the door despite the shattered lock.

Calmly, Malthus examined his chest. Two scorched holes punctuated his starched shirt side by side, like eyeholes in a child's Halloween costume. Returning his gaze to Thiel, Malthus' eyes flashed, and as he spoke, his voice dropped in pitch until it resonated inside of Thiel, choking the air from his lungs and threatening to still the beating of his heart.

"I should kill you, but I will not." Thiel was transfixed. Malthus' face, it—shifted, changed, twisted out of true. The transformation was horrible enough, but the shape, the awful *shape*...

Thiel shut his eyes, hard, but not quickly enough. The hellish vision was burned deeply into his mind, forever, and Thiel knew that his hold on reality had come loose.

A leathery vise gripped his throat and lifted him from the floor, choking him, crushing his larynx, but Thiel would not—*could not*—open his eyes. As he struggled in vain, the voice, an aggregate of many sounds, many tongues speaking at once, shredded the veil that Thiel's mind desperately sought to pull between them.

"Your memory of our few moments together," it said. "A souvenir of our partnership. That will serve as punishment. You were, after all, useful for a time. Sweet dreams, Captain Thiel."

The world suddenly shifted as the hellish creature hurled Thiel across the room. He hit the wall hard, and collapsed to the floor gasping and clutching his throat.

A moment later, screams of mindless, unspeakable agony shattered the remaining fragments of his mind. The cries were distilled from pain far beyond physical. Thiel was dimly aware, in a dark, unreachable part of himself, that the horror now visited upon his sergeants by Malthus was a torment more excruciating than any living thing should know.

Thiel knew he should get up and help them. He was responsible for them. He was their captain, and his men needed him now more than they ever had.

But Captain Alan Thiel could not move. He curled helplessly against a mahogany file cabinet in a corner of the office, eyes closed, head down, arms wrapped tightly across his chest. His mind had recoiled and turned inward upon itself, and he could do nothing but weep with fear, and shame, and despair.

THIRTY-FOUR

Cindy Moore couldn't believe her eyes. Sick of tossing and turning after a sleepless night, she'd turned on the television and switched to a cable news channel, looking for something to drown out the restless turnings of her worried mind until she could finally get some rest. That had been a mistake.

The top story, of course, was the situation in the Middle East. It had been quiet for twelve hours, but the tension at the United Nations and in the great capitals of the world was the nervous calm of a hurricane's eye.

Just as Cindy's mind began to wander, the blow-dried news anchor said something that caught her attention. Too late—in her drowsy state, she missed it. The anchor droned on a few moments more before the picture cut to some kind of protest rally.

Awfully early for that, Cindy thought. And then the banner flashed across the bottom of the screen: *Scott AFB, Illinois.*

Cindy bolted upright in bed, scrambling for the remote in the folds of the comforter. She finally found it and turned up the volume until she could hear the TV clearly.

"...self-described patriots, protesting what they call the illegal and unconstitutional arrests of hundreds and perhaps thousands of men supposedly kept in a secret detention camp located just off the base. Now, swing the camera over to the right, Jeff—that's it. In the distance, maybe a mile from our position, you can see smoke rising into the sky. Witnesses here say it was a small helicopter that was shot down by a surface-to-air missile, but we have no official confirmation of that. We do know that a local radio station lost contact with its traffic copter during a broadcast early this

morning. We can also hear—and you should be able to hear it, too—gunfire coming from that direction. We don't know the source of the gunfire, and we haven't been able to find a spokesperson for the military to talk to us."

"Go and look!" Cindy shouted at the television.

"We may find out soon, however," the reporter continued. *"The leader of the crowd behind me, identified by witnesses as former Indiana University basketball player and fringe, right-wing Internet broadcaster Barney Ison, is marching the group toward the sound of the fighting. Unless base security stops them, we may learn firsthand just who is shooting at whom. Let's hope cooler heads prevail before this turns even more violent. Live at Scott Air Force Base, I'm Dan Noble. Back to you, JoAnne."*

Cindy Moore jumped out of bed and dashed downstairs to the phone. She had to call Susie Thornton and Michelle Schiebold. The hour didn't matter. They probably hadn't slept any better than she had anyway.

"Which way?" Terry Norlock looked at Harris expectantly.

Harris hated to admit that he didn't have a clue. He wanted to flank the UN unit, but Harris wasn't sure where its flank was. Or where they were, for that matter.

"This way," he said, trying to sound confident.

"Are you sure?" Norlock asked with one eyebrow raised.

"I—okay, no. I've only been here four days, okay?"

"Sorry," Norlock said. "I just noticed that the shadows are pointing the opposite direction from the way they were when we started. Unless the earth flipped on its axis in the last few minutes, we've circled back."

"At least the shooting is farther away."

"You speak truth. Let's try this way," Norlock said, stepping off. "I think there's a road over there."

Something was wrong. Thiel should have been out by now, frog-marching Green to a rendezvous with a Night Stalker helicopter. Captain Tom Wetzel checked his watch as he waited impatiently at the top of the stairway that led down to Green's offices. Ten minutes. Way too long.

Wetzel took a couple of deep breaths and then headed back down the stairs, hoping to meet Thiel and his men on the way up.

No luck.

At the door to Green's outer office, Wetzel was assaulted by greasy black smoke and a stench so foul that he recoiled backward, retching. It was an odor he'd encountered once before, in Afghanistan, and one he'd hoped never to meet again.

Charred human flesh.

Forcing himself to take a deep breath, Wetzel blinked his burning eyes to clear the tears and charged into the room. Two blackened heaps of ash smoldered just outside Green's office. The door and the ceiling above it were scorched. So completely incinerated were the masses of smoking residue that it took several moments before Wetzel identified the shapes—the two sergeants who were with Thiel just ten minutes ago.

Malthus' guard was gone.

Pushing forward, Wetzel stepped around the remains of Thiel's men and grabbed the knob of the office door.

He pulled back his hand with a curse. It was too hot to touch. It didn't matter; the door swung open anyway. Only then did Wetzel notice the bullet holes in the shattered frame.

He stepped inside and was immediately brought short by the sight of the A-team captain sitting against the wall, hugging his knees as he rocked forward and back.

"Thiel?" Wetzel knelt in front of the other man. There was no hint of recognition in his unblinking eyes. Whatever Captain Alan Thiel saw, it was very far away.

Wetzel stood and scanned the room. Green was gone, Thiel was catatonic, and his men were dead. Now what?

A hollow wooden thump drew Wetzel's attention to the back wall of the office. He moved quickly to the source of the sound, retrieving Thiel's M4 from the floor as he went.

Listening closely along the wall, Wetzel heard the thump again, followed by a muffled cry.

Quickly, he examined the wall. There—nearly invisible, a seam. Too thin for a fingerhold.

Another thump. Wetzel searched along the wall. Behind a portrait of the White House, he found a small panel recessed into the drywall. He pushed a small red button, and a section of the wall quietly slid open to reveal a room not much larger than a walk-in closet.

Gagged and bound to a wooden chair in the darkened room was a thin, disheveled white-haired man wearing only a T-shirt and boxer shorts.

Wetzel set the weapon on the desk and hurried to the man's aid. He untied the strip of cloth fastened across the older man's mouth, and he had the duct tape around the man's wrists halfway removed when recognition dawned.

"Hey, aren't you—"

"Harold Benson," the man said, coughing.

"Congressman Benson?" Wetzel asked as he struggled with the duct tape around Benson's thin ankles.

"Yes, yes, that's right. And who are you?"

"Captain Tom Wetzel, sir. Army intelligence."

"What happened out there? I heard shots. And—" Benson grimaced, "God, what is that smell?"

"I—I don't know, sir." Wetzel pulled the tape free from Benson's legs as gently as he was able.

"Well, Captain," Benson said, rubbing his wrists, "I assume you're not here to kill me, so you just earned yourself either a promotion or a court martial depending on who's behind this. Help me get back to Washington so we can find out."

He was surprised they'd made it this far. Ison and his followers, trailed by a TV reporter and a local producer for a cable news network, had walked at least half a mile into the base unopposed. Judging by the gunfire that still split the clear morning air ahead, Ison guessed that base security was occupied with other things.

The asphalt path they followed appeared to be a service road recently added to carry traffic to a remote part of the base. It led through a wooded area that screened the gunfire and the thick black smoke that rose like a totem into the October sky.

"Mister Ison? Mister Ison, can I get a word with you?" A young man wearing khakis and a dark blue polo shirt appeared at Ison's elbow, a radio reporter waving a handheld digital recorder in Barney's face.

Without breaking stride, Ison grabbed the device from the reporter and began taking it apart.

"Hey!"

"You'll get it back," Ison said, turning it over and examining the pieces carefully. It was clean. "Here," he said, returning the parts to the young man. "Here. Can't be too careful. Who are you?"

The reporter accepted it nervously. "Uh, Bill Artos. I'm with All News 670 in Saint Louis. What do you hope to accomplish with this march on the base?" The kid juggled the pieces of his recorder, trying not to drop any as he struggled to keep up with Ison's long legs.

"I thought I made it clear back there."

"Yes, but I thought—"

"Open your eyes, kid," Ison interrupted. "Look around and piece it together for yourself. And if you need help, look up my show on the Internet. Audio and video, goes back more than fifteen years. And do some homework on Project BioShield."

"But—"

Ison stopped cold. "Learn some history. Research these names: Charles Hilliard. Thomas Foil. Maggie Taylor. Rex Grayson. Remember—Project BioShield. End of interview."

Just ahead, something that looked like a refugee from a bad Seventies movie stumbled out of the trees and onto the road. A soldier, a muscular black man, had his arm around the shoulders of a tall, blond man in an orange jumpsuit. The soldier was obviously hurt. What wasn't clear was how the guy in orange had escaped the camp.

"Hey! Little help here!" The blond guy looked exhausted, but the soldier looked worse. Ison rushed up to meet the odd couple, his long stride leaving Popeye Bailey and the radio reporter in the dust.

"Barney Ison, host of *The Barney Ison Show*, worldwide daily on the Internet," he said to the pair, getting under the soldier's other arm. "Tell me what's going on back there."

The soldier gave him a quizzical look, but he said, "Lieutenant Tony Harris, Three Sixty-Ninth Military Police. Two companies of United Nations troops are trying to fight their way into a detainment camp."

"Which I broke out of," the man in orange said proudly.

"And then saved my life," Harris added.

"UN troops," Ison repeated. "You're sure they're blue hats?"

Harris nodded. Ison closed his eyes for a moment, savoring the sweet taste of vindication. He couldn't wait to see how the mainstream media would spin *this*.

Popeye and the radio reporter finally caught up with a dozen others close behind. Ison turned to the reporter and said, "All right, young man, there is your story. Tell it well and you'll make your career."

It was all over the Internet within an hour. Before Joe Unes made it home, the all-news station had a reporter at Scott Air Base, and information from other hot spots around the country made it clear that somebody in Washington had some explaining to do.

Right now, though, Unes didn't care. The caffeine and adrenaline were fleeing his system like rats from a sinking ship, and it was all he could do to stay awake for the half-hour drive back to West County. He'd done his job and lived to tell about it—how, he didn't know. There'd be time to dwell on that later.

Cathy greeted him at the door, obviously relieved. Unes gave his wife a hug and a long, slow kiss, and then wearily let her guide him upstairs to bed.

They still hadn't heard anything about his dad. Eric's mom had brought him over to the Thorntons' to wait for news, and Mrs. Schiebold had come over, too. Eric sat on a couch in the living room, watching the cable news channel while the three ladies talked and talked.

The news announcers and a parade of talking heads argued about the battles at the air base and a few other places that morning. Even though the military police at Scott had been outnumbered two to one, it sounded like they put up a really good fight.

It was really sad about the helicopter traffic guy, though. Eric wished they'd quit playing the recording of when he was shot down. It made him want to cry every time.

The tall man at Eric's house the night before was on the news a lot, too. They kept playing clips from a speech he made, and another of him helping a soldier who was hurt. Eric wondered if Mr. Ison was the reason they found the prison camp with his dad. And then he realized Mr. Ison might not have come to help if Eric hadn't sneaked that old computer out of the attic and posted that picture of his dad to social media.

Eric smiled to himself, feeling proud. He couldn't wait to tell his dad about that when he came home.

The good news was that nobody inside the camp got hurt. But nobody would say when they were going to let them go.

The Thorntons' phone kept ringing, and everybody jumped when it did. But every time it was just somebody else wondering if Mrs. Thornton had heard anything, or to see if she was watching the news.

Finally, around three o'clock, a call came, and Eric knew right away it was Sheriff Thornton. Mrs. Thornton started crying almost as soon as she picked it up. But she was smiling when she cried, which Eric never understood even though he'd seen his mother do it a thousand times. Some weird grown-up thing.

He waited patiently until Mrs. Thornton was through. She didn't keep him in suspense.

Wiping a tear from her eye, she said, beaming, "They're coming home tomorrow."

He watched the media circus as long as he dared. Reporters, local and network, jostled for position in front of the chain-link and barbed wire enclosure like turkey buzzards squabbling over a dead armadillo, each one claiming to be first with the breaking story. But with each passing minute the danger grew. Barney Ison pulled Popeye Bailey away from the euphoric crowd celebrating its victory, small though it was, over the forces of oppression.

"We need to leave," Ison said.

"Aw, Barn, can't we hang out for awhile? I'm tired."

"We've been on the news," Ison replied. "Our faces on TV. The web. All over the world. Remember Hitch."

Popeye paled. He'd seen the charred remains of Dave Hitchens even before Barney, and for a moment his eyes looked old. A pang of regret jabbed at Ison for bringing the kid along and putting him in danger, but he knew that Popeye wouldn't have had it any other way.

"Okay," the young man said. "Where to?"

"West," Ison said. "There's a seismologist we need to see about the Cascadia Subduction Zone. The media keeps running stories on the Yellowstone supervolcano. Spectacular, but it's clickbait. I have it on good authority from a friend in Bozeman, Montana that Cascadia is the big one."

"Sounds big."

"Yeah," Ison said. He flipped the keys to the Winnebago to the younger man. "You drive. A friend in the Alliance just texted some intel on the Shadow King."

Bailey's eyes opened wide. "Sinclair?"

"Charles Robert Arthur the Seventh," Ison confirmed. "We need to know if we can trust this Inner Circle. The Alliance needs all the help it can get against Redwing."

The crowd, distracted by a reporter doing a live shot, never saw the two men slip away and disappear into the bright October morning.

He could have slept longer, but he didn't want to put off the phone call. "Fred? Joe Unes. I wanted to follow up on those computers I left for you this morning. Have you had a chance to look at them?"

"What computers?"

"I put a note on your desk early this morning," Unes said. "I left a couple of desktop computers in the evidence locker for you to look at. It's urgent."

There was a pause, and Unes realized with a sinking heart that Fred Schuler had no idea what he was talking about. "Joe," Schuler said, "There was nothing for me here this morning."

"I signed the computers in," Unes insisted. "Check the log. Seven-fifteen this morning."

"I checked the log," Schuler said. "There's nothing there."

"My signature's not on the log?"

"No."

"And no computers in the locker."

"Uh uh."

"You're not joking with me?"

"I was going to ask *you* that," Schuler said.

Unes took a deep breath and blew it out. "Okay, thanks." He set his phone on the table and stared out the French door to the back yard.

Cathy, seated across from him at their breakfast table, asked, "Is everything all right?"

Unes got up, walked around the table, leaned over, and wrapped his arms around his wife. "I don't know," he said. "Barney Ison would say nothing is ever all right. Maybe he's got something. Me, I'm heading back to bed."

THIRTY-FIVE

He didn't want to show it, but Jared Gruner was intensely jealous of Terry Norlock's adventure after he'd vaulted over the barbed wire fence the previous day. All was forgiven, though, by the chance to meet with the man Norlock rescued—and get his autograph. A former NFL player! Even if he'd only been a third-stringer.

"What were you guys thinking when you realized those UN troops were coming right at you?" In the back of his mind, Gruner thought this would make a pretty good book, and a couple of stories about the bravery of the 369th MPs would really punch it up. Thanks to the Internet, you didn't need an agent and a publisher anymore. Maybe it was time to finally finish a manuscript.

"I wasn't thinking at all," Tony Harris said, shifting to find a comfortable position in the hospital bed. "Mostly I was scared spitless."

"Oh." That wasn't the answer Gruner had hoped for.

"I mean," Harris continued, "We did our jobs. We didn't turn and run. We pulled back when they overran our position, but we kept steady fire on them. That slowed them down long enough for base security to jump in. Our captain pulled in the platoons on the flanks. It was textbook, considering. It took a while, but the blue hats finally figured out they were surrounded and a long way from home, so now they're inside the camp until we work it out with the UN."

"Why were they even here?" Stauffer asked.

Harris shrugged. "No idea," he said. "Somebody at DHS lost his mind, I guess. Figured we couldn't do the job because we didn't force you all to take those shots."

"Typical," Gruner grumbled.

"How is your knee, Mister Harris?" Vijay asked.

"Call me Tony," Harris said. "It hurts, but it's a lot better than it would have been if Terry hadn't been there. I thought for sure I'd never see my son—" His voice abandoned him then, and his four visitors discreetly looked away while Harris wrestled his emotions back under control.

After a moment, Stauffer cleared his throat and asked, "So, what are you going to do next?"

Harris sighed. "Well, my knee is well and truly shot now, so I doubt I can stick around with the Guard. We'll see. Being a P.E. teacher is okay, but I've been thinking about going back to school. Maybe law school. Or teaching history, American history. The country's got a lot of problems, but a lot of them lately come from forgetting how we got here."

"Dad!" A young voice from the doorway was followed by a blur of colors that streaked across the room and planted itself in the arms of the man in the bed.

"Come on, guys," Norlock said. "We should probably go."

Harris untangled one arm long enough to wave goodbye to his visitors. His broad smile was infectious.

In the hall, Gruner turned to the others with an expression of supreme self-satisfaction. "Now do you believe me? Was I not right about these things all this time—the hidden agendas, the deep state, the experiments in mind control?"

"Yeah, yeah," Stauffer said, dismissing Gruner with a wave. "Let's get something to eat. And then I've got to pick up a new rig."

"Indeed," Vijay said. "And please, let me install some privacy safeguards on this new computer so we do not have to break you out of jail again."

Stauffer was shocked. "What do you mean?"

"Surely this is not the last time we will use our abilities for a just cause," Vijay said, looking surprised. "I am beginning to enjoy the adventure."

It felt like a long time since he'd set foot in his own home, but the drive down from the airport in Des Moines seemed to last even longer than the time they spent in the camp. Bob Moore was glad it was over, free and at peace again with the world.

He and Cindy sat together on the couch in the upstairs family room, the television's volume low, steaming mugs of decaf on the coffee table in front of them. An exhausted Eric had collapsed into bed early, finally able to relax, but not before he'd described his secret rescue plan in great detail.

Cindy saved her account of the mysterious, threatening phone call until Eric was safely tucked in bed.

"No idea at all who it was?" Bob asked.

"No," Cindy said. "The FBI agent said to call if we hear from him again."

"Maybe now that this is over, whoever called will just stay hidden."

"I hope so." After a long silence, Cindy finally asked, "Was it bad?"

"Not physically," Bob said. "The guards were okay. I don't think they really knew what was going on. They seemed just as surprised as us that we'd been dragged in there. We didn't look like your typical prison population, that's for sure. But being away from you and Eric—that was bad."

Cindy leaned up against him. "Well, praise God you're home. And Ted, and Pastor Schiebold, too. I pray we never have to go through anything like that again."

"Me, too."

They sat quietly for a while, just enjoying the nearness of one another, words completely unnecessary to communicate their emotions.

A bright red stripe appeared across the television screen announcing that the president was about the address the nation. Bob reached for the remote on the coffee table and turned up the volume.

"Good evening," President Bell began. He sat at his desk in the Oval Office, wearing an expression of confident concern, a

nuanced and practiced look that so many politicians seemed to have mastered.

"As you know, my administration has been working tirelessly with our colleagues in the United Nations to bring a peaceful resolution to the conflict in the Middle East. I am pleased to report that progress has been made, and that both parties in the conflict have honored a tentative cease-fire for the last twenty-four hours. It is my sincere hope that this cease-fire is the beginning of a lasting peace.

"This afternoon, I was made aware of actions that were taken in the interest of apprehending those responsible for the evil plot that killed so many American men, women, and children last weekend. Unfortunately, those actions were ill advised and poorly executed. Mistakes were made. Many innocent Americans were arrested without due process of law, and this violation of basic constitutional rights cannot and will not be tolerated.

"Furthermore, inviting foreign troops onto American soil was a grave error. The sovereignty of the United States of America is sacrosanct. Accordingly, the Joint Chiefs of Staff have launched an inquiry and those responsible for issuing this illegal order will be punished in accordance with the Uniform Code of Military Justice.

"In addition, within the last hour I asked for and received the resignations of the Secretary of the Department of Homeland Security, the Director of the Federal Emergency Management Agency, and the commanding general of the United States Northern Command. Their actions, while well-intentioned, were wrong. As president, it is my responsibility to—"

Bob switched off the television and tossed the remote aside.

"Don't you want to see the rest, honey?" Cindy asked.

"What for?" Bob said. "He's saying the right things, but is it because he means them, or because he knows it's the only way to keep 'we the people' from rising up and forming a more perfect union?"

"Hmm, that reminds me," Cindy said, untangling herself from her husband's arms and pulling a scrap of notepaper from the pocket of her jeans. "A couple passing through town earlier today asked me to give this to you when you got home. I forgot all about it until now."

Bob took the piece of paper and unfolded it. The words inside were composed in block-lettered pencil, as though someone had tried to conceal their handwriting. It read:

> WELCOME HOME, MR. MOORE. PRAY HARD. THIS WAS ONLY THE BEGINNING AND THE EYES OF THE ENEMY ARE ON YOU NOW.
> *THE ALLIANCE*
> *—EPHESIANS 6:12—*

"The Alliance?"

Cindy shrugged. "They seemed nice enough. They asked a few questions about you, Ted, and Pastor Dave. I figured they heard about it on the news."

"They wouldn't have known about me coming home," Bob said.

Cindy's head tilted. "I hadn't thought about that. That's weird."

"No weirder than anything else this week," Bob said. "Come here, you."

Cindy giggled and snuggled in. Bob was grateful that E.J. was asleep.

Joe Unes hadn't expected to see Pastor Ed Harper again, especially in a professional capacity. But word had gone out from the Justice Department that law enforcement, from the FBI on down, was to make amends to the more than eighteen thousand people who'd been arrested without warrants after the weekend of terror.

Since Unes had called on Pastor Harper before he was arrested, SAC Clay tasked him with the official apology. It wasn't the worst assignment he'd ever drawn. Besides, Unes had been unpleasantly surprised to find out that they'd pulled Harper in. Telling him so wasn't difficult.

A lot had changed in the two weeks since the explosion at Grandy's. Unes had reported to SAC Clay what he found in Iowa, and the disappearance of the computers from the field office's evidence locker. Clay had seemed genuinely surprised and angered by the attempt on Unes' life. They'd agreed that this raised disturbing questions about how Joe's sudden trip to Iowa had outside knowledge. Also disturbing was that a follow-up visit to that cornfield turned up no evidence. Joe's phone and gun—gone. The corn had been harvested and tracks in the field erased by recent rains, so Unes couldn't even corroborate his story of Barney Ison's insane rescue with a weaponized Winnebago.

The Israelis had pulled back to the Golan Heights, in spite of some continued violence, and peace talks had begun in Geneva. The European Union had offered to guarantee Israel's security by sending a peacekeeping force from its new standing army and it held out membership in the EU as an incentive.

At home, the president's hands were full with the upcoming election. It didn't look good for Bell. Public pressure had forced the president to appoint a commission to investigate the causes of Ten-Thirteen, but Congressman Benson of Iowa had made it clear he intended to broaden the probe to include the government's response—especially the vaccination campaign that seemed much too conveniently prepared and ready for what was officially the sudden and unexpected detention of thousands of people.

Meanwhile, FBI Special Agent Joe Unes had developed a nagging sense of unease and discontent. What began as an official visit with Pastor Ed Harper quickly became a long personal chat.

"So, you haven't heard anything more about this Captain Thiel?" Harper sat in his office chair, hands steepled in front of him. The room was filled with a low hum as a couple of church members used a pressure washer to remove spray-painted graffiti from an exterior wall of the church.

Unes shook his head. "It's like Thiel dropped off the earth. I know Special Forces protect their soldiers' identities for security, but with our tools at the Bureau I should be able to find something on him. But everything within the last eight months is gone."

Harper nodded, frowning. "Well. This is interesting stuff, Joe—may I call you Joe?—but why are you telling me this? *Should* you be telling me this?"

"I'm having some trouble sorting things out," Unes admitted. "My background is in chemistry. Science—quantifiable data, reproducible experiments. Everything precise, carefully measured and recorded. That's how I got into law enforcement. I thought I could do more good for the world by applying my background to bringing bad people to justice."

"And you're learning you work for the bad people."

"I'm not sure."

"And what happened doesn't fit into neat little packages of quantifiable, reproducible data."

Unes nodded.

Harper leaned back. "This is what the apostle Paul meant by wrestling with powers and principalities. Sounds to me like Brother Ison has already figured that out."

Joe frowned. "You're saying…?"

"I'm saying the ones behind this are not born of woman."

Unes chewed on that for a moment while he studied the pastor's solemn face. "You're serious."

Harper paused for a moment, considering his words. "You believe in God, don't you?"

"Yeah, I think so."

"So you believe in the supernatural."

"Well—"

"That's not negotiable," Harper said. "You can't have it both ways. It's either yes or no. If you believe in God—who is, by definition, supernatural—then you believe in the supernatural. And intelligent evil is part of that world. Powers and principalities. Paul wasn't speaking in abstract terms. He meant real, live beings. Call them fallen angels or demons, if you prefer, but God calls them 'gods' in the Bible: Exodus 12:12, Numbers 33:4, Psalm 82, just to name a few. They're the spirits He assigned to the pagan nations as their gods. Deuteronomy 4:19. Baal? Astarte? Molech? Chemosh? The gods of Greece and Rome? The Jews and the early church understood that they were real. *They* are the enemy. We enlightened people in the modern world, we've forgotten what our ancestors knew."

Unes blew out a deep breath. "This is a lot to absorb. It's like I've just stepped into *The X-Files*."

"Well, let me pile on," Harper said. "A fella in Ohio has been trying to warn us about something just like Ten-Thirteen for a few years now. People you'd never suspect suddenly turning violent, thousands of them, maybe millions. Mass chaos. He calls it 'the black awakening'."

"Who is this guy? Counter-terror specialist?"

"No," Harper said, "He's a deliverance minister. What you'd probably call an exorcist."

"An exorcist? For real?"

"Powers and principalities, Joe. Cosmic rulers over this present darkness. They're all around us."

It sounded too much like a horror movie to Unes. "So, this guy thinks people possessed by demons will suddenly start killing and creating chaos with no warning?"

"Yep," Harper said. "This fella says he's run across a number of them during deliverance encounters—demons, literally, who talk about the same thing, a mass uprising. Bloody, terrible, like Ten-Thirteen but even bigger. Much bigger. They call themselves Chosen Ones."

Unes' eyebrows lifted on their own. "Chosen Ones?"

"Yeah."

"The kid in Iowa said the phony email from God he got told him he was one of the Chosen."

Now Harper's eyebrows lifted. "Maybe there's more to that email than just some fancy electronic hypnotism."

"What are you saying? Possession by email?"

Harper shrugged. "People in the occult, practicing sorcerers and witches, believe they can charge physical objects with power by performing rituals over them or by marking them with runes or sigils. We're talking about the supernatural here. Why should sending an email be any different than sending a letter?"

"But an email is just electronic information," Unes protested. "Electrons decoded and displayed as photons so the eyes and the brain can understand it."

"And an amulet is just a whole bunch of molecules, which are just atoms stuck together. Now, you've got a degree in chemistry. What are atoms when you get right down to it?"

"I—hmm. Atoms. Electrons, protons, and neutrons."

"Yep," Pastor Harper said. "So, what's the difference? And why are certain symbols supposed to give them power—supernatural power?" Unes shook his head, so Harper continued. "Because the magicians invited the spirits and gave them permission. Like those old vampire stories. You had to give the monster permission to cross your threshold and come into your house. I think it's the same in the spirit realm. It's not the spell or the ritual that empowers the user, it's the desire of the person who wants to make a deal with the devil, so to speak."

Unes lightly rubbed the recently healed scratch on his cheek. "That reminds me." Unes fished a small object from the pocket of his sport coat and handed it to Pastor Harper. "Here's another piece that doesn't fit. This came by mail to the office yesterday."

Harper turned the small metallic object over. It was a lighter. It looked expensive, engraved with an unusual geometric pattern of rectangles, like crenellations on a castle wall, topped with an oddly stylized cross.

"Do you know what that is? The symbol, I mean. It looked sort of religious to me."

"Just a second." Harper stood and pulled a slim volume from a shelf on the back wall of his office. He opened the book as he sat and began flipping through the pages. "Here it is," he said, handing the open book to Unes. "This is *The Lesser Key of Solomon.* Occultists believe they can use it to conjure up demons."

The design on the page matched the one on the lighter. "It's the same pattern," Unes said, returning the book. "What is it?"

"It's the symbol for one of the seventy-two demons supposedly summoned by King Solomon."

"What?"

"That's what it says," Harper said. *"Halphas, or Malthus: He is a Great Earl, and appeareth in the form of a stock-dove. He speaketh with a hoarse voice. His office is to build up towers, and to furnish them with ammunition and weapons, and to send men of war to places appointed."*

Unes felt a chill on the back of his neck. "Malthus? Did you say Malthus?"

"What is it?" Harper asked.

"That's the name of the man Captain Thiel was going to find when he left Mayfield."

The pastor's eyes widened but he said nothing.

"Pastor," Unes said, "Do you really believe this stuff?"

Harper took a deep breath before answering. "There's more to the world than what we see, Joe. Is this book really a step-by-step instruction manual for summoning demons? I doubt it. It was probably compiled in the sixteenth century and translated into English by a couple of occultists, Aleister Crowley and Samuel Mathers, around Nineteen Oh-Four. Did Solomon really call up demons from the pit? No, I don't think so. Can demons travel by email? I don't know. That's a new one. But could it trigger something in someone who isn't protected by the Holy Spirit? Possibly. Have you boys looked into the faith of the people who snapped? I mean, really looked?"

Unes frowned. "Other than the theory that they were connected to an apocalyptic death cult—"

Harper raised his hand to cut Joe off. "My turn to ask: Do you really believe that stuff?"

"No, not really," Unes admitted. "I told my boss I didn't see the connection. At least not here. But somebody in Washington really pushed it."

"Or something behind somebody in Washington."

"What do you mean?"

"Principalities and powers." Pastor Harper took off his glasses and rubbed his eyes. He looked tired. It had been a rough couple of weeks. "I'm not saying we should look for demons behind every corner, but their influence is undeniable. Do demons and fallen angels walk the earth and try to do us harm? You bet your life. The apostle Paul made it clear—they were the gods of the pagan world. And most people never hear this in church. In fact, most Christians in America don't believe Satan even exists, much less these other small-G 'gods.' But like I said, God calls them 'gods,' so I don't have a problem using that word or believing they're real."

Unes didn't know how to respond. It felt like the ground was shifting under his feet as they talked. Was this plot really the work of a supernatural being? How in the world do you investigate one of those? And who'd believe it?

"Let me ask you something," Pastor Harper said. "For all of your schooling and scientific training, when you stared down the barrel of that gun, you had no idea what was going to happen the moment after that man pulled the trigger. Am I right?"

Unes nodded slowly. "Yeah."

Harper leaned back and smiled gently. "Well, brother," he said, "Why don't we start there?"

EPILOGUE

Three weeks later – Somewhere in northern Libya

Sand in all directions. It reminded Malthus of the old days. He missed the ziggurats on the plains of Shinar.

Through expensive aviator shades, he looked over a group of recruits just arrived from Syria. Underfed, but their hunger wasn't physical. It burned in their spirits. Americans had an abundance of resources, but their lack of commitment to anything but themselves had been a constant nuisance.

Zealots, now—he could work with those.

New face, new plan. He'd gambled in America and lost. If only he'd had some of the fire he saw in these men, it would have worked. *Civil rights. As maddening as giving the Lessers free will.*

His satellite phone chirped. Malthus frowned. He wasn't expecting a call. Very few knew the number.

"Yes?"

"Well, there you are." Ryder's ingratiating tone set Malthus' teeth on edge. "I was beginning to think you were hiding from me."

"You flatter yourself."

Ryder chuckled. "Let me be clear. The council has tolerated you for lo, these many years because you have been useful. At times, for specific tasks. But never forget your place. Your epic failure in America jeopardized a long operation to bring together key bloodlines for our endgame. If you work without sanction again, or if you get in the way of the stratagem…well, unlike the

Lessers, Malthus—is that still your name?—*you* can burn for a very long time."

"You have no authority over me."

"I do."

Malthus bristled. "I am a god!"

"You are a jumped-up *malak* who needs to respect his betters," Ryder said calmly. "Remember, the Lessers called the half-breeds gods, too, even after the giants were destroyed in that Flood. It's rather amusing, really. The Lessers have performed rituals and held festivals for those miscegenated spirits for millennia. Halloween, Day of the Dead, ancestor worship… I love that one. Watching the old giants pretend to be dearly departed grandmas—it is *endless* fun! Some of them have even gone into show business, in a sense. Hercules, for example. You know he's a cartoon hero now? He hates it, of course, but then, the Rephaim hate the Lessers as much as you do. Maybe even more."

Ryder's voice took on an ominous chill. "The difference is they know it's in their best interests to do as they're told."

Malthus seethed, too angry to speak.

"Mister One has taken notice of your activities. You won't get another warning."

Malthus crushed the phone in his hand. Staring across the sand, he vowed that he would relive the days of old. *Ryder. Pretentious ass. It's time for a change in the infernal order.*

ABOUT THE AUTHOR

 DEREK P. GILBERT hosts the nationally broadcast program *SkyWatchTV*, and co-hosts the weekly programs *SciFriday* and *Unraveling Revelation* with his wife, best friend, and sometime co-author, Sharon K. Gilbert.

Derek is the author of the groundbreaking books *Bad Moon Rising*, an analysis of the spiritual forces behind Islam, *The Great Inception*, and *Last Clash of the Titans*, which explores the convergence of Greek mythology and end-times Bible prophecy.

He's also the co-author with Sharon K. Gilbert of *Veneration*, a study of the cult of the dead in ancient Israel and its impact on our world today, and with Josh Peck of *The Day the Earth Stands Still*, a book that traces, step by step, the occult origins of "ancient aliens."

Derek is a popular speaker at churches and conferences in on topics such as end times prophecy, Dominion theology, Transhumanism, and the Gilberts' mind-blowing research that connects the ancient Canaanites to the Nephilim, the Watchers of the Bible, and the old gods of the Greek pantheon, the Titans.

He's always been fascinated by the way things work and how things got to be the way they are. It was his study of the documentary evidence for the New Testament that awakened him to the battle raging around us. Now, he focuses on archaeological evidence that supports the history of the Bible.

Derek is a lifelong fan of the Chicago Cubs, prefers glasses to contacts, and he's been known to sing the high part in barbershop and gospel quartets.

Contact information:
derek@gilberthouse.org
www.gilberthouse.org
www.derekpgilbert.com